DEADLY DANCE

The Warships had been engaged in a close-quarters battle that alternately resembled a graceful waltz and a brutal slugging match. The Clan *Whirlwind*, with her superior speed and maneuverability, danced around the ponderous battle cruiser, pricking the *Invisible Truth*'s hide with weapons better suited to destroying fighters than attacking a capital ship.

"He's swinging around again!" the *Truth*'s tactical officer shouted. "Cannons firing."

On a secondary monitor, minute flashes sprang from the Clan warship's bow. "For what we are about to receive, the Lord make us truly thankful," one of the bridge crewman quipped, seconds before a volley of autocannon shells slammed into the *Truth*'s port bow.

Armor shattered. The *Invisible Truth* trembled under the impact of the explosive shells. Then it replied with a PPC blast.

Seconds later, a pair of gray-painted missiles left a thin layer of black soot on the *Truth*'s outer hull as they leapt free of their launch rails. There was a brief explosion, as bright as the flare of a match. A heartbeat later, a brighter fireball flashed into existence, expanding until it seemed to engulf the *Whirlwind*, and then dying out.

THE HUNTERS

BATTLETECH®

Twilight of the Clans III:

THE HUNTERS

Thomas S. Gressman

A ROC BOOK

ROC
Published by New American Library, a division of
Penguin Putnam Inc., 375 Hudson Street,
New York, New York 10014, U.S.A.
Penguin Books Ltd, 27 Wrights Lane,
London W8 5TZ, England
Penguin Books Australia Ltd, Ringwood
Victoria, Australia
Penguin Books Canada Ltd, 10 Alcorn Avenue,
Toronto, Ontario, Canada M4V 3B2
Penguin Books (N.Z.) Ltd, 182–190 Wairau Road,
Auckland 10, New Zealand

Penguin Books Ltd, Registered Offices:
Harmondsworth, Middlesex, England

First published by Roc, an imprint of New American Library,
a division of Penguin Putnam Inc.

First Printing, December 1997
10 9 8 7 6 5 4

Series Editor: Donna Ippolito
Cover art by: Bruce Jensen
Mechanical Drawings: Duane Loose and the FASA art department

 REGISTERED TRADEMARK --MARCA REGISTRADA

BATTLETECH, FASA, and the distinctive BATTLETECH and FASA logos
are trademarks of the FASA Corporation, 1100 W. Cermak, Suite B305,
Chicago, IL 60608.

Printed in the United States of America

BOOKS ARE AVAILABLE AT QUANTITY DISCOUNTS WHEN USED
TO PROMOTE PRODUCTS OR SERVICES. FOR INFORMATION
PLEASE WRITE TO PREMIUM MARKETING DIVISION, PENGUIN
PUTNAM INC., 375 HUDSON STREET, NEW YORK, NEW YORK 10014.

To Jonathan Powers or Catherine Elizabeth,
whichever you are.
I'm looking forward to meeting you.

Thanks and a tip of the hat to Blaine Pardoe and Bill Keith for all their encouragement, and to Mike Stackpole and Donna Ippolito, who forced me to think about what I was doing and to be the best I could. Thanks to Brenda for her patience, and thanks to you, Lord, I know where the opportunity to write this book really came from.

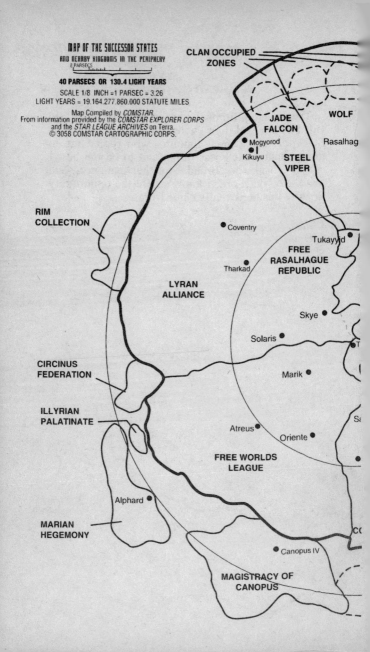

MAP OF THE SUCCESSOR STATES
AND NEARBY KINGDOMS IN THE PERIPHERY

40 PARSECS OR 130.4 LIGHT YEARS

SCALE 1/8 INCH =1 PARSEC = 3.26
LIGHT YEARS = 19.164.277.860.000 STATUTE MILES

Map Compiled by *COMSTAR*.
From information provided by the *COMSTAR EXPLORER CORPS*
and the *STAR LEAGUE ARCHIVES* on Terra.
© 3058 COMSTAR CARTOGRAPHIC CORPS.

CLAN OCCUPIED ZONES

JADE FALCON

WOLF

Rasalhag

Mogyorod

Kikuyu

STEEL VIPER

RIM COLLECTION

Coventry

Tukayyid

FREE RASALHAGUE REPUBLIC

Tharkad

LYRAN ALLIANCE

Skye

Solaris

CIRCINUS FEDERATION

Marik

ILLYRIAN PALATINATE

Atreus

Oriente

FREE WORLDS LEAGUE

Alphard

MARIAN HEGEMONY

Canopus IV

MAGISTRACY OF CANOPUS

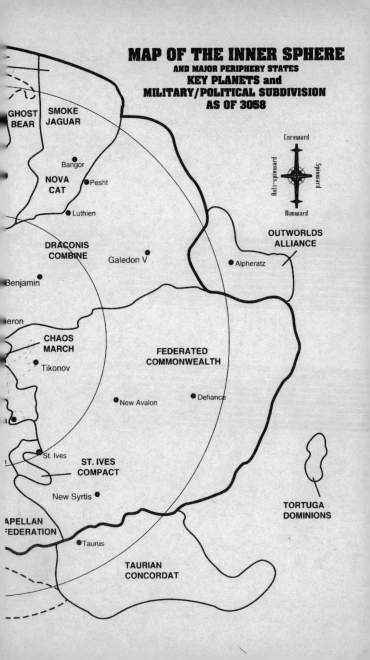

Prologue

It is the year 3058. After centuries of warring against one another, the Great Houses of the Inner Sphere have joined forces to defeat the greatest threat humanity has ever faced—the invading Clans. But this time they will do so as a united force. And they will do it under the banner of a new Star League.

When the leaders of the Inner Sphere gathered on Tharkad to decide how they might defeat the Clans once and for all, it was not long before they came up with a plan—to take the war to the Clans and destroy one of them utterly. They choose Clan Smoke Jaguar as their prey, most ruthless of the invading Clans.

In the midst of the planning comes stunning news—a renegade Jaguar warrior has revealed the route to the Clan homeworlds, until now a secret guarded so closely that even Clan JumpShip captains only know the way-stations and transit points they need for their own leg of the journey to and from the Inner Sphere.

The plan suddenly changes. Not only will the forces of the Inner Sphere, under the banner of a new Star League, strike boldly against the Smoke Jaguars on their occupied worlds, but they will send a second force to Huntress, the homeworld of the Smoke Jaguars, and raze it utterly.

Victor Steiner-Davion will lead Operation Bulldog, an attack on the Jaguars' occupied worlds in the Inner Sphere. Marshal Morgan Hasek-Davion is given command of a second operation, Task Force Serpent, which will secretly make its way to Huntress.

Morgan and the ships and men of his task force will be following the Exodus Road, the same path through the stars General Aleksandr Kerensky took when he led his people into exile three hundred centuries before. Kerensky had left everything behind to save mankind from itself. Now, Morgan will be following in the legendary General's footsteps, trying to save mankind from Kerensky's own descendants.

1

Smoke Jaguar Garrison Compound
Reega, Bangor
Smoke Jaguar Occupation Zone
12 August 3058
0422 hours

Tai-i Michael Ryan paused in his ascent up the high wall surrounding the Smoke Jaguar garrison compound. Three meters above his head, a massive Elemental leaned the clawed hand of his battle armor on the stone parapet and gazed out over the dense jungle blanketing the low rolling hills for as far as the eye could see.

Despite the heavy overcast that blotted out the faint starlight that would otherwise have filtered dimly through Bangor's thick, humid atmosphere, Ryan had no trouble making out the rough details of the Clan sentry's suit of power armor. Leaning out a bit, he could see the mottled darker patches of gray and dark green against the armor's gun-metal gray plasteel, though the light-intensifying equipment built into his helmet visor rendered everything in shades of gray. The Elemental, with his pot-belly and slanting viewscreen, made Ryan think of the *O-bakemono*, demons his maternal grandmother used talk about. The triangular short-range missile launchers looming over the warrior's shoulders like folded wings did nothing to dispel the image. Ryan shook off the thought as he glanced at his wristcomp. 0422 Hours. Right on schedule.

The Elemental leaned on the parapet for what seemed like an eternity, the powerful anti-'Mech laser mated to the suit's right forearm following his electronically enhanced gaze. Ryan flattened his body against the wall again, not sure whether this weapon-follows-your-eyes action was a routine part of sentry duty or whether the hulking sentry had detected the faint metallic scrape of the *nekade*'s steel claws as he'd slipped them into a shallow crevice in the thick stone wall.

Ryan glanced down past the climbing claws strapped to his hands and feet. About five meters down, he could make out the dim shadows of six other DEST commandos fanned out at the base of the wall in a cover formation. Glancing up again at the still-tracking sentry, he clucked his tongue into the headset communicator of his infiltration suit, breaking static in a short two-one-three pattern.

In immediate response, a sharp, sizzling crack ripped the humid air. A laser bolt fired by one of his men concealed in the jungle brush a hundred meters from the wall sliced through the Elemental's visor. The giant form pitched backward, a small hole melted into the faceplate of its armor. The steam was still rising from the ruined visor as Ryan climbed up and over the wall and rolled across the parapet. He dropped into the shadows, taking in the whole scene with his electronically enhanced vision.

Everything inside the thick stone wall was dark and quiet. He could detect no movement. A few lights gleamed weakly from a low wooden building off to his left, a structure his pre-mission briefing had designated as a barracks. The compound was surrounded by five-meter-high stone walls that had once belonged to the Draconis Combine. The installation, some three kilometers outside of the planetary capital of Reega, had once been a repair and refit facility for Bangor's militia, but that was before the coming of the Clans.

The Clans. Ryan gave a silent snort of disgust as he retracted the claws of his *nekade* with a quiet click. Nine years earlier, a massive invasion force, greater than any in the annals of military history, had poured into the Inner Sphere, bringing with it a level of technology and destruction the people of the Inner Sphere had believed lost through the centuries of warfare. At first, the identity of these implacable warriors was unknown. Eventually, through contact and conflict, the truth was revealed.

The mysterious invaders were the descendants of the Star League army that had followed General Aleksandr Kerensky beyond the borders of known space almost three hundred years before. They had ravaged over a third of the Inner Sphere, ruthlessly destroying any who attempted to stand in their way. There were six invading Clans, each one bearing the name of a ferocious predator native to one of their distant, unknown homeworlds. The Jade Falcons, the Steel Vipers, the Wolves, the Ghost Bears, the Nova Cats, and the Smoke Jaguars. Even among these warriors genetically bred for war, the Jaguars were the most ruthless, the most vicious.

The Jaguars had killed and burned their way across nearly a third of Ryan's beloved Draconis Combine, while the rest of the Clan invaders had sliced off another huge hunk of the Inner Sphere. The onslaught only stopped when ComStar revealed, at the eleventh hour, that not only had the once-secretive organization preserved technology for centuries, but they also had a secret military force whose technology equaled that of the Clans.

The ilKhan of the Clans and the Precentor Martial of ComStar had agreed to a proxy battle to take place on the planet Tukayyid. If the Clans won, they would claim Terra, the birthplace of humanity and the invasion's most sought-after prize. If they lost, they agreed to halt their invasion for a span of fifteen years. In three weeks of bloody fighting, the Com Guards defeated the till-now invincible Clans. But the Clanners still occupied the worlds they had taken, and they still had their own agendas.

Both sides had continued their raids, despite the truce, with the Combine inflicting any possible damage and stealing whatever technology they could carry off for study and development. That was why Ryan and his team had been sent to Bangor.

Bangor had been a relatively unimportant planet until the Clans arrived. Now, the Smoke Jaguars were using the old militia compound as a way station and clearinghouse for replacement warriors and materiel coming into the occupation zone. With so rich a target lying only so close, the Combine decided to send in a team of DEST commandos to do what they did best. Draconis Elite Strike Team Six drew the mission, and like every other team of their kind, they were some of the most highly trained, most ruthless military spies, saboteurs, and assassins ever assembled.

Ryan's survey of the compound revealed no indication that his presence had been detected. Moments later, he was joined by six other ghostly figures pulling themselves up onto the parapet with the faint shushing of fabric against stone. They were more humanoid in appearance than the Elemental his team's sniper had just killed, but only barely. Their bodies were clad in baggy fatigues, which slowly shifted color as the ghoulish forms crossed from the dark stone of the wall to the lighter gray flagstones of the walkway. Their heads were encased in close-fitting helmets made of the same high-strength plasteel as a BattleMech's viewscreen. Though the helmet visors were a dark red-black, the men inside could see through them. All but one of the intruders cradled powerful Blazer carbines in their arms. A centimeter-thick, black insulated cable linked the double-barreled laser rifle to one of the many ballistic nylon pouches hanging from each figure's black combat harness. There were a series of metallic clicks as claws snapped back into their retracted position.

Stooping over the Elemental's inert form, Ryan peered dispassionately at the ruined visor and saw that the shattered face had once belonged to a woman. That fact caused Ryan no distress. His only concern was that the potential threat to his mission and his team had been eliminated. Assured that the lone sentry was dead, he gestured sharply at the rest of the raiding party. He felt little remorse at the Elemental's execution. The massive, genetically engineered warrior would have killed him had she spotted him. The Jaguar sentry had been an enemy asset, nothing more—an asset that had to be removed. And the Strike Team's sniper had done so with as little compunction as Ryan would have shown at capturing an opponent's counter in a game of *Go*.

He motioned again to the team. Without a sound, the raiders split off into pairs, one team moving away to the left, another pair to the right, while the third team—Ryan and another man who carried a large nylon satchel over his right shoulder—slipped silently toward a flight of narrow stairs that led down from the parapet walk. Each two-man team had its own assignment to carry out within the darkened installation. A single man remained behind. Armed with a man-portable machine gun rather than a Blazer carbine, he sank into the shadows atop the wall. From his concealed position, the team sentry visually swept the inside of the compound, searching for enemy activity.

Briefly, Ryan paused in his descent of the stairs, straining to locate the source of a faint sound. Satisfied that the noise presaged no threat to their mission, the ghostly figures of Ryan and his partner crossed the large open courtyard, dodging from shadow to shadow. Eventually, the pair reached the large bay doors on the opposite side of the parade ground. Ryan paused for a moment to pick the lock before slipping inside. His companion followed close behind.

The sight that greeted their eyes was awe-inspiring. Ten new assault class OmniMechs, all freshly painted in the light and dark gray mottling of Smoke Jaguar "dress colors," stood, seemingly at attention, gleaming faintly in the dim glow of the overhead fluorescent panels.

BattleMechs had been around for centuries. Huge war machines ranging in size from small, fast, 20-ton scout 'Mechs to massive, lumbering monsters weighing as much as 100 tons. Mounting a staggering array of lasers, missile launchers, rapid-fire autocannons, and charged-particle cannons, protected by thick layers of hardened steel and composite armor, BattleMechs were the ultimate in war machines. Or so the warriors of the Inner Sphere had thought.

The 'Mechs used by the Clans were technologically superior in every way to the machines fielded by the Inner Sphere. Called OmniMechs, they were capable of being outfitted to suit specific battlefield assignments or the personal fighting style of the individual pilot. This ability, coupled with their greater scientific sophistication, meant that the double handful of 'Mechs Ryan and his partner now surveyed represented the cutting edge of military technology.

The commandos went to work. They selected the nearest 'Mech, the 85-ton monster once dubbed the *Masakari* by the Combine warriors who'd first encountered it. Only later did they learn that the Clan name for the machine was *Warhawk*. Either way, the massive vehicle, with its quartet of long-range PPCs and heavy armor, was a walking nightmare from which many Inner Sphere MechWarriors never awakened.

The shadowy figures clambered up onto the Omni-Mech's torso, their sneak suits rippling through color changes as they went. Standing on the 'Mech's left hip, they were able to reach a half-meter-square access panel in the machine's back. Lifting a manual-release lever caused the hatch to spring open, revealing a tangle of electrical conduits, coolant tubing, and myomer bundles. Ryan checked the small data display terminal set into the back of his left gauntlet, tapping in a few commands before he got the information he wanted. As he queried the device, his companion dug into his satchel to produce a small, plastic-wrapped packet.

Ryan eventually finished his calculations. Taking the package from his friend, he eased the device in through the hatch. Once he was satisfied that the object did not impinge on any of the 'Mech's vital systems, he used a set of powerful spring-loaded clamps to attach the small package to one of the power cables, then withdrew his arm. Quickly, the intruders sealed the panel and moved on to the next 'Mech, a humanoid-looking *Gargoyle*. Fifteen minutes later, all ten of the Clan 'Mechs had been visited by the ghostly pair. Each vehicle now carried an identical package somewhere in its insides. Silently, Ryan tapped a new set of commands into his wristcomp, and, with a jerk of his head, signaled his companion to follow him.

As quickly and as silently as they had come, the two men flitted back across the compound, mounted the stairs to the parapet, deftly scrambled down the wall, and faded away into the deep gloom on the other side.

Fifty meters into the woods, they stopped beneath the overhanging tendrils of a vine-covered palm. Taking concealed positions on either side of the huge tree, they watched their back trail carefully. Soon, a second pair of camouflaged troopers faded into view, betrayed only by the blurring of the jungle around them. Ryan lifted his chin slightly in a gesture of inquiry. One of the newcomers nodded as he settled into the shadow of the creeper-shrouded tree.

Before long, the last pair of commandos, along with the

machine-gunner sentry, rejoined their companions. One had a small black metal briefcase clutched under one arm. Ryan knew that no one had been carrying the case when they'd taken the stairs down from the wall-top parapet for their assigned task of crippling the installation's communications and sensor equipment. Why the contents of the case were so important that his team member had chosen to drag it along would have to wait until the team was debriefed. After getting a nod from this ghostly threesome, Ryan tapped one of the men on the back and crooked his thumb over his shoulder.

One by one, the men faded away into the jungle. After a few dozen meters, they were joined by two more black-clad figures. One braced a Blazer rifle on his right hip and gripped the straps of a small bulky rucksack with his free hand. The other figure cradled a heavy laser rifle. The high-power electronic sight fitted to the weapon's upper receiver revealed its purpose—a sniper's weapon. This was the gun that had neutralized the wall-walking sentry.

Ryan nodded his greeting to the sniper team and motioned them into line. The pair joined their comrades. Quickly and silently, the team faded into the jungle, keeping each other in sight by means of the sophisticated sensor packages mounted in their helmet visors. The helmets, whose visors were constructed of a seemingly opaque red plastic, were outfitted with light amplification gear, thermal imagers, and nearly every type of sensor that could be crammed into their two-kilo mass.

Five kilometers and five hours later, the team, which had been picking its way through the difficult terrain of the overgrown jungle, arrived at a small clearing. The commandos spread out rapidly, searching the perimeter of the glade for signs of a hostile presence. When none was discovered, Ryan spoke for the first time.

"O.K., we're clear. Hollis, call 'em in."

The team's commo-op pulled a small collection of gear from his ruck. A few moments later, he had assembled the components into a powerful directional transmitter. Then he spoke a few quick words into a pencil mike attached to the transmitter.

"Attic, this is Trawler. Request dust-off."

The touch of a few controls compressed the seven-word

message into a data package that could be transmitted in less than a tenth of a second, and sent it burning skyward.

"OK," the commo-op said, nodding. "Now we wait."

Forty-five minutes later, a gray-painted KR-61 Long Range Shuttle skimmed in low over the treetops. Even before its landing gear touched the grass in the clearing, the black-clad figures had dashed out of their concealed positions. In less than thirty seconds, all eight had rushed across the intervening space and darted through the open cargo hatch.

As the last man lunged aboard, Ryan hammered his fist against the bulkhead separating the cargo hold from the ship's control desk.

"That's it! Go! Go! Go!"

A harsh whine filled the tiny space as the ramp began to close. Before it was fully secured, the ship tilted sharply upward. The pilot lifted the craft clear of the ground. The roar of vertical-take-off thrusters tortured the ears of the passengers, despite noise-attenuation circuits built into their helmets.

Normally, the KR-61 was used to ferry eight tons of cargo in its tiny hold. Eight people, plus their equipment, made for cramped conditions. The shuttle was smaller than any normal DropShip, and her Pitban 300a drive system made her faster than most other small spacecraft. She had been selected by the operational planners for exactly those characteristics.

As the inertia of a high-speed boost lifted, *Tai-i* Michael Ryan released the seals on his sneaksuit and removed the heavy helmet and visor. Rolling his head, he stretched his neck muscles. The aching sinews that had supported the almost two-kilo mass of helmet and sensor array for the past thirty-six hours began to relax. Looking around the narrow cargo hold, he felt a sense of pride in the six men and two women jammed in beside him.

These eight warriors had accomplished what no other Draconis Elite Strike Team ever had. They had made a HALO jump onto a Clan-occupied world. The High-Altitude-Low-Opening parachute drop had allowed the DEST team to land undetected a few kilometers away from the Jaguar base. Once on the ground, they had penetrated a Clan installation, sabotaged the enemy's sensor and communication arrays, left nasty little surprises on the main gyro housings of a Binary of assault OmniMechs, and exfiltrated again, all without a single friendly casualty.

Ryan smiled to himself, imagining the shock of the Smoke Jaguar pilots the next time they tried to start up their machines. The instant the 'Mech's computer sent an interface signal to the massive gyroscope, the small charge of pentaglycerine would detonate. The prepackaged shaped charges would send a high-velocity explosion into the gyro housing, shattering the delicate equipment that provided a BattleMech with its balance. The image of the toppling 'Mechs brought a hard grin to Ryan's face. The damage, although repairable, would take the Clan techs at least four hours. And he knew that the Jaguars wouldn't have four hours.

At first, Ryan had thought it was foolish to simply damage the OmniMechs rather than to destroy them. Then the Draconis Combine Mustered Soldiery briefer had told him the purpose of the raid. Intelligence sources reported that the Jaguars were fielding upgraded versions of their standard OmniMechs. The DCMS wanted a look at these new machines. They also knew that replacement 'Mechs were shipped in from beyond the Periphery, through Bangor, before being deployed to front-line units.

The higher-ups at DCMS command had decided on a two-phase operation. Draconis Elite Strike Team Six, under *Tai-i* Ryan, had entered the Bangor system "piggybacked" on a commercial JumpShip. While the ship was recharging, the team's long-range shuttle detached, taking shelter in the thin asteroid belt occupying the system's number three orbit. Once the transport jumped outsystem again, and the hubbub died down, the shuttle crept into position for an orbital HALO drop.

As soon as the troopers started their long fall toward the planet's surface, the shuttle slipped away to hide among the asteroids. Once on the ground, the DEST team sabotaged the central communications and sensor facility at Reega, seat of the Jaguars' occupation force government. They also rendered the new 'Mechs unusable without destroying them, and exfiltrated, just as the real raid was being launched.

"Ryan-*san*?" The shuttle pilot's voice broke across Ryan's musings. "There they go, sir."

Ryan squeezed through the narrow hatch and onto the tiny flight deck.

Through the ship's viewscreens, he saw the reason the Clanners wouldn't have four hours to swap out the damaged gyros. At greater than two hundred kilometers, it was impossible to make out individual ships, but he could see the nova-bright drive flares of four *Leopard* Class DropShips burning hard for Bangor's surface. Ryan didn't know what unit was being sent to raid the planet, and he didn't care. His part of the operation was over. He and his team had cleared the way for the raiding force to arrive on-planet with no warning. They had also crippled the defenders' most powerful weapons. Now it was up to the 'Mech pilots, those high-and-mighty armor jockeys who claimed to have a monopoly on the warrior spirit of the Draconis Combine, men who never saw their enemy except through the armored viewscreen of a multi-ton pile of armor and weapons.

No, Ryan told himself, as he watched the distant Drop-Ships streaking toward the planet below, *if anyone in the Draconis Combine knows what it is to be a warrior, it is the men and women of DEST.*

2

*DEST Tactical Command Center
Pesht, Pesht Military District
Draconis Combine
22 August 3058
1505 hours*

"*Tai-i* Ryan, describe your method of entry."

Michael Ryan shook his head slightly, unable to hide the small gesture of impatience. His team had been debriefed by the on-site intelligence officer as soon as the KR-61 had docked with the JumpShip *Damascus*. He had gone over the material again with a second Internal Security Force officer when the ship stopped to recharge at Maldonado. Now, here they were, at the DEST HQ on Pesht, being quizzed by yet a third ISF officer, this one wearing the collar flashes of a *Sho-sa*. The nametape sewn above the officer's left breast pocket read Leshko, but Ryan doubted it was the name he was born with. ISF officers changed their identities as often as ordinary people changed their socks.

Ryan knew he was bound by the code of duty to continue answering questions until hell freezes over, but it was still hard to understand this need for confirmation and reconfirmation of the facts. He and his team were *warriors*. Warriors of a special stripe. Few were chosen for DEST, and even fewer survived the grueling training. DEST commandos had no rivals in the Inner Sphere, and were reserved for only the most important missions. Why would anyone doubt what he had to say?

Ryan was proud, and justifiably so, of the feat his team had accomplished on Bangor. They had penetrated an enemy camp, sabotaged his most powerful weapons, and escaped undetected. Nevertheless, he struggled to maintain a polite, formal tone of voice with his inquisitor. Proud he might be, an elite warrior he might be, but that did not excuse him from the unquestioning obedience required of any Combine soldier.

"We approached the facility from the south," he said. "Sior and Carter set up their position on a low hillock about one kilometer from the wall. My team approached the wall in sneak suits and got ready to climb. An Elemental stopped for a rest right above our position. Lance Corporal Sior fired a single shot, neutralizing the sentry. Then we went up and over the wall, using standard issue climbing-claws."

This last was not, strictly speaking true. Ryan's team had found the Combine-issue climbing claws uncomfortable, and also discovered that they often bent or broke under the weight of a fully loaded trooper. Instead they'd used commercially made climbing gear intended for civilian rock climbers and ninja-wannabes. Ryan neglected to mention this fact, knowing it would only generate a reprimand for deviating even slightly from Combine military policy. The mission was complete—a success—what good would it do to draw down criticism now?

"Once over the wall, the team paired up and headed for their respective assignments. Raiko and Wu disabled the communications and sensor systems by destroying the antenna arrays. Hollis and Akida set bobby traps on what our diagrams identified as warriors' barracks. Tanabe and I rigged the charges on the 'Mechs. Private Nakamura remained on top of the wall, covering the compound with his light machine gun."

The debriefer nodded as he tapped notes into his datapad. "Go on."

"*Hai.*" Ryan ran his hand through his thick, straight black hair. "Tanabe and I planted quarter-kilo shaped charges on the gyro housings of the target 'Mechs. The detonator circuits were attached to the cables leading to the neurohelmet interface. As soon as we finished, we exfiltrated."

"Did you engage any hostiles?"

"Aside from the sentry neutralized by Corporal Sior, we did not engage the enemy."

"*Tai-i,* your report states that Talon Sergeant Raiko and Private Wu were carrying a captured briefcase when they reached the team rally point." Leshko gave Ryan an up-and-under look without lifting his eyes from his computer screen. "Why was that case so important that they could not leave it behind for the follow-on forces?"

"Sir, it is a well-known principle in warfare that no plan of battle survives contact with the enemy." Ryan's irritation flared briefly into annoyance. He was one of the few men of non-Japanese descent to be given command of a Draconis Elite Strike Team. He had been carefully schooled in the subtleties of Combine society, particularly where it touched on the military. Still, he couldn't help but chafe at times under the weight of the ponderous command structure of the Draconis Combine Mustered Soldiery. He usually put his attitude down to his occidental heritage.

"During the course of his assignment, Raiko discovered a concealed safe in an office adjoining the communication/sensor center," Ryan continued. "He investigated the safe and found the briefcase, which held both hardcopy and datachip copies of the blueprints, maintenance manuals, and technical readouts of the 'Mechs we were sent to sabotage. He decided that the case was too valuable to leave.

"Had we left that case for the ground-pounders, they'd probably have missed it. Since we were under orders to maintain strict radio silence until we sent the pick-up beacon, we were not able to communicate with the follow-ons. Even if we'd been free to contact them, we were not informed of their tactical or command frequencies. Raiko decided that the value of the case's contents outweighed the increased risk in capturing it." Ryan finished with an impatient snap of his head.

Sho-sa Leshko's head came up sharply at Ryan's outburst. Yes, Ryan had snarled at a superior officer, but the officer had questioned the authority of an on-site commander.

Each of them had breached the rigid code of military protocol that bound every warrior of the DCMS. For a moment, the two men glared at each other. Then Leshko dropped his eyes, as though reviewing the data displayed on the laptop's LCD screen.

"You're right, of course, *Tai-i*," Leshko muttered. "The data you retrieved was invaluable."

"*Hai, Sho-sa.*" Ryan lapsed into the formal Japanese of the Combine. "*Sumimasen,* I should not have raised my voice."

"*Shigataga-nai,* Ryan-*san.*" Leshko followed suit, saying that Ryan's outburst didn't matter. "What matters is that you completed your mission in a satisfactory manner. My report will so state."

"*Arigato.*" Ryan inclined his head in the ghost of a bow. In his own mind, however, a brief prayer echoed.

The Dragon save me from bureaucratic fools.

As in every other case when a soldier expressed that fervent wish, nobody answered.

Half an hour later, Ryan was again summoned to the Command Center.

He'd been riding the thin edge of exhaustion by the time he and his team arrived on Pesht. The journey from Bangor had taken just over a week, but most of his time had been taken up in writing reports, answering debriefer's questions, and the like. After speaking with *Sho-sa* Leshko, Ryan had assumed he was finished explaining his team's highly successful, but relatively routine mission. He'd only just lain down on his bunk when the intercom let forth its sharp, unpleasant buzz.

Giri, duty, demanded that he answer the summons promptly, but fatigue had begun to take its toll on his temper, and his manners. He got up, pulled on his clothes, and took the lift to the Command Center.

By the time he reached its steel doors, he had mastered himself and was able to calmly enter the room that had by now become all too familiar.

"*Tai-i* Michael Ryan reporting as ordered," he snapped, bringing his hand up in a rigid salute.

His salute was returned not by *Sho-sa* Leshko nor by his immediate superior, *Sho-sa* Martin Chisei, both of whom were present, but by *Sho-sho* Hideki Ishmaru, the new commanding officer of the entire DEST program.

Ishmaru's presence took Ryan by surprise, putting him on his guard. The *Sho-sho* had taken over the leadership of the Draconis Elite Strike Teams following *Tai-sho* Hohiro Kiguri's death during the treachery. Ryan had heard the rumors surrounding Kiguri's involvement in the shameful assassination attempt on Coordinator Theodore Kurita during the Coordinator's Birthday celebration a few months earlier. Ryan knew that Ishmaru was, by reputation, an excellent administrator, a ruthless warrior, and fanatically loyal to the Kurita family. Still, on a personal level, the man was an unknown quantity. That uncertainty left Ryan with an uneasy feeling regarding Ishmaru's presence.

"Konnichi-wa, Tai-i Ryan." Ishmaru's greeting was cold and formal. "Is there a problem?"

"Konnichi-wa, Sho-sho Ishmaru-*sama."* Ryan stopped short and bowed, barely remembering to wish his commander a good afternoon in return. "No, *Sho-sho,* there is no problem."

"I am glad. It is not good when problems arise between junior officers and their superiors, *neh*?" Ishmaru's curt reply carried with it a thinly veiled threat, one Ryan could not miss.

Without waiting for Ryan's answer, Ishmaru plunged ahead.

"I realize your team has just come out of the field, but I have an important mission that cannot wait. It comes straight from the Coordinator."

Ryan almost forgot himself, but his training won out and he maintained a stone face as he listened to the most fateful words he'd ever heard since becoming one of the hand-picked members of DEST.

"You, *Sho-sa* Chisei, and Team Six are to report to the spaceport this evening at seventeen hundred hours. You will be shipping out on a kind of diplomatic mission. Your men should take along their dress uniforms, in addition to their regular gear. For the purposes of this assignment, your team will assume the cover of the personal security detail for a high Combine military official. Your loyalty to the Combine has been firmly established, Ryan-*san,* as has your team's. I am sure you can appreciate the position this places you in? Very few DEST teams have survived the recent loyalty inquiry intact. Yours did. That makes you and your men very valuable to the Combine. Yours is one of the few teams into whose hands we can still entrust the lives and safety of our highest-ranking officers."

Ryan felt the weariness drain out of him, to be replaced by a sense of pride. Here would be another opportunity for his team to serve the Dragon. It had been only a few weeks since the shameful attempt upon the Coordinator's life by *Tai-sho* commander Hohiro Kiguri, aided and abetted by other renegade DEST members and even members of the Otomo, the Coordinator's personal bodyguard. For Ryan and all other loyal DEST men and women, the conspiracy was a stain on their honor. Most had become even more eager to serve the Combine, hoping that loyalty and service might erase the blot. *Sho-sho* Ishmaru noticed the subtle change in Ryan's stance and nodded approvingly as he went on speaking.

"You will be met in transit by several other DCMS officers. When you arrive at your destination, you are to lend your support and expertise in the planning of a special military operation. As a field operative, your input will be most useful."

"Hai, Sho-sho, wakarimas." Ryan bowed again. "May I ask the *Sho-sho* who we will be guarding, and what our destination is?"

"Of course, *Tai-i*." Ishmaru smiled for the first time since Ryan had entered the room. "You will be escorting Coordinator Theodore Kurita to Tharkad."

3

From her place on the reviewing stand, General Ariana Winston watched the latest crop of Eridani Light Horse cadets march by in proud display, their uniforms highlighted by the gleam of the late afternoon sun. She couldn't help but smile in satisfaction. It was good to be back on Kikuyu and the Light Horse training base at Fort Telemar. It was also good to know that the Light Horse was almost up to its full strength of three combat regiments after the devastating losses on Coventry. It was hard to believe how much had happened since then.

Winston hadn't returned directly to Fort Telemar after Coventry, but had been summoned to Tharkad by Archon Katrina Steiner. There, the leaders of the Inner Sphere had gathered for the Whitting Conference, the first big summit since Outreach. Winston had arrived home only yesterday, and was pleased that her arrival coincided with the graduation ceremony. She'd come with big news, though no one else knew it yet. Watching the fresh, young faces parade past, it suddenly seemed to her that the long and proud history of the Eridani Light Horse had all been leading up to this day, this moment.

When Aleksandr Kerensky vanished from the Inner Sphere centuries before, taking most of the Star League Defense Force with him, the Light Horse regiments had remained behind. But they had never forgotten their Star League roots or their belief that one day the Star League would rise from the ashes. The unit was steeped in its illustrious history, had even added the black border to their banner as a symbol of mourning for the exodus of General Kerensky. Every Light Horse trooper dreamed of the day when he or she might, with pride, don the uniform of the SLDF. And now a new Star League Defense Force was being mustered. They were going to take the war to the Clans and drive them from the Inner Sphere forever.

It was, for Ariana Winston, a source of special pride that Marshal Morgan Hasek-Davion had selected her as his second in command of a secret task force that would strike directly into the heart of the Clans—at Huntress, homeworld of the Smoke Jaguars. It would be a difficult and dangerous undertaking, but if anyone could pull it off, it was Morgan. He was as legendary for his exploits on the field as for his expertise at the highest levels of command. He'd also been the Light Horse's high commander during the Clan War, and Winston couldn't wait to serve alongside him again.

As the Light Horse standard, a prancing black horse against a gold background, passed the reviewing stand, she and the dozen other officers crowding the small platform snapped to attention. Almost as one, they brought up their right hands, palms outward, saluting the flag they and their families had followed for more than three hundred years. The banner carrier repaid the honor by dipping the flag. The flag staff was liberally hung with colored ribbons, each denoting a battle or campaign in which the Light Horse had played a part. Most of the battle honors were brightly colored, but a few, like the one commemorating the massacre of Sendai, were made of somber black silk.

The most recent addition to the battle honors read "Coventry," the single word sending a brief chill along Winston's spine. Merely seeing the name of that blood-soaked planet was enough to bring back memories of the close-quarters, no-mercy fighting. Coventry marked the first real cooperative military effort on the part of the Successor States in nearly three hundred years. In that campaign, an expeditionary force, drawn from the militaries of each of the Great Houses, had banded together to halt the Jade Falcons' relentless drive into the Lyran Alliance.

The regimental band closed the formalities with a heartfelt rendering of the old Star League anthem. As Winston lowered her hand from the final salute, she felt an odd warming in her heart. Though the Light Horse had gone mercenary in the centuries since the Exodus, she was proud that the unit had never lost faith in their dream of the Star League reborn. Hearing the anthem never failed to move her, though today it seemed different somehow. The strains of that old, old song drifting across the parade ground sounded almost mournful, and Winston was suddenly flooded with a sense of doom.

She quickly shook off the feeling, telling herself it was only fatigue from travel across the stars. She wasn't going to let anything spoil this moment. If asked, she would have been hard put to decide which was a source of greater excitement, the mission itself or the historic decision to unite the Inner Sphere under the banner of the Star League. Taking the war to the Clans was going to be a great day for every man, woman, and child alive, yet the note of sadness in the familiar melody gave her a shiver in spite of the unusual warmth of the afternoon.

Winston waited for the other officers to leave the platform, then turned to the man who'd stood next to her during the ceremony. "Join me for a drink, Scott? I've got a bottle of forty-year old Northwind whiskey I've been saving for a special occasion."

"Why, thank you, General," Scott Hinesick replied, executing a short, formal bow. "We *do* have something to celebrate. For the first time since the Fourth War, the Light Horse is up to full strength." Colonel Scott Hinesick was one of Ariana Winston's oldest friends. He alone knew of her weakness for the whiskey distilled by the transplanted Scotsmen of Northwind. He was also the person who'd done the most to rebuild the Light Horse back up to its three full regiments in the years since the War of 3039.

Winston followed him down the steps of the podium. Physically, Hinesick was her opposite in nearly every way. She was tall, with a well-muscled, athletic build. Hinesick, on the other hand was a slight, wiry man whose skin was as pale as hers was dark. He stopped at the foot of the stairs and turned to wait for her to join him.

"You've got something on your mind," he said, a look of concern clouding his features. "And I'm sure it's got something to do with that big pow-wow on Tharkad."

Winston nodded slowly. Scott Hinesick knew her almost as well as she knew herself. "You don't miss much, Scott. Something wonderful and terrible is about to happen, and you and I are going to see it."

Ariana Winston's office was larger than those of the other Light Horse commanders, but otherwise resembled them in many ways. The walls were paneled in wood veneer and lined with shelves filled with ancient, hardcopy books. Also decorating the walls were memorabilia of Light Horse regiments dating back to Wellington's Light Cavalry regiments of eighteen-century England. A conference table fitted with holographic and flat-screen data displays dominated the additional space.

One of the few non-military items in the room was the silver picture frame that occupied a place of honor on Winston's cluttered desk. The picture showed a much younger Ariana Winston mugging for the camera with an older gentleman wearing the moon-and-star crest of the Twenty-first Striker Regiment. Despite the fact that his skin was somewhat lighter than the mahogany hue of her own, the family resemblance was unmistakable, as was the love Winston had for her father. Charles Winston had been dead for five years now. The edges of the frame were worn, indicating that she handled the picture often.

In addition to the heavy wood-veneered desk, plain office chairs, and metal file cabinets, a pair of overstuffed armchairs stood before a stone fireplace. Winston had asked her aide to start a good hot fire, knowing that despite the warming weather, Hinesick's old wounds would be paining him. A training accident in 3039 had cost her friend his right arm. Though the Light Horse had given him the best medical care possible, even providing an advanced prosthetic, his injuries were severe enough to disqualify him from combat duty. Since his skills and hard-won knowledge were too valuable to waste, he was assigned to the training cadre, eventually rising to take command of the training battalion itself. Winston knew that much of the credit for rebuilding the Seventy-first Regiment, which had been virtually destroyed in the 3039 War, went to him.

An orderly took their heavy gray-green overcoats as they entered, then respectfully withdrew. Winston strode over to an antique wardrobe, out of place next to the modern filing cabinets, and produced a green, three-sided bottle. Scott flashed her a lopsided grin from the fireside chair he'd just taken. He obviously recognized the black and gold label proclaiming the bottle's contents to be Cromarty Black, perhaps the finest whiskey produced outside of the Highlands of Scotland.

After pouring "a wee dram or two" for each of them, Winston settled into the chair facing her old friend.

The stiffness with which Hinesick reached for his glass, coupled with knowing how much he loved the Light Horse and the traditions it held dear, gave Winston a small stab of pain. She knew she was going to have to tell her oldest and dearest friend that he must remain behind while she went off to war. She took another sip of the rich amber whiskey, trying to delay that inevitable moment.

"That was a fine bunch of troopers you graduated today," she said. "I saw their test scores. Some of them placed pretty high, better even than some Sanglamore or Nagelring grads. And, after the way the Seventy-first got hammered on Coventry, we're going to need them."

Scott nodded as he savored the first sip of his Cromarty Black. "Those cadets will go a long way to getting us back up to strength, Ria." Hinesick was one of the few outside of her own family who used the diminutive form of her name. "We're almost back up to our full complement of three combat regiments. And just in time, too. With the way everyone worked together on Coventry, you and I may still live to see the Star League reborn."

The words gave Winston a start, but Hinesick didn't seem to notice. He was positively beaming at the idea. It wasn't just the Eridani Light Horse who worshipped the memory of the long-gone Star League. For most people of the Inner Sphere, it was a golden age, an era remembered with reverent awe for its legendary peace, prosperity, and technological advancement.

"Just think," Hinesick said. "Today may be one of the last times we play the Star League anthem as a mere ceremony," Hinesick gestured grandly with his glass. "By the time the next class graduates, we may have a united Inner Sphere."

"I hope you're right, Scott. I mean, that *is* the dream of

the Light Horse, isn't it?" Winston held her own glass in both hands, and stared into the flames crackling in the fireplace. She knew that in a short while she would be briefing her regimental commanders on the decisions of the Whitting Conference. With them, she would have to be the tough professional soldier. But here and now, in a rare quiet moment, sharing a drink with her best friend in the world, she couldn't help letting some of her very real, very human fears and reservations bleed off.

"What is it they say, Scott? A great and terrible day? That may be exactly what's coming. You say we're nearly back up to full strength since the pounding we took on Coventry. On paper, that's true. The Light Horse and the rest of the Coventry Expeditionary Force beat the Jade Falcons at their own game, but we lost nearly a third of our strength doing it. And what if we'd lost? Would the Falcons have pushed on to Tharkad? Would the truce still be intact? No, there's too much in this world that can go sour for me to be quite that optimistic just yet."

"Old gloomy Ria. It's nice to know you haven't changed," Hinesick teased.

"Well, I . . ."

Suddenly, he turned serious.

"Listen, Ria. You've been cat-footing around here all day, and I know it's got something to do with the big meet on Tharkad, but you don't seem to want to talk about it. Dammit! I'm Light Horse, I've got a right to know."

"You're wrong, Scott. I do want to talk about it. That's why I invited you up. But first, let's get the other regimental commanders in here too."

Hinesick got up and went over the visphone.

"What's this all about, Ria?" he said, hand poised over the buttons.

"Just get Ed, Sandy, and Charles up here," Winston told him. "I'll explain everything, then."

Fifteen minutes later, Ariana Winston was inviting all her regimental commanders to take seats at the conference table in her office. Joining her and Scott Hinesick were Colonels Charles Antonescu, Edwin Amis, and Sandra Barclay.

"I know that the rumors have been pretty thick upon the ground every since I got back," Winston began in her characteristically brusque manner. "Well, it's time to set the record straight."

"We're listening, General," said Antonescu, CO of the elite 151st Light Horse Regiment. A recruit back in 3029, Antonescu had risen up the ranks to his current post in 3050. The ink had barely been dry on the Light Horse contract with Hanse Davion at that time, and Charles had cut his teeth as a regimental commander in the war against the Clans.

"Good," Winston said crisply. "As you all know, Victor Davion began calling for the Inner Sphere to carry the fight to the Clans almost from the moment the Coventry campaign was over. That's what the Whitting Conference was about. All the heads of state were there, and many of their top military advisors. The way I hear it, it's a miracle any of them ever saw eye to eye, but the fact is they did. What's more, they came up with a plan—a daring plan. And the Eridani Light Horse is a big part of it."

Her three regimental commanders suddenly sat up straight. Alert, obviously excited by the news. Winston allowed herself a slight smile, remembering her own thrill at hearing it.

"We're to participate in a special operation task force," she went on. "They're calling it Task Force Serpent. Our entire combat arm will immediately begin preparations to ship out for the world of Defiance in the Federated Commonwealth. We're to be on-site no later than the fifteenth of February 3059. Once there, we will engage in a period of training and integration exercises with other task force units."

"What other units?" asked Ed Amis, the Twenty-first Striker's commander. He was still holding his unlit cigar. "You trying to be mysterious, General?" The veteran colonels couldn't have been more different. Where Antonescu did everything by the book, Amis was ever the maverick. That hadn't kept him from being an outstanding enough soldier that he'd won command of the Twenty-first during the War of 3039.

"No, Ed, I'm not trying to be mysterious. This is the biggest thing that's ever come our way. Bigger even than the Clan War. We're going to attack one of the Clans, fighting alongside some of the most elite outfits in the Inner Sphere. Com Guards, Northwind Highlanders, Knights of the Inner Sphere, Lyran Guards, First Kathil Uhlans, St. Ives Lancers, Fourth Drakøns—there'll be thousands of us. A huge fleet, with Morgan Hasek-Davion in command of the whole operation. Morgan's already on Defiance right now."

"Defiance?" Amis wanted to know. "What's there?"

"Not much," Winston said. "It's a backwater world that won't attract a lot of attention. But it's also got military support facilities because the FedCom has used it for war games from time to time. Our mission is top-secret, and deploying from so deep in Davion space will help cover our tracks."

Amis still looked confused. "You said we're going to attack the Clans."

"That's right. We're going to hit them where it will hurt them most. And for the biggest possible impact, we're going to hit them as a new Star League Defense Force. You've heard by now that the Great House leaders all signed a Star League constitution on Tharkad."

"We heard about it but we didn't really know what it meant," Antonescu said.

Winston smiled thinly. "Well, it means a new First Lord, and his name is Sun-Tzu Liao."

"You're joking," Amis said, but he didn't look like he thought it was funny. He still had not lit his cigar.

Winston shook her head. "No joke, my friends. The position rotates every three years. We don't know who'll be next."

"I'll never bow to that jackass, if you'll excuse my French, General."

"Maybe you won't have to, Ed. Our mission's going to take us beyond the borders of the Inner Sphere. A lot could happen before we get back."

Antonescu broke in. "Pardon me, General, but I'm still not sure what you're telling us. We're going to be part of a task force of top Inner Sphere units, both House units and mercenaries. But this is supposed to be a new Star League army? And we're going to attack the Clans from the Periphery while Sun-Tzu Liao takes over as new boss of the Star League?"

"That's about the size of it, Charles, except for the location of our target. We're going beyond the Periphery for this one."

Amis let out a low whistle as Winston turned to the

most junior of the Light Horse commanders. "You've been awful quiet, Sandy."

Colonel Sandra Barclay, commander of the recently re-built Seventy-first Light Horse Regiment, shook her head. "Me? I'm still the new kid in town. I just follow orders," she said, but her smile showed a hint of sadness. Winston had faced considerable opposition from long-time Light Horse officers over her promotion of Major Sandra Barclay to command of the Seventy-first, but the bitter fighting on Coventry had confirmed the rightness of the decision.

Barclay had performed beyond even Winston's expectations during the Seventy-first's fiercely opposed drop onto Coventry. It wasn't until later, when the Light Horse was trapped with the rest of the Inner Sphere defenders in the besieged town of Lietnerton, that Winston began to notice something eating away at the younger woman. By the time it was all over, much of Barclay's command was shattered almost beyond repair. Barclay seemed to be blaming herself for the losses, even though no one else did. Winston had taken her aside one day. "The first rule of warfare is that young people die, Sandy," she said. "The second rule is that commanders can't change Rule Number One."

Barclay seemed to accept her counsel at the time, but there was a tightness around her eyes and a grittiness in her voice that told Winston the younger woman would bear watching.

Ed Amis interrupted her brief reverie, voice full of awe. "We've been waiting all our lives for a new Star League, General."

Winston nodded. "All our lives, Ed. And the Eridani Light Horse regiments have been dreaming of it for almost three centuries. Nobody can say we didn't keep the faith." She couldn't help but feel that the Light Horse would now be vindicated in its fierce loyalty to tradition and its vow to live to see the Star League reborn.

"That's it for now," she said. "There's a lot more, but I want to get everyone together for that. Tell your battalion commanders we'll have a full command staff briefing in the conference room at 0800 the day after tomorrow."

"General," Antonescu said, rising and coming to attention as he addressed her. "I'm only on Kikuyu for the graduation ceremony. All my battalion commanders and most of my personal staff are still on Mogyorod. Nobody had a clue you'd be scheduling a meeting like this." The nearby world of Mogyorod was the other planet the Light Horse garrisoned in service to the Lyran Alliance.

"I know that, Charles. I've already sent word. Your people are coming in aboard the *Buford*. Mogyorod's only a jump away. They should be here sometime tomorrow night. Anything else?" She saw Antonescu's eyes narrow slightly as he worked it out that she'd been pulling strings even in the short time since her return.

Unlike most mercenary companies serving the various Successor States, the Eridani Light Horse actually owned a number of JumpShips. The *Star Lord* Class JumpShip *Buford* was one such interstellar vessel, and had been assigned to Antonescu's 151st Light Horse. With Mogyorod but a few light years distant, the trip would be instantaneous. Still, it would take a high-speed shuttle some time to make the trip insystem from the jump point.

"No, General, nothing else. Thank you." Antonescu returned to his seat.

Winston nodded once.

"Dismissed."

The MechWarrior colonels saluted and left quietly. Only Scott Hinesick kept his seat.

"I know you, Ria." He leaned back in his chair as he spoke. "There's more. Something you didn't tell them."

Winston nodded. "I didn't tell them that Marshal Hasek-Davion personally requested that I serve as his second-in-command. And I didn't tell them that the Eridani Light Horse, as one of the few combat units able to trace its heritage back to the Star League, has been asked to help draft a set of general regulations for the new Star League Defense Force."

"C'mon, Ria. That's not all. You're still holding back something else . . ." Hinesick's grin faded as realization set in. "Unless you mean . . ."

"Yeah, Scott, that's what I mean." Winston took a deep breath, trying to delay the moment of actually uttering the words. "You won't be coming with us."

Hinesick stared at her for what seemed like an eternity. "Well, General," he said finally, fighting for control of his voice, which had become as brittle as frozen iron. "A little while ago you told me something wonderful and terrible was about to happen. You didn't lie."

Without another word, Scott Hinesick rose from his chair and crossed to the door. As the door clicked shut behind him, Winston wanted to call him back. But what was the use? Nothing would change. She shook her head sadly, knowing how painful it would be for Hinesick to be left behind while she and the rest of the Eridani Light Horse rode off to meet their destiny.

4

Fort Telemar
Kikuyu, Tamar March
Lyran Alliance
15 December 3058
0900 Hours

As Ariana Winston had predicted, the senior and staff officers of Charles Antonescu's 151st Light Horse Regiment arrived less than twenty-four hours after the meeting in her office broke up. They came aboard the *Cossack,* a Union Class DropShip assigned to the JumpShip *Buford.* That put all the various Light Horse commanders on Kikuyu.

DropShips were an absolute necessity for space travel. With the collapse of the Star League, the secrets of building starships that could both jump between star systems and travel within those star systems had been lost. Only the occasional discovery of a forgotten Star League library core gave any glimmer of hope to those longing for a return to the glory days of yore. The latest, and perhaps greatest, discovery of these vintage storehouses of information was the so-called Gray Death memory core. With the decoding of the information recovered by the famous (or infamous, depending upon who you talked to) mercenary company, Inner Sphere scientists began to unlock the secrets known to their forebears. Adding to this already staggering wealth of information, ComStar broke its centuries-old veil of silence, revealing that they retained at least part of the old knowledge.

The combination of the two, along with equipment recovered following the rare Clan defeat, went a long way toward returning the Inner Sphere to a shadow of its former glory. Still, it had been only six years since the Truce of Tukayyid, and just three decades since the discovery of the Gray Death memory core. WarShips and intra-system capable JumpShips were being built, but at a painfully slow rate.

Thus, most in-system travel was accomplished by means of DropShips, massive spacecraft capable of transporting cargo and passengers between an inhabited planet and a JumpShip hanging in space above the local sun. Even in the heyday of the Star League, such ships were necessary, as no JumpShip could ever land on a planet's surface.

Colonel Antonescu had met his officers at the spaceport and given them a synopsis of General Winston's briefing of day before.

In the short time since that meeting, Fort Telemar, the spaceport city of Brandtford Heights, and the surrounding region had been transformed. Gone were the small knots of soldiers in Light Horse dress-greens lounging around sidewalk tables in Brandtford's central shopping district. In their place were pairs or trios of armed troopers, all wearing the age-old black brassard emblazoned with the white block letters "MP." At Fort Telemar's main gate, a black- and yellow-striped steel barrier had been placed across the roadway. Four armed troopers manned the checkpoint.

As Antonescu's command car drew up to a halt before the closed gate, two of the troopers stepped forward, leveling heavy laser rifles at the vehicle's occupants. A third soldier, this one wearing the divided white and green square of a corporal, strode to the hovercar's left side, his right hand dangerously close to the holstered sidearm slung low on his right hip.

"Identification." The corporal rapped out the word, as though daring anyone in the car to make trouble.

Antonescu bit back a snarl and glared darkly at the young man for a moment before handing over his papers. The corporal seemed unimpressed by the Colonel's angry gaze. If anything, he took far more time than necessary to review Antonescu's identity card and gate pass. The rest of Antonescu's staff barely got a glance.

"Thank you, Colonel." The guard returned the papers, stepped back, and motioned to the fourth man, who had remained in the guard shack.

As the barrier rose with the whine of an electric motor, the guard corporal snapped a salute. Antonescu didn't return the courtesy, but merely nudged his driver, who engaged the car's fans and drove off.

"For cryin' out loud, Colonel." Major Gary Ribic shook his head in disbelief. "What was that all about?" Rib was commander of the Eighth Recon Battalion.

"It's General Winston's idea," Antonescu told him. "Did you notice? The only Light Horse personnel you saw in town were the MPs. All leaves and liberties have been canceled, quote 'for the duration' end-quote. Anyone with even the hint of a shadow on their security check has had their clearance revoked. No one outside this compound, and only a few inside, know what's about to happen, and we'd like to keep it that way."

"So what *is* going on?"

"Major Ribic, you will learn everything you need to know at tomorrow's briefing." That said, Charles Antonescu leaned back in his seat, closed his eyes, and began to gently massage his temples, leaving Ribic's curiosity no more satisfied than before.

The next morning, Major Gary Ribic and the rest of the senior Light Horse officers were getting their answers.

The first to speak was, of course, Ariana Winston.

"Gentlemen, what I am about to tell you cannot leave this room. As you all know, I have only recently arrived from Tharkad. There's been a lot of speculation about what went on there. Well, from here on, it's not rumors anymore."

For the next few minutes, Winston outlined what she knew of the Whitting Conference. She didn't dwell on the political wrangling that invariably occurred between the crowned heads of the Inner Sphere, but stuck to the issues important to the men and women under her command. They learned about the plan to reestablish the Star

League and that Sun-Tzu Liao would serve as the new First Lord of the League.

Then she said, "That's not all. The biggest news is that the armies of the Inner Sphere will unite to attack and destroy one of the clans so totally that it will shock and terrify the rest. The Clan chosen was the Smoke Jaguars."

Winston paused to let her words sink in as absolute silence descended over the briefing room. She let the silence hang for a moment before continuing. "This invasion of the Clans will be carried out under the banner of the Star League Defense Force. It will consist of two carefully timed operations. Operation Bulldog will be headed by Victor Davion—a surprise attack on the Smoke Jaguar occupied worlds. The other will be a secret task force under the command of Marshal Morgan Hasek-Davion. The Eridani Light Horse will serve as a principal member of the second force, which will include units drawn from each of the Successor States, ComStar, and the Northwind Highlanders. We will be billed as the reserve force for the first operation, but that will be just a smoke screen."

A murmur ran through the room. Though no one spoke aloud, Winston could sense the excitement and pride rippling through her officers.

"The target of this coalition task force is one the Clans wouldn't expect in their worst nightmares. We will be launching a strike against a planet known as Huntress, the homeworld of the Smoke Jaguars!"

"God in Heaven." Antonescu's voice was hushed and full of awe. The news was so momentous that the utterly proper Colonel abandoned military protocol, interrupting his commander with his stunned utterance.

"The overall objective of both operations will be the same," Winston continued, unfazed by her subordinate's uncharacteristic breach of custom. "To destroy the entire Smoke Jaguar Clan."

Again, there was silence in the briefing room. Even the normally unflappable Edwin Amis looked dumbfounded. The scope of the mission was so huge, and its objective so far reaching, that Winston's subordinates could scarcely comprehend it. She had felt almost exactly the same way at first. Colonel Charles Antonescu broke the silence.

"How is all this possible?" he asked. "Nobody knows the location of the Clan homeworlds. Did the Explorer

Corps and Teddy finally find what they've been looking for?" The Draconis Combine had been hit hard by the Clan invasion, and Theodore Kurita had long been insisting that the way to defeat the Clans was to find their homeworlds and destroy them there. He had been actively working with ComStar's Explorer Corps to discover the route to the Clan homeworlds.

"Not exactly, Colonel," Winston said. "Seems it was actually a Smoke Jaguar who gave up the information needed to map a route. Believe it or not, a Jaguar warrior defected to ComStar not long ago."

Scott Hinesick was shaking his head in wonderment. "The various units could probably pull together enough JumpShips to do something like this, but what happens when the Clanners send out their capital ships against the task force attacking Huntress? Nobody in the Inner Sphere's got the WarShips for this kind of operation."

"Nobody except ComStar, Scott."

"What?"

"I still don't know the whole story," Winston said, "but ComStar has apparently held and maintained a secret fleet of WarShips ever since the Exodus."

Now it was Hinesick's turn to be speechless. He sat back in his chair with a start, gaping at Winston as though she'd just demonstrated that pigs could fly.

"General, did we hear you correctly?" asked Sandra Barclay. "Did you say that we're going to destroy the entire Smoke Jaguar Clan?"

The Smoke Jaguars were considered to be the most bloodthirsty of the Clans. Like their namesake, they had raced across the Inner Sphere, gobbling up worlds and warriors with appalling speed and ferocity. Only Clans Wolf and Jade Falcon had matched or exceeded the Jaguar conquests. None matched them for ferocity. During the invasion, the Jaguars had directed a naval barrage against the city of Edo on Turtle Bay as a means of suppressing rebellion. The entire city had been leveled by the massive energies generated by the Clan WarShips. Such a thing hadn't occurred in the Inner Sphere for centuries.

"That's the plan, Sandy," Winston confirmed. "The Whitting Conference figures that if we wipe out the Jags, a Crusader Clan, it will make the rest of the Clans see us differently. Not only as the new Star League, but as a force to be reckoned with instead of barbarians to be conquered. In effect, wiping out the Jaguars will make us their peers."

Winston heard a muted oath of surprise, but couldn't determine which of her officers had spoken.

"*And,*" she continued, "by destroying a Crusader Clan, we'll hurt the Crusaders' credibility as a whole. We will also be sending a message to all the Clans. How can they claim to come here to restore the Star League if we've already done it? And how can they maintain their taste for the fight if we destroy a whole Clan?"

"Well, damn, General," said Edwin Amis. "I don't exactly know what to say. I don't think any of us do. First, you stand there and tell us that we're going off to re-form the Star League Defense Force—and that makes me want to raise six kinds of ruckus.

"Then, you say that our first job as the SLDF is to *wipe out a Clan*. Do the politicians really think we can pull that off?"

"Yes, Ed, they do," Winston said. "They've got this model of something they call 'entropy-based warfare.' I'm not going to go into it all right here and now, but, given what I heard in the military briefing on Tharkad, it sounds like we're going to grind the Jags down and then destroy every trace of their ability to make war."

"Whew," Amis said, for once at a loss for words.

For the next fifteen minutes, Ariana Winston answered questions and responded to comments, most of which ran to elation at the reformation of the Star League or awe at the prospect of trying to wipe out a whole Clan. When the last of her officers had taken his turn to speak, she addressed the whole group again.

"As the entire combat arm will be involved in this operation, the Lyran Alliance Armed Forces will be sending a couple of their line units to relieve us here and on Mogyorod. They will be arriving in a week or two, so you gentlemen will have to shoulder the task of getting the replacements up to speed, as well as getting our own people ready to move. The whole idea is to have them move in as quickly and as quietly as possible. We're awful close to the Jade Falcons, especially here on Kikuyu. The Clanners may not be up to the level of the Fox Fives or Loki, but you can bet your last C-Bill that they're watching every garrison along the border. Remember, it was a Clan intelligence officer who got Waco's Rangers wiped out on Coventry.

"We will make our way, with all possible speed, to the planet known as Defiance, in the Crucis March of the Federated Suns. That world is currently ungarrisoned, but it has all the 'Mech-handling facilities necessary to serve a task force of the size that will be training there. I gather that the base at Fort Defiance was constructed to service the Armed Forces Federated Suns, which has occasionally used that world for military exercises.

"While Defiance's environment isn't hostile, it's not pleasant. The atmosphere has moderate concentrations of sulfur and sulfur dioxides—enough to require the use of respirators and filter masks. Officially, we are being assigned as part of a 'reserve force' to be commanded by Morgan Hasek-Davion. So, even if word of our move leaks out, troop deployments to and from Defiance will be explained as our going to join the main body of the assault. I'm told that the various intelligence services involved are going to launch a disinformation campaign to cover troop movements and the training exercises on Defiance. They'll also try to explain away our absence once we launch the operation."

Winston steeled herself for the firestorm of protests she knew would follow her next announcement.

"The Sixth Donegal Guards Regimental Combat Team will be moving into our garrisons here at Fort Telemar and at Fort Shannon on Mogyorod."

The room erupted into a riot of shouted objections. Many of the complaints were identical to those Winston had voiced in a blistering protest to Field Marshal Nondi Steiner, commanding officer of the Lyran Alliance Armed Forces. The Field Marshal's answer had been less than polite. It was also the answer she was now prepared to give her own troops. The answer hadn't entirely satisfied her, nor did she expect it to satisfy the men and women under her command. But first, she had to get control of the situation in the briefing room.

"Ten-hut!" The shouted words rose over the babble of fifteen voices all talking at once. Most people forgot that Winston had come up through the ranks, and had never heard the drill-sergeant bellow she could still muster at a pinch. The arguments ceased as though a switch had been thrown.

"I don't like this any more than you do, but this is a military organization, not a quilting circle. I was given an order, and I passed it along to you. There is no room for debate."

Winston was surprised at the heat in her own voice. She'd thought she had put the resentment at having to entrust the lives and safety of the Light Horse's dependents to others behind her. Now that she had given the order, the feeling of anger came creeping back.

"General, you've given the order, and we will obey it." Major Kent Fairfax got to his feet and stood at rigid attention. "But may I remind the General that responsibility for the lives and safety of Light Horse dependents is solely the province of the Fiftieth Heavy Cavalry and Eighth Recon Battalions?"

"I know that, Kent." Winston's voice softened as she gazed at the blood-red "50" embroidered on the younger officer's left sleeve. "But we need the whole Light Horse, especially considering that we're under-strength already. If we leave the Fiftieth, or the Eighth, behind, it'll be like going into battle with one boot off."

"I'm sorry, General, it just seems to me that we'll be abandoning our charges to the care of others. We haven't done that since Sendai."

"I'm aware of that, Major. So is the Archon. She is also aware of what happened on Sendai following the massacre. She has assured me that the Sixth guards will take very good care of our people. I, in turn, assured her that they'd better." Winston's voice dropped to a kind of low growl as she spoke the last few words.

Grudgingly, Fairfax gave in with a nod.

Major Hinesick quietly murmured from his corner seat, "My God, Ria, I hope you're right."

5

Many light years away from Kikuyu, on the planet Atreus in the Free Worlds League, a similar scene was being played out. The Knights' Hall of Marik Palace was vastly different in appearance from the warm, wood-paneled briefing room in Fort Telemar. The Hall was a large, stone-walled edifice, modeled after the Knight's Hall of a medieval castle back on Terra. Thomas Marik, Captain-General of the Free Worlds League, had ordered the building constructed in the spring of 3055. He had founded the Knights in 3054 as a response to what he viewed as the wave of barbarism consuming the Inner Sphere. To Marik, and to many others, the Knights were the figurative reincarnation of Arthur's Round Table, the embodiment of the ideal that "right *is* might," and "might *for* right." The ancient code of chivalry was their guide in all circumstances.

Seated at the chief place in the hall was Colonel Paul Masters, a dark-haired man of forty years or so. His uniform tunic was devoid of any decoration save one, the crest of the Knights of the Inner Sphere. Around him sat his fellow Knights, warriors gathered from all across the Inner Sphere, bound to one goal, the rebirth of the chivalric ideal. Of the one hundred fifty seats lining the Hall, there were a number of empty places. Most of the vacancies belonged to warriors away on missions whose critical nature prevented their recall. A few of the elaborately carved, wooden chairs were occupied only by an archaic barrel helmet, mantled with somber black silk. These were silent memorials to those who had fallen in battle and whose places had not yet been assigned to new, younger Knights.

Seated to the right of Masters was an older man, gray of hair, with a horribly scarred face. Though he occupied the second place in the hall, the fire in his brown eyes and the air of authority that he wore like his purple mantle revealed that he was second to none of those gathered in the stone-walled chamber. This was Thomas Marik, Captain-General and ruler of the Free Worlds League. Though he was liege lord of the Knights and their chief commander, he graciously allowed Paul Masters to sit at their head. Thomas Marik's presence in the Hall, though not a rare occurrence, lent an air of solemn magnitude to the gathering.

When the last of the Knights had filed silently in, Marik got to his feet, rising with an ease and grace that belied his sixty-eight years.

"Sir Knights," he began slowly, quietly. "By now, you have all heard some of the momentous events that transpired at the Whitting Conference. The Star League has been reborn. A new era is dawning over the Inner Sphere. The first action of the renewed Star League will be to strike out at the greatest threat to its future existence. You, sirs, the Knights of the Inner Sphere, will take part in ridding the Inner Sphere of that threat." Thomas half-turned to face the man on his left. "Sir Masters?"

Thanking the Captain-General, Masters stood as Marik resumed his seat. He surveyed the assembled warriors, collecting himself. He knew it was a great honor that the Captain-General was permitting him to deliver the news. A feeling of pride swelled in Masters' chest, a proper, righteous pride, born of the knowledge that the Knights were being included in the task force both as a powerful combat unit and to act as its conscience.

He knew that an operation whose goal was the destruction of an enemy's war-making capability would have the tendency to overstep the boundaries of "civilized warfare";

that, once the destruction started, the possibility existed that it would not stop until the Smoke Jaguar homeworld had been reduced to a smoldering cinder, and every last Jaguar warrior as well as every civilian man, woman, and child lay dead. Masters was determined that this would not come to pass, not so long as he had breath enough to oppose it.

When he had gathered his thoughts, he began.

"Knights of the Inner Sphere, we stand on the threshold of a new era. The Star League has been reborn. Even as we speak, the best combat units of the Inner Sphere are gathering for one powerful, crushing strike against the greatest enemy mankind has ever faced, the Clans. We, the Knights of the Inner Sphere, have been asked by our liege lord to join with them in this quest. Sirs, this quest is the one we were born to undertake, just as Arthur's Knights of the Round Table dedicated themselves to the quest for the Grail."

The Knights listened intently while Masters recounted the events of the Whitting Conference. When he revealed the Conference's intent to launch an all-out offensive against the Smoke Jaguars, a quiet ripple ran through the Knights. The gist of the comments was, "It's about time."

The Jaguars were the most hated of the invading Clans. The memory of the savagery of the destruction of Edo burned like a signal fire in the minds of the Knights. Warfare against those who could fight back was an honorable thing. But the wanton slaughter of civilians or prisoners and the indiscriminate destruction of non-military targets was despicable. Long had the Knights burned for the chance to strike out at the Clans, but for political reasons, the Free Worlds League had held itself apart from the fighting during the Clan invasion. To many of the Knights, the Jaguars were an abomination among men.

"As of right now," Masters continued, "security will be tightened around the Hall until all preparations are completed. All available Knights are to take ship for the planet Defiance in the Federated Suns, and must arrive no later than mid-February. There, we will begin a brief period of training and integration exercises before setting out on our mission."

"What exactly is our mission?" Sir Robert Dunleavy

stood to face his commander, as tradition dictated. "And who are we going to be integrated with?"

"What I am about to tell you cannot leave this room," Masters said. "The Knights of the Inner Sphere have been asked to participate in a long-range strike against the Smoke Jaguars. We will be following a route laid out for us by a ComStar agent. The target of our strike will be the Jaguar homeworld, a planet named Huntress."

Masters paused, taking the opportunity to consult his notes, while the uncharacteristic hubbub of surprise ran through the Hall. When the murmur subsided, he continued, choosing his words carefully.

"Even as we are departing the Inner Sphere, another push will be led by Prince Victor Steiner-Davion against the Smoke Jaguar Occupation Zone here at home. While Prince Victor grasps the Jaguar by the throat, our objective will be to break the Jaguar's back by striking at his homeworld. We are also to destroy all war-related industry, and thus destroy the Jaguars' ability to attempt any further aggression against the Inner Sphere."

"Sir Masters," a Knight interrupted. "It sounds as though we will be attacking civilian areas. That cannot be true."

"No, Sir Anropov, that is not true." Masters knew that what he was telling his subordinates was only partly accurate, and the half-truth rankled. The Knights would not be attacking civilian areas of Huntress. Still, invasion on a planetary scale and the destruction of a culture's war-making capability would certainly result in civilian casualties. "In fact, I broached that very subject with Marshal Morgan Hasek-Davion, the man who will command this operation. I told him that the Knights are not given to the sort of wholesale destruction this operation might involve.

"The Marshal assured me that he had no intention of crossing that line, which leads me to the second aspect of our role. This comes straight from the Marshal himself. The Knights of the Inner Sphere are to serve as the conscience of the task force."

Another murmur ran through the Knights' Hall. This rumble of hushed voices carried with it a note of pride and relief. Here at last was a task worthy of the Knights and of the ideal that had spawned them. They were going to face an opponent possessing considerable strength and questionable honor. The Knights had been tasked with freeing the Inner Sphere of a ruthless oppressor and with seeing to it that the liberators did not themselves become butchers.

"As far as the other units making up our task force," Masters called over the quiet babble of voices, "I can tell you that we will be joined by some of the most illustrious warriors from each of the Successor States, as well as two of the most famous mercenary companies in the Inner Sphere."

"The Dragoons . . ."

"No, Dame Marta, Wolf's Dragoons will not be joining our expedition," Masters told the woman from Tamarind. "I am referring to the Northwind Highlanders and one other.

"We will be fighting alongside the last vestiges of the old Star League, and the firstborn of the new, the Eridani Light Horse."

It is amazing how beautiful it looks from here, was the thought that ran through *Tai-i* Michael Ryan's mind as he stared through the *Tengu's* forward viewport. Before him hung the cloud-shrouded capital of the Draconis Combine, Luthien, the black pearl of House Kurita. The high, heavy cloud cover swirled slightly in places, possibly indicating a storm. Ryan tried in vain to place the location of the storms, but was frustrated in his attempts until he realized that he was looking at the planet "upside-down." Once he mentally corrected his orientation, he was able to place the largest of the spiral cloud formations over the Shaidan River Basin.

"Attention, all personnel, making final course corrections. Atmospheric interface in five minutes."

In response to the intercom's metallic announcement, Ryan took a firm grip on the polished brass rail that ran along the tough polymer viewport. Through the rail, and in the soles of his feet where they touched the deck, he felt a noticeable shudder in the *Nagumo* Class DropShip's airframe. Luthien shifted its position toward the bottom of the viewport by about thirty degrees, as the *Tengu's* captain brought the ship into a more favorable "glide-slope" for entering the planet's atmosphere. The maneuver had the added effect of obscuring the lower quarter of the green and white disk, forcing the tall DEST officer to lean forward over the rail to see the planet's southern pole.

As he stood there, the top of his head pressed against the viewport, the observation lounge's door hissed open.

Feeling vaguely foolish, Ryan straightened. A slight burning sensation on the back of his neck told him he was blushing slightly. He'd been caught gaping dreamily at his homeworld, like a school boy on his first space flight. It took a moment to recover his composure. Ryan turned to face the newcomer, hoping that the lounge's dim lights would hide his embarrassment.

When he saw the lean face and tall, spare form of the man making his careful way across the lounge, Ryan's embarrassment gave way to surprise and a sense of awe.

"*Konnichiwa,* Kurita Theodore-*sama.*" Ryan executed a surprisingly deep and elegant bow, given the difficulty of doing anything gracefully in freefall. "I was just leaving."

"Wait, Ryan-*san*. Please, stay. Make yourself comfortable." Theodore Kurita returned the bow, though his was a nod compared to Ryan's. Straightening, the Coordinator of the Draconis Combine moved effortlessly to the viewport.

"Thank you, *Tono,*" Ryan said, making his way toward one of the synthleather-covered chairs bolted to the deck near the large window.

For long moments he sat, held in his seat by the lightly padded straps installed by the vessel's designers to keep the chair's occupant from floating away in zero- or micro-G environments. Trying not to stare, Ryan watched the face of the man who was the embodiment of the Dragon, the heart and soul, and ruler of the Draconis Combine.

Theodore-*sama* was no longer a young man, but his sixty-one years barely seemed to have touched him. His face was somewhat lined and more drawn, to be sure. There was also a great deal more silver in his thick, black hair than on the day he ascended to the throne of the Draconis Combine. But, there was a youthful spring in his step, and a bright, sharp gleam in his eye. To Ryan, it seemed that the Coordinator exhibited the strength and timeless grace of a Masamune katana. Here was the man whom he and countless others had sworn their very lives to protect.

A thin, almost invisible, scar creased the Coordinator's left cheek, the legacy of a failed assassination attempt less than six months ago. The memory of the attack on Theodore Kurita still kindled a fire, made of equal parts anger and shame, in Ryan's belly. Dissidents who hated the Coordinator for his recent military and political initiatives had made a dramatic attempt to end Theodore-*sama*'s life during the annual holiday celebration of his birthday. The fact that many of the would-be assassins had been members of DEST still caused Ryan even more shame and anguish. To think that men who had once sworn to defend the Dragon, and by extension, the Coordinator, could turn on and betray him filled him with a hunger for revenge.

Ryan had been among the millions thronging the streets of Imperial City on that shameful afternoon. How fortunate he had felt to have a place so near the Coordinator's reviewing stand. He'd seen the huge, white *Sunder* Omni-Mech turn its weapons on the Coordinator's position. He'd heard *Tai-sa* Kiguri's treacherous words. He'd even witnessed the close-quarters brawl between the Coordinator, his few loyal bodyguards, and the men Ryan had once called comrades. Through it all, there was nothing he could do but watch in helpless fury. Ryan would have leapt, barehanded to Theodore-*sama*'s defense, but Tai-*sho* Yoshida had raised a thick transpex shield around the reviewing stand, cutting the Coordinator off from outside help.

Since that day, the entire Internal Security Force had been purged of disloyal agents, some of whom had been "invited onward," the polite euphemism for being ordered to commit *seppuku*—ritual suicide. Many DEST commandos had likewise been purged. Most of this latter group had simply disappeared. Ryan himself had been interviewed no less than five times by surviving loyal Internal Security Force agents, seeking to determine where his loyalties lay. When it was all over, DEST had been reduced to its smallest numbers ever. Only eight teams remained in operational readiness. Ryan, a mere *Tai-i*, was now one of the most senior field operatives. Still, what the teams lacked in numbers, they more than made up for in their utter devotion to Theodore-*sama*, to the Dragon. It was because of this newly confirmed loyalty that Ryan had been ordered to accompany the Coordinator to Tharkad as part of his bodyguard.

"Ryan-*san* . . ." Theodore broke in on his thoughts. "Michael . . . May I call you by name?"

"Of course, *Tono* . . ."

The Coordinator cut him off with an upraised hand. "Just Theodore right now," he said. "We are both soldiers, *neh*? I'd like to talk with you like a soldier, not Coordinator to *Tai-i*."

"Of course, *Tono* . . . Theodore." Ryan stumbled in his reply, but his mind was racing far ahead of his words.

The Coordinator wants a man-to-man talk, but why me? What of Sho-sa *Yodama? Or* Sho-sho *Ishmaru? Why should he want to talk to me?*

"Michael, what is your estimate of the Whitting Conference?"

Ryan's racing thoughts came to a screeching halt. Little of what had transpired at the conference had been revealed to the public, for obvious reasons. The only information to be released was that the heads of the Successor States had gathered on Tharkad to discuss how they might deal with the Clans.

Owing to his newfound position within the Draconis Elite Strike teams, Ryan had become privy to information normally unavailable to a mere *Tai-i*. He knew that he was shortly to be given command of not just one, but three full strike teams. That these strike teams would represent the Combine in a coalition force aimed for the heart of Clan Smoke Jaguar, their homeworld of Huntress. The teams were being sent both because their specialized training suited them to the task, and because the Combine could not spare any front-line units from the Inner Sphere phase of the overall operation. *Sho-sho* Ishmaru had already told him as much.

Being asked to give counsel to the Dragon himself was another matter entirely.

"*Tono,* I believe that the leaders of the Inner Sphere have made a wise decision in their plan to force the Clans to go on the defensive—"

"That isn't what I asked you, Michael. I want a simple, direct answer. No politics, just straight from the shoulder."

"*Hai, Tono.*" Ryan took a moment to cast his thoughts into some frame of order. "I think the idea of a deep-penetration strike against the Clan homeworlds is a strategically sound move. Striking at the enemy's homeworld puts him off balance. It lets him know he is not safe anywhere, either on the front or snug in his bed at home.

"In hitting his rear area, we will force him to pull units off the front line to meet our attack. That will surely benefit the other half of the overall operation.

"History bears out the notion that the destruction of a combatant's rear area, particularly his civilian areas, have a massively negative effect on his morale."

As he spoke, Ryan began to relax. Suddenly, he was no longer addressing The Dragon, but chatting with a fellow officer, a man who had commanded troops in the field and who had faced death at the hands of his enemies. Leaning forward in his seat, he rested his elbows on his knees.

"Tactically, this is going to be Hachiman's own nightmare," he said, naming the ancient Japanese god of war.

Theodore Kurita blinked at the frankness of the words, but made no comment. "This task force is going to be made up of—what—eight regiments, give or take? Each of them from a different Successor State. Until the Clans appeared, most of these people were trying to kill each other. Now, it is expected they will band together, like nothing ever happened, to attack a common enemy.

"Next, you've got ComStar. Yes, I know they defeated the Clans on Tukayyid, but a lot of mainline troops don't trust them. Why did they keep their army a secret for so long? Why didn't they step in sooner against the Clans? We all know their 'official answers,' but are the 'official' reasons the real reasons?

"Then, just to round out this traveling carnival, you've got the Eridani Light Horse and the Northwind Highlanders. Mercenaries. Hired soldiers who fight for nothing more than pay. I've heard all the stories about the Light Horse, how they are the 'last vestige of the Star League,' but I don't believe it. Neither do a lot of other people. Why didn't they ever bother to join one of the Great Houses? I know I'd have more respect for them if they'd signed on with Davion, or Steiner, or even Marik, rather than fighting for whoever waved the most money in front of them.

"So what have we got? Something like eight full regiments, each with its own strategic and tactical doctrines, different weapons, equipment, procedures. Just re-programming everybody's IFF is going to take weeks.

Focht and the others expect this hodgepodge of wildly different units to jell into an effective striking force in the space of a few months of training? Not likely.

"Then, this band of warriors will set out on a mission that will take God knows how many months even to reach the target, strike a technologically, and possibly numerically, superior foe, destroy his military, industrial, and logistical base, incidentally damaging his morale. Then, assuming the task force survives up to that point, it has to hold out against certain reprisals and counterattacks by every Clanner that Kerensky ever spawned.

"One of our mission objectives, as I understand them, is to drive home to the Clans the idea that war is neither a game nor a ritualized series of 'trials.' In effect, we are to teach the Jaguar homeworld the full horrors of war. I understand that, even agree with it. Wasn't there some ancient general who said, 'War to the knife, and the knife to the hilt'? That is what we are being told to visit upon the Smoke Jaguars, and that is good. If one is going to fight a war, nothing can be held back, no target can be declared off limits. One must strike first, and without mercy.

"But, at the same time, we are told that we are to avoid unnecessary civilian casualties. I am even told that the Knights of the Inner Sphere are to accompany us to ensure that a wholesale slaughter of supposedly 'innocent' Clan non-combatants does not occur.

"What will happen when the realities of war collide with the Knights' high moral tone? Which course of action will be followed? The highway of victory, or the footpath of mercy?

"Begging the Coordinator's pardon, but it sounds like the devil's own circus."

Suddenly, a horrified thought leapt into Ryan's mind. He had just delivered a gritty, line-soldier's opinion, in all its colorful glory, to one of the most powerful men in the Inner Sphere. And to the man who was his lord to the death. With a jerk, he sat up, assuming the stiff, formal posture dictated by the complex rules of Combine society.

Theodore stood quietly, watching Ryan with a veiled expression. Then, a smile creased his lips and he broke into quiet laughter.

"I asked for an honest opinion. I guess that will teach me to be careful what I ask for.

"If it is any comfort, *Tai-i*, I thought the same way when I first heard this plan, though I was a bit more diplomatic in my response. Precentor Martial Focht has assured me that the other Clans will be very slow to aid the Jaguars, if at all. He tells me it has something to do with their strange sense of honor. The Clans as a whole will not intervene in events affecting only one specific Clan, or in events between two separate Clans.

"Remember that Clans Wolf and Jade Falcon have recently concluded a long intramural war. 'A Trial of Absorption,' I believe the Precentor Martial called it. None of the other Clans interfered in what was essentially a squabble between two Clans. Add to this 'hands-off' policy the fact that Focht's intelligence agents report that the Smoke Jaguars have become so ruthless in both their internal and external policies that the rest of the Clans are beginning to consider them as somehow tainted, and I don't think we'll have much to worry about concerning the other Clans getting involved.

"I, like you, was more concerned with the rather diverse makeup of the task force, especially, as you say, mixing together troops who have up until now been bitter enemies. Now, having discussed it thoroughly with Prince Victor, the Precentor Martial, and the others, I believe that the diverse mix of troops is exactly what this operation needs to succeed.

"That, and the special talents of a few friends of mine."

Ryan wasn't sure if he should ask, but did so anyway. "Who do you mean, *Tono*? The yakuza?"

The Coordinator smiled politely, shaking his head.

"You will understand in time."

6

Brandtford Heights Spaceport
Kikuyu, Tamar March
Lyran Alliance
05 January 3059
1330 Hours

The low gray clouds were a perfect match for the bleakness of Ariana Winston's mood as she watched the second of a pair of massive *Mammoth* Class DropShips slow to a stop over landing bay fifteen of the Brandtford Heights spaceport. It hadn't taken much time for her to travel the few kilometers from Fort Telemar to the planetary capital, arriving just in time to witness the landing of these huge ships.

The DropShips bore the logo of Black Swan Lines, a low-cost shipping company that was a wholly owned subsidiary of White Swan Trans-Stellar Inc. Despite the fact that it was now mid-spring, the temperature had yet to reach eighteen degrees centigrade. After the false thaw two weeks earlier, which had made graduation somewhat bearable, the weather had degenerated into a series of cold, rainy days. The foul weather darkened Winston's normally positive disposition.

Slowly, ponderously, the enormous ship drifted to a halt. It seemed to be balanced on top of a pillar of silver fire and billowing smoke as its powerful engines strove to keep the fifty-thousand-ton beast aloft. Gradually, the ship began to settle toward the steel-reinforced ferrocrete surface of the landing bay.

The term "bay" was something of a misnomer, as it would seem to indicate a kind of semi-recessed area in which the ship landed. In some of the older spaceports, this was the case. Ferrocrete rings, some as much as three hundred meters across and twenty high, had been constructed at the spaceports on Terra, Mars, New Earth, and other places settled during the early days of interstellar travel. These installations were capable of handling even the largest *Mammoth* Class ships. Here on Kikuyu, a landing bay was nothing more than a wide expanse of pavement, with special laser-trackers installed at various places. Information from these devices, developed by the technical support arm of the Eridani Light Horse, added to the DropShip pilot's knowledge of exact altitude, heading, and speed. This aided in performing their landing maneuvers. The laser-trackers were especially critical to pilots of the larger spheroid or ovoid ships, since the bridge of those vessels were usually located at the top of their superstructure. From that vantage point, the bulk of the ship blocked the pilot's view of the ground, forcing him to rely on his instruments and navigational aids in order to accomplish a safe landing.

When at last the ship touched the ground, and the smoke of her drives began to blow away on the damp cold wind, Winston felt an unusual tightness in her chest. She realized that she'd been holding her breath as she watched the aerodynamically impossible spectacle of a huge steel egg flying through the air and touching down safely on a ferrocrete landing pad.

"Bu-uh!" Her breath came out in an amazed half-laughing exhalation. She shook her head in amusement. For a few seconds, she stood gazing out through the glass front of the observation lounge while her breathing returned to normal. Quietly, she laughed at herself for getting tensed up over a scene she'd observed hundreds of times before.

As the distant DropShip began to open its cargo bay doors—a scene displayed on a bank of flatscreen television monitors at the north end of the observation lounge—she could see the figures of heavy and assault class BattleMechs debarking from the vessel's darkened bowels. The monitors were necessary to pick out any but the grossest details of the grounded ship, because landing bay fifteen was a kilometer away from the spaceport's main terminal building. At that distance, in this foul weather and with her naked eye, Winston could distinguish the movement of the ten-meter-tall war machines, but could not identify the particular color or even model of the 'Mechs.

The tap of footsteps in the empty observation lounge announced the visitor's arrival before he spoke. Winston knew who he was. The Lyran Alliance Armed Forces liaison had pestered her a dozen times before that day, informing her of every petty detail of his landing and off-loading operations. Studiously, she ignored the man's presence, studying instead the gloom-shrouded, uninteresting vista of the Brandtford Heights spaceport.

"Excuse me, General."

Let him wait, Winston told herself. *It's not very professional, or military, or even courteous, but this little toad is really beginning to irritate me.*

"General Winston?" A pause, "Ma'am?"

Winston looked over her left shoulder at the LAFF officer, as though noticing him for the first time.

"Oh, General Jolar, I didn't hear you come in." The lie felt somehow satisfying.

"I'm sorry to intrude, General . . ."

Then why do you do it, you officious little pain in the neck?

". . . I just wanted to inform you that the ships carrying the last of my troops has just touched down, and we'll be ready to go on line in a couple of hours."

Winston nodded and turned back to the window. Even the ugly weather was better than having to deal with this moron.

Jolar had arrived a full week earlier, with the Donegal Guards' advance party. For the first couple of hours, he'd been tolerable. By the end of the day, his constant presence had begun to wear, first on Colonel Antonescu, then on Colonel Barclay. By the time thirty hours had passed, even the good-natured Edwin Amis had wanted to stake Jolar out on a landing bay slated for an incoming Drop-Ship. It wasn't just the man's incessant questions that made him unbearable. It wasn't his grating nasal voice, made even worse by the head cold he had developed immediately upon setting foot on Kikuyu. It was his obvious military incompetence. He was a political officer, pure and simple. The Sixth Guards' *real* commander, Marshal

Seamus Kinnell, told Winston that Jolar had been an albatross to him ever since the general's brother-in-law, Clarence Astra III, the Duke of Poulsbo, had finagled a post for the man to get him out of the palace.

Political officers had been the bane of professional soldiers throughout the history of warfare. Most often, they were incompetent fools with more imagination than brains. As a rule, they were incapable of any real battlefield decisions other than a valiant, glorious charge straight into the enemy's guns, and a hero's grave. Of course, it wasn't the political officer who would end up in the hero's grave, it was the men under his command.

As political officers went, Leftenant General Hiram Jolar was not at the bottom of the list, but Winston had a hard time remembering anyone lower on that lengthy roster. She was sure there had to be somebody less competent and more annoying, she just couldn't bring him to mind at that moment.

Jolar was still behind her. She could hear him shuffling his feet, like a little boy wanting to ask his mother a question. Might as well get this over with.

"What is it, General?" Winston did not turn around.

"Frankly, Ariana, this entire operation has me puzzled." The use of her first name irritated her, but she made a conscious decision to let it pass. "The Sixth is a good unit, not an experienced one, mind you, but a good one. My question is this: Why are we replacing elite, battle-hardened troops with a Combat Team full of relatively inexperienced recruits? I mean, it just doesn't make sense, does it?"

Winston rolled her eyes in amazement, glad that her back was to the LAAF colonel. For a long time, she didn't answer. When she heard the Colonel take a breath to restate the question, she turned to face him.

"We all have our orders, Colonel. Dismissed." Winston sketched a vague wave of her hand, which could have been interpreted as a salute, and turned back to the window.

His curiosity apparently unsatisfied, Jolar remained where he was for a few more seconds. Winston could practically hear the wheels spinning in his head as he debated pressing her further for an explanation of the extraordinary events. She continued to stare out the window, pretending to be lost in thought. Her lack of response finally sent him shuffling out of the lounge.

For a long while, Winston remained at the window, gazing out across the puddle-infested tarmac. Most of the Sixth's 'Mechs had been broken out of their cocoons, and were lumbering their way across the tarmac toward their assembly point. On the monitors, she could make out the individual 'Mech types.

A pair of sharp beeps sounded from her wrist chronometer. A glance at the instrument told her that if she left the spaceport right away, she'd be able to make it back to Fort Telemar in time for evening mess. With a sigh, she turned away from the rain-streaked window and left the lounge.

Now, if I can just get to my car before . . .

"General Winston."

"Dammit, now what?" Her patience snapped as she whirled to face the officer who had just called out her name.

"Geez, Ria." Scott Hinesick sounded stricken. "I just wanted to tell you that Antonescu reports the One hundred fifty-first is nearly finished loading, and is preparing to leave Mogyorod for Kikuyu."

"Oh, Scott, I'm sorry." Winston touched her friend on the shoulder. "I thought you were Jolar. He's been in and out of the lounge all day, bugging me with every petty detail and problem with the Sixth's offloading."

"I don't know if that makes me feel better or not, thinking I was Jolar." Hinesick pulled an exaggeratedly hurt expression. "Besides, I just saw him climb into a runabout and head out across the landing stage. Maybe one of the Guards will step on him."

Winston laughed in spite of herself.

"Now, Scott, that's one of our allies you're talking about. Where've you been all day?"

Hinesick shook his heavy gray overcoat. A thin spray of rain water spattered the tiles beneath his wet boots.

"On the observation deck, mostly. It seemed like you wanted to be alone today. And, after the third time I saw Jolar come out of the lounge, I figured you wouldn't want any witnesses when you killed him." Hinesick chuckled, but there was a note of uncertainty behind his banter. He paused. Then came a rush of words. "General Winston, I respectfully request permission to join the combat arm."

The unexpected seriousness of his tone took her by surprise.

"Say again?"

"Ria, the Light Horse is going off to war. I don't want to get left behind."

Winston knew it was breaking his heart. It would have broken hers not to go, but she'd made the only decision possible.

"Scott, you know that all noncombat personnel are to remain at Fort Telemar, to help ease the transition between the real Light Horse and the Sixth Guards." Winston laid a comforting hand on her friend's shoulder and smiled gently. "You're the commandant of the training academy. You, above anyone else, are the best-equipped to make this thing work.

"And remember, the Light Horse is going to take a pounding on this mission. There's no getting around that. I need you right here, doing what you do best—training new recruits. When we get back, we're going to need every trooper we can lay our hands on. I'm counting on you, Scott. There's no one else I can trust to teach them right."

"I know all that, Ria. But, this might be my last chance to pilot a 'Mech. I scored an eighty-seven on my last simulator run. That's aggregate—time, accuracy, and piloting. I can handle it."

"Scott, I saw your scores. I know what you're capable of. But the Light Horse needs you here." Winston stepped close to Hinesick and lowered her voice. "I want a combat-experienced officer here, on-planet, who can command the training cadre."

"Why?" Hinesick caught the note of concern in her voice. "You aren't expecting any trouble out of the Sixth?"

"Expecting it?" Winston shook her head. "No, but Fairfax was right. I can't leave the safety of the Light Horse dependents in the hands of outsiders. I want you right here to protect them, just in case."

"Very well, General. And thank you." There was a hitch of emotion in Hinesick's voice.

She returned his salute, formally correct to the millimeter, all the while smiling broadly at her old friend.

With a last look at the Guards' 'Mechs, Winston sighed again, turned, and stepped out into the steadily falling rain.

═══ 7 ═══

"Incredible." The single word, breathed out as though it were a curse, carried with it more meaning than a thousand profanities. "How can anybody live here?"

"I know what you mean," the portmaster replied. "I've been stationed on seventeen worlds since I got hired by the Ministry of Commerce, and this is by far the ugliest, hottest, smelliest, all-around nastiest post I've ever had."

Kasugai Hatsumi chuckled politely at the man's bitter humor as he accepted his passport back from the clerk.

"And what did you do to get yourself assigned to this garden spot?"

"Do? I didn't *do* anything. That was the whole problem. I *was* on New Syrtis. I was planning on being there until I retired. Just two years to go, this little skinny guy comes up to me and offers me half a million C-Bills to let a couple of crates go through customs uninspected. At first, I turned him down. Then I got to thinking about it, y'know? I mean half a mil. I'd been pullin' freight for House Davion for twenty-three years and what did I have to show for it? Retirement, a half-salary pension, and two grand in the bank, so I figured, what the heck? I let the crates slip through."

Like the Ancient Mariner, the customs inspector seemed compelled to recount the tale of his transgression to any stranger who would listen.

"Anyhow, I got the cash, and thought that was the end of it. I found out later that the crates were full of guns and bombs for Liao terrorists. When they blew up that 'Mech plant, back in '49, there was an investigation, and the Fox Fives traced the explosives back to my part of the yard. Somebody had to take the blame, and I got picked. Suspension, probation, reduction in grade, the whole nine yards. Then, when I tried to bid up again, the big bosses shuffled me off here. And here I'll stay for the next four months, twelve days, two hours, and fifteen minutes. After that, Prince Victor can kiss my feet."

Hatsumi laughed again to cover the chill that ran down his spine. "Fox Fives" was a common slang term for the agents of M15, the counter-insurgency branch of House Davion's Department of Military Intelligence. So far the Davion security agents had yet to develop a security net so tightly woven that Hatsumi or one of his comrades could not slip through. Still, no covert operative, no matter how well trained and proficient, could penetrate every safeguard, every time.

Picking up his carryall, Hatsumi headed for the terminal's main door. He hadn't gone three steps when the portmaster called out to him.

"Son? 'Less you like breathin' sulfur oxides, you'd better put on a respirator."

Hatsumi grinned sheepishly as he pulled a pyramidal device constructed mostly of rubber and metal from a pocket of his faded AFFC field jacket.

"I wasn't thinking. Thank you."

The portmaster waved once and turned back to the news-fax he'd been reading when Hatsumi entered the terminal.

Standing just inside the building's airlock-type double doors was a slightly built woman, wearing the stained jumpsuit and canvas jacket of a common laborer. Her plain appearance was relieved only by the slightly oriental cast to her features. A commercial-grade respirator mask hung by its neck strap below her chin. Her eyes flickered in recognition as Hatsumi approached.

"Ready?"

She jerked her head toward the doors. "What about your luggage?"

"This is it. The rest of our materials will be arriving in a few days."

Rumiko Fox shrugged, pulled her respirator over her nose and mouth, and stepped into the lock. Hatsumi followed her example.

It took only a few seconds for the outer doors to cycle open. Defiance suffered from a slight taint in her atmosphere, as the portmaster had warned, but the pressure was well within the so-called normal levels of human tolerance. Hatsumi was grateful for that. He was fully qualified in the use of pressure suits and other hostile environment equipment, but he loathed the restrictiveness of the suits.

A five-year old Gienah sedan sat next to the curb a few dozen meters from the door. Fox walked straight to the vehicle and climbed into the diver's seat without saying another word. Hatsumi followed silently. After tossing his carryall into the back seat, he settled down next to the silent woman.

Fox pressed the vehicle's starter, eliciting not the quiet roar of a well-tuned internal combustion engine, but a high-pitched, mechanical whine.

"It's the pollution," she said to the windshield, her voice muted by the mask. "The gunk in the air makes fuel-burners run rough. Most of the cars here are electric, even the heavy haulers."

Without another word, Fox put the vehicle in gear and pulled away from the curb.

The drive into Jerseyville took forty minutes. During that time, Fox never spoke again, leaving Hatsumi to stare at Defiance's scenery. As scenery went, it wasn't inspiring. The long stretch of macadam-paved highway ran, laser-straight, through rocky flatlands. Here and there, hardy bushes sprouted in clumps, giving refuge to whatever reptilian and avian life could tolerate the mephitic atmosphere.

From the datachips he'd reviewed while in transit, Hatsumi knew that the planet's main spaceport was located on the site of the original settlers' first landing. The flatlands wedged in between on the Pearce Sea to the east and the Devil's Backbone Mountains on the west would be some of the richest farming lands in the Inner Sphere, if not for the taint in the atmosphere. Though the sulfur content was not high enough to prevent plant life from growing, even flourishing, in the black, volcanic soil, it was sufficient to be absorbed into the crops, giving any foodstuff grown there an unpleasant, bitter taste. It was ironic that the volcanoes that provided the richness of the soil made it unusable.

That was not to say that Defiance was without economic value. The planet was rich in mineral wealth. The almost constant eruptions that had marked its early life had brought many rare earth elements up out of the young planet's core. Transuranic elements were especially common in the now mostly extinct volcanoes of the Devil's Backbone.

Jerseyville itself was only marginally more interesting to look at. A large cluster of small houses, shops, and office buildings huddled in the foothills of the Backbone range was the site of the first settlement, named for its founder, Malcolm Jersey. The settlers, most of them prospectors, had come to Defiance during the early days of the Star League. They came seeking mineral wealth. Many of them found it. Over the years, the hundreds of small, independent mines were acquired by large corporations, until eventually the greatest portion of the planet was owned outright by Solar Metals Limited, who sold it to the Davion family in 2748.

Eventually, Fox brought the car to a halt in front of a small single-family house in Jerseyville's northern suburbs. Indistinguishable from any of its neighbors, the house was a small, two-story structure, with plastic-coated metal siding manufactured to look like wood. The only thing that distinguished this house from its cousins on a thousand civilized worlds was the large pressure lock taking the place of its front door.

Hatsumi climbed out of the vehicle, retrieved his bag, and strode up the walk. At the door, he had to pause to allow Fox to tap in the proper access code.

As silently as ever, the woman punched a seemingly random series of buttons on the ten-digit keypad. The door rewarded her with a series of heavy thuds before swinging open.

It took a full minute for the residential model airlock to run through its cycle. It was the same story everywhere; bigger and faster meant more expensive. The designers of the house intended for it to be built cheaply. Thus, when the inner door began to swing open and Hatsumi removed his respirator mask, he could still smell the rotten-eggs odor of sulfur oxide.

"Kasugai!" The cry of greeting was laced with joy. Hatsumi looked up to see a small, powerfully built young man leaping out of an armchair. He, like Fox, was dressed in the clothing of a common laborer.

"Honda Tan. It is good to see you again."

"Stormcrow told me that I would be working with an old friend, but I had no idea he meant you." Tan threw his arms around Hatsumi in a crushing bear hug.

The man Tan called Stormcrow was the *jonin,* the clan leader of the Amber Crags nekekami. Hatsumi knew as much of Stormcrow's reputation as any other of his clan. During the days prior to the Fourth Succession War, as a field operative, Stormcrow had slipped into the HQ of the Fourth Skye Rangers, rifled that regiment's secure rooms, and escaped undetected, leaving behind only confusion and a small origami cat. Later, as a *chunin,* or cell-leader, he had ordered the assassination of a nosy reporter who had written an exposé revealing the long-hidden secrets of the nekekami.

The nekekami. Hatsumi mused over the word, and what it had come to mean throughout the Inner Sphere. Roughly translated, the word meant "Spirit Cat." The nekekami were the indirect descendants of the *ninja*—the secret society of spies and assassins of feudal Japan. Like their predecessors, the nekekami had raised intelligence-gathering, sabotage, and assassination to an art-form. All their lives, the nekekami trained, studied, and practiced their skills. A warrior would work his whole life, honing himself into the perfect weapon, a weapon that might be expended in a single mission.

The legends about the Spirit Cats were many. It was said that they could walk through walls, breathe underwater, sink into the ground, and become invisible at will. Some of the more outrageous tales said the nekekami were apprenticed to Death himself, or to powerful necromancers who could kill with a glance.

When at last he released his grip, Tan nodded at Fox. "I see you've met our talkative Rumiko."

The woman glared at Tan, but spoke not a word.

Tan, unimpressed, flashed a toothy smile in return.

Hatsumi felt a certain relief at seeing Honda Tan again. The two had been together for a number of operations, including a few covert operations against the hated Smoke Jaguar Clan.

"You might as well get to know the whole team all at once." Tan took his friend by the arm and ushered him into the house's tiny kitchen. There, seated at the table, was a handsome young man who was bent over a bundle of wires and circuit boards, a soldering iron in his left hand. A small, plasticized paper-wrapped bundle rested in his lap. Just enough of the parcel was visible for Hatsumi to read the lettering: "Block, Explosive, M26A1."

"Is it safe for him to have that stuff around a soldering iron?" Hatsumi's training had included only limited instructions in the handling of explosives, and he treated anything with that much destructive capability with awe and respect.

"I don't know," Tan shrugged. "That's Kieji Sendai, our resident explosives expert. Kieji, this is Kasugai Hatsumi, our team leader."

Sendai looked up, nodded once, and went back to work.

"Is it safe for you to have explosives sitting in your lap while you're working with a soldering iron?" Hatsumi repeated his question for the demolitions man.

"Hai," Sendai answered. Finishing the joint he was working on, he sat back and tossed the explosive to Hatsumi. "That's Davion-issue C-8. It's mostly Cyclonite, with a few stabilizing agents. The stuff is completely stable until it is initiated by means of a blasting cap. Then, it gives you a good high-speed explosion, somewhere around sixty-eight thousand centimeters per second."

The plastic explosive was stiff, gray-green putty, wrapped in olive drab paper. Hatsumi knew the stuff could be used for any number of applications. It could be used as is, or smoothed over the object to be destroyed. It could be molded into a shaped charge, or wrapped with chain to make an improvised fragmentation bomb. Rigged with a short fuse-type detonator, it could be bundled together in a satchel charge and stuffed into the vulnerable knee and ankle joints of a BattleMech. Only pentaglycerine was a more powerful blasting agent.

Returning the block to the table, he asked Sendai to be careful.

"It wouldn't do for us to get ourselves blown up before we started our mission.

"Pardon me for asking," Tan said, handed his team leader a cup of tea poured from the pot that had been warming on the stove ever since Hatsumi had arrived. "What *is* our mission?"

Hatsumi sampled the tea and nodded his thanks before answering.

"We are to link up with the Second Com Guards Division, posing as combat support personnel assigned to their second battalion.

"I have been assured that the Second will arrive on Defiance within the week. Places for us have already been established. When they arrive, we will report to the old Defiance Militia compound west of Jerseyville to take our places. We are to remain with the Second until our contact gets in touch with us. Once contact is made, we will receive all of our specific orders through this agent."

"That's all very good." Tan was unimpressed with the secrecy shrouding their mission. "What I want to know is, what is the specific nature of our mission?"

"I do not know, Tan-*san*. I have told you all I *do* know. The Amber Crags Clan was contacted indirectly, through a representative of our client. The client, who I have been told is very important, insists that there can be no connection between our team and himself. We are to hook up with the Second, and wait until contacted." Hatsumi took another sip of tea. "After all, waiting for our prey is a large part of being nekekami."

As Hatsumi was passing his instructions to his team, a pair of *Overlord* Class DropShips was touching down at the spaceport.

Before the smoke and steam of the landing jets drifted away, a small personnel ramp was lowered to the pavement. A tall, dark-haired man, wearing an AFFC officer's uniform, strode down the metal walkway, the dark blotch of the respirator over his face. No rank or unit insignia adorned his jacket. The large gear bag slung over his left shoulder was equally nondescript. Before his feet left the ramp, a battered green hover transport bearing the sun-and-fist logo of the Federated Commonwealth rolled to a stop at the edge of the landing stage. The driver was, like the new arrival, dressed in the green and brown fatigues of the Armed Forces of the Federated Commonwealth. The single, narrow white stripe on his gold epaulets indicated he was an aerospace fighter pilot holding the rank of captain.

Climbing out of the vehicle, the driver of the transport jogged up the ramp.

"Colonel Masters? I'm Robin Pennick, MIIO." He pronounced the acronym for the Ministry of Information, Intelligence, and Operations, "mee-oh." "I was sent to greet you and your staff. If you'll follow me, sir, we'll go over to the portmaster's office and make all the arrangements for off-loading your 'Mechs and equipment."

The Commander of the Knights of the Inner Sphere grunted in reply as they secured their respirators. Meanwhile, Masters' command staff and a number of his Mech-Warriors also filed down the ramp. Off to his right, he could hear the loud, high-pitched *skree* of heavily taxed hydraulics as the DropShip's 'Mech bay doors swung slowly open.

"All right, Mister Pennick," Masters said, gesturing at the hovercar. "After you."

Pennick climbed in, the Knights' officers piling into the vehicle after him. Then Pennick engaged the vehicle's fans and sped away from the landing stage. Pushing the car to its limit, he sent it careening across the tarmac, dodging small patches of melting, dirty ice. Just before the Knights' arrival, a nor-easter had hit Defiance's main spaceport. While the sudden snowstorm was unusual in Jerseyville's normally temperate winter, the thin layer of snow and ice that had blanketed much of the spaceport and nearby town was a dusting compared to the conditions the Knights had left on Atreus some weeks before.

During the ride to the portmaster's office, the Knights' officers glanced around suspiciously. Major Sir Gainard, one of Masters' battalion commanders, asked Pennick when the rest of the units would be arriving.

Pennick half-turned as he replied, and it was all Masters could do not to lunge for the wheel. "You Knights are the first combat unit to get here, though Marshal Hasek-Davion and his personal staff have been here for some time now. He arrived shortly after the conclusion of the Whitting Conference." Pennick allowed a rueful chuckle to escape his lips. "It must be nice to have the Prince of the Federated Commonwealth as your cousin."

"How do you mean?" Masters asked. The hovercar's open passage forced him to squint his eyes against the wind. *If he was going to drive like a maniac, Pennick might have chosen an enclosed vehicle, or at least provided crash helmets with face shields.*

"How do I mean?" Pennick laughed again. "I mean he got here less than a week after the conference was over. I'm told that Prince Victor set up a command circuit of JumpShips to carry the Marshal straight here."

Masters nodded. JumpShips could travel instantly between star systems, but what slowed down travel was the fact that it took about a week to recharge the ship's Kearny-Fuchida jump drives. Sometimes, on rare occasions, a so-called "command circuit" would be established. This costly method of travel stationed JumpShips at each star system along the planned route of travel. Each ship would make a single jump, then the important passenger or cargo would be handed off, usually by the simple expedient of transferring a DropShip to the next starship in line.

"Anyway, we expect the DEST contingent to arrive in a couple of days. The Northwind Highlanders, the Fox Teams, and the Com Guards are in transit. I expect them to be in-system by the end of the week. Most of the others, including the Eridani Light Horse, won't be here for at least fourteen days."

"Are they all going to be arriving at Jerseyville?"

"Yes, sir. It's Defiance's only spaceport."

Masters turned his head to stare at the man. Pennick was leaning back in his seat as though he hadn't a thing to worry about.

"Are you sure it's wise to bring such a large number of troops through the planet's only port facility?"

"Of course, sir." Pennick sounded positively bored. "I've been here ever since the Whitting summit as part of the advance team. When they decided to use Defiance for a staging area, MIIO went right to work. We've been using the rumor mill to spread it around that we're running joint military exercises here. It's been used for that before. That's part of the reason they chose Defiance as a mustering point. That, and the fact that it's the back corner of nowhere. The rumor we're spreading is that ComStar, the AFFC, and a bunch of mercs are concocting a plan to recapture Terra from the Wobbies."

"Excuse me, who?" Masters had never heard the name before.

"The Wobbies. Word of Blake." Pennick laughed. "Anyhow, we've been telling the locals one story, and other agents have been spreading different rumors. The whole effect is that no one outside of Fort Defiance knows what the heck is going on. The more confusion there is, the better. In fact, that's why they've got you dressed as FedCom troops, to help feed the rumor mill."

"Yeah," Masters agreed sourly as the car came to a sudden stop in front of the portmaster's office. "As long as the confusion stays outside the fort."

8

Fort Defiance
Defiance, Crucis March
Federated Commonwealth
18 February 3059
1740 Hours

Where the devil are they? Colonel Edwin Amis searched
the primary and secondary sensor monitors studding his
ON1-M Orion's cockpit. He knew that somewhere out
there in the vast cold hills of Fort Defiance's training
ground lurked two Trinaries of the Com Guard's Invader
Galaxy. Under the eye of Morgan Hasek-Davion, the
widely disparate units of Task Force Serpent would now
be engaged in several months of exercises to integrate
them into a single, cohesive unit.

The Invader Galaxy was the perfect foil. Sometime
after the Clans were stopped in Tukayyid, Anastasius
Focht had established a special unit of Com Guards,
equipped with captured Clan equipment and schooled in
Clan tactics. Configured like a Clan unit of its size, it was
named the Invader Galaxy. Its mission was to fight the
Clans on their own terms, using their own weapons and
tactics against them. As such, the Invader Galaxy made to
order for training the individual units comprising the task
force, and the task force as a whole.

That was how the Com Guards and the Light Horse
came to be stalking each other through the low, rolling

hills and flatlands aptly named the Plains of Sorrow. Amis squinted his eyes, peering through the squat, scrubby brush around him for signs of life.

It had taken a few days less than the estimated time for the task force to assembly on Defiance. The command staff immediately tossed their troops into a series of training and integration exercises. The first few of these exercises had ended in "Clan" victories, when first the Lyran Guards and then the Second St. Ives Lancers faced off against the Invader Galaxy. Then it was the Eridani Light Horse's turn.

Morgan Hasek-Davion had cooked up the overall exercise plan, and Colonel Amis knew that meant the mission wouldn't be a cakewalk, but he was beginning to wonder if the Marshal hadn't sent the Invader Galaxy to the wrong part of the battlefield. For several hours, the combatants had maneuvered, each seeking to gain a tactical advantage. The Light Horse, with its doctrine of maneuver warfare, drew on their experiences on Coventry to devise their counter-Clan tactics. In a stand-up fight, the Horsemen stood little chance against the technologically superior Clans. So the mercenaries opted for a mobile battle, launching fast hit-and-run raids, backed up by air strikes and artillery fire. Rather than meeting the Invaders in head-on single combats, as the Clans seemed to prefer, the Light Horse would use its speed, maneuverability, and massed firepower to overcome their enemy.

The Invader Galaxy had been assigned the part of Clan Smoke Jaguar. Their 'Mechs, many of them genuine Clan OmniMechs captured on Tukayyid, had been painted the mottled off-gray common to that Clan's combat machines. The ComStar unit was the natural stone against which to whet the task force's fighting edge. Dubbed OPFOR, for Opposing Forces, several companies of Com Guard infantry had been equipped with the latest battle armor, which had been painted to resemble that of Jaguar Elementals. Such techniques had been used for centuries when training soldiers, beginning with the light fiberglass visual modifications to tanks and armored personnel carriers made by the old American army during the late twentieth century. These bolt-on "vis-mod" panels, when attached to friendly machines, provided at least the rough outlines of enemy equipment.

Still, all the cosmetic alterations to the ComStar 'Mechs

didn't matter at the moment. There had been no sign of the Com Guards for the past ninety minutes.

Amis cursed vilely, scanning his readouts. Three of his four scout teams had reported "no joy," an ancient phrase indicating that there was no sign of the enemy. The last team, commanded by a young Lieutenant with the unlikely name of Tubal Caine, hadn't reported in.

Defiance's yellow sun, stained an ugly burnt orange by the sulfur contaminating the atmosphere, was already low in the sky. Amis knew that if his troops didn't locate the Com Guards soon, the Light Horse might find itself embroiled in a night action. Worse yet, if they failed to locate the OPFOR BattleMechs, his beloved Twenty-first Regiment would end up on the receiving end of some not so good-natured kidding from those units who'd already faced the Com Guards in mock battle.

All right, Amis told himself, *we gotta do something.*

"Beggar One, this is Stonewall. Move your company out to the west. Sneak Four hasn't reported in, and I'm afraid the bogeyman got 'em."

"Stonewall, Beggar One. Will comply." Captain Martin Izzat paused a moment. "Contact! Contact! Beggar One has many targets, fifty plus heading our position. Sensors indicate contacts to be hostiles. I read at least five assault 'Mechs. Beggar One requests orders."

"Beggar One, Stonewall. Beggar is to engage as targets come into range. Slow 'em up, Marty. Give us time to get the Strikers in line." Tapping in a command, Amis cued up a prerecorded message, added a few lines of data, and hit the Transmit key. The Irian communications system fired off the zip-squeal in a burst lasting only a fraction of a second. Returning to his regiment's tactical frequency, Amis passed orders to his battalion commanders.

In moments, the entire regiment—over one hundred BattleMechs, with their attendant tank, infantry, and armored infantry support units—was eating up the ground as they swung into action. One hundred meters passed, then three hundred. The regiment was up to nearly full speed when Captain Izzat informed Amis that Seventh Company was engaging the enemy.

"Stonewall, Beggar One. Beggar is engaged with the enemy. Beggar One counts thirty BattleMechs, at least eight of assault class. Enemy force has many Elementals.

"Boss, you'd better get here pretty quick."

"Hang on, Marty," Amis replied, as he struggled to keep his lurching, 75-ton machine on an even keel. "Help is on the way."

The mock battle was taking place a kilometer away. Amis' lead elements had finally made contact with the Invader Galaxy, but things were *not* shaping up according to plan. Amis had hoped that the Invaders would come straight at the Seventh, pursuing the mercenaries as they staged a fighting withdrawal. Then, when the OPFOR 'Mechs were strung out and vulnerable, the main body of his regiment would swing in on the Invader's flanks. Unfortunately, the Com Guards weren't cooperating. Instead of letting their lighter, faster 'Mechs run ahead of the slower, more powerful heavy and assault elements, the Guards stayed together. The combined weight of the attacking forces was too much for the single detached company. Izzat's Company was falling back in disarray, and getting chewed to pieces in the process.

Finally, his *Orion*'s balky tracking system painted small red triangles on his primary sensor array. The onboard computer scanned each sensor trace and matched the combined data to a Warbook program. The nearest bad guy was a 40-ton *Hermes II*. At maximum magnification, Amis watched as the man-like giant slowed from its run. A puff of smoke gouted from the machine's chest. The first hadn't even begun to disperse when a second plume of blue-gray fumes filled the air.

Then Amis heard the voice of one of his own men. "I'm hit, primary systems out, switching to ba . . ." The words betrayed no fear on the part of the young trooper who spoke them. It reminded Amis of a calm he had seen dozens of times in real battle during his career as a professional soldier. Sometimes, in the face of your own destruction, comes a tranquillity. Psychologists said it sprang from a feeling of "I'm going to die, and I can't do anything about it, so why get upset?"

Amis called the headshrinker who forwarded that particular theory foolish. No one, he believed, least of all a professional MechWarrior, simply sits back, waiting for death. He does whatever he can to prevent his demise, or at least to take a couple of the enemy with him.

The tiny blue spot representing Private Henry Stano's

Valkyrie on the Colonel's tactical monitor flashed once and went out.

Seconds later, the *Orion*'s external sound pickups conveyed the thin whistling shriek of incoming artillery shells to the Colonel's ears. The round burst short, over one hundred meters to the right of the target.

"Paladin, this is Stonewall. Splash!" Amis informed the battery that their spotting round had dropped within his line of sight. "Up thirty, right seventy-five, and fire-for-effect."

Again, the howl of incoming shells filled the cockpit. This time the 'Mech's tactical display flared red as the computer traced the flight path of the incoming rounds with delicate scarlet threads.

Four rounds landed almost directly on top of the Com Guard position. Instead of the booming detonation of forty kilos of high explosive per shell, Amis heard a sharp, flat crack. Tendrils of thick, dirty gray smoke rose and enshrouded the bogus Clan 'Mechs. Two of the aggressors flashed and died from Amis' HUD. Somewhere nearby was a neutral referee, drawn from the Kathil Uhlans, armed with a "god-gun." The hand-held laser was used to designate which enemy 'Mechs had been knocked out by the incoming "artillery."

Amis watched the smoke rise. *Interesting,* he thought. *That new stuff the Uhlans brought with them rises higher than standard smoke.* A glance at his sensors told the mercenary that the charges also carried fine metal powder, which, borne aloft by the burning phosphorus, clouded sensors. The I-Smokes, as the shells were called, would hopefully give Inner Sphere combat units an edge against the Clan's superior sensors and active probe equipment.

Amis found comfort in the old adage, "If you can't see 'em, you can't shoot 'em." Even though he knew that in this age of radar, infrared, and a host of other electronic sensors, the proverb no longer had much meaning.

"Crowbar, this is Stonewall." Amis called to his entire regiment as his rangefinder counted down to five hundred meters. "Weapons free! Lock 'em and rock 'em."

Pulling his lumbering 'Mech to a stop, Amis grasped the targeting joystick, deftly bringing the cross hairs linked to his *Orion*'s shoulder-mounted missile system up to rest on a misshapen blob of color his computer tagged as a Com Guard/Jaguar *Loki*. With a touch of the trigger, a coded laser message flashed from his targeting and tracking systems to the OPFOR 'Mech's computer. On his displays, the enemy battle machine staggered as the electronic damage took its toll. His systems guessed that the Com Guard had taken severe damage to its right arm and torso.

The system the combatants were using was an old one. Each machine in the engagement was fitted with special low-power lasers that fired, not megajoule lances of coherent light, but coded pulses. If one of these "bullets" of light hit a battlefield unit equipped with special receptor gear, the 'Mech or tank's computer would take note of the hit and record the amount of damage. Once the damage on a particular system passed the tolerance of that component, the computer would shut it down. To add to the realism of the engagement, autocannons and missile launchers could be fitted with blank-firing simulator pods that belched smoke and flame each time that weapon was fired. The entire system, called MILES, or Multiple Integrated Laser Engagement System, had been in use since the latter half of the twentieth century.

Goading his ponderous mount into a run, Amis closed the distance while the enemy was still disoriented. A brief survey of his tactical display showed that the "Jaguars" had fallen back under the Light Horse's initial rush, but were now beginning to recover their composure. Three enemy 'Mechs were out of action, but an equal number of his own force had been reduced to dull gray-blue spots on his monitor. Two more Light Horse 'Mechs flashed and died. Half a dozen "Elementals" were killed when a *JagerMech* from Stockdale's Company swept their position with computer-generated autocannon fire.

An aggressor loomed large in his HUD. Without trying to identify the machine's model or class, Amis tightened his finger on the trigger, pickled in a different weapon, and fired again. Twenty missiles leapt from their tubes to splinter the enemy's armor. Smoke spat from the *Orion*'s side as a burst of autocannon fire ate greedily away at the OPFOR 'Mech.

The enemy shuddered a bit, but turned slowly to face Amis' charge. Now, given the chance to observe his opponent, Amis realized that his target had been an old Com Guard *King Crab* altered to resemble a *Daishi*. Either way, his *Orion* was outgunned, outarmored, and outclassed by the 100-ton death machine.

The Clanner raised his arms. Xenon strobes flashed from the box-like vambraces of the vis-mod *Daishi*. Amis' computer told him that the armor on his torso and legs had been scorched, but not breached. Four bursts of virtual autocannon fire made his 'Mech stagger. Now, the damage was becoming more critical.

A shower of simulated missiles leapt from the *Orion*'s left wrist, followed by a double blast of laser light and a hail of computer-generated, high-explosive armor-piercing shells.

The *"Daishi"* was hurt, but not bad enough to prevent it from savaging Amis' 'Mech again.

From the corner of his eye, the mercenary saw a large black shape move in. Azure lightning generated by his computer flooded his cockpit as Major Eveline Eicher, his second-in-command, blasted the aggressor with her *Hercules'* particle projection cannon.

The huge assault 'Mech staggered, the simulated loss of nearly a ton of armor affecting its balance. Another blast from Eicher's weapon, augmented by a burst of cannon fire, sent the enemy 'Mech crashing to the ground.

Once he got his reeling *Orion* back under control, Amis' first thought was for his unit. One look at the tactical display told the story. Most of his light 'Mechs were either gone or badly damaged. His unit was being scattered and picked to pieces.

For the length of one second, he stared at the monitor. A curse escaped his lips. With regret, Amis keyed his transmitter.

"Stonewall to Crowbar, Stonewall to Crowbar." He spoke each word distinctly, pitching his voice a bit higher than usual so it would be heard and easily understood amid the noise and confusion of battle. "Signal: X-Ray, Tango, Hotel. I say again, X-Ray Tango Hotel. Break off engagement and withdraw."

Reluctantly, the Light Horse 'Mechs began to disentangle themselves from the bitter struggle. A few, Captain Izzat among them, lagged behind, victims of simulated damage to their legs. Only two crippled machines, neither one of them Izzat's, made it back to the Regimental Rally Point. The captain's shot-up machine had been engaged and killed by a Com Guard *"Ryoken."*

Before the last of the stragglers limped into the RRP, General Winston's voice crackled from the commline.

"Crowbar, this is Nail. Signal Six. Romeo Tango Bravo. That is Signal Six, return to base."

Three quarters of an hour later, Winston and Colonel Paul Masters were waiting in the Light Horse commander's office for the exercise leaders to arrive. Seated in the corner of the dreary, sparsely furnished room was the overall commander of the task force, Marshal Morgan Hasek-Davion of the Federated Commonwealth. Morgan had arrived quietly, with no fanfare, before many task force units had even left their garrison worlds. In his capacity as task force commander, it was his place to oversee the training, plan the combat exercises, and conduct the commanders' debrief following the first integration exercise.

Morgan was one of the most experienced battle commanders in the Armed Forces of the Federated Commonwealth, if not the entire Inner Sphere. He had begun his career over thirty years earlier as a company commander with the Davion Heavy Guards, rising quickly through the ranks until, in 3049, he was appointed overall commander of the armies of the Federated Commonwealth.

Even at fifty-three years of age, he was no desk pilot. An excellent and inspiring leader of men, his reputation for quick thinking and stubborn courage made him one of the best battlefield commanders ever to pilot a 'Mech. The combination made him the natural choice to lead the task force. Over the years, his flaming red hair had begun to fade into a silvery-gray, and deep lines of care and worry had etched themselves into his once-smooth brow. But the green eyes beneath that brow were still as bright and as sharp as a well-honed razor, and he still cut a tall, impressive figure.

Morgan knew the image most people had of him: the tough, competent, compassionate warrior. He laughed quietly to himself as the thought drifted across his mind. *If only they knew the guy I see in the mirror every morning.*

He harbored no illusions about his infallibility or his immortality, knowing that he was prone to the same failings as anyone else. He also knew that when *he* made a wrong decision, he didn't pay the price. His mistake could cost men their lives. That thought might have cost him his edge had he not been groomed to lead fighting men from the day he was born. But there had also been times when he'd have liked to go off with his beloved Kym and live out his days as a retired gentleman at his family's home on New Syrtis, with nothing to do but watch his children grow up.

If he hadn't done so, it was because he would never have deserted Prince Hanse Davion, and later his son Victor, in a time of need. And the times had so often seemed needful these past thirty years.

Colonel Edwin Amis and Demi-Precentor Regis Grandi, the Com Guard commander, arrived together. As Amis marched his 'Mech into the Fort Defiance 'Mech bay, Morgan could hear the change in the mercenary Colonel's voice from the command center where he'd been monitoring the radio traffic on both sides. Morgan recognized in Amis' post-battle transmissions the note of exhaustion and melancholy that so often accompanied an unexpected defeat. In the forty-five minutes it took for the combatants to walk their 'Mechs the twenty or so kilometers separating the site of the mock battle from the Fort's main 'Mech facility, Amis's depression had faded, leaving the Colonel his usual optimistic self. Amis and Grandi were discussing the engagement as they walked through the briefing room's sliding door.

"Colonel Amis," Morgan began without preamble. "I was told that the Twenty-first Striker was one of the best regiments in the Inner Sphere. What happened out there?" He smiled to rob his words of any offense.

"I'm not really sure, sir." Amis shook his head as though to clear it of the image of his regiment dying around him. "I've fought the Clans before and Colonel Barclay's regiment battled them on Coventry, giving as good as she got. There is absolutely no reason why the Twenty-first shouldn't have kicked the stuffing out of the Guards. No offense." The last sentence was directed to Demi-Precentor Grandi.

"None taken," Grandi assured him. "As much as I hate to admit it, I was expecting to sustain heavy losses. The degree of our success surprised me."

"So what happened? Why has every unit we sent into the field fared so poorly against our OPFOR Clanners?" Morgan fixed each of the commanders in turn with his level, green-eyed stare.

Before either of the field commanders could answer, Paul Master spoke up.

"Sir, I think I have one possible answer.

"We've been running exercises for a couple of weeks

now. In each case, we've detailed one of our own regiments to play the part of a Clan unit. Then, we assign another outfit the task of attacking the 'Clanners.' The problem is not that we can't beat the Clanners. The problem is that we can't beat the Clanners when they use Inner Sphere tactics."

For a moment, Amis looked quizzically at the Knight commander, then realization dawned.

"Go on, Colonel Masters," Morgan said.

"You see, in each of the exercises, we asked our OPFOR Clanners to defend a given position. That only makes sense, since the real Clanners will be defending when the operation gets under way.

"The problem is that we've done visual modifications on the OPFOR 'Mechs, and programmed our simulation computers to reflect the superior range and firepower of their weapons, but what we haven't done is instructed the 'red team' to fight strictly according to Clan doctrine. I mean, they're great on the offensive. They put their heads down and charge right into you, just like the real thing. When they're forced onto the defensive, they seize up. I mean, we're not really sure what the Clans will do if they're forced to defend, are we? We have something of a model, based on what happened on Coventry. But that was such a mess that we can't really draw any conclusions.

"In every case, the OPFOR has either dug in and held their ground rather than meeting the attackers head-on, or they've forced the 'blue team' to maneuver until the attackers were spread out and unable to support each other.

"Either way, what OPFOR has been doing is 'un-Clanlike.' "

The commanders sat quietly for a long while, digesting the Knight commander's observations. After a time, Morgan spoke.

"So, Colonel Masters, how do you propose we overcome this problem?"

"Let's try putting together another exercise for tomorrow. My Knights will take the part of the Clan warriors." He consulted a comp pad. "The Seventy-first Light Horse hasn't been engaged yet. Let's give them a crack at playing the aggressors.

"My staff and I will try to come up with a model suggesting how the Clanners would respond to being on the defense for a change."

9

Nadir Jump Point
Defiance, Crucis March
Federated Commonwealth
18 February 3059
0955 Hours

The *Achilles* Class DropShip *Bisan* shuddered as 160 tons of aerospace fighter blasted free of its needle-shaped hull. The sleek *Bisan* was an assault ship, a kind of cross between a 'Mech-carrying DropShip and a heavy fighter. Most vessels of this type were smaller, faster, and more maneuverable than the clumsy 'Mech transport vessels. Like every other DropShip, however, assault ships were dependent upon JumpShips to move them from system to system. Only recently had a long-forgotten technology necessary for the construction of WarShips, combat vessels capable of jumping between the stars, been rediscovered.

Michael Ryan was observing the action on a monitor set into the forward wall of the ship's troop bay, situated one deck below, and just aft of the *Bisan*'s bridge deck. From his ready position in the NL-42 battle taxi, he watched the delta-hulled *SL-15R Slayer* fighters, each massing 80 metric tons, pull around in matching tight arcs, to fall into the standard "scissors" formation. The fighters' drives flared white as they sped away from the *Bisan*'s position at the jump point. Somewhere up ahead, under two hundred kilometers away, the *Alkmarr,* an *Invader* Class JumpShip, lay in geosynchronous orbit around Resistance, the third of the Defiance system's eight planets.

At this range, it was impossible to make out the *Alkmarr* against the star-dusted blackness. The *Bisan*'s computer painted a small red diamond on the monitor screen. The icon was labeled TDI-1741, for Transport, DropShip, Interstellar. Had she been a WarShip, the *Bisan*'s Identify Friend and Foe systems would have rendered her icon as a red wedge. DropShips were portrayed as elongated "U" shapes and fighters as tiny daggers.

At first, Ryan found the whole system confusing. But, as he came to work more closely with the *Bisan*'s captain, he rapidly assimilated the information. Now, he could tell at a glance that their fighter escorts, codenamed Arrow One and Two, were already more than halfway to the target. No DropShips had been detached from the *Alkmarr,* and there were no more vessels operating in their sector.

In an exercise jointly designed by Marshal Hasek-Davion and Precentor Alain Beresick, the Com Guard ship captain assigned to lead the task force's naval assets, Ryan's DEST commandos were ordered to capture the JumpShip intact, or at least as intact as possible. Ryan's plan called for the *Slayer*s to make a couple of high-speed attack runs past the *Alkmarr,* crippling her drives. While the defenders were busy with the fighters, the *Bisan* would lay alongside and launch a pair of NL-42 battle taxis. Each of these small craft carried a specially trained and equipped boarding party whose job it was to assault and capture the JumpShip. To increase the chances of approaching undetected and docking with a larger ship, the DEST team's taxis had been given a coat of dead, nonreflective black radar-absorbent paint. Boarding and seizing a starship was just the kind of small, specialized operation that a DEST team of commandos were especially trained to pull off.

Ryan looked around the compartment at the men and women under his command. Instead of just his regular team of ten packed in here, he now commanded a full DEST detachment of thirty other highly trained commandos. When the support personnel attached to the unit (including the *Bisan*'s crew) were figured in, Ryan's total command came to sixty-five.

His superiors had considered that it would be improper

for a mere *Tai-i* to command such a large number of highly trained personnel, so they had promoted him to the rank of *Sho-sa*. Ryan had protested the increase in rank, fearing that the promotion would interfere with the tight-knit community of his own team, while seeming to be an intrusion upon the integrity of the other teams under his command. Combine cultural mores dictated that there should be distance between the commanding officers and the men. To a degree, the DEST teams avoided this mandate, operating instead on a level similar to that of a well-adjusted family. A promotion, and the increased authority that came with it, might disrupt the closeness that was so important to the proper functioning of the special forces squads. Ryan tried to argue that he was unworthy of such an honor, and that he felt his place was with his team. *Sho-sho* Hideki Ishmaru silenced his protests by pointing out that the order came straight from the Coordinator.

With a sense of pride, Ryan shrugged and rolled his shoulders, feeling as though he could actually perceive the weight of the apple-green katakana *ichi* painted on the shoulders of his Kage suit. He was relieved to see that his promotion hadn't come between him and his men, as he had feared. Instead, the increase in rank had become an additional source of pride for Team Six. They seemed to feel that an extra measure of honor and respect was due them, since the commander of the overall DEST detachment had been picked from their Team.

Each of the ten troopers crowded into the cramped troop bay of the NL-42 battle taxi were identically clad in the black power armor recently developed by the Imperial Institute of Technology. Similar to the light scout armor fielded by the Gray Death Legion, the Kage suits had been created with the assistance of the Draconis Elite Strike Teams. The suits were made up of a compact exoskeleton covered with kevlex and articulated ballistite plates. The whole thing was capable of being sealed against a hostile environment, and fitted with so many sensors that the helmet alone required its own manual. The outer surface was treated with the same mimetic camouflage as the standard DEST infiltration suits. Ordinarily, a powerful jump unit completed the kit. For this operation, the jump pack had been replaced with a specially modified manned maneuvering unit.

"Arrow, is commending their attack, sir." The *Bisan*'s captain spoke in a calm professional tone, which startled Ryan. "Expect Yari to be on station in three minutes."

"Very well." Ryan acknowledged the pilot's report via the suit's built-in comm system. Yari was the code name for a *Leopard* Class DropShip assigned to transport DEST Team Four to the *Alkmarr*'s after section. Team Four had been assigned the task of capturing the JumpShip's engine and drive rooms. Ryan glanced at the chronometer bolted to the bulkhead above the monitor. It read 0957. Their mission orders called for rendezvous with the target vessel at 1000 hours. They were right on schedule. Switching channels, he informed the rest of his team, "Three minutes."

"Three minutes." The words crackled in Ryan's radio headset as each battle-armored trooper repeated and acknowledged the warning.

"Remember, people, fast and hard," he cautioned. "No playing around. A bad guy sticks his head out, you blow it off. We aren't looking for prisoners on this trip. Got it?"

A series of *"Hais"* and "Yes, sirs" confirmed that Team Six understood their mission.

The *Bisan* rocked slightly, taking simulated damaged from the *Alkmarr*'s PPCs.

Twisting slightly in his seat for a better view of the monitors, Ryan watched one of the *Slayer*s, still discernible only by its IFF icon, swoop in on the *Alkmarr*. He knew that the pilots were some of the Com Guard's best, but he still harbored a distrust of the warriors of the once-secretive organization.

The seconds ticked by slowly, punctuated only by the computer-generated shudders marking a hit by one of the *Alkmarr*'s weapons. A brief message from the *Bisan*'s pilot sounded in his ears. He passed it on to his men.

"Thirty seconds."

Before the warning could be relayed to the last DEST trooper, Ryan was punched back in his seat as *Chu-i* Yacob Grimm ignited the NL-42's engines.

The battle taxis shot free of the *Bisan*'s hull and streaked across the narrowing gap between the assault ship and the *Alkmarr*. The monitors went momentarily blank as the *Bisan*'s feed was lost. It was replaced by an image captured by the taxi's own cameras.

For the first time, Ryan realized how huge an *Invader*

Class JumpShip was. Longer overall than the height of many tall buildings, she massed an incredible 152,000 tons. Yet, for all her fantastic bulk, the *Alkmarr* was still smaller than any but the lightest WarShips.

"And they expect us to be able to capture that?" The incredulous thought flashed through his mind.

"Grapple. Hard lock in ten seconds. Get ready, *Sho-sa.*" The pilot's call jarred Ryan out of his stunned reverie.

The taxi, which, until moments before, had been floating gently in space, slammed hard onto the *Alkmarr*'s hull.

"Lock!" Grimm's voice screeched in Ryan's ear. "Go!"

Before Ryan could begin to repeat the command, Private Wu had wrenched the taxi's aft hatch open and leap onto the JumpShip's outer hull. A silent flicker of light told him that his advance man had just "blown" one of the target vessel's pressure hatches using a simulated explosive.

If the *Alkmarr*'s defenders had missed the team's approach, they certainly knew they were aboard now.

"Go! Go! Go!" Ryan shouted across his teams' tactical frequency. A quick tap on the suit's wrist-mounted control unit switched channels. "Ronin One commencing operation."

"Roger, Ronin One," came the acknowledgment. "Be advised, Ronin Two is now aboard." The Com Guard officer in charge of the exercise seemed to be almost bored with the operation.

"One acknowledges." Ryan propelled himself through the taxi's open hatch.

The marine pilot had brought them down five meters from the *Alkmarr*'s forward maintenance hatch. Using his suit's maneuvering unit, the commando shot across the intervening space and through the opening. Just inside the ship's "ruined" pressure hatch floated the "corpse" of one of her defenders. A small red light was flashing from the crown of his helmet. As Private Wu had lunged through the open hatch, this AFFC marine had appeared to oppose the boarders. Wu, using the low-wattage laser clipped to his suit's right vambrace instead of the normal Blazer rifle, fired a single shot. The marine was "killed" by the burst of coherent light. His suit's Laser Engagement Simulation Equipment interrupted power to the man's weapon and set off the strobe. Had Ryan not been wearing his helmet, he would have also heard a high-pitched beeping that declared the enemy to be dead.

"Move out." In response to their leader's snapped order, the DEST troopers jetted away.

Following the deck plans loaded into their suits' onboard computers, the team headed for the *Alkmarr*'s bridge. Further aft, Ronin Two was using an identical method to lead them to the vessel's engineering spaces.

"Contact!" Wu shouted, his message breaking off in mid-sentence.

"Sho-sa," Talon Sergeant Raiko called. "We have enemy contact. Wu is down."

Without needing an officer to lead them, the commandos of DEST Team Six swung into action. Corporal Hollis armed and threw a stun grenade. The resultant explosion lit up the JumpShip's corridor. Before the enemy could recover, the commandos stormed forward. A hail of laser "bullets" crisscrossed the enclosed space. Several of the marines "died" without firing a shot in return.

A flash of movement caught Ryan's attention. Quickly he spun, bringing up his right forearm. As the weapon mounted in his vambrace came to bear, the sighting cross hairs superimposed on his visor settled over the torso of a defending marine. Ryan pressed the trigger. Nothing happened. A low insistent tone sounded in his ears. *Sho-sa* Michael Ryan had been "killed in action."

The feeling of gravity was disorienting, as Ryan swung through the access port into the *Alkmarr*'s grav deck. Already present in the compartment were the ComStar JumpShip's captain and a stocky man with pale blonde hair wearing the insignia of an AFFC Colonel.

"Have a seat, *Sho-sa*." The captain gestured to an empty chair. He seemed to be in charge of the meeting. "I'd like your assessment of today's operation."

As he took his seat, Ryan quickly noted that the captain wore a small gold *pi* pinned to the collar of his uniform that declared him to be an aerospace pilot. A pair of golden wings displayed on his left breast told Ryan that the officer was considered by ComStar to be a hero.

His impression of the FedCom Colonel was far less admiring. The man wore the red disk of the Robinson Medal of Valor. At one time, he had apparently been decorated for his actions against the Draconis Combine, most likely in the War of 3039.

That so-called war was actually little more than a bloody border skirmish. Hanse Davion had launched a series of attacks on worlds belonging to the Draconis Combine in an attempt to crush his lifelong foe and to recapture planets lost during the Fourth Succession War. Though the offensive met with some initial success, a counter-thrust led by Theodore Kurita blunted the attacks. The war was over in six months, with only a few worlds changing hands. Ryan felt a flush of pride as he recalled an assault by DEST commandos on the Lyran command post on Vega. The attack had stalled the Lyran phase of the operation and left Field Marshal Nondi Steiner seriously wounded.

Though a faint ripple of disgust rose along his spine as he regarded the Davion officer, but he pushed it aside. With difficulty, he forced himself to sit at the table with the man, unfolding his comp pad on the surface before him.

"The mission was a success, as far as it went," Ryan ran a hand through his hair, wishing he'd had a chance to clean up before the meeting. The Kage suits were state of the art, but they always left him feeling sweaty.

"Please continue, *Sho-sa*."

"It took six minutes to launch the battle taxis, grapple them to the *Alkmarr,* and blow the hatches. My team secured the bridge nine minutes after effecting entry." There was a note of pride in that last sentence. "Team Five took eleven to capture engineering. We took over sixty percent casualties, including *Tai-i* Asihiro and myself. I checked the computer logs." Ryan glanced at the comp pad. "The *Bisan* took four hits to her armor from the *Alkmarr*'s point-defense weapons. She was in no real danger of being breached, but damage was inflicted. One of the *Slayer*s was damaged, as was Team Five's battle taxi.

"We committed twenty of our forty DEST troopers to the capture of a single transport. We got the ship, but lost twelve men in the process. If we use these tactics against a WarShip, we'll lose the whole team."

"And, do you have any suggestions, *Sho-sa*?" The *Alkmarr*'s captain smiled slightly, giving Ryan, the impression that he'd come to the same conclusions himself.

"Nothing solid yet," Ryan confessed. "I would like to see some way of delivering a larger boarding party in a shorter amount of time. Six minutes would be more than enough time for a WarShip to blast the *Bisan* and the NL-42s straight to hell. I'd increase the fighter cover assigned to escort the assault DropShips to at least five pairs. And, I'd recommend not even trying to board a WarShip unless there was no other choice."

"Is that all?" The FedCom Colonel spoke for the first time.

"Yes, Colonel," Ryan closed his comp pad with a snap. "For now."

"All right *Sho-Sa*." The AFFC officer leaned his forearms on the table. "I'll let you in on a few 'trade secrets.'

"This isn't the first boarding exercise against a Clan JumpShip we've run. The AFFC has been staging mock boarding parties for six months now, always with the same result. We can capture any kind of transport intact, but we take unacceptable casualties in the process. If we try taking on a WarShip, we get our heads handed to us.

"Like you, we decided that we need larger, more powerful vessels to transport the assault teams. The problem with ships like the *Hannibal* Class is their lack of small-craft bays and/or grappling equipment. If we use a larger ship, they have to lay alongside the target vessel while the marines cross using manned maneuvering units. All that time, the enemy is beefing up his defenses, firing on the assault ship and boarding party, and generally making life miserable.

"Our shipyards at New Syrtis and at Atreus are working at adapting the 'Mech bays on some of the larger assault ships to serve as taxi launch bays. If we can lick a few structural problems, we should be able to field a couple of the refitted ships with our task force.

"I wouldn't worry too much, though." The FedCom Colonel smiled as he dismissed Ryan. "None of us on the planning staff anticipate having to board any Clan WarShips."

Ryan turned to leave, but couldn't help muttering something in Japanese.

"What did he say?" he heard the FedCom officer ask.

The *Alkmarr*'s captain chuckled. "It's an old proverb, Colonel. Loosely translated, it means, 'famous last words.' "

Ryan swung out of the access port.

* * *

"Baka!" Ryan cursed the FedCom officer for a fool as he stormed through the hatchway leading to the *Alkmarr*'s passenger deck.

"Something wrong?" Ralph Carter, predictably, was the first to notice Ryan's arrival. The man's sixth sense made him a natural choice to serve as a spotter/observer for Lo Sior, the team's sniper.

"Cursed Davion officers." Ryan's contemptuous snort conveyed more to the assembled troopers than an hour-long discourse. "He actually had the nerve to critique *our* performance on the exercise."

Talon Sergeant Raiko, sensing his commander's mood, stood up with a groan only utterable by senior noncommissioned officers.

"Well, no wonder they gave you a hard time." Raiko grinned, robbing his words of any offense. "A senior officer, supposedly one of the best in the teams, goes charging full tilt into a fire-fight and gets himself greased by some no-rank marine." The Talon sergeant adopted the put-upon, Father-knows-best attitude common to every sergeant "saddled with" an officer.

"When are you going to listen to me, *Sho-sa*? Sergeants belong in combat. Officers just get in the way."

In the face of Raiko's good-natured kidding, Ryan's anger melted away.

For a moment he glared at his senior noncom. In any other branch of the Draconis Combine Mustered soldiery, such impudence toward an officer on the part of an enlisted man was a court-martial offense. Though the DEST teams that had survived the purge were perhaps the most loyal element of the DCMS, and clung more fiercely to the traditions of the Combine, within their own ranks there was often a camaraderie found nowhere else in the Kurita military.

"Huh." Ryan shook his head, amused by his Talon Sergeant's age-old jibe.

Carter interrupted the banter. "So what did you tell them, sir?"

"I told them just what happened," Ryan said. "They sent a platoon to do a company's job. Do you know what they told me?" Bitterness crept into his voice. "They said not to worry about it. We probably won't have to board any Clan WarShips anyhow."

Carter rolled his eyes. "I wonder if my life insurance is paid up?"

"I'd check on that real soon if I were you," said a strange voice from the hatchway.

Ryan turned to see a tall, muscular man with close-cropped black hair, wearing the uniform of a Davion marine, swinging his feet through the opening. As he pulled himself upright, Ryan saw the unadorned blue epaulets of an infantry officer clipped to the man's shoulders. What especially caught his attention was the black fox's mask pinned to the man's collar. The nametape on his right breast read "Fuentes." A ripple of distrust and hostility flashed through Ryan's mind as he realized the collar flash's significance.

"We haven't met yet, *Sho-sa*." Fuentes bobbed his head in what could have been interpreted as a bow. "I'm Leftenant Miguel Fuentes. I was the officer in charge of the marines you fought today. I just wanted to come by and congratulate you and your boys on your victory. Sorry you didn't 'live' to see it, sir."

"Those were your men, Leftenant?" Ryan struggled against his wounded pride, making the conscious decision to let the jibe about his "death" pass.

"Yessir, they were. And they were mighty upset at getting beat by a bunch of Dracs, if you'll pardon my French."

Ryan repressed his distrust of the Davion trooper long enough to snort out a laugh. "I see. You aren't really Davion marines, are you?"

"No sir, we're not." Fuentes tapped his collar pin. "Your guys beat up on Fox Team Four."

Those of Ryan's squad who heard the quiet confession were open-mouthed with surprise. The men they'd fought and defeated were members of the Federated Commonwealth's elite M16 commandos. The "Rabid Foxes" had a reputation rivaling that of even the Draconis Elite Strike teams.

"Listen, *Sho-sa*." Fuentes approached Ryan, and he clearly had something more than congratulations on his mind. "We've got to talk. Your op went down with, what, fifty-five percent casualties? That seems to be about standard.

"A couple of years ago, my team had to recapture a

civilian DropShip that had been seized by Liao Death Commandos during that mess in the Chaos March. We waxed the DCs, but took a lot of damage doing it.

"Between us, we've got some of the best soldiers and officers in the Inner Sphere. Captain Montjar, that's my company commander, thinks it might be a good idea for us all to put our heads together and hammer out an alternative to Extra-Vehicular Activity or battle taxi assaults."

For a moment, Ryan hesitated, fighting the ingrained response. Just a few months ago, he would have killed Leftenant Fuentes without a second thought. The man was M16, and M16 was the enemy.

No, Ryan forcibly reminded himself. *The Clans are the enemy.*

"Very well, Leftenant." Reflexively, Ryan began to bow, but caught himself. Instead, he offered Fuentes his hand. "It will be a pleasure to be working with you, instead of against you."

10

Fort Defiance
Defiance, Crucis March
Federated Commonwealth
22 February 3059
0615 Hours

"'Ten-hut!" Master Sergeant Carole Cole barked out the command as the steel briefing room door hissed open.

The officers of the Knights of the Inner Sphere shot to their feet as a token of respect for their commander.

"Be seated." Colonel Paul Masters waved his officers back to their places. Most of the Knights had large mugs of coffee or tea in front of them. He envied his men the luxury of that small pleasure. It had been a few days since he'd offered his challenge to the Eridani Light Horse, and he'd spent every minute since then reviewing debriefing tapes, battle ROMs, and personal accounts of combat encounters with the Clans. Using this data, he and his people had put together what they believed was an accurate model of how the Smoke Jaguars would react if they were suddenly forced onto the defensive.

Masters had spent most of the night planning his regiment's part in the coming operation and was feeling the effects of the lack of sleep. He knew the Knights' martial prowess, and had little fear that they would fail to execute the plan he had devised. What concerned him was the Eridani Light Horse. If they acted as he expected them to, his plan would work. If the wily mercenaries pulled off one of the battle-tricks for which they were so famous, his carefully constructed strategy would fall apart. Masters knew this was only an exercise, designed to familiarize members of the task force with one another and to prepare them to meet and overcome the highly aggressive Clan tactics. Still, this was not a contest he wanted to lose.

The Knights were unique in all the Inner Sphere. They were a combat force built not only on military strength, but also on the ideal that a man might fight, kill, and even die, without losing his humanity. Masters viewed this exercise as a means of validating that theory before the fighting men of the task force, and, thereby, the rest of the Inner Sphere.

Pushing aside his fatigue, Masters strode to the head of the conference table, thumbed a datachip into the proper slot, and without preamble began his briefing.

"Gentlemen, today we will be taking the role of the Smoke Jaguars in a field combat exercise." A holographic map sprang up before the Knights as he spoke. "This is the Crossmolina Highlands, the site of today's operation."

As Masters reeled off the particulars of the mission, a ComStar technician who had been assigned to the Knights manipulated the holoprojector's controls, causing various features on the laser-generated map to glow briefly. The map displayed a portion of the rocky upland region two score kilometers east of the Fort Defiance compound, separated from the installation by a line of tall, craggy hills labeled the Crossmolina Mountains.

"We, as the Jaguars, will be defending the abandoned Basantapur mining facility near Darom." He pointed to a spot in the middle of the uplands, rocky and distinctly lacking in vegetation. "Our opponents will be the seventy-first Light Horse Regiment of the Eridani Light Horse." Masters' voice was level and even. He spoke clearly and slowly, making sure that each of his commanders understood exactly what was expected of him.

"We will deploy by battalions. The First will take the center, about one kilometer south of the installation. Sir Gainard, the Second should deploy along this ravine to the east, and the Third, that's you, Dame Yanika, behind this line of hills to the west."

As he laid out the details of his plan, tiny three-dimensional images of the mine and an array of Battle-Mechs popped into existence on the map. The terrain around the mine concerned Masters. The jumbled off-tan shading indicated rough ground, which would limit the speed of units moving across it, restricting his ability to respond to any unexpected moves by the Light Horsemen.

"The Light Horse should be approaching our position via the Laurelton Gap. That is the easiest route into the Highlands." The gap appeared as a narrow defile, through which ran the centimeter-wide red line illustrating the Light Horse's projected line of approach. "Still, I wouldn't count on it. Colonel Barclay is no fool. Her regiment faced the Jade Falcons on Coventry and fought them to a standstill. She's just as likely to send a flanking force out through the Tel Burnas and hit the Third from behind." A red arrow arced in from the west edge of the map, through a series of low, rolling hills, and into the line of Knights' 'Mechs concealed there.

"We'll have to be ready to react to whatever tactics the Light Horse throws at us. Now remember, today we're not the Knights of the Inner Sphere, we're the Smoke Jaguars, one of the most aggressive of the Clans. Nothing in their doctrine seems to indicate any defense strategies. Even when faced with an aggressor, the Jaguars attack. So, to make this exercise as real as possible, you are ordered to close with the Light Horse as soon as they are spotted.

"Any questions?" Masters looked around the room.

"Yes, Sir Masters," Sir Pracha Seni, a lance commander from Yanika's Battalion and a chronic joker, raised his hand. "Are we to follow the Clan rules of engagement?"

Many of the Knights chuckled quietly at Seni's question. Even Masters smiled. The Clans traditionally favored a system of fighting that emphasized personal valor above all. Their complex code of conduct required Clan warriors to engage each opponent one-on-one until he was eliminated. If an enemy warrior fired on more than one Clan target, or if an enemy tried to interfere in one of these single combats, then all bets were off and the Clan warriors could attack any foeman in sight.

"Only until the Light Horse breaks them. Anyone else? No?" Masters clapped his hands and rubbed the palms together in a gesture of eager anticipation. "That's it. Equipment check in thirty minutes. Dismissed."

Now, Masters told himself, *I have time for that coffee.*

On the other side of the compound, Ariana Winston was finishing up her meeting with the Seventy-first's officers. Throughout the meeting, her tone had been one of quiet professionalism, mixed with apprehension.

"This will be a standard deployment. The Eleventh Recon will move out ahead of the column, conducting patrol sweeps to locate the Knights. When you make contact, hit them and fall back, maintaining contact. If I know Masters half as well as I think I do, he'll be pushing the Knights to respond just like the Jags would—attack. Keep them entertained, but don't get mixed up in a cat fight. Keep moving. Draw them out, get them to overextend. When they get strung out, the Eighty-second Cav will jump them. I want the Seventeenth Recon to draw up in reserve to catch any leakers.

"Any questions?"

Winston looked around the briefing room. Her gaze settled on the Seventy-first's commander, Sandra Barclay. Sandra sat leaning forward, her hands folded on the table in front of her. White smudges on her knuckles and a tightness around her eyes and mouth told Winston something was wrong. Barclay always seemed to be second-guessing herself since the bloody siege of Lietnerton on Coventry, and Winston had hoped that the exercises on Defiance would shake Barclay out of her funk.

A question jerked Winston's attention back to the meeting.

"I'm sorry, Captain Avilla, say again?"

"Has there been any progress with getting the APCs to run in this rotten-egg soup they call an atmosphere?" The Eighty-second's commanding officer repeated. "I'd like to know if I'm going to have a motor-infantry company or just foot-sloggers."

"Captain Zeek, that's your department."

Telemachus Zeek, Jr. was, like Winston, second-generation Light Horse. The young man with the nearly unpronounceable name had started out as an armored personnel carrier driver in his father's infantry company.

When Captain Zeek Sr. retired in 3045, his son "inherited" command of the Kingpins.

"Well, General Ma'am, the techs are still fighting with the filtration systems for the ICE engines. Anything with a fusion engine is okay. That means that the Blizzards and Maxims are limited to about fifty percent power output. You can push those hover transports to about seventy-five if you have to, but you'll double the breakdowns. It'll also mean twice as much down time for maintenance."

Winston rubbed her eyes, a bad habit she'd developed under the stress of command. Suddenly self-conscious, she forced herself to stop, putting her hands as casually as possible into her pockets before replying to the infantry captain's discourse.

"All right, Captain, keep them at it. Have your chief technicians write me up a report. I'll bring it up at the next command staff meeting."

Winston pulled her hands from her pockets. She'd just caught herself toying with the spent pistol cartridge she carried as a good luck piece. Another bad habit.

The compulsive gestures told her how worried she was. Not only about the coming exercise, but Task Force Serpent as a whole. The Light Horse was more than a combat unit under her command, they were her family. Now, more than at any other time, she felt the great trap of soldiering. You had to love the army to be a good soldier. And to be a good commander, you had to be willing to order people you loved into a situation that would certainly kill some of them. She'd certainly ordered people into combat before, knowing that some of them wouldn't come back. Even during the dark and dreadful days of the Coventry campaign, which had nearly seen the destruction of the Seventy-first Regiment, she had been secure in the knowledge that the Light Horse, as a body, would survive. This operation was different. Failure meant the total destruction of the unit. Even if the task force succeeded in wiping out the Smoke Jaguars, there was no guarantee that the Light Horse would survive the attempt.

"Okay, people, if there's nothing else, have your companies formed up at the rally point in one hour.

"Dismissed."

11

Crossmolina Highlands
Defiance, Crucis March
Federated Commonwealth
22 February 3059
0845 Hours

"**W**atch it, Boss!" Corporal Penelope Greene's voice cut sharply across the Light Horse's communications channels. "*Gladiator* on your 'nine.'"

Captain Stanley Crosetti wrenched the controls, as though twisting his own body would hurry the seemingly millimetric rotation of his *Hunchback*'s torso. As the machine continued its turn, he could see the Knights' *Zeus* that the battle computers and vis-mod shells reconfigured into a Smoke Jaguar *Gladiator*. Flame belched from the boxy autocannon perched bazooka-like on his 'Mech's right shoulder. The simulated armor-piercing explosive shells stitched a bright, flashing line across the aggressor 'Mech's hips. Even that huge war machine designed for close-assault battles couldn't stand the kind of punishment Crosetti's huge gun could dish out. Armor shattered and spalled away, leaving the enemy with little protection on his lower torso.

A veteran of several campaigns, Crosetti was impressed with the realistic images generated by the mock-engagement computer programs. His long combat experience hadn't, however, helped him against the Knights.

His company had, according to plan, spearheaded the advance of the Eleventh Recon Battalion. They had tracked down the Knights a few kilometers to the west of the abandoned Basantapur mine. Instead of pulling back into a tight defensive position, the OPFOR 'Mechs lunged after him. By the time he had pulled his company back to what he thought would be the protection of the Tel Burna Hills, he'd lost the entire Recon and half of the Strike Lance.

The Knights' response to his advance had been so ferocious that Crosetti had a brief feeling of *déjà vu,* going back to that fiery hell of a battle on Coventry. That campaign had left him in charge of the Slashers, as the Third Recon Company was nicknamed. Captain R.C. Gutjahr, his former commander, was killed by a Gauss slug from a Falcon *Mad Cat.* During the all-too-brief rebuilding period, General Winston had bumped Crosetti into the driver's seat of the Third at Colonel Barclay's request.

The *Gladiator* lifted its left arm. An actinic flash glared from the stubby muzzle replacing the machine's left hand.

Crosetti's *Hunchback* reeled under the simulated impact of a 125-kilo chunk of metal accelerated to supersonic velocity. The virtual Gauss slug "splintered" the reinforced steel armor on the 50-ton 'Mech's left leg. Before Crosetti could get his staggering machine under control, the ersatz Clanner completed the destruction with another blast from his weapons. Unable to withstand such punishment, the engagement program determined that the *Hunchback's* leg had snapped off in mid-thigh. The machine froze up as the battle computer determined that Crosetti would have been knocked unconscious by the 'Mech's fall.

Over his still active radio, Crosetti heard Corporal Greene's stunned shout.

"The boss is down! Slasher One and Two, form up on me and withdraw to Phase Line Tamarack."

Four kilometers away, General Ariana Winston, ensconced in the cockpit of her CP-11-C *Cyclops,* turned as far as the command couch would allow to look at the neurohelmetted figure of her passenger. As the command 'Mech for the entire Light Horse, her *Cyclops* had been refitted to include a command console. Normally, the slot would be occupied by a sensor and communications technician. Today, her back-seater was none other than Morgan Hasek-Davion.

Morgan had known Winston by reputation for much of her military life. The relationship became more personal when he'd called a number of units to Sudeten at the start of the Clan invasion. In the course of that strategy session, the two had come to appreciate each other's military acumen and integrity. Ever since, when time and location permitted, they exchanged the odd personal message, developing what had started out as a professional acquaintance into a long-distance friendship. Morgan had barely thought twice about selecting Winston as his second in command of the long strike. The Light Horse's dedication to the traditions of the Star League was icing on the cake.

Today, Morgan had decided to hitch a ride with her to observe the day's exercises.

"They're coming," she said over the internal communication system.

Morgan bobbed his neurohelmetted head once in reply. He had been watching the remote feeds as the Knights, in an uncharacteristic display of brute fury, smashed the Third Recon Company aside as though they were nothing more than unarmed AgroMechs. The battle had developed according to plan, with the Eleventh Recon Batt locating the Knights and drawing them out, away from the mine. The plan began to unravel as the Knights, responding to Colonel Masters' forceful interpretation of Clan tactics, ripped the Eleventh to shreds.

Three times since the first shots of the running battle were fired, Winston had to first urge, then order, her troops to stand fast. Morgan knew how difficult it was for warriors to remain in a prepared position while their comrades were dying only a few kilometers away. He'd experienced that feeling of helpless rage in 3039, and later, during the desperate early days of the Clan War. Even now, part of him wanted to override Winston's control of the 90-ton command 'Mech and charge off to rescue those men and women who were being shot to pieces over the next ridge. He knew it was just a simulation, but he couldn't escape the urge to take action. From the creaking of Winston's safety harness, which filtered back from the front cockpit seat, Morgan knew she was experiencing the same compulsion.

"Stand fast, Light Horse." Winston's voice on the radio seemed to be directed as much at herself as the rest of the regiment. "Let the enemy come to us."

"Gold Three, Gold One. *Whitworth* on your right. He's locking you up."

Sir August Mangini swung his *Enforcer* to face the threat and took a full volley of guided missiles. The combined impact of the missiles on his right arm and torso made the red and silver 'Mech stagger. With a skill born of long practice, Mangini brought the 50-ton machine back under his control. Smoothly, almost arrogantly, the Knight dropped his targeting cross hairs over the green and tan Light Horse 'Mech's center of mass and fired.

For Corporal Greene, struggling to maintain control of her damaged, overheating *Whitworth*, the results of the combined laser and autocannon hits were disastrous. A simulated explosion touched off by a laser hit to her portside magazine gutted her 'Mech. Instantly, the computer shut the machine down, and an irritatingly polite, computer-generated voice informed her that she had been killed.

"Thanks for the tip," Greene snarled as she pulled the release handle, opening her egress hatch. Even the tainted air of the Crossmolina Highlands seemed cool and refreshing after the stifling heat of her cockpit. Through the open hatch, she watched a Knights' *Wolverine* finish off the last of the Third Recon's 'Mechs.

"Well, General," Corporal Greene said to the Light Horse's distant commander. "It's all up to you now."

"Here they come!" The alarmed shout echoed the words and emotions of soldiers since the dawn of time.

Ariana Winston wasn't sure who gave the warning. She never had time to figure it out. No sooner had the alert sounded across the regimental communications channel than every sensor in the cockpit lit with warnings.

Half a kilometer away, the shattered remnants of the Eleventh Recon Battalion poured through the roadway gap in the ridge. Winston could see that less than half of the battalion's thirty-six 'Mechs had survived the running battle with the Knights.

She keyed the radio.

"All units, this is Dancer." The use of the codename assured that there would be no confusion over who was issuing the order. "Let Hawkeye get clear of the kill zone before we open fire. When I give the word, let 'er rip."

Seconds crawled by. The limping 'Mechs of the Eleventh Recon slowly crossed the open area between the easternmost ridge of the Tel Burnas and the concealed positions of the Eighty-second Heavy Cavalry.

Suddenly, a computer-generated explosion consumed a hobbling Light Horse *Rifleman*. Winston flinched at the abruptness of the 'Mech's demise. Instantly, her IFF painted a dozen or more red squares on her head's up display. Each tiny icon bore the label THREAT and an alphanumeric string intended to identify the type of 'Mech or vehicle being displayed. Most warriors Winston knew disregarded the tag or even reprogrammed their display to leave off the identifier. Being a field commander, she thought it prudent to know the exact nature of her opponents. Now, she wished she had disabled the system. So many OPFOR 'Mechs were pouring through the cut that her HUD was becoming too cluttered to be of any use. She tapped in a command, ordering her computer to display only the information on the closest threat unit. The HUD immediately cleared, revealing only a single scarlet marker. The label DRGFLY identified the lead OPFOR element as a 40-ton *Dragonfly*.

The range indicator placed him at seven hundred fifty meters. Slowly, the enemy closed. Morgan, seeming to enjoy his role as Winston's sensor technician, reeled off the distance to the target from his back seat. "Seven hundred meters. Six-fifty."

For her part, Winston was happy to let him deal with the flood of data coming in through the *Cyclops'* sophisticated communication and sensor systems. Having him along as a sensor tech made her job a lot easier. Morgan, with his wealth of tactical experience, was able to determine which information she needed and what could be ignored. They'd never fought side by side on the field before, but she suddenly felt the kinship only known between soldiers under fire.

"Six hundred, in range of LRMs." Morgan, to Winston's amusement, had adopted the flat tone so typical of sensor operators. "Five-fifty. Five hundred meters. At the rate he's closing, his probes will pick us up in about thirty seconds."

"Thank you, Marshal. You know, I *have* done this before," Winston growled, though with an overtone of good humor. Keying her communicator, she sent a wide-band message to her troops. "Eagle, this is Dancer, open fire."

At that order, every MechWarrior in the Eighty-second Heavy Cavalry Battalion, codenamed Eagle, triggered his weapons at whatever targets were in range.

On Winston's HUD, the DRGFLY icon winked out as five Light Horse 'Mechs poured fire into the visually modified *Cicada*.

Keying in another command, she brought up her own targeting display. This computer-generated image identified only those targets that were within the 660-meter range of her Gauss rifle.

For a few moments, she scanned the display, then settled her sights over the icon of an OPFOR *Puma*. She tapped the trigger, used a thumb switch to toggle up a different weapon, and fired again.

With the sound of a thunderclap, a simulated Gauss slug smashed into the *"Puma."* A second later, eight out of ten long-range missiles arced in to complete the destruction the Gauss rifle had started.

Winston's display told her that the OPFOR 'Mech was badly damaged. A second Gauss slug put it down for good.

"General, on your 'nine'!" came Morgan's excited shout from the *Cyclops'* rear cockpit.

"I see him!" Winston shouted back.

Swinging her 'Mech through a ninety-degree left turn into her "nine o'clock" facing, she searched out the pseudo-OmniMech Morgan had detected. Her cross hairs settled over an icon tagged CLBRN. From the back seat, Morgan shouted. *"Cauldron-Born.* That's a new Jag heavy. The Com Guards are really putting us through it."

Winston didn't reply

Indeed, the Com Guards, who had developed the computer programs that allowed the conducting of full-scale war-games, were putting the Light Horse, and all the rest of the task force units, through the full rigors of battle.

The inclusion of a brand-new OmniMech, first seen during the failed Clan invasion of the Draconis Combine capital of Luthien, showed the seriousness with which the training was being carried out.

The Knight/Clanner didn't appear to have noticed Winston's camouflaged 'Mech lurking behind its screen of trees. As carefully as she could, Winston settled the scarlet cross hairs over the bird-like 'Mech's backward-acting knee joint. With a feather touch, she caressed the trigger twice, reversing the order of her previous volley.

Still, the computer-generated hypersonic Gauss slug arrived before the slower missiles. The computer figured out the amount of damage each shot should have done in the 65-ton OmniMech, named for the nearly unkillable monsters of Irish myth. Like its namesake, the *Cauldron-Born* shrugged off the damage and turned to face its assailant.

"Hurry up and shoot, he's locking weapons." For all his years of combat experience, Morgan's warning shout sounded like some green recruit facing his first enemy, full of excitement, fear, and the joy of battle. She guessed that he must have sorely missed real action in the cockpit of a 'Mech.

Even as Winston fed the OPFOR 'Mech a second helping of Gauss and missile fire, the *Cauldron-Born* returned the same fire, adding to it a burst from its autocannon for good measure.

Winston felt confident that she could defeat her opponent. Her *Cyclops* outweighed the vis-mod Clan 'Mech by twenty-five tons, and she had better field position and the psychological advantage of having drawn first blood. Suddenly, the Knight was not alone. A second 'Mech, this one labeled MDCT-D, stepped up beside the *Cauldron-Born*.

Splitting her fire, she punched another simulated crater in the *Cauldron-Born*'s armor while peppering the *Mad Cat* with long range missiles.

By way of reply, both Knights/Clan 'Mechs leveled their weapons, and fired.

"Dancer, Dancer, this is Saber. I say again, the enemy is withdrawing in disorder, what are your orders? Over." Major Ron Jenkins switched frequencies.

"It's no use, Colonel Barclay. I can't raise Dancer."

Sandra Barclay gnawed her bottom lip, anxiety welling up in her stomach like acid.

"All right, Ron," she said at last. Dialing in the Light Horse's tactical frequency, she sent out a broad-beam signal. "All units, all units, this is Phantom. Dancer is off the air. I am assuming command. We will allow the enemy to retire. All units will pull back to alternate position Alpha. Get me your butcher's bills as quick as you can. They may decide to reform and hit us again.

"Major Jenkins, send someone from one of your fast lances to find out what happened to Dancer."

Blast it, General. Where are you? Barclay hunched forward in her command couch, scanning her tactical displays. There was no sign of Winston's *Cyclops*. There could be any number of reasons for that. Her communications system could be down, or her computer. Her 'Mech could have overheated and shut down.

Forcing herself to relax, Barclay leaned back, releasing the control sticks and stripping off the nomex gloves to ease the cramps stabbing through her hands and up her wrists. She continued to stare at the tactical display, so she wouldn't have to look at her hands. She didn't need to. It had been the same after every battle of exercise since Lietnerton. Her once-steady hands were shaking like autumn leaves.

Ten minutes later, Barclay's communicator crackled to life.

"All stations, all stations, this is Control." The voice of the Com Guard adept was clear and strong. "All stations, Code Seven. Exercise completed. Return to base."

"Control, this is Phantom. Message received and acknowledged."

Looking at her hands, she saw that the pronounced tremor had settled into a slight occasional twitch.

"Phantom, this Saber."

"Yeah, go ahead, Ron. What did you find out?"

"You're going to love this," Jenkins laughed. "The General went toe-to-toe with a couple of Clan heavies and got her head handed to her. Literally."

"Keep it up, Major," came Winston's voice over commline, her usual strong, clear tone slightly fuzzy and tinny over the speakers. "I have an opening in the support company on the kitchen staff. How would you like to command a lance of potato-peelers?"

"Glad to have you back, General." Barclay hoped the metallic effect of the radio would hide the tremor in her voice. "What happened?"

In the cockpit of her *Cyclops,* Winston exchanged a pointed glance with Morgan, who shrugged. He too had caught the unnatural quaver in Barclay's transmission.

"Major Jenkins was right." Winston tried to cover her concern with a self-deprecating laugh. She succeeded where Barclay failed. "We tried to take on a couple of bad guys. The computer says I've got a broken back, but at least I'm better off than our observer."

"How's that, ma'am?' Barclay's voice had a guarded quality as though she were oblivious to Winston's deadpan humor.

"The Eridani Light Horse is sorry to inform you of the death of Marshal Morgan Hasek-Davion. He died in battle, with his face to the enemy."

"What?' Barclay's surprised yelp startled her commanders.

"That's right, Colonel. I guess he'd been playing with the politicians too long. He forgot how to duck."

Morgan laughed at Winston's jibe. "I'm sorry, General. I guess I just need a little more time to adjust. I'll be more careful next time.

"After all, it wouldn't do for me to die before we even start this business."

12

Fort Defiance
Defiance, Crucis March
Federated Commonwealth
25 April 3059
1025 Hours

The officer's briefing room at Fort Defiance was as drab and depressing as the rest of the base. The wall, once painted a pleasant desert tan, had faded, the paint oxidizing to a mournful off-mustard color. Near the ceiling, the paint had darkened to a black-brown, stained by years of smoke and grime. The mid-morning sun filtering through the dusty windows did little more than magnify the dinginess of the scene. The only bright spot in the room was a white piece of cloth draped against the wall behind the briefer's podium. Even that clean sheet took on the look of a burial shroud in the bleak chamber.

Morgan Hasek-Davion leaned forward in his chair, looking around the conference table. He could tell that the assembled unit commanders felt subdued by the somber surroundings. At the same time, he sensed an air of expectation that warred against the depressing ambiance of the room. He felt the same contradictory spirit. The individual units that made up the task force were as combat-ready as they'd ever be. They had been ready before they'd arrived on Defiance, otherwise the leaders of the Whitting Conference would never have selected them for the mission. That knowledge gave him a feeling of confidence—that and the three months' worth of training and integration exercises the task force had just completed. But his confidence was tempered by an underlying concern that the task force, as a whole, was still not ready to embark upon its mission.

Morgan, though eager to finally come to grips with the Clans, had known there was an edge of desperation surrounding this mission, had known that even as he'd been the one to propose the ideas to the Whitting Conference. Though Victor Davion had disagreed at first, Morgan had known it was the right move, despite the risks and the difficulties. He knew that once such a decision was made, the only proper course was to go forward with it, resolving problems as they arose and drawing on every shred of one's will and courage so as not to lose heart. He had undertaken the task of welding a total force strength of eight regiments composed of eleven units drawn from across the Inner Sphere, into a single, deadly weapon. And he had never looked back. The training and integration exercises had gone a long way toward accomplishing this purpose, and if there were still areas that needed work, well, there were always areas that needed work.

The time allowed for that phase of Operation Serpent had run its course. Now was not the time to wallow in doubts and fears. They were on a schedule, and Morgan knew he must continue full speed ahead and trust that they'd accomplished enough in the time allotted. He looked around the room at the assembled commanders, silently assessing them.

Andrew Redburn, commander of the First Kathil Uhlans, slouched in his chair, absently pecking away at the data unit lying open on the table before him. Andrew was one of Morgan's oldest friends. They had been together since the Fourth Succession War, when the Uhlans had been formed out of the fragments of three Davion combat units.

Andrew Redburn's presence on this mission was comforting to Morgan. He was one of the finest soldiers Morgan had ever met, steady, stubborn, and as loyal to House Davion as Morgan himself. Though Morgan's responsibilities as commander of the AFFC army had kept them apart in recent years, it had done nothing to dim their friendship. Andy was always ready with a word of support, a dry-humored jest, or a scathing reproof, if he felt one was needed. Their experience on Kathil thirty years ago had bonded them, and Morgan felt they were as close as any brothers.

Feeling Morgan's eyes on him, Redburn gave his old friend a smiling thumbs-up.

His gaze traveled next to Marshal Sharon Bryan, the staunchly pro-Katrina leader of the elite Eleventh Lyran Guards, who returned his gaze defiantly. Sitting next to her was Paul Masters, the ever-proper commander of Thomas Marik's Knights of the Inner Sphere. Colonel Masters did not look up from the quiet chat he was having with Major Marcus Poling, commander of the First Battalion of the Second St. Ives Lancers.

Masters and the Knights had been included in the task force for several reasons, the most important being the fact that they comprised a reinforced regiment-sized unit with their own transportation, in the form of several DropShips and the JumpShip *Bernlad*. A secondary, but no less important, reason for the Knights' inclusion was their high moral code. When it was first proposed to send a task force on a long, roundabout march to strike at the Smoke Jaguar homeworld of Huntress, Morgan had asked the Knights to act as the conscience of the task force. He'd never doubted that Masters would take the job seriously or that the man might rapidly become a pain in the butt when it came to matters of military expediency, such as dealing with displaced Clan civilians and managing prisoners.

Across the table from Masters and Poling sat Överste Carl Sleipness, whose Fourth Drakøns had been whittled down to one battalion when the Clans had overrun the Free Rasalhague Republic eight years ago. Keeping his own council, the Överste stared morosely into the coffee cup grasped between his scarred hands.

A burst of laughter drew Morgan's attention to the far corner of the room, where Captain Roger Montjar of the Fox Fives exchanged gibes with DEST commander Michael Ryan. To Morgan, this seemed the strangest of all the friendships that had sprung up between the unit commanders during their short time on Defiance. Montjar and his two squads of "Rabid Foxes" would have killed Ryan or any of his thirty DEST commandos had they met anywhere else prior to the Whitting Conference. Now, the special forces leaders laughed together like close comrades.

Morgan had heard, as had most of the command staff, of an incident in Jerseyville, where the DEST troops on liberty, despite the AFFC uniforms worn by way of a disguise, had been set upon by a number of local miners. He'd been told that the assault had less to do with any suspicion that the commandos were "Dracs," than with the fact that they had apparently "stolen" a couple of the miners' girls. Though outnumbered, the DEST troopers had given a good account of themselves, until a few of the miners' friends joined the fray. At that point, according to the "unofficial" story, a half-dozen or so Rabid Foxes leapt into the melee on behalf of the Combine commandos. By the time the local authorities arrived, the brawl was over, and the soldiers were nowhere to be seen. That incident seemed to have sealed the friendship between the Rabid Foxes and the DEST members.

Morgan was less willing than Montjar to accept Ryan at face value. He had always been uncomfortable around zealots of any stripe, and the cold, ruthless killers of the Draconis Elite Strike Teams were perhaps the most rabid of an essentially fanatic type. The presence of the DEST officer couldn't help but raise Morgan's hackles.

Well, Montjar seems to trust him, Morgan thought wryly, *I suppose that's what they mean by friendship forged in battle.*

Their quiet laughter drew the attention of Colonel Samuel Kingston. Of all the unit leaders assigned to the task force, Morgan trusted him the least. Neither Kingston nor his regiment of Capellan troops, the Legionnaires, had done anything to earn Morgan's enmity. He knew it had to be some old bitterness left over from the days of the Fourth Succession War.

Only the mercenaries seemed at ease. Ariana Winston chatted easily with the officers commanding the Eridani Light Horse's three regiments. Occasionally, Colonel William MacLeod added his rolling burr to the mix, boasting of the exploits of his regiment of the Northwind Highlanders.

Beside MacLeod sat Major Loren Jaffray, commander of the recently formed Northwind Hussars. The unit had been formed expressly to fight the Clans after Jaffray had encountered the Smoke Jaguars on the Periphery world of Wayside V. Morgan knew that much of the Hussars' equipment had been acquired by the mercenary regiment during that expedition. The experience gained in that campaign was almost as valuable as the captured Omni-Mechs were. The Hussars had put their knowledge to good use during the training. Between them and the Invader Galaxy, Task Force Serpent had gained much insight into the Clans, and the Smoke Jaguars, in particular.

Whatever distrust Morgan felt for Kingston, the feeling was magnified five-fold where Loren Jaffray was concerned. Though Jaffray had never given Morgan any reason to doubt him, the man had once been a House Liao Death Commando, one of the fanatical warriors sworn to give their lives for the Chancellor of the Capellan Confederation. In Morgan's mind that put Jaffray in the same catagory as Michael Ryan, a zealot and a stone-cold assassin. Colonel MacLeod had personally vouched for Jaffray's integrity as well as his loyalty to the Highlanders and to the task force. Morgan hoped that MacLeod was right.

The briefing room door hissed open to admit Demi-Precentor Regis Grandi, the commanding officer of the Com Guards Second Division. "Sorry I'm late," he muttered. "I got tied up in a meeting with my technical staff."

As the commander of Task Force Serpent, Morgan had no doubt that the men and women under his command would obey his orders in combat, once the time came. What worried him was that long march to war. Trent, the Smoke Jaguar MechWarrior turned ComStar informer, who had provided the task force with the navigational data to take them to the Jaguars' homeworld, said it would take nearly a year to make the outward journey.

For himself, Morgan was eager to jump out on what would be the most important mission of his career. There was a special anticipation in his heart. For years he had served House Davion and the Federated Commonwealth as a line officer. More than once, he had placed his life on the line in attempting what Andrew Redburn often called, "crazy, impossible stunts." But with his promotion to the head of the Armed Forces of the Federated Commonwealth, his opportunities to actually face an enemy in 'Mech-to-

'Mech combat had dwindled away. Now, at last, he faced the possibility of having a hundred tons of fighting steel beneath him once more, and the prospect filled him with the anticipation and joy that only a warrior can know.

A lot can happen in a year, Morgan thought. *But nothing's going to happen unless we begin.*

"All right," he said, then took a moment to be sure he had everyone's attention. "Let's get started. Status reports. Colonel Masters?"

"The Knights are ready to go, sir," Masters said confidently.

"I wish the Light Horse was that ready," General Winston chimed in. "A number of our 'Mechs were damaged during the training, especially during that class-A malf-up with the Knights. Six of our light 'Mechs went down with leg and ankle damage. The ground in the Tel Burnas was a lot rougher than the maps showed. Some of the Eleventh's recon units got twisted up pretty bad. Most of the repairs are pretty well finished.

"Our biggest problem is RSM Young's *Archer*. When the computer shut down his 'Mech during that last exercise, the blasted thing didn't lock up the legs. So, a 70-ton 'Mech took a header into a big pile of boulders. Young's OK, just bruises and a broken nose. The problem is his 'Mech. The fall bent the left-knee driver rod almost in half. The damage was so bad that he couldn't get the thing back on its feet. We had to drag it into the repair bay on a flatbed. When the techs tried to do repairs, they couldn't get the rod free of the yoke assemblies. We had to swap out the entire left knee joint. That meant removing all the armor on that leg, cutting the joint shaft and bearings free of the strut yokes, and welding new ones in place. None of that was especially tricky, just hard, physical labor.

"The real problem is getting the leg to move. Our techs can't seem to get any power to the lower leg now. They've put in three different actuator packages and completely rewired the power harness, but they still can't find the problem. I'm giving them two days to trace it. If they can't get it fixed by then, we'll either have to replace the entire leg or leave the 'Mech behind."

Morgan nodded as he scribbled a memo on the comp pad on the table in front of him.

"Um-hum," he looked up from his notes. "Do we have any spare legs for an *Archer*?"

Winston checked her own portable data unit. "Not on planet. The nearest AFFC garrison big enough to have the equipment we need is the Crucis March Militia post on Tsamma. If we get an HPG message to them stat, we could probably have the replacement leg here in a week."

"Too long." Morgan looked up from his comp pad. "Any equipment that can't be made ready by oh-one May can be moved aboard the DropShips and repaired in transit. Those that can't be moved will have to be left behind. I'll make arrangements for picking up replacement 'Mechs from an AFFC garrison somewhere en route."

Winston shifted uncomfortably in her seat. The Light Horse had a reputation for being one of the most efficient, reliable units in the Inner Sphere. The balky left leg on Regimental Sergeant Major Young's *Archer* wasn't anyone's fault. That didn't make it any easier to tell Morgan that her unit was not one hundred percent ready to start the operation.

"Don't worry, sir. We'll be ready when the balloon goes up, even if we have to carry Young's 'Mech aboard."

"Uh-huh." Morgan's reply carried a note of playful skepticism.

"Colonel MacLeod?"

The Northwind Highlanders commander shot a grin at Ariana Winston. Since their arrival on Defiance, the mercenary companies had been involved in a friendly rivalry. Morgan knew that several thousand C-Bills had changed hands as a result of wagering on the outcome of the engagements fought by the mercs. Andrew Redburn had sheepishly confessed to winning two hundred C-Bills on the Light Horse's last exercise. Morgan's only comment was his relief that Redburn hadn't bet against him.

"Well, Marshal, the Highlanders are a champin' at the bit. We're ready to mount up as soon as you give the word."

"I'll take that as a 'ready.'" Morgan said, to the accompaniment of laughter from the other officers. The Scots burr of MacLeod and many of the other Highlanders had been the subject of many good-natured jokes since their arrival.

"I have to go along with General Winston, sir," *Sho-sa* Ryan interjected without being asked. "All of the special teams could use a bit more time, both to develop more integrated tactics, and to build a bit more trust. I know it's different for you 'Mech-jockeys, but with us special ops guys, trust is kind of hard to come by. We have to count on each other implicitly, especially in the field. We have to know what the other guy is thinking without asking. That kind of relationship is hard to build in a few weeks."

Morgan raised one hand to stop the DEST officer's flow of words. "I know what you're saying, Major, but we simply don't have the time it takes to build that kind of tight-knit integration."

"Yes, sir. I know that, But . . . "

"No buts, Major Ryan. I need to know if your people are ready to go."

"Strategically, I'd have to say yes." Ryan paused, lifting his hands in apparent concern and frustration. "Tactically? No. We could use more time to get more fully integrated."

"I'm sorry, Major, but you heard what I told General Winston. All repairs and drills will have to be done en route. You'll have plenty of time for integration while we're on our way to the target. You can conduct boarding exercises to your heart's content while the fleet is sitting at recharge points, but May first remains the jump-off date."

"Yes, sir."

Morgan nodded and moved on. One by one, he queried the various unit commanders regarding their troops' state of readiness. Each assured him that their units would be ready to take ship when the time came, and each stated their wish for more practice time. Finally, Morgan looked straight at the Com Guard commander.

"Demi-Precentor Grandi, what about the Guards?"

Grandi reviewed his notes before speaking.

"The Second Division will be ready to go by the first. I received a message from the Precentor Martial yesterday. Marshal Hasek-Davion, sir, you already know the contents of this message. I'd like to inform the other commanders."

Morgan nodded. "Go ahead, Demi-Precentor. But just the first section." Morgan paused as a faint grin tugged at the corners of his mouth. "I want to tell them the rest myself."

Grandi smiled in return.

"The Precentor Martial informs me that the additional JumpShips necessary for the transportation of this task force will be arriving on or about the twenty-seventh of this month. The bulk of this fleet will be made up of ComStar vessels, under the command of Precentor Alain Beresick. The fleet is to include the ISS *Invisible Truth,* the last *Cameron* Class battle cruiser known to exist in the Inner Sphere."

A ripple of surprise ran through the briefing room. General Winston, whose Eridani Light Horse maintained one of the largest fleets of JumpShips outside of any Successor State navy, stared open-mouthed.

It was now known that ComStar had for centuries maintained a small fleet of WarShips left over from the old Star League, hidden away among the many uninhabited systems of the Inner Sphere. But no one imagined that the organization had managed to preserve one of the most powerful WarShips ever built.

Grandi waited until the murmuring had ceased before continuing.

"The Federated Commonwealth has agreed to send two *Fox* Class corvettes, while the Draconis Combine has assigned their newest *Kyushu* Class frigate, *Haruna,* to the task force."

Andrew Redburn stirred at this last announcement. "I thought the Combine only had seven *Kyushu*s," he whispered to Morgan. "I don't remember seeing that name on any intelligence reports."

"Neither did I," Morgan replied, equally *sotto voce*. "When Theodore told me he'd be sending me his newest frigate, I thought he meant the *Victory at Wolcott*. When I told him so, he reminded me of their Phoenix Program. Who would have guessed that they were building WarShips in secret to go along with all their new ground units?"

Again, Demi-Precentor Grandi was forced to stop his briefing until the whispered conversation subsided. Morgan felt a subtle flush of embarrassment, but he was also glad that, after all the campaigns and battles he had seen, he could still feel fear and excitement at the beginning of an operation.

Before Grandi could resume his briefing, a low chuckle rippled through the room. Colonel Kingston looked up, meeting Morgan's questioning gaze.

"At least we can repay the Jaguars for Turtle Bay," he

said, grim satisfaction glittering in his dark almond-shaped eyes. "*We* have the WarShips now. If we have to, we can level their whole planet."

"No, we will not," Paul Masters said through gritted teeth. "Not so long as my Knights are part of this task force."

"Sir Masters is right." Morgan raised his right hand, forefinger extended, curtly silencing Kingston's reply. "We will *not* use the war fleet's weapons to level Huntress. If we do, we're no better than the Jaguars."

"I must agree with the Marshal," Demi-Precentor Grandi added. "Remember, ladies and gentlemen, that the success of this mission depends upon speed and secrecy rather than raw firepower." Grandi paused to consult his notes. "Those units possessing their own JumpShips, like the Knights and the Light Horse, will be expected to transport DropShips carrying combat troops from other units.

"The Precentor Martial has urged me to send his regards, and wishes us good luck and godspeed."

Grandi sat down in silence while the assembled commanders digested the message they had just received.

A few moments later, Morgan rose and cleared his throat before speaking. He knew the import of the message he was about to read and was, frankly a little awed by it. He cleared his throat again, tugging at the collar of his tan uniform jerkin.

"As you know, there was a second half to that message. By agreement of the various heads of state represented by this task force, all officers and men of Task Force Serpent shall be issued new uniforms.

"Ladies and gentlemen, the members of this task force will be the first in almost three hundred years to wear the uniform of the Star League."

A second wave of excited murmurs rumbled across the briefing room.

No one in the briefing room was more pleasantly surprised than the Eridani commanders. Colonel Amis took the cigar from his gaping mouth. Winston, a huge smile creasing her face, leaned toward Colonel Antonescu, whose hands had frozen in mid key-stroke on his comp pad.

"I can't wait to see Scott's face when we tell him."

Antonescu smiled thinly. Colonel Hinesick was one of

the staunchest proponents of a return to the Star League. Only Sandra Barclay showed no reaction, sitting with hands clasped on the table in front of her.

When the commotion quieted, Morgan continued.

"Since ComStar is providing the uniforms, there is a side note here from Precentor Martial Focht. He says he is sorry that these new uniforms will not be the technological equals of the originals." The original Star-League era uniforms were made using the same lostech knowledge as the 'Mechs of that bygone era. Neurohelmets were lighter and more efficient. Infantry and armor uniforms afforded the soldiers a greater degree of protection with less bulk. Even the helmets worn by the humble ground-pounders were a marvel of technology, boasting voice-controlled sensors and anti-laser glazing. Even having the Gray Death memory core and the technology gleaned from the Clans hadn't granted Inner Sphere developers the ability to replicate such advanced equipment.

"All personnel will be granted Star League ranks equivalent to that which they currently hold. All personnel will wear the Star league crest, in addition to their Successor State and/or unit insignia. All 'Mechs, fighters, ships, and other vehicles will have the Star League crest painted on them, in addition to their original markings.

"Finally, all personnel and equipment will bear the insignia developed for this task force."

With that, Morgan turned and pulled away the white sheet that had been tacked to the wall, covering the large, painted crest. It showed a black serpent, its fanged jaws open, ready to strike, coiled around the Cameron Star.

13

Fort Defiance
Defiance, Crucis March
Federated Commonwealth
25 April 3059
1350 Hours

Ten minutes later, after Morgan had dismissed the meeting, a Com Guard infantry sergeant slapped Kasugai Hatsumi on the shoulder.

"Hey! You Seida?" the soldier yelled over the noise in the 'Mech bay. The nekekami leader, responding to his alias, nodded. The man jerked his thumb over his shoulder. "There's a call waiting for you in the Officer of the Day's office."

Without waiting for an acknowledgment, the soldier walked off in the direction of the office. Hatsumi followed a few moments later. Though he had been trained to operate nearly any type of vehicle, from motorcycles to BattleMechs, the one device his instructors had left out was exoskeletons. In his role as a Com Guard astech, Hatsumi had been assigned to work in the Guards' 'Mech bay. He had been loading cassettes of cluster ammunition into a *Champion*'s LB 10-X autocannon when the call came through. The job required the use of a heavy exoskeleton. Adapting to the ungainly "mini-Mech's" slow, clumsy movements had been a major task for one who had been trained to walk with the smooth, easy grace of a hunting cat.

Hatsumi felt a tremor of anticipation as he switched off the exoskeleton's power cell. It had been easy to fit into the role of assistant technician that his employer had provided for him. Out of habit, he had picked up some valuable information on the everyday goings-on of the Com Guards, but he had yet to learn the nature or target of his mission. His training prohibited him from speculating on these subjects. Prior notions, however accurate, would influence how he and his team responded when it was time to carry out their assignment.

Hatsumi required a few minutes to power down the machine, loosen the numerous safety straps, and dismount. By the time he reached the Officer of the Day's tiny station at the back of the cavernous ferrocrete structure, the call had been waiting for some time.

The Com Guard Adept, a short wiry man with a scarred face, plainly regarded OOD duty as a waste of his valuable talents. He glared at Hatsumi, and pointed sharply at the phone.

"Line four." The Adept's voice was tight and hard. "Voice only, so use the handset. You know you're not supposed to get personal calls here, don't you?"

"Yes, sir." Hatsumi bowed his contrition. "I'm sorry. It won't happen again."

The Com Guard officer harrumphed and turned back to his console.

"Yes?"

A haze of gray snow covered the viewscreen. Hatsumi saw a small red pilot light indicating that the video portion of the call had been blanked at the point of transmission. The handset must have been manufactured before the last Succession War. The audio-only carrier was laden with static, and hissed or crackled with every sibilant or plosive the caller uttered.

"Hatsumi? Get your people ready. It is time to start your mission." The caller's voice was unrecognizable, but Hatsumi suspected he wanted it that way.

"Yes?" The flatness in his voice did not betray the sudden tension writhing through his guts.

"I also have a message from your friend on Peacock.

He said to tell you 'He travels the fastest who travels alone.' "

"I see." Hatsumi's tone was neutral and impassive. Before he had left his home on the Combine world of Peacock, his *Jonin* had given Hatsumi a simple code phrase, a line from an ancient poem by someone named Kipling. The verse, spoken as a message from a friend, served to authenticate the speaker as his contact. "Thank you for calling."

Replacing the handset in its cradle, Hatsumi once again thanked the Adept, who didn't deign to reply. The nekekami walked at a leisurely pace across the 'Mech bay without a backward glance. His study of human nature told him that the Com Guard, so impressed with his own perceived importance, had already forgotten the presence of the low-level worker who had received an unauthorized call. If Hatsumi hurried or showed signs of furtiveness, he would attract unnecessary attention to himself. He strolled casually as though he was returning to his work station.

As soon as he was out of sight of the OOD's office, he altered his course, heading for one of the hangar's numerous side entrances. Five hundred meters away was the Guards' primary communications shed. As Hatsumi entered, the communications adept on duty rose, opening his mouth.

"I'm looking for Adept Kipling. I was told he'd be here." Hatsumi spoke first, preempting the man's challenge. The name was the one he'd been told to give.

The duty officer's mouth snapped shut, and he stared blankly for a moment. "I'm sorry. I don't know anyone by that name.

"Ah. Sorry to bother you." Hatsumi was gone again before the adept could speak. None of the four men in the communications center showed any reaction to the brief visit, save one. Honda Tan, wearing the triangular patch and silver Z of a Com Guard Acolyte Technician, betrayed himself only so far as to narrow his eyes at hearing the poet's name.

Twice more, Hatsumi repeated the charade, once in the base infirmary, where Rumiko Fox was posing as a hospital corpsman, and again in the ammunition storage bunker for Keiji Sendai. Though he never spoke directly to his teammates, the message he had for each of them was clear.

Twenty minutes after being called to the OOD's office, Hatsumi was struggling to strap himself once again into the hated exoskeleton.

Three hours later, Hatsumi was bending over a different pile of equipment. The base at Fort Defiance, though quite large, was strained almost to its limits by the presence of, not the three regiments it was originally designed to house, but nine. Still, the nekekami team had managed to find a disused storeroom in what used to be part of the aerospace fighter maintenance facility. Each of the "Spirit Cats" had staked out a corner of the room for himself, and was now busily engaged in checking over his or her own gear.

As the team leader, Hatsumi had the least heavy equipment to deal with. He had his sneak suit and personal weapons, but little more. His role was to observe and direct the team's three specialists, rather than to engage in direct action. Still, as a nekekami, he was fully capable of assuming any of the others' posts, should one of them be killed or incapacitated. Hatsumi's only major piece of equipment was a palm-top data unit, similar to those carried by most field commanders. His was a bit different in that it boasted far more onboard memory than most note-puters. The unit's optical chips held data on each of the regiments attached to the task force and the officers commanding those regiments. The information had been supplied through agents of the Amber Crags Clan augmented by Hatsumi's own observations.

Honda Tan knelt on the floor in the midst of a bewildering array of electronic devices, night scopes, and recording equipment to support his station as an intelligence agent. This was the gear with which Hatsumi was most familiar, having used most of it during his long career as a field agent. The small, black plastic mushroom humming quietly by the storeroom's single door was one of Tan's toys. The device contained counter-surveillance equipment and a number of security sensors. Should someone approach the storeroom, the machine would let out a soft growl, giving the nekekami several seconds' warning—and several seconds would be more than enough for the trained agents to prepare a response. The device also generated a short-range electronic cloud that would scramble any sensors directed at the storeroom. As unlikely as surveillance of the team's hiding place might be, Hatsumi had lived long enough to develop a healthy dose of paranoia where security was concerned.

Rumiko Fox, as silent and unsmiling as ever, sat at the storeroom's one table. Carefully, the assassin unpacked, inspected, and replaced numerous vials, bottles, and parcels. Each of these containers held one of the drugs or poisons she had come to favor in her career as a professional killer. Hatsumi knew that not all of the substances in those bottles were deadly. Some, like the compound called "dragon's tears," were powerful drugs. The "tears," for example, were a hideous psychoactive, which, when administered over the course of a few days, would cause permanent and irrevocable insanity in the victim. Hatsumi suppressed an internal shudder as he watched Fox work. The woman was quite lovely, beautiful even, but there was a cold emptiness in her eyes that reminded him of a viper.

A large aluminum briefcase lying open on the floor beside her reminded Hatsumi that not all of Fox's assassinations were silent deaths brought about by subtle poisons. A disassembled Minolta 9000 advanced sniper system lay nestled in its foam cutouts. The flat black finish on the high-tech rifle seemed to absorb the diffused light of the room's illumination strips, giving the weapon a cold, evil look. Hatsumi knew that the rifle was, like all firearms, only a thing, a complex mechanism of steel and plastic, with no will of its own. Still, the very nature of the weapon gave him the distinct feeling that the rifle was watching him, waiting for the chance to snuff out any life that came beneath the cold, lifeless eye of its electronic sight.

Hatsumi shivered again, as he noticed the similarity between the sight's objective lens and Fox's light brown eyes. Hatsumi bore no illusions as to who and what he was. He understood that the nekekami were viewed as ruthless spies and assassins, considered as something of an aberration by so-called "normal" society. He accepted that as having a strong basis in fact. But, there was something in Rumiko Fox that set her just that much more beyond the pale of civilization's mores.

Forcibly, he tore his eyes away from the assassin and her deadly toys, turning them to the corner where the team's remaining member sat.

Sendai leaned against the far wall of the room, smiling happily, humming a little tune as he stuffed breaching charges, booby traps, and a few directional mines into a large nylon duffel bag. The demolitions expert had packaged up explosives of every size and description, ranging from small, lock-breaking charges, no bigger than a shot glass, to heavy destructive devices weighing as much as ten kilos. A separate aluminum case fitted with a thumbprint lock held the detonators.

The case's lock was keyed to the right thumb print of each of the team members. No one else could open it without destroying the lock. Such an attempt would probably detonate one, or all, of the detonators, destroying the case, and likely the intruder as well. Sendai had carefully explained that the case and the kit-bag holding the explosives would be stored in separate compartments aboard whatever vessel to which the team would be assigned, making the likelihood of an accident remote.

When each had finished inspecting his own gear, he switched with a teammate and repeated the examination. Though every one of them was a specialist in one field of operations, every nekekami received a degree of cross-training sufficient to familiarize him with the equipment used by his fellow agents.

The rotation was executed twice more, until each operative had reviewed the equipment being carried by all of his partners. That finished, they began working on the team's common gear. Every weapon was broken down, cleaned, inspected, and reassembled. Every sneak suit was examined. Each communicator was tested.

At last, predictably, it was Honda Tan who broke the silence.

"Kasugai, who is our target?"

"I'm sorry, Honda, I don't know yet." Hatsumi spread his hands in a gesture of innocence as he confessed his ignorance of the team's objective. "I was told we would be contacted on a step-by-step basis. This step is to prepare to move aboard our DropShips.

"Remember, we must blend in, stay out of trouble, and be ready to strike when the time comes."

For a moment, Tan chewed on his leader's reply. "That's it?"

"That's it." Hatsumi noticed that Fox and Sendai had stopped working to listen to the exchange. Each of the nekekami agents, including Hatsumi himself, were naturally curious about their mission. Unfortunately, the team leader had no more indication as to the team's objective than any of the others. "I won't speculate on the nature of our task. What I will say is the target must be very important, and the client very powerful, for such a veil of secrecy to have been drawn across our mission."

"All right, Colonel, I'm here." Morgan Hasek-Davion returned the Northwind Highlanders' commanding officer's salute as he stepped from his command car. "What was it you wanted me to see?"

Following the final pre-mission planning session, Colonel William MacLeod had sent a message to Morgan's quarters personally inviting him to be present for a little ceremony scheduled to take place in the Highlanders' assigned section of the Fort. MacLeod's invitation had specifically stated that Morgan should meet him in front of the Highlanders' main BattleMech bay at seventeen hundred hours. By the time Morgan arrived, Defiance's yellow sun had sunk low enough to the horizon that it was shining almost directly on the 'Mech bay's main door, washing the plain gray concrete with a pale orange-gold light caused by the taint in Defiance's atmosphere.

"A grand sight indeed, sir," MacLeod said.

Though Morgan knew MacLeod could not see beneath the ugly black respirator mask covering his face, he was sure the Highlander commander recognized the expression in his eyes for he returned Morgan's grin with one of his own. Lifting a small, hand-held communicator to his mask's speaker grille, MacLeod then spoke a few quick words that sounded to Morgan something like, "Alba gu bragh." MacLeod turned to Morgan and translated, "Scotland forever."

Moments later, there came a deep scraping rumble that was so familiar to Morgan that he didn't need to see the fifteen-meter-tall bay doors sliding ponderously open to identify the sound. At twenty-five meters, the movement of the massive doors could be perceived through the soles of the feet as a faint trembling in the ferrocrete beneath them.

There was nothing faint about the sensation that followed. At that long stone's throw distance, the whine of servos and actuator packages pierced the sulfur-laden air and stirred Morgan's heart like a bugle call. The heavy thudding of marching BattleMechs shook the ground.

Sunlight glinted off armor as a monstrous humanoid figure moved from the shadowed interior of the bay onto the ferrocrete apron.

That's a Highlander. The thought flashed across Morgan's mind like a laser bolt.

The huge, barrel-chested, square-headed assault 'Mech had originally been designed for the Star League Defense Force. With its wrist-mounted Gauss rifle, lasers, and missile launchers, the *Highlander* had been one of the most popular designs of a long gone era. The 90-ton monster was also one of the few assault class 'Mechs capable of bounding into the air on jump jets, covering ninety meters in a single leap. Sadly, the design had been lost in the chaos following the fall of the Star League and the Exodus of Kerensky's armada. Only recently, with the discovery of the Gray Death memory core and the unveiling of ComStar's military arm, had the *Highlander* had its rebirth.

Even more shocking to Morgan was the complex checked pattern of green and blue bands decorating the 'Mech's armored hide. At times called plaid, at others tartan, the pattern was one as old as the term Highlander. The crest on the 'Mech's right shoulder dispelled whatever doubts Morgan may have had about its unit affiliation. The green and blue plaid and the silver crest had only ever belonged to one unit, the Royal Black Watch.

Following the *Highlander* was a company's worth of heavy and assault 'Mechs, each painted in the same green and blue tartan. Most of the battle machines were standard Inner Sphere 'Mechs, but a few were recreations of older models whose original design stretched back to the time of the Star League. Morgan recognized the ugly hunch-shouldered outline of a PPC-armed *Thug* as well as a gangly *Black Knight*.

"Aye," MacLeod answered Morgan's questioning look. "They're the Royal Black Watch. Or at least what's left of 'em."

"I thought they were wiped out when Stefan Amaris seized the Star League throne."

"They were, laddie. They were." A note of maudlin anger crept into MacLeod's voice as he told the tale. "Most of 'em were cut down in the palace by the Usurper's guards. Them as made it out of that trap, tried to hold off the Amaris Dragoons, hopin' to let Richard Cameron, the First Lord escape. Poor bastards didna know he was already dead at the hand of the Usurper. In the end, Amaris used a nuclear weapon on 'em. T' my knowledge, no Black Watch warrior survived that day."

"Then how. . . ?"

"Well, a long time later, a couple of the Highlanders came t' believe that they were *still* a part o' the Star League army. Understand that *all* of the Highlanders consider themselves t'be *upholders* of the ideals of the Star League. These folks believed they *were* part of the SLDF. It became an obsession wi' them. They formed what they called an 'order' within the Highlanders, considerin' themselves t' be the Royal Black Watch. Most of the Highlanders officers have known about this secret society among our ranks. A few of 'em were even *members* of the Black Watch.

"Their goal all along has been the rebirth of the Star League. Now that it's happened, they've decided t' reveal themselves. I understand Neil Campbell, their leader, who ye'll be meetin' in a bit, had something of a dilemma on his hands. Some of the Watch wanted t' go right off t' Sian and swear allegiance t' Sun Tzu the moment they heard the Star League charter had been signed. After all, the Royal Black Watch was the First Lord's personal bodyguard, and Chancellor Liao is the new First Lord. Captain Campbell did some fast talkin' and persuaded them t' stay with the Highlanders until this mission is over an' done, *then* they'll have something t' show the First Lord."

As MacLeod recounted the history of the Black Watch, Morgan felt an odd sense of pride welling up in his heart. He knew the history of the Black Watch—every Mech-Warrior who'd ever attended a military academy did. Oddly perhaps, the pride came not from the knowledge that he was taking such a prestigious unit as the Black Watch into battle, but from the honor Colonel MacLeod was affording him. Morgan was the first non-Highlander officer to learn of the existence of yet another link to the long-gone golden age of the Star League.

The tartan-clad 'Mechs had fallen into a line abreast, with the *Highlander* in the center. As Morgan watched, a small ingress/egress hatch in the side of the 'Mech's boxy head swung open and a powerfully built young man wriggled out onto the machine's armored shoulder. With speed and agility he swarmed down a narrow chain ladder that he had released from a compartment in the 'Mech's shoulder. As he strode across the pavement, Morgan noted that the Highlander was a bit shorter than his own good height, although the solid, corded muscles of the younger man's physique made him seem somewhat taller.

"Marshal Hasek-Davion," MacLeod intoned formally. "May I present, Captain Neil Campbell, company commander of the Royal Black Watch?"

Campbell snapped off a smart salute, which Morgan returned with no less formality.

"Captain, I'm proud to have you with us," he said. "With the Eridani Light Horse, the Northwind Highlanders, and now your Royal Black Watch, the Star League Defense Force is truly here."

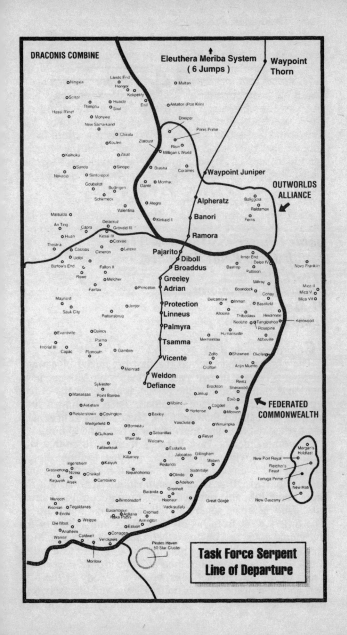

14

Battle Cruiser ISS Invisible Truth
Zenith Jump Point, Defiance
Crucis March
Federated Commonwealth
01 May 3059
0800 Hours

"**C**ommander on deck."

The phrase dated back to the first organized blue-water navies of Terra's distant past. Instinctively, Morgan hesitated and glanced around the bridge, looking for the officer whose entrance had been heralded. Then, feeling a little foolish, he realized that the Com Guard petty officer who had barked out the announcement was referring to him.

As commander of Task Force Serpent, a force that was part of the newly reformed Star League Defense Force, Morgan had retained his title of Marshal rather than assuming the old SLDF rank of Commanding General. All the units under him also retained their original command structure, with Morgan generating all operational-level orders. The orders went from his office to the commanders of the individual units, and on down their chain of command. Morgan knew that truly integrating the task force into a single army would take far more than an edict from the crowned heads of the Successor States, however. Many of the officers and men of the various units still viewed themselves as part of their own Successor State's military. It would take still more work, arguments, compromise, and patience for them to become one army. Without integration, the task force would fall apart under the strain of combat, and the Jaguars would eat them alive.

I've got a year to work on that, Morgan told himself as he stepped onto the battle cruiser's control deck. In the meantime other matters were even more pressing. Matters like the departure of his huge task force from the Defiance system, as they began their long trek through the stars.

The *Invisible Truth*'s bridge was like none Morgan had seen before. Having been a soldier most of his adult life, he had been on the bridge of every type of transport-type JumpShip. He'd even been privileged to tour the prototype *Fox* Class corvette while she was still under construction at the Galax shipyards.

The *Truth* was different from all those. Where a transport ship might have four or five bridge stations, and a corvette as many as ten, the *Truth* boasted fifteen consoles for bridge personnel. The center of her spacious control deck was dominated by a high-resolution holotank. Morgan had seen such devices before, but always on a smaller scale. The three-dimensional laser-generated image of the task force, its ships hanging motionless in space above Defiance's GV sun, was easily six meters across. Surrounding the tank's raised platform were a series of smaller flatscreen and tri-D monitors displaying everything from the current tactical situation to the status of the jump sail. A second battery of instrument panels ran around the outside of the bridge deck. These were occupied by still more ComStar techs going about their routine tasks, from monitoring radio traffic to guiding a Com Guard DropShip into her berth.

Standing in the center of the holotank was a rather unimpressive figure of a man. His slight build and height and thinning mouse-brown hair made Morgan think of a low-level tax clerk instead of the commander of one of the most powerful fighting ships ever built.

At the petty officer's shout, the man turned away from the image of a Lyran *Monolith* and descended the short flight of steps leading into the tank.

"Marshal, welcome aboard the ISS *Invisible Truth.*" A silver star gleamed on the right shoulder strap of the man's khaki and white jumpsuit, balanced by a Cameron

Star on the left. "I'm sorry I didn't meet you myself, but I was somewhat busy here."

"That's all right, Commodore Beresick. I . . ." Morgan never got to finish his statement.

"Precentor, ahm, Commodore," a Com Guard commtech stumbled over the rank change. "The *Cabot* is calling again."

Beresick immediately forgot all about Morgan as he turned to reply. "You tell Marshal Bryan I don't want any more excuses." Beresick snapped at the equally frustrated technician. "No, better yet, I'll tell her myself."

Morgan left Commodore Beresick to deal with the problems of organizing so large a fleet into a coherent body in preparation for jumping outsystem. Crossing to the holotank, he mounted the stairs to the platform. From up close, the holographic model of the Defiance system was equally as confusing as it looked from across the room. Tiny JumpShips hung nose-down above Defiance's single star. Smaller points of light, representing Drop-Ships, shuttles, and aerospace fighters, drifted between the miniature starships. Each laser-generated blip was tagged with a short alphanumeric code that identified the vessel. It had taken several days following the close of the final pre-mission briefing to get the task force's 'Mechs, vehicles, and soldiers, not to mention technical and support personnel, billeted aboard the transports they'd occupy during the long march to Huntress. Each JumpShip and DropShip was laid out before him in faintly glowing miniature. One of these images, labeled LC0057 - *CBT,* was highlighted with a faint scarlet glow. The *Cabot.*

Morgan glanced around the control stations until he located one bearing an engraved brass plaque reading "Holotank Control." The tech seated at that station had a green-cornered white square sewn to his shoulder and a nametape that read "Daum."

"Mister Daum." The tech looked up in response to the commanding officer's call. "Can I please see a map of the coreward half of the Inner Sphere, including the Clan occupation zones?"

The technician punched a few buttons before looking up. "Display vertical or horizontal?"

"Vertical, please, and put Terra at the bottom."

"Yessir."

A few more taps sounded from the tank controller's station, and the image of the Defiance system winked out, to be replaced by a flat image of the coreward Inner Sphere.

"Pull back a bit, so I can see Defiance."

The tech acknowledged his command, and the image shrank. Unasked, Seaman Daum had highlighted Defiance in red against the gold field of the Federated Commonwealth.

For a long moment, Morgan stood back, surveying the holographic map, his chin cupped in his right hand. With his eyes, he traced the task force's projected route. From Defiance, they were to jump into the Weldon system. From there, they would hop to Vicente, Tsamma, and then Palmyra. The dog-leg series of jumps, forced upon them by the thirty light-year maximum a JumpShip could leap from star to star, would eventually carry the task force across the Federated Commonwealth's and into the Outworlds Alliance of the Periphery. The Task Force would then jump out of the Periphery, heading into virtually uncharted space, by the end of June. Owing to the time necessary to recharge jump drives, they would barely make it.

As he surveyed the task force's planned route out of the Inner Sphere, Morgan began to feel the weight of his responsibilities settling heavily on his shoulders. Until that moment, all the training, integration exercises, meetings, strategy sessions, all of it, had been something of a blue-sky project, something that would be undertaken some-time. Now, it *was* sometime. In all too few moments, Morgan would be asked to give the command to launch the most important military operation since the Exodus.

My god, the Exodus. The thought rang in his mind like a cathedral bell. Somehow it had never truly hit him till now. The Exodus Road was what the Clans had named Kerensky's route away from the Inner Sphere, and Task Force Serpent would be following a slight variation on that road through space. He and these thousands of warriors, support personnel, and ship crews would retrace the route that Kerensky took almost three hundred years ago.

Morgan shivered as he imagined what it must have been like, centuries ago, in the control center of the *McKenna's Pride,* the battleship that had carried General Aleksandr Kerensky into the mists of time and myth. What had Kerensky felt as he looked out through the viewscreen into the black void beyond? Did he fear for the men and women under his command? Did he ever expect to return? Did he mourn the loss of the only home he had ever known? The questions had been asked thousands of times by historians, writers, political commentators, and common people, but there had never been a satisfactory answer, until now.

As Morgan Hasek-Davion stood in the center of the *Invisible Truth*'s holotank, a flash of revelation shook him. He was experiencing exactly what must have gripped Kerensky so long ago. Fear and excitement, sorrow and pride, loss and honor; these were surely the emotions that had swept through the General as he stood on the brink of the unknown, without even the sketchy maps programmed into the *Truth*'s navigational systems. A sense of fear and wonder gripped Morgan as he considered the past. Kerensky had left everything behind to save mankind from itself. Now, Morgan was about to follow in the legendary Kerensky's footsteps trying to save mankind from the General's own descendants.

"Like our little toy?"

Morgan jumped, his heart in his throat, as his thoughts snapped back to the present. For a brief moment, he wasn't quite sure where he was.

"What?"

"I asked if you liked our new toy." Commodore Beresick had joined Morgan in the holotank.

"Very much." Shaking his head to clear it of the lingering images of the long-ago journey, Morgan turned his attention away from the map and faced Beresick. "I wasn't aware that the Com Guards had any ships of this class."

Beresick chuckled, looking like a proud father. "As far as we know, and we know a lot, the *Invisible Truth* is the last of her kind. At one time, we had two *Camerons:* the *Lady Shandra* and the *Electa.* An early Explorer Corps mission found them lying 'in mothballs' in a deep Periphery system. We aren't really sure why the Exodus fleet abandoned two perfectly good battle cruisers, but there they were."

Morgan gave the Commodore a quizzical look, but said nothing. Beresick either failed to see the "you're-not-telling-the-whole-story" arch of the Marshal's eyebrows, or else he didn't care if Morgan believed him or not. The man just kept right on talking.

"Once the ships were in our hands, we gave them an overhaul and rechristened them *Invisible Truth* and *StarSword.* Over the years, age, decay, wear and tear, just got to be a bit too much for the old girls. ComStar made the decision to cannibalize the *StarSword* in order to maintain the *Truth.*"

As Beresick described the dismantling of a proud old fighting vessel to keep her sister-ship in fighting trim, a misty, faraway look crossed his face. Morgan had never really thought about how painful a lost ship might be to a naval man. He suddenly realized that their journey through unknown space to Huntress was going to be a no man's land for him in more ways than one. On the ground, Morgan was in his element. His slightest order could set great armies in motion, could tip the balance between defeat and victory. But he was no spacer. Commander of Task Force Serpent or not, aboard the *Invisible Truth,* he was often going to be no better than a mere passenger.

"I heard you talking to Bryan a moment ago," Morgan said. "What's her problem?"

"Aah," Beresick's tone revealed his frustrated disgust with the Lyran Marshal. "She's still griping about having St. Ives DropShips docked with her JumpShips."

Morgan snorted. Sharon Bryan was a fanatical member of the Katrina Steiner faction. During the planning stages of the operation, she had more than once voiced her opinion that no units other than loyal Steiner troops should be transported aboard Lyran vessels. Since the St. Ives Compact had been established primarily through the efforts of Prince Hanse Davion, Morgan's late uncle, Bryan viewed the St. Ives troops as pawns of the FedCom. To her mind, they were little better than spies.

Morgan, Beresick, and others had tried to make her see the light, but to no avail. Eventually, Morgan had to exercise his command authority, ordering Bryan to accept the Second St. Ives Lancers as passengers aboard her ships. Bryan gave in grudgingly. Arguments of that type had slowed the boarding process, which had already consumed most of the three days since the final pre-mission staff meeting.

"Any other problems?"

"Lots. You want them in alphabetical or chronological order?" Beresick waved down Morgan's surprise. "Listen, sir, any operation of this size is going to have problems, lots of them, but nothing that can't be handled. I wouldn't worry too much. We'll jump outsystem on time."

Morgan knew he might still worry, even though it was useless. He'd be the one to give the order to jump, but the rest of it was out of his hands. From now until they reached Huntress, his life was going to be very, very different.

Commodore Beresick was true to his word. Just over three hours later, the last DropShip, a *Leopard* assigned to the Rasalhague Republic contingent, the Fourth Drakøns, docked with the ComStar JumpShip *Asturias,* the last carrier to do so.

At Beresick's command, a ship's tech opened a communications channel.

"All commands, this is Spanner. Report status."

One by one, beginning with the Eridani Light Horse's command ship, the *Gettysburg,* the ships of the fleet reported their state of readiness. Each account was a variation on the same theme; "All commands squared away and ready for jump."

When the last vessel had checked in, Beresick turned to face Morgan. Responding to the enormity of the moment, the Precentor-turned-Commodore drew himself to full attention, saluted, and said, "All stations report manned and ready, sir."

Morgan drew in a deep breath, held it for a moment, let it out again in a long sigh, and gave a single nod.

"All right, let's be on our way."

Morgan's command was almost a suggestion. Beresick was far more dramatic.

He snapped another salute, executed a crisp about-face, and began barking out commands in a fashion befitting the captain of a sail-powered frigate of an age gone by. With his left hand clenched tightly around the brass rail surrounding the raised holotank platform, Beresick rapped out his orders.

"To all commands: initiate jump procedures. Mr. Hivlan, lock course into the navputer, Mr. Ng, engage the K-F drive."

Tension was thick in the air. Grim-faced men and women sat rigidly at their consoles. Morgan saw that a faint sheen of perspiration had broken out on Beresick's high forehead. As surreptitiously as he could, he reached up to wipe his own brow. His hand came away slick with sweat, which he wiped off against the leg of his jumpsuit uniform.

Sharp commands were given and repeated as various systems were brought on line. Some of the tight-voiced acknowledgments stepped on each other, as anxious crewmen readied the ship for jump, making it necessary to repeat the messages.

"Course plotted and laid in."

"K-F drives charged and on line, sir."

At last, the *Truth*'s executive officer turned from his control board, faced Beresick, and saluted crisply.

"Sir, all systems are on line. The ship is ready to jump."

"Sound the horn."

In response to Beresick's order, a raucous honk rang through the WarShip. Twice more the klaxon tortured the ears of the *Truth*'s passengers and crew.

In the miniature world of the holotank, a scarlet flare of light bloomed and vanished in less than a second, leaving flash-bulb afterimages swimming before Morgan's eyes. More crimson flashes dotted the projection, as the *Invisible Truth*'s powerful computers translated the electromagnetic and tachyon flares of the departing JumpShips into a visible-light display.

"Marshal, we are ready to jump," Beresick said.

Morgan nodded again, and with an edge in his voice for the first time since arriving aboard the *Invisible Truth*, spoke a single word.

"Jump."

"Aye, sir. Jump," Beresick repeated. Turning to the chief engineering officer, he snapped, "Mr. Ng, activate field initiator. Jump."

"Initiator active, Captain." The small man with fine Asian features sent his fingers dancing across his control panel. "Jump in five . . . four . . . three . . . two . . . one . . . Jump!"

Ng's final exclamation slurred, as though played through a recorder that had suddenly run out of power. The field initiator, a massive system of electronics and quantum mechanics buried deep within the *Truth*'s hull, drew power from the ship's engines, and, focusing it through the Kearny-Fuchida drive, translated it into an expanding field of energy that soon enveloped the ship. In a burst of electromagnetic and tachyon radiation, the gate snapped closed, as the WarShip materialized at the nadir jump point of its destination system, nearly thirty light years away.

Morgan's senses cleared quickly, throwing off the disorienting effects of having been hurled across the void between stars. The holotank was still flickering, with bright red flashes proclaiming the arrival of the balance of his task force.

His task force. For the first time since the summit had picked him for this daring mission, the enormity of the job before him came crashing down upon him. There were fifty-five thousand men and women, over a thousand 'Mechs, aerospace fighters, and armored vehicles, thirty-four Drop-Ships, and thirty starships under his command. It wasn't the size of the task force that shook him; it was the mission he had undertaken. He was leading one of the largest military operations since the fall of the Star League, to launch an assault on the homeward of a foe who had rolled up half of the Draconis Combine as easily as a man might roll up a carpet.

Out there, beyond the farthest mapped stars of the Periphery, they would be alone, cut off from home, support, and reinforcement. Succeed or fail, the responsibility would be his alone.

A few hundred kilometers away, aboard the *Invader* Class JumpShip *Circe,* Colonel Sandra Barclay had no need of subterfuge. She'd been on the *Circe*'s grav deck in a meeting with her regimental command staff when the warning klaxon sounded. She'd been susceptible to the curious ailment of jumpsickness from the first time she'd traveled in space, and had never overcome her sensitivity to the extraphysical anomaly of the experience.

Many doctors believed that Transit Disorientation Syndrome, usually simply called jumpsickness, was some sort of psychosomatic reaction to the precipitous, and wholly unnatural, process of instantly being translated across thirty light years of space. Most people felt a momentary discomfort, like being on an elevator making a sudden and rapid descent. Even normally healthy individuals who had never suffered from motion sickness could suddenly find themselves sick to their stomachs when the starship they were aboard vaulted through the netherworld of hyperspace.

Some few, Sandy Barclay among them, were subject to painful and often debilitating abdominal cramps, blinding headaches, and deep-seated, fiery aches in their joints for as long as thirty minutes after a hyperspace jump. Usually, these symptoms could be controlled, or at least lessened, with medication. The regimental surgeon had prescribed a synthetic meclizine analog that reduced the effects of Barclay's severe jumpsickness to the annoyance level experienced by most others who suffered from the condition. While grateful for the reduction of her symptoms, she hated the dry mouth and drowsiness that accompanied that relief.

Despite the medication, when the *Circe* phased in at Weldon, a wave of nausea hit Barclay, her normally fair complexion now an odd waxy gray as the blood drained from her face. A strange hiccoughing catch in her breath forced her to break off in mid-sentence.

"Colonel?" Captain Daniel Umsont's dark brown eyes were full of worry.

"I'm okay, Dan." Barclay sucked in several deep breaths, her right hand pressed against her roiling stomach. "Let's take a five, okay?"

Without waiting for a response, Barclay pushed her chair back and quickly left the lounge. On unsteady legs she made a beeline for the nearest head.

Umsont's eyebrows drew together, his handsome black-skinned face a portrait of concern, as he watched his commander depart.

"She'll be fine, Dan," Captain Brian Fornal, the regiment's chief surgeon, laid a hand on Umsont's arm. "TDS."

Umsont relaxed slightly. He'd been with the Light Horse for eight years, the last three of those as Colonel Barclay's adjutant. But, in all that time, he'd never been with her during a hyperspace jump. As a matter of military decorum, she'd been careful to keep to her quarters until the nausea and disorientation wore off.

After a few moments, Barclay returned to the meeting. Her gait was steadier, and a bit of color had returned to her face, but there was still a tightness in the skin around her blue eyes.

"I'm sorry, folks." Her voice was steady and clear, but carried a note of embarrassment. "I guess it can happen to the best of us."

"Aw, forget it, Colonel." Kathy Lykken, the Eleventh Recon's commander, waved aside Barclay's apology. "Next time, stay away from the hard stuff. Hangovers and hyperspace are a bad combination."

Barclay smiled thinly at Lykken's attempt to lighten

the mood, appreciating her efforts to deflect everyone's attention from her condition.

"That's right, boss," Dallas Bell chimed in, adding his own brand of gallows humor to the mix. "Listen to Major Lykken, she knows what she's talking about."

Lykken growled sharply and flung an empty plastic coffee cup at the armored infantry officer, who easily dodged the harmless missile.

"All right, people." Barclay controlled her impulse to laugh at the antics of her subordinates, knowing that they were carrying on like first-year cadets to take her mind off her own discomfort. "Can we get back to business?"

Before the meeting could continue, a rolling beep sounded through the grav deck. Moments later, Corporal Ufko, her commo tech, handed Barclay a telecommunications handset.

"It's General Winston."

"General? Barclay."

"How are you holding up, Colonel?" The metallic effect of the ear piece gave Winston's matter-of-face tone an eerie, alien quality.

"Fine, General." Barclay was beginning to feel like herself again. "Is anything wrong?"

"No, Colonel, everything's fine. I want you to get a breakdown of your regiment, indicating those troopers who are susceptible to jumpsickness." Winston paused, giving Barclay the impression that she was checking some sort of database. "I know this is only the first jump of many, but I'd like to keep track of how many of our people go down every time we jump. It may not make a difference now, but it sure will in the future. I'd rather not wait until we jump into the middle of a Clan battle fleet to discover that half our fighter pilots are out of commission."

"Okay, General, I'll have my staff get right on it." Barclay's stomach did a slow flip-flop at the mention of jumpsickness.

"Good." General Winston hesitated a moment. "And how are *you* doing, Sandy?"

"Not too bad, ma'am. I had a bout with the green queasies, but I'm coming around."

"Good," Winston repeated. "You're one officer that I can't afford to have out of commission when things start heating up. Get me that report as soon as you can, Colonel. Winston out."

The commline went dead.

Barclay sighed as she passed the handset back to the commo tech. Returning to the conference table, she fell heavily into her chair and began explaining the General's request to her staff.

The order to take a census of the jumpsickness-prone troops did not originate with Ariana Winston. It was issued by Morgan Hasek-Davion. When he received the final report four hours later, he learned that less than two percent of the soldiers under his command had suffered adverse effects from the jump.

Seated in the large, synthleather chair behind Commodore Beresick's ready-room desk, Morgan used an electronic stylus to scrawl his signature across the bottom of the computer screen displaying the report.

"Well, Alain, what do you think?"

Beresick, who had also seen the report, shrugged. "Two percent? That's not too bad. The average among the general population is somewhere between nine and fifteen percent, so I guess we're doing pretty darn good."

The Commodore scanned his copy of the database, which his staff had assembled from the various reports it had received.

"The greatest incidence of TDS seems to occur among the technical and support personnel. The least likely to be hit are ship crews and fighter pilots. Must have something to do with being a warrior."

Coming from any other source, the statement would have sounded callous and self-serving. From what Morgan knew of Alain Beresick, the man hadn't a gram of conceit in his entire body. What Beresick had meant was that indefinable something that makes some people willing to strap themselves into twenty or more tons of armored steel, or a high-performance aerospace fighter, or a physics-defying JumpShip and push both the machine and themselves to the limit of their performance envelope, even if it meant dying in the act. Everybody knew the arrogant swaggering MechWarrior or fighter jock from countless B-grade trids and holoshows. Granted, there were some warriors who fit that stereotype, but neither they nor their attitude outlasted their first major engagement. Most professional warriors, whether they piloted a BattleMech, flew fighters, or slogged through the mud, were calm, quiet men and women, with a self-deprecating attitude and a real sense of their own mortality.

Beresick had supposed that whatever drove these men and women to risk their lives in combat was probably the same factor that help shield them from the effects of Transit Disorientation Syndrome. Of course, this theory didn't answer the question of why some soldiers, like Colonel Barclay, suffered more severely than was the norm.

"Okay, Commodore, we'll halt here and make a normal recharging stop. That'll give us time to fully recharge our jump drives and let these folks recover," Morgan said, gesturing to the report.

"All right," Beresick nodded his agreement. "I wasn't too eager to push it anyway. Double jumps, quick charging, hot-loading—they're all bad for the drives. This mission is risky enough without straining the drives."

One leader not polled about the health of his force was perhaps the most worried. Fifty percent of his unit had been adversely affected by the jump. Though they were recovering as quickly as any other task force member, Rumiko Fox and Keiji Sendai were too important to the success of his mission for Kasugai Hatsumi to pass their illness off lightly. The effect of losing Fox and Sendai to jumpsickness was amplified by the fact that the entire team had not been assigned to the same starship. For reasons best known to their employer, he had been billeted aboard the *Invisible Truth,* while the rest of his team had been assigned to the *Banbridge.* Hatsumi shrugged and cursed whoever thought of dividing his team to the lowest regions of the Christian hell for their stupidity.

Using what medicines they had at hand, along with those they could covertly pilfer from the ships' medical facilities, the nekekami treated their stricken comrades as best they could. Hatsumi fretted over his mission the whole time. Should they be called upon to carry out their assigned task immediately after a jump, or worse, a double jump, two of the nekekami would be out of commission, making the job that much more difficult.

15

***Battle Cruiser ISS* Invisible Truth**
Nadir Jump Point, Pajarito
Draconis March
Federated Commonwealth
29 June 3059
1525 Hours

The intercom unit built into Morgan Hasek-Davion's desktop emitted a sharp buzz. He acknowledged the signal with a brief flash of irritation.

"Sir, all commands report insystem, and no problems."

Morgan had given a standing order that he be advised of the fleet's status each time it jumped into a new system. It had taken eight weeks for Task Force Serpent to crawl across the Federated Commonwealth. In that time the routine reports had become boringly repetitious. The monotony was beginning to wear on Morgan's nerves. He had no formal reply to the message, merely a muttered "uh-huh," before returning to the mound of paperwork before him.

Having been a soldier all of his adult life, Morgan was aware of the fact that an army traveled not on its stomach, as the old saying had it, but on its paperwork. Though paper had largely been replaced by noteputers and optical chips, the archaic term remained. Morgan was amazed at the amount of red tape he was expected to deal with, even considering the size and diversity of the task force. The weeks spent since leaving Defiance had been occupied by reading the reports submitted by the various unit commanders and writing summary reports of his own.

There are times when I think I'm little more than a high-priced clerk. Morgan snorted ruefully at the thought.

The rear area bean-counters, who were the bane of every army since Hannibal, had insisted that accurate records be kept of the amount and kind of supplies consumed, the length of time spent recharging jump engines, which unit was running combat simulations on which date, and the outcome of those virtual battles. He knew there was some kind of purpose behind the requests for incredibly petty details, but he had yet to see it.

For the average member of the task force, who did not have Morgan's mound of paperwork to occupy his or her time, an effort had been made by the mission commanders, through their respective quartermaster corps, to keep the soldiers and sailors, pilots and MechWarriors occupied during their long march to war. Most of the JumpShips had seen a cargo bay remodeled into a sort of high-tech training center, outfitted with the latest in BattleMech combat simulation pods.

Morgan was fascinated by the level of realism these training units provided. Developed during the latter part of the twentieth century, partially for the military, but more for use by the entertainment industry, each cockpit-sized pod was tied into a central computer, and could be configured to simulate any type of BattleMech or aerospace fighter currently in use by the various Successor State armies. There was also programming available to emulate the function of Clan OmniMechs captured by the Inner Sphere. As many as two dozen pods could be tied into the same processing unit. This allowed combat simulations on a company-to-company level.

During his first run using the state-of-the-art simulators, Morgan, piloting a computer-generated model of his captured *Daishi* had squared off against Andrew Redburn in a simulated *Atlas*. The 'Mechs were evenly matched at one hundred tons, though the *Daishi* boasted greater firepower. Andrew fought fiercely, from the head, as he always did. He made Morgan work for every hit he scored. By the time Morgan had reduced his friend's assault 'Mech to electronic scrap, he was soaked in sweat. Cramps tugged at his arms and legs from manipulating the pod's realistic controls.

Morgan had played many a simulated battle against Redburn, and had beaten him as often as not. Still, the level of realism provided by the pods caused him a pang of guilt at blasting his friend's 'Mech into smoldering junk. He breathed a small sigh of relief when he saw Redburn, his auburn hair matted with sweat and tousled by his neurohelmet, emerge from the pod next to him.

"I'm glad we're on the same side, Morgan," Redburn said, nodding a jerky, smiling greeting. "I'd never want to fight you for real."

Morgan waved aside the compliment. "Ah, Andrew, you were just being nice to an old man." Morgan smiled broadly. At fifty-three, he was only a year older than his friend, and the effects of time, and an inherently dangerous profession had yet to catch up with him.

"You're not *that* old." Redburn's grin widened until it threatened to reach his ears. "But I *was* just being nice to you. Mmumph."

Any further gibes Redburn wished to level at his friend were stifled by Morgan's thrown towel striking him in the face.

A smaller, less sophisticated version of the pods had been installed in the rec-rooms of most of the task force's seven WarShips. These simpler machines could be used to play more than two hundred computer games, including a commercial version of 'Mech combat. Understandably, this was the least used of the simulator's programs.

Every effort had been made to keep the men and women of Task Force Serpent occupied. A rigorous training schedule, which included intramural 'Mech simulator combats, had been established. Sergeants and petty officers winked at, or, in some cases, bet on the outcome of these mock-combats. Every stowage space not holding vital stores was filled with chip and hardcopy books. An enormous library of vids and tri-D shows, including every recording of the past season's 'Mech games on Solaris, had been made available to off-duty personnel.

Occasionally, while the task force ships were recharging, they were able to pick up a news or entertainment broadcast from the inhabited planets far below. Morgan was fascinated to see the depth and degree of the disinformation campaign being propagated by the Ministry of Intelligence and Information. Unlike the Draconis Combine, which held the news media as a branch of the government, the Federated Commonwealth had a free, civilian-owned press. Morgan knew that a free press was often the bane of the military, but it could also be a useful tool.

Based upon the news reports, Morgan figured that the MIIO was giving out just enough information to make the media suspicious of the press releases. In turn, carefully placed and well-developed agents were "leaking" information to the media, telling them what they "really wanted to hear."

The gist of the reports was that the units of Morgan's task force had been called to Defiance for training. Once that training had been completed they were being moved to "an undisclosed location," ready to back up the coalition force now battering its way through the Smoke Jaguar occupation zone.

In what Morgan considered a brilliant move on the part of the MIIO disinformation officers, the various news media were getting reports from all over the Federated Commonwealth. "Reliable sources" claimed to have sighted the task force everywhere from Aldebaran to Broken Wheel. Some of these sightings were genuine, most were not. The carefully crafted and timed reports coming out of the Ministry had spawned a rash of copycat reports. The latest sighting, it seemed, claimed to have spotted the task force lying dormant at the nadir jump point of the Hyalite system on the border between the Commonwealth and the Taurian Concordat, just about as far from its actual position as you could get.

At least the disinformation campaign is going well, Morgan thought with a sigh.

To maintain the intentional confusion over the task force's actual location, the Whitting Conference had also imposed a total communications blackout. No one in Task Force Serpent had been permitted to post or get letters, send or receive HPG messages or maintain any of the usual contacts with the outside world. Morgan knew personally of at least one case where such contacts perhaps should have been allowed. A young tanker in the St Ives Lancers had been sent a priority HPG message telling him that his father had passed away. For security reasons, the message was not delivered, the blackout was that complete.

Two more casualties of this bloody war. Morgan cursed vilely to himself. *Truth and compassion.*

Everyone involved in planning Task Force Serpent knew that, for the first several months of the year-long mission, the greatest enemy they faced would be boredom.

After a few more minutes of desultory pecking away at his keyboard, Morgan sighed, heavily slapped the Save key, and pushed his chair away from the desk.

I'll finish up the reports later, he told himself as he snatched up his green uniform jacket. Unlike the fatigues he'd worn as an officer of the AFFC, this new uniform dispensed the synthleather jerkin in favor of a hip-length, long-sleeved jacket. Despite the fact that he'd been wearing the new uniform for several weeks now, he still felt a bit strange wearing fatigues designed for the legendary Star League army.

As he passed out of his office and into the corridor encircling the flag officer's quarters (to which he was entitled as task force commander), Morgan silently cursed the lack of gravity. Of all the aspects of space travel, he hated the prolonged periods of weightlessness that must necessarily be endured by passengers on commercial or military transport vessels. The average JumpShip could generate just enough thrust, using its station-keeping drives, to orient itself above a system's star, and to hold that position while its jump sail gathered the necessary energy to charge the massive Kearny-Fuchida drives. A WarShip, with its larger, more powerful maneuvering drives, could generate enough forward thrust to give the illusion of gravity, but that burned up so much fuel that it made acceleration-induced gravity impractical.

Of course, the passengers and crew of a transport ship could use magnetic boots to move about the ship with relative ease, but such devices gave no impression of gravity. Morgan could remember a number of times when he was rounding a corner aboard a Jump or DropShip, only to bump heads with another passenger who was coming from the other direction, walking on the vessel's wall or overhead. Then, of course, there were the physical effects of prolonged exposure to freefall. To combat the loss of muscle tone, neurological atrophy, and bone decalcification, most large ships carried so-called grav decks. These large, doughnut-like sections revolved around the ship's central structure at a specific rate, imparting a kind of centrifugal gravity. By allowing each crewman and passenger a certain amount of time each week to use the recreation facilities housed in the gravdecks, the ill-effects of long zero-G missions could be averted, or at least reduced.

As Morgan approached the elevator in the port-dorsal corner of the corridor, the lift doors opened, allowing a pair of Com Guard officers to exit. Each touched his brow in the palm-outward salute used by the Guards (and the long-ago Star League Defense Force). That was something else Morgan hadn't yet grown accustomed to—receiving salutes from everybody in sight, including the Com Guards, who had for so long held themselves aloof from the other militaries of the Inner Sphere.

At the last moment, he returned the salute and slipped into the elevator. Leaning back against the wall of the lift, he hoped that the Guards officers didn't think he was trying to put on airs by delaying his response until he was almost out of sight. Even after all these weeks in transport, he was still trying to adjust to the strangeness of the situation.

Punching the button that would send the lift to the bridge, Morgan leaned back against the wall of the car. Briefly, he closed his eyes, recalling to his mind the comforting thoughts of hearth and home. All too often, his career called him away from that which he held most dear. Now, he'd be gone for heaven only knew how many months, maybe even years. It would take almost a year to get to Huntress, but what they didn't know was how long they'd be there, either fighting the Jags, or waiting for Victor and his relief forces to arrive. "No plan of battle survives contact with the enemy intact," ran the ancient proverb. Morgan snorted a bitter laugh. *Sometimes it doesn't survive contact with your own troops.*

Maybe Kym was right, maybe he was getting too old for this line of work. In a moment of melancholy, he wondered if he'd ever see Kym again.

The elevator car slid smoothly to a halt, the barely perceptible jerk bringing him back to full alertness.

"What's our status, Mr. Ruiz?"

"Afternoon, sir." The Com Guard officer of the watch offered his greeting without turning away from the con-

sole before him. "All commands are in system. We're unfurling the sail. It should begin charging in about an
hour."

"Very good, Mr. Ruiz. Is the Commodore in his ready
room?"

"No, sir. Commodore Beresick left the bridge about ten
minutes ago. He said he wanted something to eat, a hot
shower, and a couple of hours in the rack." Ruiz looked
up at last, reading the look on Morgan's face. "I guess
he's not going to get it. Should I call him back to the
bridge?"

Morgan had been pacing back and forth through insubstantial images of the holotank, a device that had come to
hold an odd fascination for him. He stopped abruptly and
shook his head.

"No, Lieutenant, let him be. I'm sure he could use the
rest. Just make sure to send someone to fetch him for the
staff meeting."

"Yes, sir." Ruiz tapped a reminder into the memory of
the bridge noteputer.

For a while, Morgan stood in the center of the holotank
watching the tiny starships drifting placidly in space.
Then, with a heavy sigh, he left the bridge.

16

Battle Cruiser ISS Invisible Truth
Nadir Jump Point, Pajarito
Draconis March
Federated Commonwealth
29 June 3059
1825 Hours

For the first time since Task Force Serpent had left Defiance, the full command staff had been called together for a briefing. With the fleet poised on the rim of the Inner Sphere, Morgan felt it was time to nail down the last details of their mission: objectives, tactics, and so on. He knew that all of his commanders were familiar with these factors, but he wanted to make all things clear before definitively leaving the Inner Sphere and the borders of known space.

Two subjects still sent a ripple of unease through Morgan's soul. The first of these was broached even before the entire command staff had taken their seats.

"Sir, have you given any more thought to the subject of orbital bombardment?" Predictably, it was Colonel Samuel Kingston who raised the question. The commander of the Capellan Confederation regiment that bore his name had been the most vocal promoter of using the warfleet's powerful weapons to "soften up the defenders before committing ground troops."

Morgan had developed a quiet dislike for the Liao officer. At first, he had put his feelings aside, believing them to be nothing more than the product of a lifetime spent looking through a BattleMech's HUD at an enemy wearing the colors of the Capellan Confederation. But, as time and proximity made him more familiar with the man's attitudes and personality, Morgan found himself developing an intense dislike for the dark-haired commander of Kingston's Legion.

Kingston was an excellent field commander and tactician. He had integrated both his regiment and himself almost flawlessly with the rest of Task Force Serpent. Still, there was something quite disturbing in the man's cavalier attitude toward the safety of enemy civilians. Morgan tried to put it down to the Capellan's lack of experience with the sheer destructive power of space-based weapons. But, after reviewing several hours' worth of testimony recorded by individuals lucky enough to have escaped the Clan firestorm that had destroyed the city of Edo, on Turtle Bay, the man's attitude became even more heartless and bloodthirsty.

To make matters worse, Commodore Beresick, Major Michael Ryan, and even General Winston had variously suggested the idea of preceding the main task force landings with a naval bombardment.

"No, Colonel," Morgan said at last. "I haven't given it any more thought, because I thought we'd settled this issue. I saw the vids that ROM smuggled out of Turtle Bay." Beresick's eyes widened a bit at Morgan's offhand reference to data supplied by ComStar's intelligence service. ROM did not share such information gladly or frequently.

"I saw the burning buildings," Morgan continued. "The devastation, the wholesale slaughter. I *will not* be responsible for that kind of barbarity, and *that,* ladies and gentlemen, is *final*."

For several moments, Morgan brought his level gaze to bear on each of the officers present, daring them to voice a challenge to his decision. When no one opposed him, he nodded and continued.

"All right. Our mission, as you all know, depends almost as heavily on stealth and secrecy as it does speed. The Inner Sphere phase of this operation is set to jump off at about the same time as we launch our mission. Our objective is the Smoke Jaguar homeworld, known as Huntress.

"Our operational plan calls for us to make our way into Clan space via a long, roundabout route. In this way, we intend to avoid the Clanners' main lines of supply and communication. Most of the star systems we will be using as jump points have been classified as uninhabited by the Explorer Corps." Morgan paused for a short, bitter laugh. "Most of them don't show up on navigational charts. Even the charts that we got from old Star League records only show the closest of them.

"We plan to be insystem at Huntress no later than the middle of February. As soon as we come out of hyperspace, we'll launch the assault."

Again, Morgan paused. This time, there was no humor in his long hesitation as he surveyed his command staff. The next subject was not an issue he looked forward to facing. Taking a deep breath, he continued.

"Since security must be of paramount concern, the summit decided to take this out-of-the-way approach. But the danger of contacting a Clan force still exists. Therefore, any Clan forces encountered prior to our arrival at Huntress must not be allowed to escape. They must either be captured or annihilated."

A tense hush fell over the room. For a while, none of the officers spoke. Sir Paul Masters finally broke the silence.

"Say that again, sir?" he said, glaring at Morgan. "I must have misheard you."

"I'm sorry, Colonel Masters, but that's the way it's got to be. We cannot allow one Clanner to escape to warn the enemy of our presence." Morgan had been expecting the Knights Commander to give him an argument every time he broached the subject of the task force's "scorched earth" policy, but now Masters was taking the principled, chivalrous knight routine just a little too far.

"I understand matters of security," Masters said sharply, taking a deep breath. "What I do not understand is the military necessity of 'no quarter,' especially in this case. If we begin by destroying an enemy force, without pity, or exception, then we risk becoming the barbarians the Clanners believe us to be." He shook his head, as though in disbelief.

"I have to agree with Sir Masters." Marshal Sharon Bryan stood at stiff, formal attention as she spoke. "You're talking about troops who've had the Ares Conventions drilled into their heads from the first day they put on the uniform. If, all of a sudden, you order them to ruthlessly annihilate the entire enemy force, you'll destroy the morale of this task force. You're likely to end up with a mutiny on your hands. For the love of God, they're soldiers, not assassins." She looked pained.

"There's something else at work here." Överste Carl Sleipness, of the Fourth Drakøns, was speaking before Bryan had resumed her seat. "If you give the order for the troops to annihilate an enemy's fighting force, you run the risk of losing control of your soldiers. It's happened time and time again throughout history. When an army is released from part of the restraints placed upon it by the common decency, none of the restraints are observed. If you tell our soldiers to take no prisoners and leave no survivors, you will soon have a rioting mob on your hands, rather than an army. You run the risk of annihilating the entire Clan culture."

"Good."

Morgan could not determine who had made the muttered comment, but it strained the bounds of his temper to hear it. Before he could snarl out his response, Colonel William MacLeod of the Northwind Highlanders was putting in his two credits' worth.

"There's somethin' else you might want t' be considerin'. We'll be operatin' far behind enemy lines, alone, and with no back-up. Now, if we let any of the *sassanach* get away an' warn their superiors, every Jag warrior not currently involved in an operation will be out, huntin' us down."

"There is still one consideration that has yet to be discussed. Morgan-*sama*." Major Ryan adopted the formal, almost stilted cant used in the Draconis Combine when addressing a superior on a sensitive matter.

"We are assuming that any Clansmen we take prisoner will be attempting to escape. That is what you or I would do if we were captured. But the Clans often make bondsmen of captured enemies, and these bondsmen consider themselves members of their new 'Clan.' We've done the same thing with them in the Inner Sphere. I shouldn't worry too much about escape.

"There *is,* however, one major problem with the notion of taking either bondsmen or prisoners. This task force has substantial but limited resources. Most Clansmen would never willingly surrender. They're captured after being so badly wounded that they cannot resist any longer. We would have to render medical aid and comfort, as is required by the Conventions. We are also limited in the amounts of food and fresh drinking water available to this task force. I know our operational plan calls for us to replenish our water stocks from whatever secure sources we may encounter along the way, but that still leaves food. If we're forced to fight, and decide to grant quarter, I suspect that we'll all be down to eating packaged field rations before this operation is over.

"Once this task force crosses the border, we can hold nothing back. We must be committed to an all-out effort, or we might as well have stayed at home."

"As much as I hate to admit it, sir, I have to agree with Major Ryan." Captain Roger Montjar toyed with the black fox's mask pinned to his collar as he spoke. "We can't let any Clanners escape to warn their bosses, and we just don't have the resources to care for prisoners who don't have a substantial logistic, strategic, or tactical value."

Bryan began to protest, but Montjar cut her off.

"I'm not advocating the wholesale murder of helpless prisoners, and unarmed civilians, but a policy *must* be set."

Bryan was once more on her feet, shouting angrily at the Fox Team leader. Montjar had risen as well, leaning over the table to bring his face as close to hers as he could. His hands were clenched into fists. Masters leapt to stand beside Bryan, while Kingston took sides with Montjar. When Andrew Redburn added his rich tenor voice to the quarrel, Morgan had had enough. He ordered the squabbling commanders back to their seats, but to no avail.

Schweeee! The piercing whistle yanked the shouting officers' attention back to the head of the table, where Morgan was just taking his fingers from his mouth.

"I said, sit down and shut up!"

The commanders, shocked into silence, quietly returned to their seats. Masters was the last to go. He gave Morgan a look that seemed to say, "This isn't over yet." In his place next to Morgan at the head of the table, Commodore Beresick lightly rubbed his left ear, as thought he suspected Morgan's shrill whistle had somehow damaged the eardrum on that side.

"*That,* by God, is enough!" Morgan was generally slow to anger, but right now he felt as if he could shoot all of the commanders and start again from scratch.

"I am the commander of this bloody expedition. When I make a bloody decision, I expect it to be bloody well carried out.

"Now, Captain Montjar, you want a policy set, fine, here it is. As of right this second, no Clan forces should be allowed to escape from a battle area, either on the ground, or in space. If any Clan warriors are rendered helpless, or if they surrender, they will be taken prisoner. If they wish to become bondsmen to this task force, that's fine. Otherwise, they will be treated according to the Ares Convention guidelines regarding the treatment and handling of prisoners of war. We can feed and care for them out of captured supplies. There isn't much else we can do."

Morgan glared around the room at the unit commanders, the set of his jaw a challenge to any who dared oppose his decision. As he caught each officer's eyes in turn, he read the same message, in varying degrees of intensity. *"None of us are happy with this, but you're the commanding officer, and we'll abide by your directive."*

"All right, that's settled." Morgan gave a short, disgusted sigh. "Now, let's get back to business. Readiness reports. Marshal Bryan?"

Bryan stood, her dislike of Morgan's command decision clear on her face. But she was too good a soldier to let her personal feelings interfere with her job.

"The Eleventh Lyran Guards are at one hundred percent readiness." Bryan began her report, speaking smoothly and steadily, occasionally referring to the notes displayed on the screen of her personal noteputer.

One by one, each unit leader checked in, giving a detailed report on the status of their units. General Winston reported that the problem plaguing the knee of Sergeant Major Young's *Archer* couldn't be solved. During the layover at Tsamma, a pair of *Leopard* Class DropShips had been dispatched to the Crucis March Militia base on that planet. There, they had picked up five brand-new 'Mechs in exchange for five damaged machines, Young's battered *Archer* among them. The Crucis Militiamen hadn't been too pleased at the prospect of trading new 'Mechs for old, but Morgan's signature on the orders made the swap indisputable. Overall, the Militia came out ahead on the deal. Of the five 'Mechs dropped from the task force's roster, there were three heavies, one medium, and one light. In exchange, the Militia turned over two heavy and two medium 'Mechs and one 35-ton *Panther*.

RSM Young, because of a clause in the Light Horse's contract, was given one of the heavies, a 65-ton *Catapult*. While carrying less armor than his heavy missile platform, the new *CPLT-C3* had undergone an extensive refit. Gone were the bird-like 'Mech's boxy Holly long-range missile packs. A massive Luxor Mobile Battery system had been installed in their place. Though now limited to five rounds of ammunition, Young did not complain much. The Arrow IV system was far more accurate than the old fifteen-found volley-fire racks carried by the original *Catapult* design. Using a designation system such as the Target Acquisition Gear mounted in a number of lighter 'Mechs, pinpoint accuracy could be achieved out to the maximum range of the big missiles. If he ever got into a brawl, the lack of articulated hands and arms would hurt, but the four lasers sprouting from the 'Mech's torso would keep many aggressors at bay.

Young had complained a bit about being moved down in weight, but Ariana Winston knew her Regimental Sergeant Major well enough to recognize the gripe as a cover for his delight. She'd been a noncom once herself. It didn't do to let the officers think you were happy, they'd just find something for you to do, something guaranteed to make you miserable.

Eventually, the status reports wound to a close. All commands were ready to begin their mission.

"Thank you, Överste." Morgan rose as Sleipness sat down. "All right, folks, that's it. We jump out of here as soon as the engines are charged."

"Three hours at the outside," Commodore Beresick said quietly from his seat next to Morgan.

"Okay, three hours to jump. Dismissed."

One after another, the commanders filed out of the briefing room, until only Beresick, Ariana Winston, and Morgan were left.

"Sir," Winston began as soon as the other leaders were out of earshot. "I know you've made your decision, but you'd better think long and hard about any 'no quarter' policy. I've got troopers who are descendants of survivors of the Kentares and Sendai massacres. They aren't going to like the idea of wasting everyone who doesn't surrender."

Before Morgan could reply, Ariana Winston had swept into the passageway, and was gone.

"Well, Commodore? Aren't you going to chew me out too?"

"No need," Beresick said. "Remember, I command a WarShip. That means that any time I engage the enemy, it is to destroy him. We depersonalize things by telling ourselves that it's just a ship, or fighter, or 'Mech. We tell ourselves that we're destroying a machine, not the pilot or crew. It's not until you search the debris field for survivors, but there aren't any, that you comprehend how many lives you snuffed out And when a WarShip is destroyed, most of its crew goes with it."

"Mmmm," was Morgan's only statement.

"Well, sir," Beresick stood up, working the kinks out of his lower back. "I'd better get back to the bridge. See you in a couple of hours."

As the door to his berthing space hissed open, Kasugai Hatsumi swept the compartment with his eyes, more out of habit, ingrained, cultivated, and developed over long years of training, than out of any fear of actual attack. It had been almost four hours since he had helped secure Överste Sleipness' DropShip to its docking collar on the *Banbridge*'s spindle-like mid-section. Now, coming off watch, Hatsumi was dog-tired. He had no idea that there was so much work to be done aboard a JumpShip. In his role as an able spacehand, he had been called upon to accompany a senior jump tech as she crawled through the narrow passages surrounding the ship's Kearny-Fuchida jump drive.

The huge spindle-like drive core made up most of the *Monolith*'s bulk and needed to be checked over carefully before and after each jump. It was a hot, sweaty, dirty job, one which, on most other vessels, was usually reserved as punishment detail. Aboard a ComStar ship, however, crew members were assigned to whatever details came up as their names appeared on a duty rotation roster. Since his cover was that of a mere able spacehand, Hatsumi was tapped to go with the jump tech, lugging her heavy tool kit and testing gear so she could maneuver more freely in the claustrophobic confines of the drive compartments.

Hatsumi didn't envy the tech her freedom of movement. She needed to be unencumbered so she could squeeze in between the massive coils and power leads, where it was hotter and dirtier than it was in the tight passageways. By the time they'd thoroughly checked each component of the K-F drive, the jump tech was smeared with far more grit and dust than Hatsumi.

After stripping off his filthy jumpsuit, Hatsumi reached into his locker to retrieve a clean uniform. From the bottom of the flat, chest-like locker came a faint, barely audible hum. Suddenly, Hatsumi was no longer tired. Searching blindly through the scant belongings stored beneath his zero-G bunk, he located a flat plastic box, six centimeters square and one centimeter thick. The device was similar in appearance and function to paging units that had been in existence for centuries. This one could only be accessed by a single transmitter, operating on a very narrow, very specific wavelength. Even then, a message from that unit had to be compressed to the right pulse-length, or the receiver would refuse to accept it.

Touching a mini-stud on the device's top edge, he silenced the tone. Another touch caused a single word to be displayed on the device's tiny LED screen.

"Mandrake."

A third touch blanked the screen. The single cryptic word had spoken volumes to the nekekami leader. It told him that the time for his mission was at hand, and his team should be ready to move at a moment's notice.

At the moment Hatsumi was returning the device to its hiding place, Morgan was receiving a message of his own.

"Sir." Commodore Beresick came and stood next to him at the *Truth*'s main bridge viewscreen. "All commands report charged, stowed, and ready."

"Very well, Commodore." There was an odd ring in that brief sentence, an emotion that Beresick could not place. Perhaps it was the enormity of the moment. The task force had, up until that point, been operating deep within friendly territory. Now, it was about to take its first jump out of the Inner Sphere. Granted, they were merely crossing into the Periphery. But, since the Clan invasion, the Periphery had become a dangerous place to travel. There had been a resurgence in the number of pirate bands and the ferocity of their raids. Then there was that business with the bogus Knights and their so-called "Star Lord." Perhaps it was these concerns that created the strained note in Morgan's voice.

Whatever was bothering the Marshal, he shook it off quickly, for when he spoke again it was in the full, steady voice Beresick had grown accustomed to, making him wonder if he'd really heard the strange tone.

"Communications officer, give me a clear channel to talk to the fleet."

The technician acknowledged Morgan's command. Within seconds, Morgan had drawn himself up, looking as though he was preparing to give some grand address about the momentousness of the occasion. This belied the simplicity of the message.

"Cavalier to all commands, attention to orders. Initiate jump sequence, now, now, now."

Morgan stepped back from the communications panel, laying a hand on the tech's shoulder in a token of thanks for his assistance. Beresick took note of the simple gesture with admiration for the Marshal. It was little things like acknowledging a subordinate's efforts that were the mark of a good commander, one the troops would be willing to follow into the teeth of perdition, if necessary.

Even as Morgan's hand fell back to his side, Beresick was turning to bark out the orders that would begin the sequence of events geared toward translating the *Invisible Truth* from rational space through the nonexistence of hyperspace, to a system that was nothing more than a pinpoint of light barely glimpsed through the WarShip's viewscreens.

"Lock course into navputer."

"Lock course, aye, sir. Course plotted and locked in."

"Charge the drives."

"Charging drives, aye. Drives are charged and on-line. Ready to jump."

"Sound the horn, and jump."

Even as the klaxon blared its grating tone throughout the ship, Morgan and Commodore Beresick, standing side by side in front of the main bridge viewscreen, watched as the *Rostock*, a *Fox* Class corvette bearing the fist-and-sunburst emblem of the Federated Commonwealth, winked out of sight, the first Inner Sphere WarShip to carry the fight to the Clans.

17

Battle Cruiser ISS Invisible Truth
Zenith Jump Point, Waypoint Juniper
Deep Periphery
19 July 3059
2045 Hours

Three times, the process of sending the *Invisible Truth* through the physical anomaly called hyperspace had been repeated in the Task Force's slow march across the Periphery realm known as the Outworlds Alliance. The Alliance, along with a half-dozen or so others, clung to the outer rim of the Inner Sphere. Unlike the larger Successor States, the Periphery states were largely unknown areas, occupied by adventurers, pirates, and scoundrels. Sandwiched between the outer rims of the Draconis Combine and the Federated Commonwealth, the Alliance clung precariously to existence. Were it not for increased aid from its more powerful neighbors, isolation and predatory bandits would have sent the Alliance into collapse decades ago.

It had take nearly three weeks for Task Force Serpent to make its way across the Alliance, avoiding systems with large populations for fear of accidental, or purposeful, betrayal to the Clans. It was well known that the invaders had finally taken steps to deploy their own version of intelligence agents, called "The Watch." Whether the Clans were spying on the Alliance was not known. Still,

Morgan Hasek-Davion thought it prudent to avoid all unnecessary contact.

Within seconds of the *Rostock*'s disappearance from the zenith jump point of the Alliance's Alpheratz system, Lieutenant Commander Phat Ng, the *Invisible Truth*'s chief engineer, called out. "Engines on line, ship ready to jump."

"Sir?" Beresick looked at Morgan, transferring command of the vessel to him for a moment.

Morgan nodded. "Jump."

"Aye, sir. Jump."

Morgan knew that the transit between worlds was instantaneous, at least according to the way clocks ran in rational space. Still, the instant Commander Ng engaged the huge Kearny-Fuchida drives, he felt a rapid, but gradual, prickling sensation run through his body, as though he had passed through a field of static electricity. His vision blurred, and the sounds of the chaotic bridge dopplered into a distorted moan. A sudden, coruscating wave of color and noise exploded from nowhere to engulf him. The light and sound seemed to batter his chest, belly, and head. The sensation was like ejecting from a burning BattleMech into a carnival clown's mad dream. For a moment, it seemed his mind would shut down from sensory overload.

Then, as abruptly as it began, the assault on his consciousness was over. Only the faint afterimages of nameless colors, and a slight tremor deep in his guts, remained.

Blinking away the lingering shimmers, Morgan glanced at the *Truth*'s navigational display. A string of alphanumerics told him that the WarShip had emerged from hyperspace in the right spot.

"General quarters."

Commodore Beresick echoed Morgan's command. An amplified, metallic voice rang throughout the ship.

"General quarters, general quarters. All hands, man your battle stations."

Again, the bridge was flooded with sound and motion. This time, the commotion was entirely natural. As each section called in, a bridge officer confirmed the report, and a green indicator came to life on the ship's status board. When all of the indicators in a department showed green, the officer responsible for that department sang out.

"All gunnery stations manned and ready."

"Engineering, manned and ready."

"Pri-fly reports all fighters ready, and standing by for launch."

And so the litany went, until Captain Joshua Greystone, the *Truth*'s executive officer, after reviewing the status board, called across the babble of voices.

"Commodore, all stations report manned and ready."

Beresick turned to face the bridge officers.

"Sensor operator, report all contacts."

"Sir, my only contacts are those belonging to the task force."

"Navigator," Beresick called to another technician. "What is our position?"

The officer reeled off a series of numbers, few of which had any significance to Morgan. He could see, by means of a monitor screen, that the fleet had emerged from hyperspace somewhat rimward and spinward of the Outworlds Alliance, at a single M-type star, with no inhabitable planets.

Beresick interrupted Morgan's study of the star map.

"Sir, we are right on time, and on target. All commands report in system, with no problems. We have no stray sensor contacts. I have passed the order to secure from general quarters and begin the recharging process."

At the opposite end of the *Truth*'s 839-meter length, a complex dance of man and machine was beginning.

In response to a series of commands, the ship's powerful maneuvering engines came on line. Slowly, the massive vessel began to swing around her head, until her nose was pointed directly at the star below. The thrusters fired a second time, bringing the starship to a stop. Thereafter, the drives would be used sparingly, only enough to keep the battle cruiser on station.

No sooner had the *Truth* ended her orientation burn than a complicated series of servomotors, myomer bundles, and hydraulic systems began to deploy the ship's jump sail.

To the uninitiated, the term "jump sail" was confusing. Not really a sail at all, the immense disk was a complex machine. Sandwiched between thin layers of plastic and wire mesh were sensitive collectors designed to gather solar energy, which would be transmitted, via specially designed power conduits, into the ship's jump drives.

With a diameter of nearly one and a half kilometers, but a thickness of only a few millimeters, the *Truth*'s sail was delicate in the extreme. Unfurling the high-tech gossamer was no job for fools or the impatient. Though many Jump-Ships now mounted a bank of lithium-fusion batteries that could be used to power the vessel through a single jump, damage to the sail could be a death sentence, particularly for a ship operating alone and in the void between inhabited systems. A damaged jump sail would inhibit the ship's ability to recharge its engines. If the sail was destroyed, the jump drive could only be recharged by drawing power from the ship's massive fusion engines.

This particular process, while just as efficient as sail recharging, had its own peculiar set of problems. If power from the ship's fusion engines was sent too quickly into the jump drives, the delicate Kearny-Fuchida systems could be damaged beyond repair. Starship captains had been known to use this so-called "quick charge" technique, especially in a dangerous situation, but most preferred to rely on the safer method of recharging their drives using the jump sail. The thought of being caught with spent engines and a badly damaged sail was enough to give the most hardened spacer nightmares.

That was why it was ninety minutes after Beresick gave the command to begin recharging the *Truth*'s engines that the report came back, "Sail is deployed. Recharging is underway."

Morgan looked across the bridge at a visibly relieved Beresick. Not being a spacer himself, he didn't have quite the dread of a damaged jump sail that the Commodore did.

"I really hate to add to your problems, Commodore, but maybe we'd better think about launching a BARCAP." Morgan smiled as he gestured at the holographic representation of his task force, floating above the glowing mass of the star, tails up like a school of some bizarre kind of gigantic, bottom-feeding fish.

Beresick grinned in return and passed the order to the primary flight control center. Several decks below, in the compartment by naval tradition still called "Prifly," the Aerospace Controller (given the traditional title of "Air Boss") ordered a double pair of the *Truth*'s fighters launched.

Within moments, two big *Thunderbird* aerospace fighters were hurled clear of the WarShip's hull by the ship's catapult system. Minutes later, a second pair of fighters were launched.

The *T-Bird*'s potent mix of laser and missile armament made it a logical choice for Barrier Combat Air Patrol duty. Though neither Morgan nor Commodore Beresick were expecting contact with hostile forces, there was always a chance. If any aggressors should appear, it would likely be pirates, who would turn tail and run rather than take on so large a fleet. But, contact with the Clans was possible. The task force's present position was close to the truce line, and no one was really certain exactly how the line applied to areas beyond the Inner Sphere.

While Morgan watched, tiny icons representing the fighters appeared in the holotank. As the other ships of the task force launched their own fighter cover, more blips were added. Eventually, there were twenty fighters describing endless loops around the starships they had been assigned to protect.

The system had been designated Waypoint Juniper during the planning phase of the operation. It was indistinguishable from a thousand others across known space, and millions beyond the human sphere. With an M4 star and no habitable planets, the system had little to attract settlers.

It was that M4 star that worried Commodore Beresick. Because of the vagaries of the physics involved in operating a Kearny-Fuchida drive, it would require at least 205 hours for the jump sail to collect, convert, and store enough solar radiation to power the fleet's jump drives for their next hyperspace transit. That meant the fleet would be lying doggo for eight and a half days.

Up until this particular recharging stop, no one had paid much attention to the length of time the fleet would be lying quiet, gathering solar energy to recharge their K-F drives. Now, in the no-man's-land of the Periphery, with the danger of encountering pirates—or possibly even a Clan raiding party hanging over them—the tension among the officers and men of Task Force Serpent began to mount.

At first, the effects were subtle. Restlessness and the inability to concentrate were easily countered with shorter watches and extra time allotted on the vessel's grav decks. But, as the hours mounted, so did the stress level.

Before the mid-point of the charging process had been reached, Captain D. C. Stockdale, the Eridani Light Horse's chaplain, had already been asked to speak three times with

troopers who had become embroiled in bitter arguments.
The last of these, sparked by a disagreement over the outcome of a 'Mech combat simulation, had nearly brought
two veteran warriors to blows. Stockdale, with the aid of
Sergeant-Major Young, had to separate the men before they
could inflict damage on each other.

Even the officers were not immune to the drain of tension on one's patience. Once, during a change of watch,
Morgan asked Commodore Beresick to check on the rotation schedule of the pilots flying the BARCAP. As Morgan tried to explain his concern for the alertness and
combat readiness of those badly overworked aviators,
Beresick snarled, asking him why he wasn't so concerned
for the ships' crews.

Aboard the *Bernlad,* a *Star Lord* Class JumpShip belonging to the Knights of the Inner Sphere, Paul Masters
spent fifteen minutes dressing down his personal technicians for not completing a scheduled maintenance procedure on his *Phoenix Hawk* when he thought it should have
been done. When the Knights' chief technician heard that
Masters had reprimanded the techs, he tracked the Colonel
down and gave him a scathing rebuke of his own. During
the profanity-laced diatribe, the tech became so incensed
that Masters feared a physical assault.

These tension-provoked incidents came to a head thirty
hours before the fleet was due to jump outsystem.

A pair of *SL-17R Shilone*s belonging to the Eridani
Light Horse's Third Striker Battalion had just completed
a long patrol swing around the *Ericsson,* an *Invader* Class
JumpShip attached to the First Kathil Uhlans. As they
began the inward leg of their patrol sweep, Warrant Officer Leonard Harpool spotted a blip on his sensors, where
no blip should have been.

"Wildman, I got an unknown here." Known as "Hedgehog" for his spiky, unruly hair, Harpool reported the contact to his lance leader, giving range and bearing in proper
military fashion. "He's at three-three-seven, mark sixteen.
Three-nine-zero and closing."

Lieutenant "Wild Steve" Timmons, the lance commander,
glanced at his sensor display. The blip was slightly to port,
and above his plane of travel, at ten o'clock high. The display told him that the unknown was about three hundred

ninety kilometers away. The combined velocities of the bogie and his fighter lance meant that they would be in visual range in a very few seconds.

As Timmons watched, the bright trace divided, suddenly becoming two. Neither blip displayed an Identify Friend and Foe signature.

"I got 'em, Leo. Hang tight a minute."

Timmons tapped in a command, sending out a powerful coded pulse of microwave energy. The transponder squawk should have triggered a similar pulse in a friendly ships. This time, there was no response.

"Negative IFF response. Lock and load, Hedger, we got us a gunfight." Switching channels, Timmons sent off a brief message to the "Air Boss" aboard the *Invisible Truth*.

"Courtyard, Courtyard, this is Echo Five. Two bogies, possible bandits, at one-six-even, mark forty-five. Echo Five and Six are engaging."

"I got a sensor lock." Harpool called even before Timmons had finished his report. "Warbook calls 'em Clan OmniFighters, prob'ly *Sabutai*s. Eighty percent certainty. Target lock."

"Hedger, wait . . . " Timmons shouted, half a second too late.

"Missiles away."

As Harpool's cry rang across the commline, twenty Shigunga long-range missiles leapt from the rack beneath the *Shilone*'s recessed nose. In the vacuum of space, there was no launch flare, as there would have been if the missiles were launched in an oxygen-rich atmosphere. Only a bright scarlet thread generated by the fighter's tracking system, projected onto Timmons' heads-up display, marked the missiles' flight path.

Three hundred kilometers away, a computer-generated voice rang in the ears of Lieutenant Richard Norgan. "Missile launch. Take evasive action."

An experienced combat pilot, Norgan needed no such prompting. He had noticed the missile track on his HUD a fraction of a second earlier, and was already standing hard on his right rudder pedal. Norgan slammed the stick right and forward with such force he was afraid he'd bend it. With his left hand, he shoved the throttle all the way forward, into the overthrust détente.

Instantly, his 75-ton fighter responded, dropping away into a rolling dive to starboard.

"Courtyard, Courtyard, Sierra Nine is taking fire!" Norgan shouted into his communicator. His desperate evasive maneuver had almost worked. Only three of the incoming missiles slammed into his *Hammerhead*'s fuselage. Reversing his turn, Norgan brought the fighter's massive Imperator autocannon to bear on his attacker. The target was out of range, but it wouldn't be for long. A few more seconds at this speed, and he'd unleash a storm of high-explosive armor-piercing shells capable of disabling all but the heaviest of opponents in a single pass.

Dimly, through his outrage at the unprovoked attack, Norgan heard the furious shouting of the aerospace controller. The Air Boss seemed to be ordering him to break off his attack.

For a brief, confused moment, Norgan continued to close with the attacking fighter, his finger tightening on the trigger.

"Dammit, Sierra Nine, I said break off your attack! Your target is a friendly, I say again; your target is a friendly. Acknowledge!"

With a shake of his head, Norgan safed his ship's weapons.

"Courtyard, Sierra Nine acknowledges, target is a friendly. Breaking off attack, but if that son of a buck fires one more blasted missile at me, I'm going to blow him straight to hell."

The Air Boss didn't acknowledge Norgan's threat. He was too busy reading the riot act to Warrant Officer Harpool.

"I don't give a bloody damn in hell what your sensors told you! You violated every rule of engagement in the bloody damn book! Now, you get your butt over here, and I mean right now!"

Harpool tried to protest, but the Boss wasn't having any of it.

"I don't give a rat if you're Light Horse, Com Guard, or the bloody king of Kashmir. You came within a red cat's hair of starting the biggest furball this side of Tukayyid. I gave you an order, Mister, and if you aren't in my office in the next half hour, you'll be lucky if they even let you *think* about flying a fighter again. Do you read me?"

With a snort of disgust, Commander Frank Kazeva

yanked off his headset and threw it on the communications console, cutting off Harpool's glum acknowledgment.

"Danny, get me the bridge."

An hour later, Harpool and Timmons were standing at rigid attention in the Air Boss' office. Kazeva paced angrily back and forth before them. Seated in the hard, straight-backed chairs lining one side of the room were Ariana Winston, Commodore Beresick, and Morgan Hasek-Davion. The presence of the three flag-rank officers told the pilots they were in deep trouble.

"All right, boys," Kazeva's voice was a threatening snarl. "Why don't you tell me how you came to fire on a Com Guard *Hammerhead*?"

"Sir, it was my fault," Lieutenant Timmons began. "I was the flight leader. It was my responsibility to ascertain the nature of the contact before engaging."

"That's a load of drek, Lieutenant, and you know it." Kazeva came to an abrupt halt, his face less than a decimeter from Timmons'. "This hero here was too quick on the trigger, too eager for his first kill. Isn't that right, Harpool?"

"No, sir," Hedgehog answered, hardly daring to look at the Air Boss. "The Warbook gave us an eighty percent probability that the targets were *Sabutai*s. There was no IFF response, and we were closing way too fast to take any chances of letting the enemy get the jump on us."

"So you just threw out the ROEs, and made up your own, is that it?"

"Well . . . no sir. You see . . . "

"Did you even bother to read the posted ROEs, Mister Harpool? Did you read where it says that, in the case of an unidentified contact, CAP pilots will make visual contact with any unknowns *before* engaging?"

"Yes sir, but . . . "

"Then which are you, Harpool, a traitor, or stupid?" Kazeva glared at the young warrant officer, his face twisted into a mask of rage When he spoke again, his voice was level, his emotions under control.

"You gentlemen are grounded until further notice. In the meantime, I want each of you to provide me with a hand-written copy of the posted Rules of Engagement and a freehand drawing of each fighter and DropShip type in this task force. When you finish with that, you can give me a set of freehand drawings of each type of Clan Omni-Fighter. Once I am satisfied that there will be no repeat of this 'unfortunate incident,' then maybe, just maybe, I'll consider putting you two yahoos back on flight status."

Kazeva looked questioningly at the flag officers behind him, silently asking if any of them had something to add. Though none of the three replied, the Air Boss knew that General Winston would have some very special duties for the pilots when they got back aboard their own vessel.

"All right, get out of my sight."

Timmons and Harpool saluted smartly, executed crisp about-faces, and gratefully fled the office.

Winston sat, gazing at the closed door. Then, with a snort of laughter, she got to her feet, shaking her head.

"Thanks for not being too rough on them, Boss."

"I'd have liked to let them off entirely," Kazeva said, sitting heavily on the corner of his desk. "*Hammerhead*s look an awful lot like Clan *Sabutai*s, even on scanners. They're about the same size, same mass, almost identical configuration. Then, when I got the maintenance report on Sierra Nine, I almost did let 'em go. Still, a busted transponder is no reason for violating the ROEs."

When Sierra Nine returned to the *Alkmarr,* the astechs had discovered that the *Hammerhead*'s transponder wasn't working. A fuse protecting the relatively delicate instrument had burned out sometime after launch. Without the benefit of that electronic identification tag, the Echo Flight had no way of identifying the unknown sensor trace, other than by making visual contact. In most cases, by the time a fighter could see another, the identity of the unknown had been established, either by gunfire or voice contact.

"Well, I'm glad you didn't let them off," Winston answered. "We got lucky this time. Next time, I might have to buy the Com Guards a couple of new fighters."

"I was thinking the same thing," the Air Boss grinned, "only it was me who had to buy the ships."

The next day, while Timmons and Harpool were still struggling over their freehand drawings, the ships of Task Force Serpent furled their sails and jumped.

18

Captain Helen Lamus' eyes darted rapidly across the bewildering array of controls, gauges, and displays before her, shifting constantly between her attitude display, radar altimeter, and rate of descent indicator. Other displays told her that she was fighting a relatively mild fifteen-kph cross wind and a gravitational pull slightly greater than that of Terra. Despite the fact that she was an experienced Com Guard pilot, with over a thousand hours in the *Mule* Class DropShip, Lamus had to occasionally release the controls to swipe the palm of one hand, then the other, across the leg of her olive drab flight suit. By the time she returned her hands to the controls, a thin sheen of sweat was already beginning to reform. Landing a spherical DropShip on an unfamiliar planet, and without benefit of a landing beacon, was always a dicey proposition, one that caused her stomach to do somersaults.

One of the greatest hindrances to a large operation such as Task Force Serpent was the need for fresh water. It had been a little over four months since the task force jumped beyond the border of the Outworlds Alliance. The long voyage had depleted the fleet's water supply to the point that Marshal Hasek-Davion had decided to, as he put it, "stop for a drink."

Based on intelligence provided by ComStar and the Explorer Corps, they knew that there were a number of systems along the task force's projected route where fresh water could be found in abundance. Morgan and Beresick had decided that, whenever possible, a collection team would be dispatched to replenish the task force's water supply. To that end, a pair of *Mule* Class DropShips had been specially modified, with huge storage tanks, high-speed pumps, and filtration systems—everything needed to collect and purify water from local sources.

Finally, a tiny red indicator on the altimeter began flashing. The *Mule* was less than one hundred meters above ground level. Lamus licked her lips as she watched the numbers tick down. Seventy-five meters . . . fifty . . . twenty-five . . . ten . . . the ship shuddered once as it came into contact with the ground. The four massive landing legs flexed within their housings, cushioning the effect of the 11,000-ton vessel coming to rest on the planet's surface. When the altimeter flashed zero, Lamus let out the breath she'd been holding in one long exhalation.

"Facet, this is Barleycorn. Grounding now."

As the flight controller aboard the *Antrim* acknowledged that Lamus' vessel had reached the planet's surface safely, the pilot began unstrapping herself from the vessel's command couch.

Far beneath her feet, in the *Mule*'s vast cargo bay, a ComStar technical crew was undoing a complex series of nylon harnesses. These were not intended to hold passengers in their seats. The bindings were too large for that. These tiedowns, along with magnetic clamps, secured three M-1537 prime movers. Each of these vehicles, capable of carrying ten tons of equipment, was loaded almost to capacity with a bewildering array of pumps, filters, hoses, and couplings. Each also sported a crane and winch powerful enough to lift twice the vehicle's cargo capacity.

As large as these vehicles were, they occupied only a fraction of the *Mule*'s cargo hold. The bulk of that cavernous space contained a titanic holding tank.

At last free of the restraints, Captain Lamus looked out through the bridge viewport. The second *Mule* had grounded two hundred meters to the south of her position. To the west, stretching farther than she could see, was an expanse of blue water. The surveys said that this lake, the size of a sea on some worlds, was the largest source of fresh water to be found in this Deep Periphery star system. Named "Sweetwater" by the task force, the lake was bordered by a line of rough, rocky crags on the north. South and east, the terrain was more gentle, a series of low, rolling hills. The command staff had opted for a landing zone on the westernmost shore of the lake, due to the mostly level ground there, which stretched for some distance before giving way to a light, scrubby wood. Three kilometers further west, the scrawny hardwoods gave way to a denser forest of tall, majestic variform oak and maple.

A few hundred meters north, south, and west of the landing zone, Lamus could barely make out the camouflaged shapes of BattleMechs. Pulling a pair of compact, seven-power binoculars from a cubbyhole next to her command console, Lamus scanned the combat machines. At nearly a kilometer, the details of the 'Mechs escaped her. She knew from her briefing that if she were to turn the *Mule*'s visible light scanners toward them, she would see that the 'Mechs were painted with the prancing black horse and the blue moon of the Eridani Light Horse's Twenty-first Striker Regiment. The huge egg-shaped bulk of an *Overlord* Class DropShip loomed dark and ominous just a few thousand meters east of her much smaller *Mule*. Lamus knew that the massive vessel, like the 'Mechs, belonged to the Eridani Light Horse. The *Overlord* was capable of transporting a full battalion of BattleMechs along with their supporting infantry and fighters. The Light Horse troops had been detailed by Marshal Hasek-Davion to provide security for the watering party.

The MechWarriors who were tapped to escort the foraging parties regarded the opportunity to leave the confines of their starships almost as a reward or favor bestowed upon them by their officers. As a measure of the frustration, if not outright claustrophobia faced by the MechWarriors cooped up for long months aboard a ship, it was rumored that among some regiments, a turn at guarding a foraging party could be bartered for almost anything a person could want. One of the more outrageous, and probably untrue, tales had a member of the Fourth Drakøns trading a brand new *Jager-Mech* for an older model *Javelin* and the chance to get real solid ground beneath him.

* * *

Even as Captain Lamus was focusing her glasses on the distant 'Mechs, Major Paul Calvin was entering a command that would bring the Matabushi Sentinel sensor and tracking system installed in the head of his *Victor* up to its full fifty-power visual light magnification. He could get more power out of the system's combined radar/ladar sensors, but the resolution of the image would suffer. The computers that converted the combined radio- and laser-gathered data into visible images couldn't pick out the fine details of a target. The result was a grainy representation rendered in shades of gray. With the vis-mag system, at least he could see colors.

Calvin's Battalion, nicknamed "The Dragonslayers," had been detailed to provide security for the water party. With three companies under his command, the Seventh and Fourth 'Mech and the Twenty-fifth Heavy Assault, protecting the DropShips from anything less than a full heavy BattleMech battalion would be an easy job. It was a pretty standard assignment, with his light recon elements deployed a couple of kilometers away from the landing zone, while the rest of the units formed the main line of defense. His two air lances remained aboard the *Overlord* DropShip that had brought them to the planet's surface.

As the sensor monitor cleared, Calvin could see the low-slung shapes of the detachment's prime movers making their way to the water's edge. General Winston said it would probably take twelve to sixteen hours to purify enough water to fill each of the *Mules*. That was a long time—too long for a MechWarrior to sit in the hot, cramped confines of his cockpit.

Major Calvin was a life-long Light Horseman, having been "raised in the saddle," as the aphorism for someone born into the mercenary company had it. Though the Twenty-first Striker Regiment, the parent unit of Calvin's Dragonslayers, was still part of the Eridani Light Horse, and still received its orders from General Winston, he had a few reservations about this so-called renewed Star League. The Light Horse rank structure and chain-of-command remained intact, with orders coming down from Marshal Hasek-Davion through General Winston. There was just something different about this mission, something of a permanence that made Major Calvin a little distrustful, almost as though the Eridani Light Horse might lose its unique character under the covering of the Star League banner.

"Lieutenant Vitina," Calvin called to his adjutant. "As soon as the techs have their gear up and running, we'll start spelling the troops. It's going to be a long time until they get those tanks filled, and I don't want anybody going down with the heat."

"Yessir," Vitina answered, turning his *Apollo* to face his commander's 'Mech, in a very human gesture. "I'll see it gets done."

"Thanks, Tony."

As the lead M-1537 ground to a halt in the pebbly sand of the lake shore, ComStar Tech Ferro Machak jumped out of the cab, sinking to his ankles in the loose soil. Machak, a bear of a man, vaulted easily into the bed of the transporter, using the lugs of one huge, knobby tire as a kind of short ladder.

Grabbing the meter-long stage-one filter-head, Machak gently lowered the device to the ground beside the transporter. Other adepts and acolytes swarmed over the truck unloading hoses, hooking up pumps, moving like a well-oiled machine.

Dropping lightly to the ground, Machak lifted the seventy-kilo filter head with ease and carried it to the water's edge. Another pair of techs dragged a twelve-centimeter hose from the bed of the transporter, while a third group used the powered hoist to offload the booster pump.

The theory was simple enough. The filter head, and about twenty meters of its attached hose, went into the lake. From there, the line ran to a booster pump on shore, and eventually, to the DropShip, where the main purification unit was now being deployed. Even with the high-speed pumps and filters, it would take most of the day to collect enough water to fill the huge storage tanks.

Machak sighed with pleasure as the pumps started their rapid thudding. The sun was warm, and the air was fresh and clean. Best of all, he got to spend a whole day on a planet with real, honest-to-Blake gravity, instead of the couple of hours a week he was allowed in the odd, rotating environment of a ship's grav deck to combat the effects of prolonged freefall exposure. As far as Adept Machak was concerned, all was right with the world.

* * *

Ten kilometers away, Trooper Alan Vaux was laboring under a different opinion than Adept Machak. Vaux had been a member of the 1172nd training company. He had signed on with the Eridani Light Horse right out of high school. Far from the typical Light Horse cadet, Vaux had squeaked through basic training with grades barely good enough to qualify him as a 'Mech pilot. His marks came up during his A-School, where he exhibited a budding talent for reconnaissance work. Unfortunately, as soon as he graduated, his old lackluster ways returned. Twice, Captain Holmes had put him in hack for goofing off while on duty. The last time, Regimental Sergeant-Major Young had a few quiet words with Vaux, which seemed to straighten him out again. Unfortunately, Task Force Serpent came up before the Light Horse officers had any real time to evaluate the young trooper's performance.

Vaux had just been posted by his Lance Sergeant, Charlotte Kempka, when his commline crackled to life.

"All units, all units, this is Dragon One. Drinker reports all systems are go."

"That's great, Major." Vaux had the good sense to switch off his transmitter before indulging himself in the derisive snort. "Now, all we have to do is sit here for the rest of the day while the techies do their thing. Brother, how I hate picket duty."

"All right, listen up," came Sergeant Kempka's voice crackling over the commline. "We're on a standard rotation schedule. Carasia, you got first watch, West, second, Vaux, third. I'll take cleanup."

A chorus of groans sounded across the lance's tactical channel.

"I don't wanna hear it." The link's metallic effect made Kempka's voice even harsher than usual. "Them's the orders, and that's what we're gonna do. Right?"

They chorused, "Yes, Sergeant," with only slightly more enthusiasm.

"And another thing. Stay sharp. Keep your scanners running, but don't forget about your 'Model 0 Mark 1s.' " Kempka used the soldier's slang for the sensors every warrior was born with, his eyes. "Just 'cause we ain't in Clan space right now, don't mean there ain't hostiles out there."

=== 19 ===

Nine hours later, the bright sunshine of morning had turned into a dull gray misting rain. It wasn't so bad for the MechWarriors, who had dry, although stuffy, cockpits to shelter in. For the water collection crew, the conditions were awful.

No one had counted on the fact that the seemingly clear blue water of what they had dubbed Sweetwater Lake was actually full of microfine silt that clogged the filter head so badly that it needed to be reeled in, detached from the pickup hose, washed clean, reattached, and replaced in the lake every three hours. The whole process took an hour to complete. A mission that should have taken twelve hours looked like it was going to stretch into fifteen or more.

Alan Vaux sat in the cockpit of his *Firestarter,* grumbling to himself about the weather, the heat, the mission, and life in general. The young trooper did not realize how lucky he was. One of the often-overlooked features of the *FS9* series of 'Mechs was the ingress/egress hatch. Where, on most 'Mechs, the hatch either swung horizontally, like a door, or slid open on runners, the hatch on the *Firestarter* hinged upward, like the lift gate on a ground car. In rainy conditions, which would normally preclude the opening of a 'Mech's hatch, the *Firestarter*'s accessway could be locked in the up position, affording the pilot with some welcome fresh air.

Vaux's cockpit was buttoned up tight. Whether he had forgotten about the built-in rain awning, or whether no one had told him about it was immaterial. The lapse that unnecessarily increased his discomfort probably saved his life.

As the rookie trooper sat, his feet up on the control panel, listening to the rain dripping against his viewport, a piercing wail filled his cockpit. A crimson THREAT icon flared to life. His HUD jumped from standby to active in a split second.

Before he could switch his startled gaze away from the blinking warning light, another automated system came on line. A tearing, high-pitched roar ripped through the rain-soaked copse of scrub trees in which he'd been sheltering, as his 'Mech's anti-missile system spat out a stream of steel-jacketed slugs at a rate of over three thousand rounds per minute. The screeching bellow paused as the weapon adjusted its aim, then the radar-aimed minigun filled the air with another cloud of bullets.

Not more than twenty meters from his 'Mech, the slugs clawed most of a missile volley from the sky. The explosions sounded like a string of monstrous firecrackers exploding in midair. Shrapnel rang off the *Firestarter*'s armor, followed by a triplet of heavy blows as the warheads not destroyed by the anti-missile system smashed into his 'Mech. Had his hatch not been dogged down, the steel splinters would have passed through the opening, slashing their way through cockpit and pilot.

"Dragon! Dragon! This is Ember One-Four. I'm under attack!" Vaux screamed into his commline as he struggled to shove his feet back into the pedal well where they belonged.

"Settle down, Four." Kempka's unpleasant voice had never sounded so sweet. "Just tell me what you got."

"Uh, I have four, no six, drek, ten, that's ten plus contacts, all converging on my position." Vaux struggled against the rising fear. Simulator runs and field exercises couldn't prepare anyone for the stark terror of hearing armor-piercing warheads detonating against your 'Mech's outer plating. Forcing himself to focus, Vaux read off the information scrolling across his data displays. "Uh, yeah. That's ten plus contacts, in two groups, four and six. Lead group seems to be four light or medium 'Mechs. Group two looks like heavies. The biggest MADs out at about sixty tons. No IFF signals, no EW emissions." Quickly glancing over the sensor display panel, Vaux confirmed that the *Firestarter*'s Magnetic Anomaly Detector had correctly interpreted the mass of metal closing on his position.

"All right, Four, just stay frosty." Vaux could hear the whine-thud of an advancing BattleMech behind Kempka's clipped orders. "Get your probes running. If a bad guy shows you a piece of himself, you blow it off, y'hear? Help is on the way."

"Right, Sarge."

The knowledge that the rest of his lance was moving to support him acted like a sudden infusion of courage to the green trooper. His scanners revealed the lead enemy 'Mech to be an old 3025 model *Valkyrie*. Mounting a Devastator Series-07 missile launcher in its chest, this was probably the 'Mech that had loosed that first volley of missiles. If so, something wasn't quite right here. A *Val* carried twelve reloads for its ten-tube missile launcher, yet the pilot hadn't fired a second pattern. The first volley had been loosed at over six hundred meters, nearly maximum effective range for standard LRMs. Perhaps the pilot wanted to close the distance before trying again.

Vaux watched as the range counter ticked away the distance between his *Firestarter* and the lead enemy machine. On the tactical situation board, three more enemy 'Mechs were painted and identified. The first was a 40-ton *Assassin,* a standard Inner Sphere design. It was the leading pair of 'Mechs that sent an icy shiver of fear rippling along trooper Vaux's spine. Less than four hundred meters away, and closing fast, were the distorted, hunched-over shapes of two Clan OmniMechs.

His Warbook program tagged the nearest machine as a *Puma-B.* The second was identified as an *Uller.* Both were light machines. Vaux felt confident that he could have taken either one of the Inner Sphere 'Mechs in a stand-up fight, but, in a four-on-one brawl, his 35-ton 'Mech wouldn't last long.

"Sarge, I hate to rush you, but this is starting to get ugly here."

As he spoke, the *Valkyrie* stopped. Flame blossomed from its torso as ten missiles leapt from their launch tubes. The missile defense system whirred to life, swatting half of the inbounds from the sky. Most of the rest fell short, scattering clods of earth, shards of rock, and shattered, burning branches in a dirty, smoke-laced cloud. A few missiles found their mark, gouging pits in the *Firestarter*'s spindly legs. Vaux fought the controls to keep the 'Mech upright.

The range indicator clicked over to two-seventy, just inside maximum range of his 'Mech's lasers. Working the firing grip, Vaux brought the orange targeting pipper up to settle over the *Puma*'s center-of-mass. A steady pulsing of the glowing ring indicated a lock. Mashing the trigger, Vaux sent a pair of laser bolts burning into the hostile's chest. Heat flooded into his cockpit, but was quickly dissipated by the 'Mech's heat sinks.

The aggressor paused, fired. Armor slagged and ran away from his right elbow joint under the fiery caress of nearly invisible laser fire.

Now, the *Uller* was alongside the *Puma*.

"That's not fair, blast you!" Vaux screamed at the enemy. Something inside him snapped. Fear gave way to blazing rage. Despite his orders to hold his position, the young trooper shoved the control stick hard forward and sent his *Firestarter* into a lumbering run. Both attackers blazed away at him, scoring a couple of minor hits, but failing to stop the charging 'Mech.

Aiming for the nearest enemy, Vaux lowered his machine's shoulder like a grav-ball player bursting through a defensive line. At something over ninety kilometers per hour, the *Firestarter* smashed solidly into the *Uller*'s jutting nose. The Clan 'Mech flailed its arms, trying desperately to keep its balance, but gravity won out. With a noise like thunder, the 30-ton battle machine crashed to the ground, falling heavily on its right side.

Vaux didn't see his victim's fall. The impact had sent his *Firestarter* reeling. As he fought to keep his balance, the 'Mech's gyro screaming in protest the whole time, he pirouetted, quite by accident, to within thirty meters of the *Puma*.

At point-blank range, the 35-ton 'Mech pumped twin bolts of coherent light into the incendiary 'Mech's armor. A stream of tracers ripped through the air a meter from his cockpit. A rapid series of laser pulses added their mega-joule caress to the destruction being wrought on his armor.

When Vaux recovered his balance, there were deep, smoking pits in the armor protecting his right side and leg.

Facing his tormentor, Vaux unleashed his full weapon complement in one devastating blast.

Suddenly, his 'Mech became sluggish as the heat threatened to fry the control circuits. A maddeningly polite, computer-generated female voice advised him that a reactor shutdown was imminent. Vaux slapped the override, praying that the heat sinks would reduce the temperature in the 'Mech's core before the computer overrode his override.

None of this mattered to Vaux's opponent, however. Three gouts of burning fuel had washed over the *Puma*. Already running hot from its assault on the charging enemy, the pilot was forced to eject from his rapidly over-heating machine.

That's one. Vaux told himself as the suddenly pilotless *Puma* crashed to the ground. *But I'm still in a world of hurt.*

A shattering one-two punch confirmed his assessment of the situation, as a pair of short-range missiles slammed into the *Firestarter*'s already-damaged torso. The *Assassin* had joined the fight.

"Dammit, Kempka, where are you?" Vaux yelled into the commline.

"Calm down, boy. We're right here."

Immediately, the sky was filled with twisting smoke trails as five volleys of short-range missiles blasted into the enemy ranks. The *Valkyrie* fell hard and didn't get up. The *Assassin* turned and fled.

"I told you to stay put, Vaux."

"Yes, you did, Sergeant. Sorry."

"Save it. You able to fight?"

"My right side's kind of toasted, but I'm okay."

"Good." Secretly, Charlotte Kempka was proud of the rookie pilot. He had taken on four enemy machines, blunted the force of their attack, and gotten his first kill all at the same time, though he had violated orders to do it. "See if you can do what you're told this time.

"We're falling back. The heavies are on the way, so let's not get ourselves killed before they get here, okay?"

Before the recon lance could begin to withdraw, Oliver West's *Javelin* staggered and fell, smoke trailing from a tight cluster of shell craters in the center of its thinly armored back. The *Uller,* damaged, but not destroyed by Vaux's mad rush, had staggered back to its feet. The machine, painted in the black, red, and gray colors of Clan Nova Cat, had seized the opportunity to unleash a volley of laser, autocannon and missile fire into the back of the unsuspecting Light Horse 'Mech.

This cowardly assault was a last act of defiance and desperation. Before West's knocked out 'Mech came to rest in the muddy grass, his lancemates swung around and blasted the *Uller* into smoldering junk.

There was little time to analyze or celebrate the victory. Even as a dazed and wounded Oliver West was clambering out of his disabled 'Mech, Kempka's THREAT board flared to life again.

"Dragon, Dragon, this is Ember One-One. Flash, Sitrep." Sergeant Kempka's voice was loud and harsh in the speakers built into Major Calvin's neurohelmet. "Grid: Juliet Seven two-six-niner. Ember One has contacted the lead enemy elements, including two Clan Nova Cat OmniMechs. Sensors indicate more bandits are inbound. Ember One-One is jamming enemy communications. We are falling back on your position."

"Ember One-One, say again, all after 'lead enemy elements.' " Half of the sergeant's Situation Report had been lost in a grating burst of static.

"I say again: Ember One has engaged and destroyed lead enemy elements, including two Clan Nova Cat OmniMechs: one *Puma* and one *Uller.* Sensors indicate ten or more bandits are inbound our position. Ember One is falling back on your position."

"Roger, Ember One." Calvin's mind raced. If the intruders *were* Nova Cats, the whole operation could be blown before it got under way. He knew from intelligence reports that all of the Clans were engaged to some degree in hunting down and exterminating the Periphery pirates that still existed along the rim of the Inner Sphere. Those same reports carried unconfirmed tales of former Clan warriors, disgraced because of some failing, who had been exiled to the Periphery to become bandits themselves.

"Ember One, fall back toward the LZ, but maintain contact with the enemy. I don't want to lose them."

A burst of static distorted Kempka's reply, again forcing Major Calvin to ask for a repeat.

"I said, losing them isn't going to be an issue," Kempka snapped. "We waxed a couple of their buddies, and they're out for blood."

Thirty minutes later, the battle was over. As soon as he heard that the recon lance was taking fire, Major Calvin ordered the watering party back aboard the DropShips. Leaving his battalion's Seventh Company to protect the DropShips, he hustled the rest of the Fourth and Twenty-fifth through the thin, scrubby woods lining the shores of Sweetwater Lake.

Whoever the mysterious attackers had been, they weren't Clanners. As the Twenty-fifth came up, they ran smack into the bulk of the enemy force, a hodge-podge of old-model 'Mechs, mixed in with a couple of updated types. The biggest of these had been a brand-new *Quickdraw*.

The fight was short and sharp, almost a classic 'Mech battle in miniature. The Light Horse recon lance had encountered the enemy's lead four 'Mechs, also light reconnaissance jobs, and destroyed them. Then, both sides brought up their heavy combat units for the main event. The Light Horse lost only two light and one medium 'Mech. The intruders had been utterly destroyed. Of the sixteen 'Mechs that had entered the fight, none had escaped. Most were taken out in the first few minutes of the engagement. A few, like the *Quickdraw,* hung on a while longer.

Now, as his infantry support platoons rounded up the few attackers who had ejected from their disabled 'Mechs, the ComStar techs resumed their task of collecting and purifying water for the Task Force.

Twisting in his seat, Calvin popped his hatch and clambered out onto his 'Mech's shoulder to watch the mop-up operation. Soldiers dressed in the dark olive and brown-striped uniforms of the Eridani Light Horse moved among the disabled enemy machines. Here and there, he could see a figure, clad only in shorts and a T-shirt, hands raised, being herded along by a few camouflage-clad troopers.

"Dragon One, this is Hatchling Leader."

Reaching through the hatch, the Major plucked the commline headset from its place next to his control couch.

"Go ahead, Hatchling," he replied, holding the boom-mike to his lips rather than settling the headset over his sweat-matted hair.

"Boss, we got a problem. These guys are pirates. They tell me they got a base about thirty klicks west of here."

"Oh, great." Calvin's tone left no doubt that the news was anything but great. "Listen, Jed, make sure your boys round up all the bad guys. I'm gonna call this in."

Before the infantry leader could reply, an alarmed shout cut across the commline.

"We got a live one here!"

Calvin swung himself back into the cockpit, where the tactical display showed an active enemy 'Mech darting into the trees on the far side of the field.

"Somebody catch him!" What the angry shout lacked in tactical finesse, it made up for in effectiveness. Three Light Horse 'Mechs, all from Recon Lance, Fourth Company, lunged into the trees after the fleeing bandit.

"All right, people spread out. Use your scanners and find this son of a buck. We can't let him get away." Sergeant Kempka's voice was hard and angry. The bandit 'Mech, a new model *Jenner,* badly battered, but still bearing the markings of the Tenth Pesht Regulars, had darted right past her *Raven* while she stood in stunned surprise. During the fighting, her battered 'Mechs had moved forward to screen the Light Horse's main body from enemy reinforcements. When none were forthcoming, her lance had been relieved of picket duty. They had just entered the main battle area, heading back toward their DropShip, when the bandit machine suddenly came to life.

Her scanners had shown that it was shut down. She had assumed that the immobile 'Mech had been knocked out. When the ugly, bird-like machine came back to life, she was so surprised that she didn't even get a shot off. Trooper Vaux had reacted first, lacing the fleeing 'Mech's back with laser fire as he shouted out the alarm.

Kempka moved her *Raven* cautiously through the trees, picking her route with care. The woods were not dense, but the ground was littered with large rocks and deadfalls, making footing treacherous. Her 'Mech, with its lanky, backward-acting legs, was especially vulnerable to knee and ankle damage. She did not want to be crippled while stalking a wily enemy through unfamiliar territory.

"Ember One-One, this is Two. I think I've got him." Carasia's whisper barely carried through the link, as though he were afraid the enemy warrior might hear him.

"Two, where are you?"

There was no reply.

Then, stunningly loud in the rain-soaked woods, the woosh-crack of a missile launcher rent the air, followed by the rapid, firecracker detonation of warheads against armor.

"Holy Mother!" Carasia was shouting now. "This guy's a freaking ghost!"

"Two, what the devil's goin' on?"

"I missed him, boss," Carasia snarled. "I had the sneaky beggar in my sights, I got a missile lock, and I missed him."

Kempka nodded to herself. Carasia's short-range missile launchers had been fitted with sophisticated fire-control systems that signaled a solid target lock with a sharp warbling tone. Once the system locked onto a target it was a rare thing to miss.

"All right, Two, keep on him."

The sergeant studied her tactical display. Carasia's 'Mech was south, and a little to the east, of her position. If the pirate was trying to get away, he'd probably head straight back to his base, which the ground-pounders said was to the west. This guy was clever. He would not want to lead a hostile force straight back to his hideout. That meant he'd probably turn. But which way, north or south?

"Two," she called at last. "Keep headin' due west, see if you can't flush him. Four, flank out right a ways, in case he tries to get by us. I'm gonna move off south. Stay in radio contact. Yell if you pop him. We don't want him gettin' away."

Kempka switched her commline to standby, and turned the gain on her *Raven*'s state-of-the-art electronic warfare equipment up to just short of the distortion point. Slowly, carefully, she slipped between the trees. Occasionally, she paused, locking her 'Mech's knees and cutting in the external sound pickups.

This was a technique she'd tried to drill into her lancemates for years. All the high-tech electronics in the world still can't match the "Eyeballs, Model 0 Mark 1" that every warrior was born with. There was something about looking and listening with the senses that God gave a person, something that allowed you to pick up on something that the best electronic sensors would sometimes miss.

This was one of those times. There he was. The *Jenner*'s dark green and gray camouflage paint job didn't quite match the background. Kempka saw her enemy five seconds before he saw her. That was all the time she needed.

With exquisite care, she deftly lined up her *Raven*'s targeting cross hairs with the bandit 'Mech's dome-shaped head. Keying in the target interlock circuits, she tapped the trigger once.

Six Harpoon short-range missiles leapt from their tubes with the hollow, singing roar that marked that particular weapon system. At the same time, a pair of scarlet laser beams snapped across the short distance to wreak their damage on the enemy's armor.

The *Jenner* staggered under the combined impact. Hurt, but not disabled, the camouflaged 'Mech turned to face its tormentor. Kempka heard a new clip of missiles thunk into place in the launcher rack. This time, it was no gentle tap. She clamped down viciously in the firing grip.

Two missile volleys crossed each other's contrails in the center of the narrow clearing, followed by the unearthly crack of air superheated by millions of joules of light energy as the antagonists exchanged laser fire.

Kempka's head swam as three warheads impacted on her *Raven*'s beak-like nose. Amber warning lights flared to life as the bandit's lasers ripped through her 'Mech's previously damaged leg armor, reducing an actuator package to slag.

The enemy suffered worse. Already hurt by Kempka's surprise attack, the *Jenner* stumbled, going down on one knee.

The bandit 'Mech never got the chance to rise. Looming out of the steaming forest behind the *Jenner* came the squat, stout form of Carasia's *Commando*. Extending the 'Mech's right arm, the Light Horseman hesitated to be sure that his missile tracking systems had locked onto the target. Then, at point-blank range, he launched a lethal barrage of armor-piercing warheads into the *Jenner*'s thinly armored back. Even over the flat, metallic bang of the exploding warheads, Kempka's external mikes picked up the odd, rackety whir of the bandit's gyro coming apart inside its housing.

The *Jenner* wobbled on unsteady legs. A flash and smoke split the dome-like head as the pilot ejected on a column of flame. His 'Mech crashed to the forest floor like a poleaxed steer. The bandit came to earth a few meters away.

"All right, that's it." The hollow sound of the *Raven*'s external speakers gave Kempka's voice an unearthly, almost demonic quality. "Put your hands behind your head, and start back toward the lake. Don't even think of running, or I'll blow you into next week."

Clearly exhausted, the bandit nodded and raised his hands.

The battle of Sweetwater Lake was over.

====== 20 ======

Sweetwater Lake Basin
Meribah System
Deep Periphery
16 November 3059
1855 Hours

"**D**ragon One, this is Ember One-One. We got 'im."

"Roger, One-One."

Major Calvin massaged his temples as he swung the boom mike away from his lips. Kempka's capture of the fleeing pirate relieved only one twinge of what was promising to be a massive headache. According to those few prisoners who were both willing and able to talk, 'Mechs that had launched the raid were only a fragment of the pirate band's real strength. Supposedly, they were a security detail left behind by the band's leader while he led a large raiding party against a rival band two jumps away. The prisoners told Calvin that the raiding force wasn't due back for at least a week. That would be plenty of time to finish recharging the task force's engines and jump outsystem. They might even be able to collect enough fresh water to last the rest of the operation, if they were careful.

What worried Major Calvin was the presence of an undetected enemy force less than a day's march from the vulnerable DropShips and technical crews he had been assigned to protect.

Rubbing the back of his neck with one callused hand, Calvin forced out the decision he'd been putting off.

"Attention all units, this is Dragon One. We are suspending operations, pending further instructions from Cavalier. Drinker, you have thirty minutes to get your people and as much as you can of your gear back aboard your ships. Be ready for immediate dustoff. Dragonslayers, tighten up the perimeter by two-zero-zero meters. We're going to hold the LZ until we hear otherwise. Dragon One, out."

Switching channels, Calvin contacted Captain Gascoine aboard the *Hussar*.

"Mike get ready to patch a message through to Courtyard, will you?"

A few moments later, the communications link had been prepared. Calvin thought carefully about what he wanted to say. With the *Invisible Truth* holding station at the star's zenith jump point, it would take at least ten minutes for his message to reach the task force flagship. With true two-way communications rendered impossible, each party in a conversation had to phrase his messages carefully.

Keying in his 'Mech's zip-squeal recorder, Calvin began to speak.

In a few precise sentences, he laid out the situation being faced by the watering party, sketching out the bare details of the skirmish with the pirates and the information gleaned from those taken prisoner.

Switching off the recorder, the MechWarrior tapped a stud, which sent the message to the *Hussar*'s communications panel. From there, it went burning off into the cloudy sky.

For a long time, there was no response. Major Calvin began to wonder if his transmission hadn't gotten through. Then came a reply.

"Dragon One, you are instructed to have Barleycorn dust off. Once in orbit, Barleycorn is to remain on station pending further orders." Calvin nodded to himself. He had already ordered the collection teams aboard their DropShips. It wouldn't take much time to ready the Mules for boost. Once in orbit, they could easily ground again, reestablishing their work details, or, if necessary, make a high-speed run back to the fleet.

"Once Barleycorn is safe, Dragon is to begin search operations to secure the landing zone and to locate the pirate base."

"Roger, Cavalier, will comply." Calvin acknowledged Morgan's instructions. "What are your instructions regarding our prisoners?"

"Dragon," the reply came after many minutes. "Place your prisoners under guard aboard Barleycorn One. They will be transferred to Courtyard for debrief."

"Roger, Cavalier. Will comply." Calvin knew that "debrief" was a euphemism for "interrogation." As a soldier, he recognized the maxim which states that intelligence is the first arm of warfare. That didn't mean he had to like the men and women who gathered intelligence. In most cases, intel officers weren't even soldiers. Unlike reconnaissance troops, who wore the uniform and made a direct contribution on a battlefield, intel-types were usually civilians who skulked around in the enemy's rear area, sneaking into military, industrial, and political centers to beg, buy, or steal the information they wanted. Whatever contribution the intelligence officers made, its impact on the common trooper went largely unnoticed. When everything went right, anyway. If a piece of bad, or out-of-date, intelligence was passed along to mission planners or field commanders, an operation could fall apart before it had begun. The cost in lives and material was usually high.

Shutting down the link to the flagship, Calvin punched up his operational frequency to relay the Marshal's orders to his team.

Fifteen minutes later, the *Mule*s carrying the ComStar techs and seven captive pirates, along with an infantry squad from Seventh Company, lifted off in a cloud of smoke and dust. As the orange-white blaze of the Drop-Ship's flares vanished into the low-hanging overcast, Calvin toggled his commline to active.

"All right, people. If you're through waving goodbye, we've got some work to do. Kempka, take your lance northwest and initiate a standard patrol sweep."

Some time later, as the recon elements of the Eridani Light Horse's Fifth Striker Battalion were searching the wooded Sweetwater Basin, a high-speed shuttle from the *Antrim* docked with the *Invisible Truth*. Aboard were a half-dozen dejected-looking men and women, dressed in a bewildering array of mismatched uniforms, paramilitary dress, and civilian work clothes. Most sported blood-stained field dressings, indicating that they hadn't surrendered easily. They also wore the hollow-eyed, weary expression common to all prisoners of war.

They were met in the small craft bay by a squad of armed men wearing the khaki armored jumpsuits and visored helmets of Star League marines. Quickly, the bound prisoners were escorted out of the bay and into a liftshaft. Seconds later, the captives were hustled through darkened corridors into cramped, three-meter-square cells. They barely had time to assimilate their surroundings, when a second, smaller body of armed men entered the detention area.

"DeVanziano." One of the faceless marines barked out the name with no preamble. "Antony DeVanziano."

A weary-looking pirate, whose fatigue was under-pinned by defiance, stepped to the barred window of his cell. "That's me. Whaddya want?"

The man, who wore the divided, two-color square patch of a corporal, gestured sharply toward that cell door. Two of his men jumped forward, unlocked the cell, dragged the defiant pirate into the corridor, and slammed the door to again, with such speed that DeVanziano's two cell-mates were forced to jump backward away from the door, or be struck by the heavy steel panel as it swung closed.

"Now, lissen, you muck-eaters," the prisoner blustered, as the marines clamped steel restraining cuffs around his wrists. "You best tell me where I am and who you are, or else."

The marines gave no indication of having heard the angry, profanity-laden string of threats their captive continued to shout. They simply frog-marched the cursing pirate into a featureless room just outside of the detention block.

Seated behind a plain metal table were a pair of stocky men, dressed in drab green jackets. One wore a black fox's mask on his collar, which earned him a defiant snort from the captive. When DeVanziano turned his gaze on the room's second occupant, his defiant obscenities froze in his throat. There, gleaming on the collar of the officer's jacket, was a tiny gold-plated Greek letter Rho.

"Very good, Mister DeVanziano, you understand exactly who and what I am." The intelligence Adept chuckled as he rose sinuously to his feet. "Very good indeed. Since we understand each other so well, perhaps you'd like to tell me everything I want to know, without my having to resort to, shall we say, more unpleasant methods?"

Two decks above, in Morgan's flag office, the Marshal looked across his desk with a thin smile.

"Don't you think he's playing the 'Grand Inquisitor' bit a little too well?"

"Just a bit." Demi-Precentor-cum-Colonel Regis Grandi let out a chuckle. "But that's exactly what our Mister De-Vanziano is expecting. To his mind, the only thing missing is the old Tiepolo robes. Ah, it's just as well. If Adept Tobin were wearing the old robes, I'm afraid we'd end up rushing our prisoner to sick bay for treatment of a coronary."

Turning back to the monitor, which gave an odd, high-and-inside perspective of the interrogation room, Grandi reminded Morgan that Tobin was one of the best intelligence officers in the business.

The interrogation process was disturbing to watch. Tobin, every inch the professional, never raised his voice. The Adept's quiet, reasonable tone reminded Morgan more of a minister counseling a parishioner than a highly skilled intelligence officer.

Seated behind the table in a position that instantly conveyed an air of authority, Tobin began the inquiry with a few simple questions: the ubiquitous name, rank, and service number. As he continued, Tobin switched to subjects of military importance. The questions came in cycles. Each time he asked for information, he phrased his queries just a bit differently, the carefully chosen words shading both the question and the answer. Without changing his level, almost sympathetic tone, Adept Tobin challenged every repeated statement, inferring that the prisoner was lying and that the interrogation team knew more than they were letting on. Throughout the entire process, Captain Montjar never said a word. He merely leaned his chair back against the wall, his eyes half-closed, as he gazed at the edge of the table.

Gradually, inexorably, DeVanziano, who had begun the session in angry defiance, began to come apart before the commanders' eyes. Less than an hour after he started, Adept Tobin brought the interrogation to a close.

After the guards had removed the prisoner, Tobin looked up at the concealed camera.

"That's the lot, sir." He smiled in satisfaction. "We want to go over our notes and talk to a couple more of them before we come to any conclusions, but, for now, it's probably safe to start water collection again. I don't think this guy was lying to me."

Three hours later, Tobin and Montjar reported to Morgan's flag cabin where they presented their findings to Ariana Winston and Andrew Redburn, as well as the Marshal. Upon receiving word that the interrogation team had concluded its deliberations, Morgan sent a message asking the other officers to be present when the findings were presented.

According to the information garnered by the intelligence officers, the pirate band numbered around one hundred. Mostly, they were refugees from the old "bandit kingdoms" that were virtually obliterated when the Clans overran the Periphery. Those pirates who had managed to escape from the main Clan thrust and the subsequent solahma units dispatched to hunt them down made their way across the Periphery, gathering strength, until they settled on the uninhabited planet they had named Eleuthera. From there, they began a new campaign of plunder and thievery. Somehow, the pirates had managed to elude detection and capture, until now. They were able to survive by striking at refugees and at other pirate bands. Lately, they had begun attacking Periphery, Inner Sphere, and Clan-held worlds.

The bandits supposedly had a force of thirty-three 'Mechs, mostly older-model machines. Some of their warriors had newer machines, outfitted with newtech systems. A few had even managed to capture Clan OmniMechs, a claim borne out by the *Puma* and *Uller* destroyed by the Light Horse security detail. According to the prisoners, the rest of their force was away on a raid. There were still a couple of pirates back at their base, sort of a security force. They also reported that the pirates were holding a number of prisoners, mostly refugees, that they were using as forced laborers. The rest of the bandit force wasn't due back for at least two more weeks.

"How certain are you of this information?" Morgan tapped the noteputer displaying Tobin's report.

"As certain as I can be, sir." Tobin spread his hands. "You can never be one hundred percent positive of anything you get from a prisoner, but I'd bet the farm on this one."

"VSA supports the conclusions, sir." Montjar passed across a second noteputer. He hadn't been at all bored by Tobin's interrogations, but had been watching the tiny screen of a Voice Stress Analysis unit secured to the underside of the table. The noteputer's liquid-crystal screen displayed a series of jagged lines, which conveyed little to Morgan. He knew, however, that the M15 officer understood the data. The lines showed a base stress level, reflected as tiny quavers in the subject's voice, imperceptible to the human ear. A second series of lines showed a second, elevated, set of stress levels, brought on by Tobin's questioning. According to Captain Montjar, this high-tech analysis revealed that each subject questioned was telling the truth as he recognized it.

"Thank you, gentlemen, that will be all." Morgan waited until the two intelligence officers had closed the door behind them before speaking again. "So now what?"

"Well, Morgan," Andrew Redburn sat back, taking a long, relishing sip of tea from the cup in front of him. "Well, here's where the bullet hits the bone, doesn't it?"

"How do you mean, Andrew?"

"I mean, we can't just walk away from this, can we? We've got to send someone in there to clean out the pirates and rescue the prisoners, right? That probably means the Light Horse, since they're onplanet already."

"That's how I see it." Morgan's tone of voice suggested that he wasn't sure where Redburn was going with his discourse, but didn't like the direction nonetheless.

"Well, sir," Redburn continued. "Unless you're going to order 'no quarter,' and I know you won't do that, you're going to end up with a batch of POWs. Now, we've got a bunch of pirates down there, not exactly the most honorable sort of people to begin with. I don't think they're going to sign on as bondsmen, if you know what I mean." Redburn gave Morgan a half-grin that conveyed his relief that it was not *his* decision to make.

Ariana Winston rose and paced across the room. "Well, we can't spare any ships to run them back to the Inner Sphere," she said. "And we can't leave them here. If they get picked up by the Clanners, God knows how much damage they could do by shooting their mouths off at the wrong time.

"Although I suppose it's possible that the pirates might mistake us for the Explorer Corps." Her lips curled into a wicked grin. "Especially if we tell them that's who we are."

She stopped pacing and thought for a moment. "But even with that, some smart Clan officer might be able to extrapolate the size of the task force by picking the pirates' brains. I mean, the pirates saw X number of 'Mechs and Y number of DropShips. The Clanners might not get it exactly right, but they might make a good guess. And remember, the 'Mechs the pirates *did* see had Eridani Light Horse and Star League markings. One of the first questions a Clan commander is going to ask is, 'What kinds of markings did the enemy 'Mechs have?' If the bandits remember enough to tell them, the Clanners will know the Light Horse aren't back on Kikuyu and Mogyorod. God knows what they'll make of that little bit of information."

"So what do you suggest, Marshal?" Redburn set his cup down with a clatter.

"I suggest we give them a choice," Morgan said. "They can sign on as infantrymen, able deckhands, stevedores, whatever. Or, they can get locked in the brig until this operation is over, at which time they'll be delivered to the proper civilian authorities."

"May I remind you all that the reason we ran into these beggars in the first place was because we had to replenish our water supply?" Regis Grandi cut in. "This task force has limited supplies of food and water. We cannot afford to be saddled with extra mouths to feed, especially those who will be doing nothing other than sitting in the brig.

"As unpleasant as the decision is, our policy must *literally* be 'join or die.' "

Instantly, both Redburn and Winston were on their feet.

"I will *not* countenance the murder of helpless prisoners," Redburn bellowed. The vehemence of his outburst surprised Morgan. Over the many years that Morgan had known Andy Redburn, his friend had mellowed from the brash young man who had once threatened to punch a Baron of the Lyran Commonwealth into a steady, reliable field commander. One thing that hadn't changed was

Redburn's sense of fair play and compassion. The idea of killing defenseless captives appalled him.

"Again, people let me remind you that these 'helpless prisoners' are pirates," Grandi shot back. "They are, by their own admission, responsible for Blake alone knows how many murders."

"And you, sir, are using a specious argument to prove an immoral point," Winston shouted, hands clenched into fists as she leaned across the desk into Grandi's face.

"God in Heaven, woman, who do you think I am? Amaris? Hitler?" Grandi shot to his feet, anger painting his face crimson. "I don't *want* to kill these people, but what *are* we supposed to do with them? We can *not* just leave them here. When the Clans find them, do you think *they'll* have any trouble interrogating the pirates? Those filthy rats will give us up just to save their own disease-ridden hides. Then what? I'll tell you what. Then, the Clanners swing around on our tails and slaughter every last person in this task force, that's what."

"That's enough, Colonel!" Morgan's angry bellow shocked the bickering officers into silence. "God's blood, I'm getting tired of this. Since you *officers* can't agree on anything, *I'll* tell you how it's going to be."

Morgan felt his stomach tighten. "General Winston, your people onplanet will locate and destroy the pirate base. All traces of this task force's presence onplanet must be eradicated. Those pirates taken prisoner in the assault will be given the option of joining this task force as laborers. Those who refuse to join will be court-martialed and executed."

Redburn began to protest, but the blistering look he received from his friend and commander froze the objection in his throat.

"That's it. Dismissed."

"Sir, I will relay your instructions to my people onplanet." Ariana Winston's voice was cold and formal. She stalked from the office without a salute, not even looking at her commanding officer. Grandi followed quickly, but Andrew Redburn lingered behind.

"Listen, Morgan," he said, voice was quiet and steady as he sank into the chair in front of his friend's desk. "I'll support your decision. You know that. So will the rest of the Uhlans. I'd never say anything against you in public. But think very carefully about what you mean to do.

"You know that the DEST and Fox teams won't have trouble with your decision. Sometimes, I wonder if those people have any soul at all. The Capellan troops aren't going to squawk, either. I'm not too sure about the Com Guards, Lancers, or the Drakøns. Of course, you know that Marshal Bryan and the Lyran Guards are going to go ballistic. She'll probably accuse you of 'barbaric mistreatment of prisoners' or some such drek. Naturally, Katherine will pick it up and try to use it against her brother. But that's not what worries me."

Redburn leaned forward, resting his elbows on his friend's desk. "You're going to have to tread carefully around the Knights and the mercenaries. MacLeod and the Highlanders are fairly pragmatic, but you heard how Winston reacted, and she's worlds more reasonable about things than Masters. I can guarantee none of them are going to be overjoyed at the thought of executing prisoners.

"If we tell Masters about the court-martial, he'll insist that he be allowed to sit on it, or heaven help us, even defend the pirates. He bloody sure isn't going to countenance executing them out of hand. We're going to have to do this thing ourselves." Morgan realized that Redburn was suggesting they leave Masters and the other commanders out of the loop during the court-martial proceedings.

"Now, the fact that they *are* pirates might, *might,* mitigate the circumstances this time, but as soon as this traveling circus runs into Clanners who don't want to become bondsmen, there's going to be trouble."

Wearily, Morgan sat forward, resting his face in his hands. Rubbing his eyes, he looked across at his friend.

"All right, Andrew, what do you suggest as an alternative?"

"The ring-leaders should be executed, of course. As for the rest, those who refuse to sign on could be held in the brig until the next time we jump into a system with a habitable planet. Then, they can be marooned."

Morgan nodded wearily.

"All right, so long as this compassion for murderers doesn't put us behind schedule."

21

Sweetwater Lake Basin
Meribah System
Deep Periphery
17 November 3059
1630 Hours

"Talon One? Hatchling One. In position, awaiting orders." Lieutenant Charles Emrys spoke slowly and distinctly into the helmet-mounted radio's boom-mike. A short burst of static punctuated the message.

Emrys and his platoon of twelve Light Horse armored infantrymen were crouched at the edge of a sizable man-made clearing. Whoever had initially cleared the ground that was now occupied by the pirate base, the bandits were less than diligent about keeping their perimeter clear. A thick tangle of brush and vines had grown up at the edge of the base, affording the armored troopers as good cover as they could have wished for. Emrys himself was hunkered down, as much as his power suit would permit, beneath a thick, thorny bush. Given the armor's camouflage and his carefully selected hide, Emrys knew he should be all but invisible at more than four meters.

He also knew that, a few kilometers to the east, Battle-Mechs of the Eridani Light Horse's Fifth Striker Battalion were waiting for his report. Scouting was one of the tasks assigned to the Light Horse's armored infantry platoons. The power armor employed by the mercenary troopers wasn't quite the equal of the so-called "toad-suits" used by Clan Elementals. The armored skin was thinner, and the suits lacked the heavy anti-'Mech missile launcher and automated medical systems of their Clan counterparts. Still, the level of protection, offensive capability, and mobility provided by the standard power suit was a quantum leap above that of regular infantry forces.

The operational plan was simple, at least in theory. The armored infantry would scout out the pirates' base and report back to Captain Martin Izzat, commander of the Twenty-fifth Battalion's Seventh 'Mech Company. Once a scan of the enclave was complete, the 'Mechs would move up to capture the base, with the armored infantrymen in support. Emrys feared that another officer was likely to be on the field as well, a fellow called Murphy, whose laws had plagued fighting men since the beginning of time.

Using information provided by the few prisoners willing to cooperate, the task force's intelligence division had pieced together a rough model of the pirate base. But when Emrys and his platoon finally reached the spot detailed by the captives, he realized that calling the ramshackle huts and corrugated metal buildings a base was giving it too much credit. The pirate enclave looked more like the refugee camps the Light Horse had helped to erect following the bloody, destructive battle for Coventry.

"Hatchling One, can you give me a remote feed?"

In response to the request from the 'Mech officer, Lieutenant Emrys activated the video transmitter built into his suit's long-range communications system. The system sent a coded signal back to the waiting 'Mechs, whose computers translated the message into a grainy image displayed on one of the many monitors cluttering a BattleMech's cockpit.

How could a man fight like that? Emrys wondered. *Surrounded by computer screens and flashing lights? It's all I could do to learn to operate this suit, let alone a BattleMech.*

The image he was broadcasting was of a collection of dilapidated shacks clustered around a broad open area. In the center of this "town square" stood a half-dozen rust-streaked BattleMechs, the heaviest of which was a 65-ton *JagerMech,* still sporting the gray and black splotches of urban camouflage.

Emrys panned the camera around, coming to rest on a small knot of women emerging from one of the huts. Their tattered clothing might once have been any color, but now it was stained an off red-tan, the color of the local clay. The women were lugging a large plastic-wrapped bale, a task made difficult by the leg irons clamped around their ankles.

His curiosity about the contents of the bundle turned into anger as Emrys realized that the women were being used as slaves by the pirates. The rage vanished when he saw the direction in which they were dragging their burden.

"Hatchling One, pull back." Captain Izzat's voice crackled in Emrys' ear. "They're heading right for you."

"No can do, Talon." Emrys' voice sank to a whisper, even though the women could not possibly have heard him through his heavily armored suit. "We move, and they'll spot us for sure. Best to brazen it out and trust in our cammo."

"All right, Hatchling, it's your call. Act at your discretion, but try to avoid any civilian casualties, O.K.?"

"Roger that."

Emrys passed the order to his platoon. He knew that most people, these women included, only saw what they expected to see. With luck, they would walk right past the green-and-brown-camouflaged troopers.

Unfortunately, neither luck nor the capricious Mr. Murphy was on his side.

The woman struggling with the front of the bundle, a tiny thing who might have once been pretty (it was impossible to tell under the layers of dirt), suddenly jerked upright, dropping her share of the load. Before any of her exhausted partners could speak, she let out a shriek and bolted back toward the compound. Or tried to. The poor wretch got about three steps before she stumbled and fell heavily, tripped by the hobbles.

Emrys thought the fall should have knocked the breath out of her lungs, but her ever-louder screams of terror and alarm proved him wrong.

"Toads! Toads! There are toads in the woods!" The woman bolted back the way she had come, having apparently mistaken the Light Horse armored troopers for Clan Elementals. "Toads" was the somewhat derisive slang term initially applied to Elementals during the Clan invasion. Given the superficial similarity of shape between

Inner Sphere power suits and Clan battle armor, the mistake was understandable.

Emrys loosed a blast of profanity fit to make a sailor blush. "That's done it. Talon One, we've been spotted. Hatchling is moving in."

The twelve armored troopers of the First Armored Infantry platoon leapt forward into the compound.

Three men dressed in fatigues and dirty body armor came out of the nearest building, through the same door used by the women. Each had a long arm gripped tightly in his hands. The lead bandit actually managed to get his weapon up before Emrys' team could react. A gout of flame thirty centimeters long leapt from the assault rifle's muzzle. Emrys flinched inside his armor as the metal-jacketed slugs beat out a dull, clanging tattoo on the hardened steel shell. Seeing that his small arm was useless against the nightmare figure that was drawing closer, the pirate began groping for the firing grip of the grenade launcher slung beneath the Kogyo-Reyerson-Toshiro assault rifle.

Emrys knew that, while the slugs stood little chance of penetrating his battle armor, the half-kilo explosive charge fired by the grenade launcher might breach his suit. He brought his power-suited left hand up, and, praying that there were no innocents on the other side of the clapboard wall, triggered a burst of machine gun fire. The slugs ripped into the pirates, spinning the lifeless bodies in a macabre dance. Behind the pirates, splinters flew through the air as the wooden frame wall virtually disintegrated.

Bolting past the still-twitching bodies, the lieutenant smashed through the door. The room looked like a slaughterhouse. Six men and two women, in various stages of undress, lay slumped on the floor. Five of them were sprawled in the huddled, shapeless way that only the dead can achieve. The others, spattered in blood, writhed convulsively with the pain and shock of their wounds. Against the far wall cowered a small knot of survivors, fear stretching their faces into death-like masks.

"Blast!" Emrys spat. He stopped for a split second, wondering if he had time to treat the injured and secure the living. He certainly couldn't leave potential hostiles behind him.

The decision was taken out of his hands by the sharp crack of missiles being fired.

"Hatchling One-Four." The cry held a note of surprise and fear that could not be wholly masked by the metallic quality of the comm system. "Enemy 'Mechs moving in fast." A pause, presumably while Trooper Crow fired a laser bolt at the onrushing enemy. "I identify three mediums. One *Blackjack,* one *Centurion,* and one *Dervish.*"

Cutting in his external speaker, Emrys barked an order at the terrified mob. "Stay put. If you leave this building, you'll be killed."

Yeah, and you stand an equally good chance of dying if you don't *leave.* The thought leapt unbidden to his mind. He forced it away. Time for recriminations later. Right now, he had a job to do.

A clap of thunder, barely deadened by the suit's noise-attenuation circuits, shook the ground, as a lightning-bright stream of charged particles lashed the muddy earth less than five meters from where Emrys had emerged from the building. For long seconds, he tried to force his mind to focus on the puzzling fact that he was now looking *up* at the overhanging eaves of the building he had just exited. Then, the realization dawned on him. The concussion of the near-miss had thrown him onto his back.

Willing his balky limbs to move, Emrys struggled to his feet.

"El-Tee, you all right, you need a medic?" The faceless head of Sergeant Grinnell's power suit appeared in Emrys' view screen.

"No," Emrys grunted as he was helped to his feet. "No, Sarge. I'm O.K."

"Right. I wouldn't try to fire your weapon, though. The barrel's clogged with mud."

"Dammit." Emrys slapped the machine gun's barrel housing with the suit's grabber claw. "Any good?"

"Nope. You must have jammed it into the ground real good when you fell."

"Aaah!" Emrys voiced an inarticulate snarl of disgust. "All right, Sarge, you get on with business. I'll stay here and try to coordinate. Maybe, when the ground-pounder comes up, I can get one of them to clear this bloody gun for me."

Emrys could feel Grinnell's eyes upon him even

through the heavy armored visors each man wore. Without another word, the sergeant turned and vaulted the wreckage of what had once been a ground car. The lieutenant dropped to one armored knee behind the smoldering, twisted metal.

Unlike its larger cousins, his suit didn't have enough room for a tactical display. From what he could determine by the brief, static-distorted radio messages, his platoon had managed to destroy one 'Mech, a 20-ton *Locust,* almost before the pirates knew they were under attack. Some of the bandits had been caught away from their machines, and had surrendered when the troopers of Second Platoon burst into their barracks. Other enemy pilots had managed to mount their 'Mechs before the attacking infantry men cut them off. Now, the pirates were engaging his men in a close-range brawl. The platoon's armored infantry were superior to any foot-slogger in the field, but even their heavy power armor couldn't last long against BattleMechs. He needed Seventh Company to relieve his hard-pressed troopers.

"Talon One, this is Hatchling One-One," Emrys growled into his transceiver's boom-mounted microphone. "Where the devil are you guys?"

"Cool out, One-One." Izzat's thick New Syrtis drawl eased from the headset ear piece. "The cavalry's on the way."

Izzat's company began closing on the pirate base before the echoes of Emrys' initial machine gun burst faded away. The first on the scene was Private Henry Stano's *Valkyrie.* The green replacement, flush with the excitement of his first engagement, had charged ahead of the Seventh 'Mech Company's main body. For a few seconds, Stano traded laser and missile fire with a pirate *Dervish.* Then, a devastating blast from a PPC caught his 'Mech just below its armored ribs. Whirling to face the new threat, Stano made a mistake. In turning to engage the *Griffin,* which had managed to flank him, he exposed his thinly protected back to the damaged, but still active, *Dervish.* The *Val*'s meager armor shattered under a merciless volley of twenty-four short- and long-range missiles and two laser bolts. Staggered by the pounding, Stano struggled furiously with his controls, fighting to keep his

'Mech on its feet. When the *Val*'s CASE panels blew away, the rookie warrior's nerve snapped.

Believing he had only seconds to live, Stano yanked the yellow and black-striped ejection handle.

For a brief, horror-stricken moment, nothing happened. Then, with a roar, the young trooper was rocketed skyward, away from his disabled 'Mech.

Stano's Lance Sergeant, Willis Rexer, rushed his *Watchman* onto the field just as the kid tumbled to the ground. The fall must have stunned the rookie, because he made no attempt to cut away from his rapidly collapsing rescue chute or to get to his feet to get away from the battle raging around him. The crackle of gunfire yanked the sergeant's attention away from his fallen trooper.

The *Dervish* loomed large in Rexer's viewscreen. A pair of short-range missiles shot past his 'Mech's hunched shoulders to explode among the variform elms of the forest. The Sergeant replied with a trio of laser bolts. As the rest of his lance came up alongside him, Rexer closed with his opponent, and, in short order, reduced the 55-ton machine to smoldering junk.

"Courtyard, this is Talon One." The *Invisible Truth*'s communications system crackled as it decompressed and replayed the short-burst transmission sent by the Light Horse officer commanding the attack on the pirate base. "STATREP: Objective secure. Talon suffered five casualties, one KIA. Three 'Mechs damaged, but repairable, one questionable. Seven enemy 'Mechs destroyed. Fifteen PW's taken." Captain Izzat paused for a moment. "Forty-five refugees secured, and in our hands. Sir, it's a mess down here. These pirate bastards were using the refugees from the Clan occupied zones as slaves. Most of them are sick, starving . . . We're doing the best we can for them, but I don't know if it's going to be enough."

Not all of the pirates' captives were wounded or at death's door because of mistreatment. But Captain Izzat was a soldier on site, one who was used to seeing prisoners treated decently. So appalled was he by the condition of the prisoners that he gave in to unintentional exaggeration. In truth, only a few prisoners were at death's door from injury or abuse, and only one or two of those were likely to die regardless of medical care. Izzat was merely voicing his frustration that some of them needed a full sick bay, and all he had on hand were a couple of combat medics.

Morgan glanced at Redburn and Winston, who had gathered on the *Invisible Truth*'s bridge to follow the progress of the battle. Redburn's face was impassive, but there was a tightness around Winston's dark eyes.

"Very well, Talon One," Morgan said. "See to the needs of the refugees. Secure the prisoners, and prepare them for transfer to the flagship."

Morgan could feel Winston's eyes boring into the back of his head as he passed his next order.

"Captain Izzat, make sure you document everything you've seen and done in that compound for possible use as evidence in a summary court martial against the pirates."

It took nearly twenty minutes for the message and reply to bounce between the flagship and the distant planet. During that time, both Morgan and Ariana Winston carefully avoided the subject of the pirates themselves, confining their talk to the treatment and disposition of the refugees.

"Cavalier, say again?"

Morgan repeated the order, and twenty minutes later received confirmation from the Light Horse officer. Returning the headset to the communications technician, he steeled himself to face Winston.

"Well, Marshal," she said, her voice raw, "it looks like you got the grounds for your court martials."

Before Morgan could reply, she snapped an angry salute, turned on her heel, and stormed off the bridge.

Several hours later, the *Hussar* thudded into the *Invisible Truth*'s number two docking collar. When the access tunnel irised open, fifteen dejected-looking pirates were herded into the cavernous cargo bay by sullen-looking Light Horse infantrymen. As soon as a squad of Com Guard security troops took charge of the prisoners, the mercenaries returned to their DropShip and departed. During the entire operation, none of the Light Horsemen had spoken a word more than was absolutely necessary. The proposed fate of the captive pirates had obviously spread throughout the fleet. The Eridani troopers, with their deeply ingrained tradition of treating captured foemen with decency and fairness, were understandably angry at the thought of executing prisoners of war. The fact that these prisoners were bandits—little more than common criminals—seemed to have little bearing on the matter.

It took several days for Morgan to complete his interviews with the captured pirates. So large was the task that Andrew Redburn and Regis Grandi were called into assist him. Ordinarily, as Morgan's second, Ariana Winston would have been part of the board of inquiry. But she refused. Soon after leaving the *Invisible Truth* for the Light Horse command ship *Gettysburg,* she had sent a message explaining the reason behind her refusal.

"Under any other circumstances, and if it was anybody but you," she gritted out between clenched teeth, "I would have ordered my troops to disregard your orders. But we are the Eridani Light Horse, and that name still means something. We agreed to take part in this operation. Since you are the task force commander, we will follow your instructions in military matters to the letter. However, we will have no more part in the 'disposition' of the prisoners."

Morgan tried to mollify Winston by informing her of Redburn's plan to maroon those pirates not convicted by the court martial. All he got for his efforts was a baleful stare.

"You think that makes a difference?" she said, then broke the connection without waiting for an answer.

The court martial was convened and concluded in two days. With Grandi, Redburn, and Commodore Beresick making up the tribunal, four of the prisoners were found guilty of piracy, theft, murder, and other crimes. For these crimes, the court martial ordained a punishment of death.

In short order, and with no fanfare, the condemned men were executed, and their bodies were consigned to space. The rest of the pirates, convicted of lesser crimes, were to be marooned. In some ways, this was a far harsher sentence than that received by their leaders. These men would be set down on an uninhabited planet, with just enough supplies and equipment to try to survive. If they managed to eke out a living from the wilderness, it would only be through hardship and toil.

While the proceedings were underway, Ariana Winston spoke only once with the flagship, In that communiqué, she asked that the Light Horse be relieved of security duty for the water collection teams. Her anger barely concealed beneath the stiff formal language, Winston explained that she did not want her men to have any further reminders of what was taking place aboard the flagship.

In an effort to make peace with her, Morgan agreed, replacing the Light Horse troops with the First Kathil Uhlans.

Later that day, he summoned Andrew Redburn to his flag office. For the first time since the operation had begun, Redburn noticed how drawn and weary his friend's face had become.

"Tell me something, Andy. What do you think is really eating Winston?"

Redburn leaned back in his chair, taking a few moments to formulate his answer.

"Well, I can't say for certain. I can only guess. I'd have to put it down to the reason the Light Horse was selected for this mission. They have a tight grip on the past, all the way back to the Star League.

"Have you ever taken a good look at some of their troops? I mean, a real close look? Their Fiftieth Battalion wears that red unit patch to remind them of the massacre on Sendai, remember? Two thousand dependents, men, women and children, wiped out, murdered by Jimjiro Kurita.

"Now, here you are, asking them to countenance the execution of prisoners. I'm not saying what we're doing is wrong, but think of it this way. After living your entire life with a tradition that protects noncombatants and prisoners-of-war, it's hard to put that aside, even for pirates, even for a couple of real bastards who deserve to die."

Redburn leaned forward and said, with a sigh, "She'll probably come around in a while. For now, I'd leave her alone."

Winston's principled withdrawal was not the end of the troubles Morgan had to face over the court martial and execution of the pirate leaders. Shortly after his conversation with Redburn, he received a visit from Paul Masters.

"Marshal Hasek-Davion," the Knights commander said, plunging in without preamble. "Are the rumors true? Have you really executed prisoners?"

God save me from idealists. Morgan pushed the thought aside as he turned to face the other man.

"Yes, Colonel Masters. I did order the execution of four prisoners. The men were the leaders of a pirate band that preyed upon refugees fleeing from the Clan occupation zones. They were tried and convicted of murder and piracy by a court martial, and executed according to the universal code of military justice. The remaining pirates, those convicted of lesser crimes, will be marooned in the next suitable system."

Masters stopped short, taken aback by the annoyed directness of Morgan's answer. He was not put off stride for long.

"Sir, I appreciate the fact that this is a military operation. I further appreciate the fact that you are the commanding officer of this military operation. Your right to convene a court martial is not at issue here.

"I am not calling the integrity of the proceedings into question. I have no doubt that the hearing was fair, and the sentence just. But, sir, I must protest the fact that the majority of the command staff was not informed of those proceedings until they were over. An action with such far-reaching consequences should have included representatives of *all* the units involved in this task force.

"Marshal Hasek-Davion, with all due respect, I must caution you, sir, in the strongest possible terms, do not undertake any further such actions without *at least* formally advising each of the unit commanders of your intentions.

"This is a cooperative effort," Masters said stiffly. "We expect you to cooperate."

═══ 22 ═══

Battle Cruiser ISS Invisible Truth
Unnamed Star System
Deep Periphery
15 December 3059
1810 Hours

Morgan's hearing returned to normal as the *Invisible Truth* phased in from the nothingness of hyperspace. The task force had come four jumps, a hundred twenty light years, past the system named Meribah by the Explorer Corps scouts who had first located it. Meribah, the Marshal knew, was a Biblical word. It was the name for the place where Moses drew water from the rock. Like so many of the places in the Old Testament, Meribah had another name, Massah. The words meant "Quarreling" and "Testing." He also knew that, because Moses failed his test at Meribah, he was forbidden to enter the promised land.

It wasn't exactly a quarrel he had going with Ariana Winston, but it had taken more then Redburn's "little while" for her to "come around." Almost two full weeks, in fact. She had studiously avoided Morgan except for essential discussions on troop readiness, fighter rotation schedules, and other military matters, but even those contacts were strained.

Though there were some on the command staff who viewed Winston's withdrawal as an ill-tempered sulk, Morgan knew differently. She was understandably angry—not because the Meribah pirates had been tried and executed; she understood the necessity of military justice. Her anger was the result of forty-seven years of living with the Light Horse principles of fair and humane treatment of prisoners being brought up hard against the realities of a new era of modern warfare, in which the only dictum was kill-or-be-killed. Morgan felt some of that turmoil as well. Even in light of the restored Star League, and all that it promised, the harsh realities of total war had to be faced. The Meribah incident was simply the first test of the task force's join-or-die policy—a policy no one had fully understood till it came time to implement it.

Morgan made every effort to restore the friendly relationship he'd shared with Winston, but to no avail. She simply refused to acknowledge any statement or question that did not directly concern task force operations.

Then, one morning two weeks ago, Morgan made a disparaging remark concerning the poor quality of the coffee provided for the staff meeting.

"Some longshoreman must have gotten mixed up over coffee and cordite," Winston said, as though nothing had ever been wrong between them. Then she took a second sip of the murky, black liquid, shuddered, and pushed her cup away. "Graagh. On second thought, cordite would taste better than this stuff."

It wasn't much, but after two weeks of strained relations, it was a beginning. Morgan had been afraid that the incident at Meribah might have opened a permanent rift between Winston and himself. That would not have boded well for either the mission or for Morgan personally.

Any further musings were cut short when a shout from the *Truth*'s communications officer rang across the bridge.

"Sir, *Ranger* reports contact with a number of unidentified starships. Captain Winslow requests instructions."

"What?" Morgan yelled in surprise above the sudden clamor sparked by the alarm. "Show me."

In response to his command, four tiny images flared scarlet as they floated above the floor of the holotank.

"Can you identify?"

"No, sir." The sensor tech was punching in commands as rapidly as he could, trying to coax more resolution out of the *Truth*'s scanners. "The nearest friendly vessel is the

Ranger. Captain Winslow reports she is unable to identify the bogies."

"Dammit all," Morgan cursed. "Sound General Quarters. Gun crews to their stations. Prepare to launch fighters."

The sounding of an alert as the task force phased in at a new system had become almost a routine measure. This time, it was different. The klaxon had barely begun to sound when the gun stations began to report in. Somehow, the men and women of Task Force Serpent had sensed that this alert was the real thing. Commodore Beresick reported "all stations manned and ready" in just under four minutes, a full fifteen seconds faster than the previous record.

"Marshal," the commtech called. "*Ranger* reports positive ID on the bogies. Now classifying target vessels as bandits."

The identification codes floating next to the images of the enemy ships flickered and changed. The largest of the figures, now obviously a WarShip, bore the label CNGRSS.

"Sir, *Ranger* IDs the bandits as one *Congress* Class frigate, two *Whirlwind* destroyers, and one *Invader* Class transport. *Ranger* is still too far away from the target vessels to get a positive Clan affiliation. Captain Winslow reports bandits may be attempting to furl their sails in preparation for jump."

"All right. Commodore Beresick, this is your bailiwick. You have command, sir," Morgan said. "I'll try to stay out of your way."

Beresick nodded, then barked out orders.

"Commodore has the conn. *Rostock* will remain with the transports. All other WarShips will initiate a high-G burn to close with the bandits. Transports will detach their designated Fleet Defense DropShips. The FDDs will come into formation with the WarShips.

"Let's get 'em, boys and girls."

Major Michael Ryan rubbed the small, painful bump on his skull, right above the hairline. When the alarm came through, he had been sound asleep in his bunk aboard the *Haruna*. Startled into wakefulness, he had attempted to vault from his bunk. Mercifully, his rank gave him the privilege of a semi-private cabin, and his bunkmate, the *Haruna*'s chief gunnery officer, was on duty. The sheets had gotten tangled around Ryan's ankles, turning his graceful leap into a headlong sprawl. His metal-framed desk chair broke his fall by striking him a glancing blow to the forehead.

Swearing like a rejected courtesan, he disentangled himself, resisting the impulse to spend a few moments ripping the sheets to shreds. At last, he bolted from the room, snatching his "jump kit" from the tiny closet next to the door on the way out. Barefoot and clad only in track shorts, he darted across the corridor to catch the lift down to his action station.

By the time the elevator jerked to a halt on Deck Ten of the frigate, Ryan had put on his olive drab jumpsuit, struggling into the garment with difficulty in the crowded lift car. His feet were still bare as he ran through the accessway into the *Haruna*'s number two cargo hold. The cavernous space was dimly lit by a series of fluorescent strips set into the overhead, a dozen meters above.

"Konban wa, Major," *Gunjin* Carlotta Sior called as she watched his dramatic, if not dignified, entrance.

"Talk to me, Bill. What's going on?"

Tai-i William Culp, Team Five's blond-haired, blue-eyed leader, was switching the bay's intercom to standby when Ryan arrived.

"We've been ordered to 'action stations; boarding,' Major." A native of Sternwerde displaced by Clan Ghost Bear's invasion of that planet, Culp had a feral expression on his thin, pale face, a look enhanced by the weak illumination of the bay. "They tell me we've run into a Clan flotilla, and Beresick is moving to engage them. The TOO said you were supposed to check in as soon as you got here."

Ryan reached past his subordinate and keyed the communicator.

"Bridge, Tactical Officer."

"Commander, this is Major Ryan. What do you want us to do?"

"Sho-sa," Lieutenant Commander Masahiro Kobayashi said. The *Haruna*'s Tactical Operations Officer was an old-line DCMS officer. He had resisted the idea of supplanting a long-standing system of rank to fit in with the idea of a coalition force, or a renewed Star League. "Get your teams ready to get aboard the *Bisan*. The orders are to prepare to launch a boarding action."

"Got it." Ryan smiled as he broke the connection. Kobayashi was a hidebound prig, who considered the Draconis Elite Strike Teams to be a necessary evil, one step above the filthy, honorless nekekami. Ryan enjoyed yanking the naval officer's chain whenever possible. His satisfaction showed on his face as he turned to his troops.

"Okay, suit up."

Thirty commandos scattered across the cargo bay. Along with the others of his command, Ryan approached an odd, boxy module, where Simon Nisimura, his personal suit tech, awaited him. At first, the idea of having a technician assigned to him had struck Ryan as strange. But the first time he tried to struggle into his Kage suit without the tech's help, he learned the value of an expert assistant.

With a total lack of regard for propriety or self-consciousness, Ryan stripped off the jump suit. He knew that the men and women of his teams were professionals who considered it beneath their station to ogle each other as they prepared for battle. One of the technicians originally assigned to assist Team Four had been transferred out after serving only one day. The man had made a few off-color remarks concerning Team Four's attractive female communications specialist. Captain Yosuke had to drag three male members of his team off the unfortunate tech before they killed him. The tech was sent home in disgrace, a heavy cast immobilizing his left arm.

The only consideration Ryan gave to modesty was to step into the shadows as he exchanged the track shorts for a thick gray bodysuit. The close-fitting garment was a modified version of a MechWarrior's cooling vest. The heavy cloth contained thousands of small tubes, which carried a variant of the coolant used to protect a pilot from the heat generated by operating a 'Mech in combat. The bodysuit, which included a tight-fitting hood, gloves, and boots, also carried a sophisticated sensor mesh, which would transmit movement and combat commands to the suit's onboard computer. The mesh also analyzed the operator's physical condition. The computer could then respond by adjusting the amount and rate at which coolant flowed through the suit, administer pain killers, stimulants, or antibiotics from a small medipack built into the armor's superstructure.

Once he was satisfied that the bodysuit wouldn't bunch

up around the arms, elbows, and knees, or chafe, as it had done in past training exercises, Ryan grabbed a steel bar mounted in the suit ingress/egress module about two-and-a-half meters off the deck. Using this handhold, he swung his les up into the lower half of the powered combat armor. The composite and steel leg armor was always cold and clammy when he first slipped into it, but it warmed up quickly, as the mesh bodysuit fed data to the armor's computers.

As soon as Ryan's feet were locked into the heavy boots, Nisimura stepped up to help him as he wormed his way into the armor's thick, heavy breastplate. As he donned each piece of the armor, the tech fiddled with the joints, making sure that all seals, circuits, and interlocks had been properly connected.

Ryan didn't hurry this process. Once, during a training exercise on Defiance, a trooper from Team Four had rushed through the suit-up process. The man's left arm harness failed to achieve a proper lock with the plastron. Private Kee had gotten a lungfull of irritant gas when the seal let loose in the middle of an engagement with the Lyran Guards.

When the last piece of body armor had hiss-popped into place, Nisimura pulled a bundle of probe-tipped wired from the pouch hanging on his left hip. Shoving the metal leads into jacks built into the suit's outer structure, Nisimura ran a fast, thorough diagnostic and calibration check on the Kage armor's systems. As the tech was coiling up the medusa-like bundle of wires, Ryan used the suit's fully manipulative hands to attach a specially modified Blazer rifle to the hardpoint built into the armor's right vambrace. Another calibration check confirmed that the weapon was aligned properly with the suit's targeting sensors and display.

The rest of the team members would be armed with Blazers, shredders, and other small arms. Private Teji Nakamura, the team's weapons specialist, carried a heavy Imperator auto-grenade launcher. Carlotta Sior was the only one who was not happy with the Kage suits. As the team's sharpshooter, she complained that the bulky armor interfered with her marksmanship. Sior even had the team's armorers modify a Minolta 9000 rifle to mate with the suit's wrist-mounted hard point. In training, Lo had managed to hit twenty-three out of twenty-five man-sized targets at one thousand meters, using the suit's improved targeting system. Today, she would be going in armed with a Blazer rifle.

Each of the troopers had a specially modified vibrokatana attached to his armor's carapace. Though the weapons might seem archaic or foolish in the modern combat arena, the DEST troopers knew better. During commando operations against the Clan invasion, some of them so secret that details had yet to be released, at least one member of each DEST team had killed an Elemental with the high-tech swords. It was rumored that captured Elementals claimed to be more afraid of a vibrokatana than a Gauss rifle.

Many of the now-armored warriors also carried bulky satchels strapped to their suit's built in cargo points. Some, like Private Akida of Ryan's Team Six, carried a canvas bag loaded with breaching charges. Lance Corporal Ringh of the Team Five carried a small, powerful plasma cutting torch.

Ryan keyed up the suit's helmet-mounted communications link.

"Comm check, Team Six?"

"Six-Two on line."

"Six-Three, here."

"Six-Four ready."

Ryan then checked in with the leaders of Teams Four and Five, wanting to be certain that all of the warriors under his command were ready to carry out their mission.

"All right, attention to orders." Ryan spoke quietly. "Our mission is to prepare to initiate a boarding action. We have been instructed to board the *Bisan* and be ready to launch.

"We will not be committed until our target vessel has been disabled. The fleet's major combat vessels will attempt to cripple the target vessel during the approach and cover the teams until they are in grappling range. At that time, the *Haruna* will move us as close as she can to the target vessel. Then, the assault ship and battle taxis will take us in the rest of the way. After that, it's all up to us."

"Any idea what the target is?" Captain Yosuke inquired.

"No, not yet." Ryan's voice held a note of concern. "If it's a transport JumpShip or a DropShip, we should be fine. If they expect us to bag a WarShip . . . there'll be the devil to pay."

* * *

"What did you say?" Star Colonel Alonso snapped at the red-haired woman seated at the *Shining Claw*'s primary sensor control station.

Alonso was the epitome of a Clan Ghost Bear warrior; tall, with a well-muscled frame. He was proud of his strength, stability, and persistence, the traits his Clan admired in the huge ursine predator native to Strana Mechty, and whose name they bore.

"Star Colonel, there are a large number of unidentified starships emerging from hyperspace, bearing one-six-five, Mark fifty-two."

"Identify."

"Sensors indicate seven warships, including one *Cameron* Class battle cruiser, three destroyers, two *Essex* and one *Lola* Class. The other warships are of an unknown class." The sensor operator punched a few buttons. "The rest of the intruders seem to be transports, including a number of *Monolith* and *Star Lord* Class JumpShips."

"Who are they?"

"Unknown, Star Colonel." The tech worked at her controls in a vain attempt to increase the gain of her sensors. "The intruders are not transmitting a recognizable transponder code, and they are still too far away for a detailed scan. If I were to make an educated guess, I would have to surmise that the intruders are potential hostiles."

Alonso rested his chin in his right palm for several moments as he considered the perplexing report. His tiny flotilla, which was transporting Clan civilians to the Inner Sphere, was well away from the main lines of communications between the Clan Occupation Zone and the homeworlds. The convoy's route had been chosen specifically because of the remoteness of the planned jump points.

Perhaps the intruders were Nova Cats or Smoke Jaguars, bringing fresh troops into their occupation zone to deal with the raids being launched by the Draconis Combine.

Still, standing orders forbade relying upon any such assumption, and Alonso had not reached the rank of Star Colonel by ignoring standing orders.

"Sensor operator, confirm your scans."

Seconds ticked by as the black-haired officer watched the technician's fingers race over her instruments.

"Scans confirmed. One *Cameron*, one *Lola*, and two

Essex. Scans also suggest that one of the unknowns conforms to the data provided by The Watch on a Draconis Combine *Kyushu* Class frigate."

"What?" Alonso knew that The Watch, the Clan version of an intelligence arm, had provided limited data on recent military developments achieved by the Inner Sphere. He simply could not believe that one of those new WarShips could be here, so far from the Inner Sphere.

"Fire Fang reports that the lead enemy vessel bears the insignia of the Com Guards . . ." The sensor operator's voice caught in her throat.

"What is it?" The olive skin of Alonso's face turned an odd brick red as anger sent blood rushing into his cheeks and forehead.

"Star Colonel . . ." The tech hesitated, perhaps fearing an explosion of Alonso's legendary temper. "The *Fire Fang* reports that the lead enemy vessel, the *Lola,* bears the insignia of the Com Guards and the Star League Defense Force."

Alonso glared at the technician. "Say that again," he hissed.

"Star Colonel, the intruders all bear the insignia of the Star League Defense Force."

"That cannot be. There is no Star League. Terra has not yet fallen. This is a trick. A dirty, blasphemous trick of those filthy, *stravag* Inner Sphere barbarians," Alonso said furiously.

"Star Colonel," a freeborn technician called out. "The enemy commander is hailing. He is calling for our surrender."

"The hell he is."

In response to Alonso's curt gesture, the tech routed the incoming message through the *Shining Claw*'s bridge holotank. The image of a tall, dignified man, wearing the drab uniform of a Star League general officer, snapped into existence. Alonso focused first on the uniform. Four tiny gold pips gleamed on the left shoulder of the jacket. Numerous campaign and award ribbons adorned its breast, including a glittering Diamond Sunburst. Above these loathsome displays of vanity, which Alonso considered degrading to a true warrior, was the ultimate obscenity. The man was shamelessly wearing a silver Cameron Star.

Finally, Alonso's senses expanded to take in the rest of the man wearing the uniform. Green eyes flashed out of a face that was proud, handsome, and strong. The man's red hair was streaked heavily with gray.

"Attention, Clan WarShips, I am Marshal Morgan Hasek-Davion, commander of the Star League Task Force Serpent. Let this be my *batchall*." There was pride in that strong, clear voice. "I call upon you to prepare to defend your fleet and yourselves. We will be attacking you with all but one of our WarShips. I name as *isorla* any ship that is rendered unable to fight or maneuver, and claim its passengers and crew as bondsmen. What forces do you bid in your defense?"

The sheer force of the man's presence caused Alonso to hesitate for a moment. It was as if he was looking through a magical window, back over three hundred years, and seeing one of the ancestors his Clan had always sought to emulate. Then, reason cleared his mind of such foolishness, reason that replaced indecision with a burning rage. If the Inner Sphere *surats* wanted to play at being the Star League, let them. They would suffer all the worse for this outrage.

"I am Star Colonel Alonso Gilmour, of Clan Ghost Bear. I do not recognize your claim to the Star League." Alonso felt a grim satisfaction in calling this Morgan Hasek-Davion a liar. "I accept your *batchall*. I will defend my fleet with every asset at my disposal."

Alonso slashed his finger across his throat, prompting the commtech to sever the connection. Before the holographic image faded, Alonso began barking out orders in a voice raw with fury.

"Send to all commands. Battle stations. All WarShips are to finish furling their jump sails if the task can be accomplished quickly. If not, they are to cut their sails adrift. They will be recovered later. Once the fleet is free to maneuver, they are to engage the enemy as he closes."

This is not good, not Clanlike. It is the angry bear who is trapped by the hunters. I must master my anger. Alonso paused, taking deep breaths to clear away his wrath and focus his thoughts. Gradually, the aching tension he felt began to ease.

"Star Colonel, should we not send the *Winter Wind* back to Arcadia? Should we not get word to the Khans?"

Alonso rounded on the crewman who had spoken.

"*Neg!* They have named all of our ships as *isorla* in this fight. We will destroy these blasphemous *surats* who claim the mantle of the Star League. *Then,* once we have washed out the sacrilege of their presence in their own gore, we will roar out our triumph to Arcadia and to every other Clan homeworld and to all Clansmen wherever they are."

Before Alonso had finished speaking, a dozen voices erupted across the *Claw*'s bridge. Orders were passed to the other ships of the flotilla. Warriors were called to battle. Star Colonel Alonso surveyed the controlled pandemonium and sighed with pleasure. Though not every member of his crew was of the warrior caste, in that moment every Clansman in his tiny flotilla was preparing to fight.

Looking at the holographic representations of the Inner Sphere WarShips as they made their deliberate, ponderous way across the cold, lifeless space separating the two fleets, an unfamiliar cold shiver ran down his spine. Along with it came the realization that he, Star Colonel Alonso, was about to be involved in the first battle of a new phase of warfare.

His lips moved as he silently recited a portion of *The Remembrance:*

None stronger, none more fearless
Than the Ghost Bear.
None can hold against him.
What we know to be true:
The Ghost Bear conquers all.

The verses withered on his lips. For some indefinable reason, the high-sounding, powerful words left a bitter taste on his tongue. The sudden attack of doubt was so uncharacteristic, so startling that the lines seemed to ring as hollow as a spent shell casing.

Suddenly, Alonso felt a sensation he had never known in his short, violent life as a Clan warrior.

And the feeling was fear.

=== 23 ===

ISS **Ranger**
Unnamed Star System
Deep Periphery
15 December 3059
1810 Hours

Captain Mercia Winslow stood beside her command console aboard the *Ranger,* hand wrapped tightly around the grab-bar attached to the panel's steel housing. On the bridge viewscreen, she could easily make out the quartet of open white circles that the WarShip's targeting and tracking computers had drawn to represent unknown contacts. As soon as the targets were classed as hostile, the icons would automatically shift to red triangles.

The *Ranger* had come out of hyperspace thirty seconds after the task force flagship, but had been the first to spot the unidentified vessels. Being the nearest to the bogies, she had been ordered to close with the unknown ships. Winslow, along with everybody else in the task force, knew that the contacts were hostile. The task force had now traveled six hundred thirty light years beyond the coreward edge of the Outworlds Alliance. Except for the small Scout Class JumpShips piloted by the Explorer Corps, no Inner Space vessel had ever penetrated so deeply into uncharted space since the Exodus. Still, the task force had to follow the procedures developed during exercises prior to their departure, procedures honed to a fighting edge with each successive jump into enemy territory.

As the order to close with the unknowns came in, Winslow ordered the crew of her *Lola III* destroyer to battle stations. Immediately, a pale blue glow replaced the white light shed by the overhead panels. Winslow knew that the light change was supposed to make it easier for the sensor and weapons operators to pick out the fine details of their displays.

She also knew that the real reason ran all the way back to Terra's first global war. In the early days of naval warfare, the primitive submarines operated by the feuding nations would, by preference, launch their attacks at night. In those days, the ships used a soft red light to allow the captain's eyes to adjust to the dim light of the surface before looking through his periscope. In the later part of the twentieth century, they found that a blue light was easier on the crew's eyes. Winslow suspected that the real reason she was not getting a mild eye-strain headache was because most military planners and ship builders were a hidebound lot. If tradition called for blue lights when battle stations sounded, then blue lights there would be.

As her eyes were adjusting to the lighting change, a low, sexy female voice sounded throughout the ship.

"General quarters, general quarters. All hands, man your battle stations. This is no drill. General quarters, general quarters."

Winslow was less annoyed by blue lights than she was by the seductive tones of the computer-generated announcement. She was aware of the years of research indicating that crew members, male and female alike, paid more attention to the husky female voice than the sharp, raspy, male bellow popularized by endless trivids and holodramas. That didn't stop her from feeling irritation at the nonexistent woman's unnecessarily suggestive quality.

It wasn't a strangely misplaced jealousy, she told herself again and again. Winslow was a good-looking woman by anyone's way of reckoning. Young, fine-featured, with long, shiny chestnut hair pulled into a tight braid at the base of her neck. She looked more like an actress in a low-budget holovid playing the part of a naval officer than the genuine article. No, Mercia Winslow disliked the phantom seductress because this was war, and war was a serious business.

One by one, the various departments reported in, using the same format heard for centuries on ships of war.

"Weapons officer reports all stations manned and ready."

"Engineering reports all stations manned and ready."

And so it went, until her executive officer, Commander Jackson Ross, said, "All departments report stations manned and ready, Captain."

"Very well, Mr. Ross." Winslow gestured toward the flickering white circles. "Engage maneuvering drive. Close to firing range with the targets."

"Captain." That was the voice of the chief petty officer manning the long-range sensor panel. "I make the unknowns to be one *Invader* Class JumpShip and three WarShips: two *Whirlwind*s and one *Congress*. All bear the markings of Clan Ghost Bear. The targets are furling their jump sails. Looks like they're going to make a run for it."

"Or close for a fight," Ross put in from his station next to the helm panel.

"Mr. Held, are we close enough for a visual?"

"Yessir," the sensor chief responded. "On screen now."

"Captain, the lead *Whirlwind* has cut her sail adrift. All three WarShips have turned onto an intercept bearing. I think they mean to engage."

"What about the *Invader*?"

"She's still furling her sail." Held never took his eyes off his displays. "Hey, I've got a power spike in her engineering section. I think she's trying to hot-load her jump engines. Captain, she's trying to get away."

Winslow flinched slightly at the news. If the *Invader* was successful in diverting power from her fusion engines to her hyperspace drives, the ship could jump outsystem before the *Ranger* could close to effective firing range. On the other hand, if the technicians working in the hot, cramped confines of the JumpShip's engine room weren't excessively careful, they could inflict serious damage on the fusion plant and jump drives. Whether they'd make it or not depended greatly upon the skill of the Clan ship's engine techs, and how much of a charge they'd been able to collect with their jump sail.

Winslow turned slightly, until she could see Lieutenant Commander Fontanazza, the weapons system officer, out of the corner of her right eye.

"Mr. Fontanazza, lock the White Sharks onto the *Invader*. We don't want her escaping."

"Yessir." The Com Guard officer's fingers flew over the weapons control panel. Like Winslow, Fontanazza was a woman. Naval tradition stretching back centuries to the blue-water navies of Terra dictated that all officers, regardless of gender, be addressed as "Mister."

"Sir," Fontanazza called as she finished her calculations. "Missile control reports that only the portside launcher will bear on the *Invader*."

"Very well." Winslow gritted out the words between clenched teeth. "Lock the portside Shark onto the target. Helm, come left fifteen degrees. Launch control, stand by to launch fighters. Gun crews, stand by to engage as your weapons bear.

"Mr. Held, call off range to target."

"Four-seven-zero kilometers, and closing."

"Mr. Fontanazza, fire the Shark when you've got optimum range for a good hit. Then reload and fire at will. Weapons will be free at three hundred-sixty kilometers."

"I do not care what your instruments tell you. I want those *stravag* drives charged, now!"

Star Captain Hector was livid. His close-cropped, white-blonde hair seemed to bristle with rage above his flashing cloud-gray eyes. It had been almost fifteen minutes since the *Ursus* reported the first faint traces of the electromagnetic pulse and infrared flare that accompanied an arriving JumpShip. Since that time, Hector had been railing at his engineering staff, mostly made up of free-birth technicians, pushing them to get the *Winter Wind*'s jump drives on line. He'd had no evidence that the incoming vessels were hostile, but no ship captain worth the name liked being caught lying helpless, with half-charged engines, by an incoming ship of unknown origin and possibly hostile intent. It sometimes happened that WarShips from one Clan would declare a Trial of Possession against those belonging to another. Not often, but often enough to make a good ship captain aware of the possible threat to his vessel.

The Star Captain had been living up to his name, treating the lower-caste techs with contempt that bordered on abuse. He could not boast that he understood the workings of an *Invader* Class JumpShip. All he knew was that the jump drives had to be fully charged before he could attempt to take his ship outsystem. He understood that by using the *Wind*'s jump sail, the engines would reach minimum usable charge in another five hours, but the unidentified WarShips appeared less than six hundred kilometers from the four-ship detachment. Though his vessel was not a WarShip, he ached to come to grips with the enemy. Only the understanding that he was charged with the safety of the *Winter Wind*'s passengers and cargo tempered Hector's lust for battle.

The *Winter Wind* had been detailed to transport three DropShips, each carrying scores of freeborn civilians being relocated to planets within the Ghost Bears Occupation Zone. He had a few Elementals aboard, simply because Clan military doctrine required the presence of security troops on all starships, whether they be combat vessels or no. Of his three DropShips, two were troop transports. The third was a *Broadsword,* loaded with a Striker Star of mixed-weight OmniMechs.

Three WarShips had been detailed to protect the civilian cargo. The flagship *Shining Claw,* a *Congress* Class frigate, was the heaviest vessel in the flotilla. A pair of *Whirlwind* Class destroyers, the *Fire Fang* and the *Ursus,* rounded out the little fleet. A fleet that was now under attack.

"Star Captain, the nearest unknown now reads as a *Lola III* Class destroyer." There was a note of horror in the sensor technician's voice. "Her markings indicate that she's a Com Guard ship."

"What? Here?" Hector wheeled on the man, nearly smashing the tech into the control panel in his haste to get a look at his enemy. "It cannot be. The Inner Sphere *surats* have no WarShips, certainly none of that class. You must be mistaken. Check your instruments."

The image displayed on the small viewscreen gave the lie to Hector's words. The approaching vessel was still too far away for even the *Wind*'s powerful sensors to make out her fine details. But the odd circle star with downward pointing beams painted on her forward superstructure was very clear. Hector could scarcely bring himself to admit it, but the conclusion was inescapable. The intruding starships could be nothing but an Inner Sphere invasion force.

Hector leapt back to his command console, where he mashed a button on the ship's intercom with a thickly callused thumb.

"Gun crews to their stations. Charge the point defense weapons. Elementals stand by, we may be boarded."

Any reply was lost in the sensor operator's alarmed shout.

"Star Captain, I detect fire control radar. They have locked their missiles onto us."

"Range to target, three hundred kilometers." Chief Held called from his station aboard the *Ranger*. Then, more sharply. "Captain, he's got his jump drives on line."

"That's it. We can't wait." Mercia Winslow whirled to face her weapons officer. "Mr. Fontanazza, confirm missile lock and shoot."

Three seconds ticked by while Fontanazza checked her instruments.

"Lock confirmed . . . missile away."

The *Ranger* trembled faintly as the forty-ton missile streaked from its launch tube.

For the first time in nearly two hundred years, an Inner Sphere WarShip had fired its weapons in anger.

"Launch, launch, launch! The enemy has launched a missile! The missile has acquired and is homing!"

"Weapons officer! Status of the PPCs?" Hector didn't need the panic-tinged shout from the sensor operator. He had seen the launch flare himself.

"PPCs are charged and manned, Star Captain," came the reply from behind him.

"Target the missile and fire as the weapons bear."

The Ghost Bear warrior knew that the *Wind*'s particle projection cannons were simply larger versions of those weapons fitted to the OmniMechs in his hold. They were intended for intercepting stray asteroids and other such space debris that might puncture the relatively thin skin of the JumpShip. Compared to an asteroid, a missile was a relatively tiny object. The PPCs, in their big, clumsy turrets, stood no chance of successfully engaging the swiftly approaching missile. Still, the alternative was to simply await the shattering impact of the massive ship-killer. To sit idly, resigned to death, was not Clan-like.

"Starboard PPC firing," Crewman Adin announced from his position at weapons control. "PPC missed. Recharging."

Before Hector could respond to the calmly rendered death sentence, the White Shark missile slammed into the *Wind*'s starboard side just abaft the bridge module. The weapon, intended to penetrate several layers of hardened armor before exploding, ripped through the *Invader*'s thin skin, shattering hull plates as it went. Then, a fraction of a second later, the warhead detonated.

Eight thousand kilos of high explosive shredded most of the *Wind*'s minimal armor. The JumpShip shuddered under the impact. Star Captain Hector was thrown to the deck, to the accompaniment of a sickening crunch, as his left shoulder dislocated under his falling body.

"Freebirth!" Hector snarled in anger as he rolled to his feet, ignoring the fiery pain of his useless arm. "Damage report . . ."

The order went unfinished as a trio of heavy naval lasers drove lances of intense energy deep into the still-smoking wound left by the White Shark missile.

Again, the *Wind* seemed to flinch in pain and surprise. A loud metallic bang resounded through the ship.

"What in the name of Kerensky was that?" Hector screamed at the chief engineer.

The technician, a trueborn who had failed his training as an aerospace pilot, faced the fuming warrior, shock, fear, and sadness gouging deep furrows in his face.

"I am sorry, Star Captain. We have lost both our field initiator and drive controller. We cannot initiate jump sequence. The *Winter Wind* is dead."

"Aye," Hector said, gritting his teeth. The physical pain of his injuries meant nothing compared to the disgrace of having his ship disabled beneath him. "To all hands, stand by to repel boarders."

24

Battle Cruiser ISS Invisible Truth
Unnamed Star System
Deep Periphery
15 December 3059
1825 Hours

Morgan Hasek-Davion watched in fascination as the *Invisible Truth*'s holotank displayed the unfolding engagement in three-dimensional real-time images. The lead vessel of the task force was barely three hundred kilometers away from the Clan *Invader* when the image flickered. Several tiny flashes illuminated the holographic ship's arrow-shaped profile. The alphanumeric string, which revealed little to Morgan's decidedly ground-bound intellect, shifted. A number that had been quickly increasing from eighty to one hundred suddenly flicked down to zero.

"Message from *Ranger*," a communications tech called out. "Captain Winslow reports enemy JumpShip engaged and disabled." The discrete Morgan had been so absorbed with had indicated the percentage to which the *Invader*'s jump engines had been charged. The missile and laser hits had reduced that figure to zero. The ship would never jump again.

A cheer rang through the *Invisible Truth*'s bridge. It was quickly snuffed out by Commodore Beresick.

"Silence on deck!" he snapped. "That's one kill, gentlemen. May I remind you that there are still *three* WarShips out there. This fight's not over."

Properly chastened, the bridge crew turned their attention back to the flickering, glowing monitors. With a "harrumph" of satisfaction, Beresick leaned close to Morgan, a thin, boyish smile tugging at the corners of his mouth.

"Truth be told," he whispered. "I wanted to cheer too."

"Me too, Commodore. Me too," Morgan said.

As Beresick straightened, the proud grin vanished from his features.

"Mister Coote, message to the *Haruna*." The Commodore reeled off a set of instructions that were recorded, compressed, and transmitted to the Combine warship via a secure laser-based communications link. When boiled down into plain language, the message was simple. "Board and capture the *Invader*."

True to the motto emblazoned in both kanji and Western letters above the *Haruna*'s main viewscreen, Captain Randolph DeMoise did "Anticipate the command." Commodore Beresick had not even finished transmitting the order to close with the crippled Clan JumpShip when the *Kyushu* Class frigate suddenly accelerated toward the disabled *Invader*.

"All batteries, stand ready," DeMoise called out. There was a ring in his voice, like the sound of a steel blade being drawn for the first time; a beautiful, joyous, deadly sound. "That JumpShip is a fat prize, and I don't think the Clanners are going to let us take her for free."

"Captain, we have an enemy destroyer moving to cut us off. The Warbook IDs it as a *Whirlwind*."

DeMoise checked an auxiliary monitor set into his command console. The detailed identification program provided by the Explorer Corps indicated that the vessel trying to interpose itself between the *Haruna* and the crippled *Invader* was a pre-Star League design, originally intended as a fast-attack ship. Heavily armored and well armed, it massed about a hundred thousand tons less than his *Kyushu*. The destroyer, with its heavy naval lasers, autocannons, and Gauss cannons, would give the lightly armed *Haruna* a good, tough fight. If there was a bright spot in the data flickering on the screen before him, it was the *Whirlwind*'s absence of DropShip support. Lacking DropShips, and with berthing space for only two Stars of fighters, the destroyer couldn't throw up much of a defensive screen. The *Haruna* could support four DropShips and a full squadron of eighteen fighters. It would be a near thing, but DeMoise had confidence in his ship and crew.

Sixty kilometers ahead of the *Haruna,* and somewhat to starboard, the *Ranger* was making history again. After firing the shots that scored the first capital ship-to-capital ship kill of the offensive, Captain Mercia Winslow ordered the helm over thirty degrees to port. In seconds, the *Ranger* was arrowing directly toward the Clan WarShips.

"Captain," Lorraine Fontanazza said excitedly. Her voice held the knowledge that she had launched the attack that scored the first major kill of the campaign. "Range to the *Congress,* now two-eight-zero kilometers. That's inside missile range."

"Very well, Mr. Fontanazza," Winslow acknowledged. "Match generated bearings and shoot."

"Missiles locked . . . One away . . . Two away." As Fontanazza proclaimed the launch of each missile, the deck beneath Winslow's feet vibrated perceptibly from the energy necessary to propel nearly forty tons of steel and high explosives across the great distance to the target. "Missiles have acquired and are homing."

The *Ranger*'s viewscreen gave the impression that the bridge crew was looking out through the destroyer's nose. In truth, the bridge was buried deep within the WarShip's armored hull. The viewscreen, mounted on the bridge bulkhead opposite the liftshafts, showed a tactical display generated by the ship's powerful Delta Trac-VII tracking system.

Winslow stared, almost mesmerized, as a pair of computer-generated blue arrowheads streaked toward the small red icon marking the faraway *Congress.* As the wedge-like symbols reached the target and merged with it, Lieutenant Held reported the hits. A moment later, he indicated that the *Congress*' thick nose armor had shrugged off the same amount of damage that had crippled the *Invader* moments before. The frigate boasted more than ten times the armored protection of the lighter JumpShip. It would take more than a pair of White Shark missiles to inflict serious harm on the massive combat vessel.

Suddenly, a new set of scarlet markers appeared alongside the Clan WarShip.

"Captain, the enemy has detached DropShips, I read both to be *Union-C*s."

"Thank you, Mr. Held. Mr. Fontanazza, bring the forward laser batteries to bear on the DropShips. As soon as the missiles are reloaded, hit the *Congress* again." Winslow returned to her command station, where she checked a few readouts. "Mr. Held, range to target?"

"Range to *Congress*, now two-zero-zero kilometers. Range to DropShips, one-five-zero kilometers."

Winslow turned, gesturing sharply at a tall, impressively built officer, whose black skin and facial scars proclaimed that he had once been a noble of the Dulolur Clan of Alcor, in the Isle of Skye, before he joined the Com Guards.

"Mr. M'Basa, launch fighters."

"Aye, Captain," The *Ranger*'s flight control officer replied. Turning to his control panel, M'Basa relayed the order in deep, booming tones. "Attention, all fighters, launch now, now, now."

Several decks below, a hardened ferro-carbide bay door split into four quarters, each of which withdrew into the ship's armored hull. No sooner had the electromagnetic clamps securing the iris port in its open position thudded into place than the cavernous launch bay was filled with the silent glare of a heavily armed GTHA-500 blasting away into the perpetual night of space. Quickly, a second *Gotha* fighter rocketed from the *Ranger*'s hull, joining his wingman as he arrowed toward the onrushing *Union*s. In short order, four more pairs of aerospace fighters pushed high-G burns for the Clan DropShips.

"Badger, this is Too-tall," Lieutenant Donald Sandoval shouted to his wingman. "I'm gonna cut across the lead bandit's nose. Try to convince him to sheer off."

"Right with ya, Tee-Tee." Elmer "Badger" Sarti, who had earned his nickname because of a natural white streak in his black hair, was enjoying himself immensely. He'd signed on with the Com Guards three weeks too late to take part in the cataclysmic battle for Tukayyid. With the truce now in force, he'd feared he would never get his chance to fly against the Clans.

Sandoval lit off his fighter's overthrusters, bringing the ship to full power. Diving straight for the *Union-C*'s blunt nose, he unleashed a shattering double volley of long-range missiles. The DropShip seemed to shudder. Then, like a ring-hardened boxer shaking off the feeble slaps of an enraged child, the big spheroid vessel struck back.

Laser pulses snapped past Sandoval's left wing as he hurled the *Gotha* into a gut-wrenching split-S. Air hissed into the legs of his G-suit as the ship's computer fought to keep the pilot's blood in his head and chest. Only a few of the Clan DropShip's volley-fired missiles struck home, pitting the thick ferro-aluminum skin of the *Gotha*'s long, straight wings.

As Sandoval eased his stick back, pulling the fighter out of its twisting half loop, he caught sight of Badger's fork-hulled ship pressing home an attack against the *Union-C*'s missile-scarred nose. Faintly, against the blackness of space, Too-tall saw the actinic muzzle flare of a Gauss rifle. Sarti's *Gotha* trembled as the giant pellet of nickel-iron smashed into its armored belly. Missiles and laser pulses laced the fighter's fuselage and wings.

"Badger, break left!" Too-tall shouted into the commline. "I'll cover you."

Slowly, far too slowly, the damaged fighter lifted its starboard wing. Something was wrong.

"Don, I—"

Sarti never finished his panicked cry. A second glittering ball slammed into the *Gotha*'s already broken armor. Ferro-aluminum shards flew from the gaping wound. Threads of unthinkably powerful light speared the lurching ship. The *Gotha*'s commline circuits melted, transmitting their own destruction as an almost human scream of pain. At least that's what Sandoval told himself that heart-ripping sound had been. The ruined fighter skittered off, out of control, thick, greasy vapor trailing from gaping rents in its armor.

Furious, Sandoval whipped his ship into a Shandel turn. The maneuver was so tight, so abrupt that the GTHA-500's airframe moaned in protest. The pilot's vision dimmed, narrowed, as his G-suit strove to counteract the centrifugal force generated by the turn. As his sight cleared, Sandoval saw the huge, bulbous nose of the DropShip looming before him. With a twitch of rudder and stick, he brought the *Gotha*'s targeting cross hairs to rest over the glowing craters left in the Clanner's armor by his last attack pass. Heat spiked into his cockpit as Too-tall unleashed a murderous volley from his ship's full weapon load.

Lieutenant Commander M'Basa called out, "Captain, our fighters are engaging the lead DropShip."

"Very well, Mr. M'Basa." Winslow struggled to keep a neutral tone of detached interest. She failed. Excitement and fear sounded in her voice.

"Mr. Fontanazza, lock forward laser batteries on the trailing *Union*. Fire as your weapons bear."

In contrast to the spiraling, darting fighters, the huge WarShips seemed as slow and ponderous as an Odessan raxx. Lances of coherent light snapped and flickered from the *Ranger*'s nose, shattering the DropShip's armor as easily as a hammer smashes crystal. The *Union* tried to reply, but the *Ranger* was built to withstand more punishment than the smaller ship could inflict. The Clan DropShip slowly collapsed in on itself. Fire glowed through gaping rents in its armor.

"Missile launch!" Commander Held's voice thundered over the babble suffusing the *Ranger*'s control deck. "They got us locked."

"Hard a-starboard, down fifteen."

A product of long training and ingrained habit, the helmsman repeated the order, indicating that he understood the command and that he was complying with it.

The deck canted as the *Ranger* swung sharply away from her original course. Lacking point-defense weapons, the destroyer's only hope of avoiding a collision with the speeding packet of destruction lay in maneuvering so sharply that the missile lost track of its target. The tactic failed.

The fifty-ton missile slammed into the *Ranger* aft of her number three missile battery.

The detonation of twelve tons of high-explosive was devastating. Winslow was pitched off her feet, barely saving herself from a fall on the deck by catching the corner of her command console with one of her flailing arms.

It was Timothy Ross who recovered first.

Wiping away blood flowing from his nose, he shouted, "Damage report!" His voice cut through the cries of fear and alarm like a PPC through construction plastic.

"Damage control reports a hit to the portside armor. No breach, but we took a helluva whack."

As Captain Winslow barked out commands to bring the *Ranger* back onto an intercept heading, a flicker of motion caught her eye. There, swooping in from the upper right side of the viewscreen, came the Com Guard *Essex* Class destroyer *Starlight*. As the *Starlight* drove past the *Ranger,* its odd, backward-raked prow seemed to erupt into flame. Eight massive naval autocannons, the modern equivalent of the quick-firing dual-purpose guns of Terra's long-defunct blue water navies, spat death at the Clan WarShip.

The heavy shells struck glittering sparks off the *Congress'* flanks and back. If not for the sheer destructiveness of the barrage, the shimmering flashes and confetti-like glint of shattered armor drifting off into space might have been considered a beautiful sight.

Aboard the *Shining Claw,* there was nothing that could be considered beautiful. The barrage had opened several gashes in the frigate's pressure hull. A number of crewmen had died horribly, their bodies turning inside out as the atmosphere in those sections of the ship was blown away into space. Quickly, emergency pressure seals slammed into place. These measures, intended to save lives, inflicted at least one casualty. A damage-control technician, a fraction of a second too slow to react, dove through a hatchway, only to have his legs amputated by the closing seal.

In a daring, desperate move, Star Colonel Alonso ordered the *Claw* brought about. Summoning all the thrust her engines could provide, the seven-hundred-meter long ship drove between the converging shapes of her Inner Sphere tormentors. As she ran past the bows of the enemy ships, which were swinging in a vain attempt to follow her maneuver, Alonso called out an order.

"All broadside guns, fire at will."

Laser, autocannon, and missile fire licked out from the *Claw*'s narrow flanks. Armor-piercing shells blasted the *Essex*'s nose, sending a shudder through her 600,000-ton frame. The *Lola III* fared better. The damage inflicted by her missiles, and the *Essex*'s guns, had crippled some of the *Claw*'s starboard side weapons.

In the half-real, miniature world of his holotank, Alonso nodded in satisfaction. His audacious gamble had paid off. The *Essex* destroyer had been staggered by the devastating broadside, and seemed to be shearing off to recover. The *Lola,* faster and more powerful, had fallen victim to its own inertia. Unable to turn quickly enough to follow the *Claw* through her attack run, the *Lola* was now trying to reverse her turn, to bring her broadside guns into action. Alonso smiled grimly. Let the Inner Sphere *surat* try.

"Helmsman, hard to port, up forty."

The man strapped into a heavily padded chair sang out his acknowledgment of the order. Against an artificial resistance, which mounted the farther the control yoke was moved away from a neutral center position, the helmsman swung the giant WarShip into a hard left turn, at the same time pulling the yoke back against his chest.

Standard Ghost Bear procedures said that the maximum up angle for a *Congress* Class frigate was thirty-five degrees. Any more than that and a captain risked inflicting stress damage on the ship's massive, but rigid, spine. Fortunately, the ship's designers weren't her commanders. Alonso knew that the *Claw* could withstand an up angle of up to fifty-five degrees before the inertia-induced stress would begin to cause structural damage.

As the big ship turned through one hundred thirty-five degrees, Alonso ordered the pilot to ease his helm into a more standard turn.

"Attitude control, roll one-eighty."

Ponderously, the frigate revolved around her long axis. The maneuver had brought the *Claw* out of her turn above, ahead, and slightly to the right of the enemy *Lola,* with her relatively undamaged port side facing the destroyer. The *Essex* was somewhere off the *Congress*' starboard quarter, probably still licking its wounds.

"Freebirth! Look at that!"

The cry came from the ship's chief weapons officer.

Dragging his attention away from the *Lola,* Alonso turned just in time to witness the awesome spectacle of a *Cameron* Class battlecruiser going into combat.

* * *

"All gunnery stations, weapons free, that is weapons free."

A few hundred kilometers off the *Invisible Truth*'s starboard bow, the flat, rectangular bulk of a *Whirlwind* Class destroyer was on the receiving end of a fusillade of PPC fire and autocannon shells. No sooner had Commodore Beresick passed the "weapons free" order than every gunner aboard the huge battle cruiser locked his sights on the much smaller enemy vessel. A powerful Killer Whale anti-ship missile slammed into the Clan ship's hull, but the heavily armored WarShip shrugged off the damage, replying with its own blast of laser and autocannon fire.

"Minimal damage, Captain," a technician called from the bridge station, where he was monitoring the ship's condition. Beresick waved in acknowledgement.

"Commodore, the *Haruna* is closing with the *Invader*."

Beresick nodded. He was too busy watching his own battle.

That didn't stop the *Haruna* from driving closer to the crippled Clan JumpShip.

Morgan, having no such constraints, was enthralled by the scene portrayed in miniature by the *Invisible Truth*'s holotank. To one side of the battle area, the *Ranger* was engaged in a deceptively graceful ballet with the Clan *Congress*. Occasionally, one or both of the tiny vessels would flash when its opponent scored a hit. The *Starlight* seemed to be recovering from her encounter with the Clan frigate, and was swinging around to rejoin the fight. Some distance ahead of the icons representing the *Invisible Truth* and the *Whirlwind,* bearing the blue-gray colors of Clan Ghost Bear, the *Haruna,* impelled by its massive Terada drives, brushed past the second enemy *Whirlwind.* The Clan *Whirlwind* had tried in vain to interpose itself between the *Haruna* and the crippled *Invader.* In turn, the Clan WarShip had been intercepted by the *Antrim* and a pair of *Avenger* Class assault DropShips.

Despite his fascination, Morgan battled with a growing sense of frustration. At Meribah, he'd been locked in a JumpShip hovering above that system's star, unable to join the MechWarriors in their assault on the pirate base. Now, in the fleet's first engagement with the Clans, he was completely out of his element, a ground-pounder among starship crewmen. Even his access to the holotank was limited by Commodore Beresick and the *Truth*'s tactical officer, who needed that particular instrument more than he did.

It was maddening. Here he was, one of the most experienced, most decorated combat officers in the Inner Sphere, locked in a battle where he could do little but offer moral support.

"Captain, the *Whirlwind* is in PPC range."

"All right. Warn him to get out of our way." Randolph DeMoise's calm was beginning to erode in a flood of excitement, adrenaline, and fear.

Several decks above his head, the coils of the *Haruna*'s Super-Rand heavy naval PPC flared with lightning-bright intensity. A coruscating beam of energy lashed out through the weapon's focusing head, striking the armor belt protecting the *Whirlwind*'s port short-range missile battery.

Undaunted by the energy blast, the Clan destroyer replied to the frigate's attack with a spear of laser light.

"Fighters! Oh-six-two neg ten."

"I see them," the *Haruna*'s chief gunnery officer responded with a coolness he didn't feel in his guts. Flipping a series of switches, he brought the *Haruna*'s point-defense weapons on line. Long-range missiles, similar to those used by BattleMechs, but capable of hitting targets at far greater ranges, reached out to swat an inbound fighter. The tiny craft bucked under the impact, but recovered quickly, only to be blown out of existence by a pair of laser blasts. As the twisting Clan fighters, identified at last by the *Haruna*'s Warbook program as *Visigoth*s, pressed home their attack, a series of small pulse lasers and multi-barrel autocannons spat streams of death into their path. Two more OmniFighters were reduced to glowing wreckage, but the rest swooped in across the *Haruna*'s back, leaving chipped and broken armor in their wake.

One of the *Visigoth* pilots must have spotted the long, dagger-like shape of the *Bisan* nestled against the *Haruna*'s forward docking collar. With his wingman in tow, the pilot flung his ship into a tight, rolling turn. For moment, the *Visigoth* was "on its back," the pilot looking *up* through his canopy at the dark gray warship. Then the *Visigoth* whipped itself upright again, vibrating as the heavy autocannon mounted in its nose spat a string of tracers into the *Haruna*. The OmniFighter's forward motion walked the strobing explosions across the *Haruna*'s broad back and into the nose armor of the docked assault ship. Lasers and short-range missiles widened the destruction.

"Bloody, damn . . ." the *Bisan*'s chief gunner rasped beneath his teeth. Angrily punching an override, which slaved all of the ship's weapons to his panel, the chief, a veteran of the Clan War, locked the DropShip's targeting sensors onto the drive flare of the retreating fighter. For a second, he hesitated, while the computer chewed on the optimum targeting solution, then fired.

Two heavy Gauss slugs smashed square into the *Visigoth*'s fuselage beneath its anhedral tailplane. The missiles and autocannon rounds that followed finished the job. The *Visigoth* disintegrated before the pilot had a chance to eject.

More laser and PPC fire slashed into the *Haruna*'s forward superstructure. The big ship shuddered under the impact of the Clanner's heavy shells. One supersonic Gauss slug slammed into the armor protecting the ship's forward starboard launch bay. Structurally, the damage was light, but the impact threw a scare into the launch crew. One young assistant technician panicked and ran toward the bay's number three escape pod. Unable to calm him, Petty Officer Third Class Jack Piet subdued the terrified youth with a well-intentioned blow that broke the astech's jaw.

On the control deck, Captain DeMoise continued to direct fire against the Clan WarShip. Several times, he considered maneuvering the *Haruna* to bring her powerful broadside guns into play. Once, he even opened his mouth to give the order. He broke off without speaking. An experienced officer, he knew that the only chance they had of capturing the *Invader* intact lay in delivering the DEST teams to the target vessel before the Clanners had a chance to entrench themselves in her narrow cabins and passageways.

Another volley of gunfire shook the *Haruna*.

"Captain, we can't take much more of this."

Before Randolph DeMoise could reply, an immense, midnight-blue disk shot across the viewscreen. At first,

DeMoise thought a fighter launched by another ship in the task force had arrived to share in the dogfight swirling around his ship. Then he realized that if it were truly a *Thrush* Class light fighter, the pilot would have had to pass so close to the *Haruna*'s sensor array that he would risk shearing it off. No, this was something else.

The transponder code painted alongside the ship's icon told the story, as did the blast of fire the vessel delivered against the *Whirlwind* at point-blank range. The new arrival was an assault DropShip, an *Avenger*. As the oddly configured vessel pulled out of its attack dive, it was joined by another of the same class.

Before DeMoise could respond to that unforeseen development, fate dealt him another favorable card.

"*Haruna,* this is *Antrim.*" The words were clipped and too loud, but sounded sweeter by far than any music DeMoise had ever enjoyed. "We'll take care of the *Whirlwind.* You bust through their line and grab that JumpShip."

Swinging in from the right side of the viewscreen came the stubby, bullet-shaped silhouette of a *Fox* Class corvette, the letters ANTRM glowing next to her tactical icon.

"All right," DeMoise growled under his breath. He barked, "Helmsman, lay us alongside the *Invader.* Full ahead."

Moments later, Lieutenant Commander Kobayashi reported in formal, stilted tones. "Captain, we are through the enemy's defensive line."

"Very well." Captain De Moise's reply was as formal, but less stilted. "Tell the *Bisan* to make ready for breakaway."

25

Draconis Combine WarShip Haruna
Unnamed Star System
Deep Periphery
15 December 3059
1840 Hours

A giant invisible hand pressed Major Michael Ryan down in his seat. If he had been clad in the old black armored jumpsuit favored by the holovid industry when portraying members of the Draconis Elite Strike Teams, he would have come away with deep pressure bruises, as the acceleration couch's thin padding failed to prevent the seat's metal frame from digging into the back of his thighs. Ryan had lost count of the number of operations he had come out of wearing the odd horizontal bruises caused by the sudden, jolting acceleration of a DropShip blasting free of its parent vessel.

A faint tremor of anxiety mixed with exhilaration ran along his spine. He and his team had gone up against the Clans a dozen times before, and each time they had come out more-or-less intact. This time, there was something different about the attack. It wasn't just the idea of combat aboard a starship, though that brought its own problems. Ryan's men had been trained to fight in every conceivable environment, and he was certain that they would acquit themselves admirably. It was something else, something more primal, that sent an unaccustomed shiver through his frame.

It was pride. Pride, in the idea that he was fighting for something larger than himself, larger than the Draconis Combine, although he was in a sense serving the Dragon as never before. He and his men were taking part in a grand crusade, not for wealth or possession, or for some half-mystical goal like a renewed Star League. They were going into battle against the greatest threat that mankind had ever faced, to destroy the enemy.

Michael Ryan smiled grimly.

In the aftermath of the fighter attack, DeMoise held a swift conference with Major Ryan and the *Bisan*'s captain, Maeda Ge. DeMoise would have preferred to run the WarShip right up alongside the disabled Clanner, possibly using the *Haruna*'s bulk to shield the small battle taxis as they made the dangerous crossing to the target vessel. Commodore Beresick had ordained otherwise. With an enemy *Whirlwind* and its associated fighters snapping at the *Haruna*'s heels, the fleet commander ordered the *Haruna*'s captain to launch the *Bisan* at one hundred kilometers, then turn to engage the Clan destroyer.

Putting the launch off as long as he dared, DeMoise carried the *Bisan* almost to within touching distance before ordering the breakaway. By that time, the firepower of the *Haruna*'s close-defense weapons, combined with the DropShip's lighter guns, had driven off most of the pursuing Clan fighters.

On the *Bisan*'s small, four-man bridge, Ge pulled back hard on his control yoke, at the same time shoving the throttle fully forward. White fire flared from the dagger-shaped ship's drive nozzle. Leaping forward with the acceleration of a fighter, the *Achilles* Class vessel cleared the boxy length of the *Haruna* in less than three seconds.

"Rick, how far out are we?"

"Eight-five kilometers, closing fast." Richard Sule, the ship's sensor tech, studied his displays for a moment. "*Tai-i* . . . ah, Captain, I see drive flares along the *Invader*'s docking module. I think the bad guys are popping their DropShips. Looks like a couple of *Union*s. Wonder why they aren't launching number three?"

Ge spared the long-range sensor display a fleeting glance.

At less than one hundred kilometers, the *Bisan*'s scanners had enough resolution to pick out the angular, brick-like mass of a third DropShip, still clamped securely to the *Invader*'s spindle-shaped hull.

"I don't know, Rick. Right now, I think we should be glad they're holding her back."

The blood staining Star Captain Hector's close-cropped blond hair had nearly stopped flowing from the ugly gash opened in his scalp by the edge of the command console. Moments before, a blast from the unknown enemy frigate had shaken the *Winter Wind* like a child's toy. The impact had hurled Hector to the deck, his skull grazing the corner of the control panel.

"Say that again?" Hector's voice held a note of challenge and threat.

"Star Captain, the *Ice Dart* failed to launch. Damage control crews are working on her right now, but they do not believe they will be able to free her in time. They say that the docking collar was warped by that last hit."

"Freebirth." Hector muttered the word between clenched teeth.

"Star Captain, without the *Ice Dart* to help screen this ship, I am afraid there is little we can do to prevent the enemy from boarding us, or destroying us at his leisure." Had he not been a trueborn, the *Wind*'s executive officer would have cringed at the idea of bringing Hector such a report.

"So shall it be," was the Star Captain's only reply.

"Watch it. They're splitting up, trying to flank us."

"I see them, Lieutenant," Maeda Ge replied to Sule's warning cry.

Faster than their shape and size would suggest, the big *Union Class* DropShips bore down on the *Bisan*. In a one-on-one fight, a *Union*'s armor and heavy weapons load would make it more than a match for an *Achilles* Class, but for the assault ship's superior speed and maneuverability. Facing a pair of the big spherical vessels left the *Bisan* at a disadvantage.

"Captain has the for'ard guns." Cutting in an override, Ge routed the firing controls for all of the DropShip's forward-facing weapons through his panel. Making delicate adjustments to the *Bisan*'s helm, she worked to bring the vessel's devastating forward weapons to bear on the leading Clan vessel.

The Clanner was coming straight and hot, bearing down on the *Bisan* as though he intended to run the DropShip down. In response, Ge twitched the stick and throttle, swinging the narrow aerodyne ship into a long shallow arc across the leading *Union*'s path, and away from his partner. The *Union* tried to follow the maneuver, but the nimble *Bisan* evaded him easily. Autocannon bursts and laser bolts dug small pits in the *Bisan*'s wings as she ran past the Clanner's nose.

Suddenly, Ge flung the *Bisan* into a tight pirouette. The ship's spaceframe groaned as she came around like a dog chasing her tail. There, before him, loomed the spherical bulk of the Clan *Union*. Ge laid the pad of his right forefinger on the control yoke's firing stud. An adjustment down and left brought the targeting pipper to bear on the big DropShip's center of mass.

Four strokes of silent lightning blazed into the *Union*'s armored flanks. Armor shattered and spalled away under the intense impact of heavy Gauss slugs. Autocannon shells and missile warheads combined to finish the devastation. The *Union* staggered, thin vapor streaming from deep cracks in her armor.

"All right, launch the fighters," Ge ordered. "Maybe they can take some of the heat off us for a while."

Second later, in response to Ge's order, the *Bisan*'s forty-five-hundred-ton bulk thrummed sharply as a pair of updated *SL-15R Slayer* fighters rocketed clear of their launch bays. Turning abruptly, the eighty-ton delta-winged attack ships raced across the void between the *Bisan* and the damaged *Union*.

"Major Ryan." Ge's voice crackled from the commline. "Get ready. We're going to swing around for another pass. As soon as we're in position, we're going to kick your taxis loose." The line went dead before Ryan had a chance to say anything.

As the *Bisan* rolled onto an approach vector, a pair of dark gray *Turk* fighters blasted free of the damaged *Union*'s cratered hull. Maeda Ge watched in horrified fascination as a black and red *F-700A Riever,* launched from the *Haruna* to support the *Bisan*'s approach to the Clan

JumpShip, cut directly across the lead Clan fighter's nose. The Ghost Bear wouldn't even have to maneuver to line up his shot.

Paired flights of corkscrewing missiles lashed across the *Riever*'s fuselage, followed by a flickering lance of laser fire. The Kurita pilot tried to maneuver away, but a gleaming ball of nickel iron blasted into the *F-700*'s tail, ripping the starboard rudder free of its moorings. Ordinarily, the loss of the tail element would not have affected an aerospace fighter, as long as it did not attempt to enter a planet's atmosphere. In any ship other than the *Riever*, this would have been the case. The Marik engineers who designed the upgraded *F-700R* version had replaced the old exhaust ports on the *Riever*'s engines with a specially designed steerable nozzle. This nozzle linked to the same controls that moved the ship's stabilizer, rudders, and other control surfaces during operation within a planet's atmosphere. The control linkage, not destroyed by the *Turk-A*'s volley, refused to acknowledge that the ship was operating in freefall, and that the second rudder was still there and functional. The balky electronics package also refused to allow either the pilot or the flight computer to alter the angle of steerable nozzles.

Ge could imagine the Combine fighter pilot cursing the Marik technicians who'd refitted the *Riever*, when a second volley of missiles and Gauss slugs tore the heart out of his shot-up fighter. As the ship broke up around him, the *Riever*'s pilot ejected. Ge prayed against hope that his tiny escape capsule would be found in the vast, empty darkness.

"Star Captain, there is an *Achilles* Class DropShip bearing down on us, at three-two-zero, mark one."

Hector, who had run out of curses, stared balefully at the tiny, dagger-like icon speeding silently toward his crippled JumpShip. The *Wind*'s PPCs were doing their best to slow or turn the enemy craft, but the *Achilles* shrugged off the damage as if the charged-particle streams were nothing more than a spray of water.

The assault ship's icon seemed to merge with the *Wind*'s as the smaller vessel darted past the JumpShip. Scant moments later, the *Invader*'s hull rang with a deep, hollow *boom*. A freeborn crewman let out a yelp of surprise as Hector's second-in-command reported that a pair of small combat transports had grappled with the *Winter Wind*. A few heartbeats later, the exec reported that Inner Sphere marines were storming aboard.

Hector merely nodded and recited the old proverb: "It is a good day to die."

"Here we go, Major!" Maeda Ge shouted over the commline.

Ryan was cut off in mid-acknowledgement.

At more than six hundred kilometers per hour, the *Bisan* streaked directly toward the bulbous nose and bridge section of the Clan *Invader*. When the *Bisan*'s navigation computer told him he was in the optimum position, Ge ordered the NL-42 battle taxis, which were nestled in the DropShip's small craft bay, to be launched.

As bumpy a ride as the *Bisan*'s breakaway from the *Haruna* had been, there was no comparison to the buffeting Ryan and his team suffered when the tiny steel ball of a battle taxi was kicked out of the *Bisan*'s armored launch bay.

"Hang on, Major!" Yacob Grimm shouted from the command deck. With gut-wrenching speed, the little taxi swung through a ninety-degree arc, until it was literally flying backward. Grimm fired the ship's maneuvering drive, chopping its speed dramatically. The two-hundred-ton craft shuddered as the powerful engines strove to override the momentum imparted by the *Bisan*'s high-speed dash along the Clan JumpShip's needle-like spine. In seconds, the tiny craft had slowed almost to a stop. Grimm yanked the throttle back, cutting the NL-42's thrust to almost zero as he worked to line the taxi up with the Clan ship's forward pressure hatch.

"Fire the grapples."

A thump, more felt than heard, marked the launch of a pair of large rocket-driven cylinders. Though they weren't weapons, the projectiles carried a payload as dangerous to the *Winter Wind* as any explosive warhead. A few meters from the hull of the Clan *Invader*, a tiny radar set triggered the grappling unit's powerful electromagnetic grapples.

"Grapples set. Reels turning." Gunner's Mate Erin Hoey looked up from her weapon panel. The magnetic hooks were tethered to the NL-42 by fifty meters of high-tensile strength steel tow cable. As powerful winches mounted in the taxi's lower structure began reeling in the cables, the transport pod began to settle against the *Invader*'s hull. Grimm fed a little more fuel to the ship's attitude controls to cushion the jarring stop, which, in the first training exercise he had flown with DEST Team Six, had sent the commandos tumbling to the deck of the DropShip's bay. This time—the result of long practice at Defiance, and while the fleet was recharging its jump engines at dozens of star systems since—Grimm brought the little taxi to rest with only the mildest of bumps.

"Lock the winches," Grimm ordered, then switched to Ryan's channel. "We're down and locked. Go!"

26

NL-42 Battle Taxi
Unnamed Star System
Deep Periphery
15 December 3059
1850 Hours

Even before the pilot had begun his excited shout, Peter
Wu yanked open the taxi's aft hatch and leapt out onto the
Invader's hull. Privates Nakamura and Akida followed
quickly, the latter carrying a large ballistic nylon satchel.
Seconds later, the taxi's superstructure thrummed as the
shock wave generated by five kilos of pentaglycerine cast
into a highly efficient shaped charge smashed the pressure
hatch's lock. As the portal cycled open, Ryan felt a second and third explosion through the soles of his feet.
Through the NL-42's open hatch, he saw Wu launch himself feet first into the open pressure hatch.

"Hatchway clear." The young commando's voice was
tight with adrenaline and the joy of battle.

"All right! Go! Go! Go! Ronin One is going in." The rest
of the assault party had already joined Wu inside the airlock
before Ryan's armored feet touched the *Invader's* hull. There,
the troopers could use more subtle methods for opening
the hatch. Leaving his bag of explosive tricks alone, Akida
simply yanked open a circuit panel, grateful for the Kage
suit's enhanced strength, and hot-wired the hatch override.

The DEST team swarmed out of the lock and into the

corridor beyond, where they were met by laser fire. A detachment of the Clan ship's security force had assembled in the crew's common area adjacent to the pressure lock. Five armored Elementals launched an attack on the invading commandos.

"*Chiksho!*" Ryan cursed as a burst of automatic weapon fire stitched a line of shallow divots in his Kage suit's breastplate. The suddenness and intensity of the Elemental's onslaught caught him by surprise. He had expected resistance, but the Clanners seemed driven more by rage than by a desire to defend their ship.

Kashira Raiko desperately pumped a half dozen shots into a charging Elemental before the hulking warrior pitched over onto the deck. The Clan warrior fell less than a meter from Raiko's position. Charlotte Sior and Ralph Carter, acting, as always, like a single pair of hands, laced the torso armor of a second Clanner with highly accurate laser fire. Only the combined assault of two Blazer rifles, firing in rapid volleys, dropped the massive trooper before he could fire his third shot. When they checked the downed warriors, the DEST troopers saw the thick black sludge that characterized the Elemental suit's reaction to severe trauma, flowing into the wounds. The Elemental which Raiko believed he had killed, or at least incapacitated, was struggling to rise. He finished the Clanner off with a point-blank laser blast to the head.

In the face of the sudden, unexpected ferocity of the strike team's response, the remaining Elementals took shelter in the open doorways of the crew quarters. Ryan's men were forced to root them out. Twice, laser bolts flashed uncomfortably close as he directed the assault. The scientists who had developed the Kage suits had tried to assure him that the armor could not be damaged by most anti-personnel weapons, but Ryan knew better. There was no body armor that was absolute proof against all small arms. The desperate street fighting in Imperial City during the Smoke Jaguar invasion of Luthien had proved that. It was proved again, right in front of him, when another Elemental was hurled back against a bulkhead, his armor shattered by a high-explosive armor-piercing grenade from the launcher carried by Teji Nakamura.

Ryan was grateful that the Elementals were limited to using light anti-personnel weapons rather than the more powerful 'Mech-killers their suits had been designed to carry. Small lasers, heavy machine guns, or flamers stood a good chance of damaging one or more of the JumpShip's vital systems. The short-range missiles normally carried in the twin triangular shoulder mounts were likewise useless. Their big, armor-piercing warheads might penetrate the ship's thin armor, opening a breach in the hull.

The DEST troopers were similarly limited in their choice of weapons. Teji Nakamura had, rather vocally, expressed his desire to carry one of the new, man-portable Gauss rifles, until Ryan pointed out the effects of explosive decompression.

The last Elemental threw himself into an insane, berserker-like charge. Talon Sergeant Raiko showed why he had lived long enough to become one of the most senior non-commissioned officers in the DEST program. Even encumbered by the Kage suit's bulk, Raiko spun like a top. A sharp hum filled the air, followed by an unpleasant screech. The decapitated Elemental collapsed in a heap. The sergeant ended his graceful, almost dance-like movement in an en garde position, with his faintly glowing vibrokatana held above his head, the blade parallel to the deck.

"Are you finished, Sergeant?"

Seeing that his opponent was down, Raiko relaxed out of his *jodan* posture, nodded at his commander, smoothly returning the weapon to its sheath.

"Finished."

Ryan grinned behind his armored mask. "All right, move out."

Quickly, following the deck plan mapped out on their suits' navigational systems, the strike team set off for the JumpShip's bridge. Once, during that short trip, they were engaged by Clan security troops.

The attack left private Ralph Carter nursing a right leg lacerated by shell fragments and splinters of his armor. An unarmored crewman had opened fire on the team from the cover of a half-closed access hatch. Careless of what damage he might inflict on his own ship, the Clansman loosed a five-shot burst from a gyroslug carbine at the advancing commandos. Three of the mini-rockets impacted on Carter's Kage suit. Though the battle armor was designed to stop all but the heaviest of small-arms attacks, the laminated steel, plastic, and ceramic armor failed to completely deflect the high-velocity explosive-tipped slugs.

Carter let out a yelp of surprise and pain as his leg collapsed under him. Peter Wu, the team's advance guard, snapped off a burst of Blazer fire, but the ambusher had already dodged behind the heavy steel hatch cover. When Wu and Corporal Hollis darted forward to engage the Clanner at close range, he slammed the hatch in their armored faces.

"Dammit! He locked it," Wu growled, tugging with all of his suit-amplified strength.

"Don't worry, Pete," Kenichi Akida said, chuckling as he extracted a pre-packaged breaching charge from his carryall. "I remembered to bring the keys."

Carlotta Sior gave no attention to the vignette being played out at the hatch. She was kneeling beside Carter's damaged suit.

"Genki des, Lo," Carter snarled, more embarrassed than hurt. "I'm all right. He just peppered me, that's all."

"He more than just peppered you, boy," Sior gazed in shocked horror at the miniature craters in Carter's leg armor. "You got a couple of good-size holes in your suit. Thank God the whole ship isn't decompressed, or you'd be painted all over the inside of your armor by now."

"I tell you I'm fine, Lo." Carter slapped his partner's claw-hands away and struggled to his feet. "The medipack is taking care of the wound, and if you'll slap an armor patch over those holes, I'll be fine."

Before Sior could reply, the cry "Fire in the hole," sounded from her commline.

Three seconds later, a sharp bang, loud enough to be heard plainly through the suit's thick helmet, resounded in the passageway. Wu and Hollis dove through the shattered hatch, rolling to their feet in the area beyond. Sweeping the room, their weapons following their eyes, the troopers saw no sign of the Clanner, alive or dead.

Carter spat out a torrent of invective, calling down curses on his assailant and his family, forgetting that the ambusher, like all trueborn Clansmen, had no real parents or family, except for his or her sibkin all derived from the same eugenics program. Winding down, Carter's voice dropped to a wicked hiss.

"Good, that just means I get a chance to kill the beggar."

Sior paused in her efforts to apply the self-adhesive patch to Carter's suit.

"Ralph, I've never seen you like this."

"You've never seen me shot before. When someone puts a bullet in me, I take it kind of personally. It's one of my faults."

"Carter, you okay to stay with us?" Ryan's voice held a note of concern, both for the condition of his injured man and for the status of his mission.

"Yeah, boss. I'll be fine." Carter gestured at the new, black square of high-strength composite his partner had affixed to his suit. "Just as long as the bad guys don't take this patch as a mark to shoot at."

Ryan nodded, forgetting for a moment that his helmet and faceplate masked the gesture.

"Okay, move out. Wu, take the point."

The DEST team had only gone a couple of dozen meters when Ryan's helmet commline buzzed with an incoming message.

"Ronin One, this is Ronin Two. Primary objective secured. Casualties light. Ronin Two is moving against secondary objective."

The brief, cryptic message meant that Ronin Two, consisting of DEST Teams Four and Five, had managed to attack and seize the *Invader*'s engineering spaces without sustaining any serious casualties, and were now on their way to assault the JumpShip's docking bays. Ryan acknowledged the report, adding that he and his team were two decks below the bridge, *their* primary objective.

Ten minutes later, Ryan transmitted his own "objective secure" message. The bulk of the Elemental security force had settled into a defensive position in the tiny secure area just outside the JumpShip's bridge. The fighting had been short, fierce, and brutal. Three of the Elementals, including one whose armor bore the double gold bars of a Star Commander, were killed during the initial assault. Two more died in the close-quarters fighting that followed. The remaining three were badly wounded.

Ryan's team did not get away undamaged. Kenichi Akida was seriously injured when an Elemental grabbed his Kage suit by its folded stub wings, hurled him against the bulkhead, and rammed the fisted battle claw into the

DEST trooper's middle. Before the Clanner could finish the job, Raiko lopped off both of the massive Elemental's arms with a pitiless swipe of his vibrokatana. Akida dropped to the deck, writhing in agony, as the Talon Sergeant sent the Clanner to greet Kerensky in person, with a thrust so powerful that the slightly glowing tip of the high-tech katana came out through the back of the man's armor. Frank Hollis was nursing a couple of cracked ribs, inflicted when an Elemental, bigger than any he'd ever seen, back-handed him into a steel bulkhead. If not for the protection afforded by the suit, Hollis would have probably been killed. As it was, the communications operator had had the breath knocked from his lungs. He recovered in time to blast a pair of deep, steaming holes into the assailant's armor.

When DEST Team Six burst through the door onto the *Invader*'s bridge, they were met by a scene of chaos and destruction. The Elementals had sold their lives to give the bridge crew a few minutes to wreck every panel, display, control, and readout they could lay their hands on.

As Peter Wu forced open the locked door, a crewman lifted a heavy half-rifle. The powerful laser bolt struck Wu's right pauldron, leaving a deep furrow in the armored shoulder-piece and a slight burn on the trooper's upper arm. A few more shots were traded, with the unarmored Ghost Bears getting the worst of the bargain, before a large Clansman with blood-stained white hair got his crew under control.

For a moment, Star Captain Hector surveyed the blank, expressionless masks of the armored troops who had burst onto his bridge. He could not help but recall how much fear Clan Elementals had once struck into the weak hearts of the Inner Sphere barbarians. And now these freebirths had overcome him, but he felt no fear of them. He had seen the face of battle and death before, had lived with it all his life. No, he felt only shame that he had lost a valuable command to the barbarians he had once helped to conquer. He was only consoled by the knowledge that he and his bridge crew had erased or corrupted every bit of data in the ship's computer core that the Inner Sphere *surats* might find useful. To make matters worse for the barbarians, Hector and his crew had smashed as much of the bridge equipment as they could before the enemy had come crashing through the door.

He understood that destroying the expensive, delicate systems would be considered wasteful by strict Clan standards. Still, the *Winter Wind* was dead. Worse, she had been captured by barbarians. By wrecking every bridge system and dumping the contents of the ship's computer core, Hector made sure that the Inner Sphere technicians would be unable to use that vital data against the Clans. He allowed himself a bitter laugh at the thought.

Taking a deep breath, he stepped forward, head held high, hands spread in a gesture of peace.

"I am Star Captain Hector of Clan Ghost Bear. In accordance with your *batchall,* I formally surrender my vessel to you, and accept service as your bondsman."

As Michael Ryan shouldered his way through his troops, he felt a deep sense of pride at the accomplishment of his mission. He had fulfilled his duty to the Dragon in a way few had ever done before. He and his men had captured a Clan JumpShip with only light casualties.

With the touch of a button, he lifted the visor on his helmet. "Sir," he said to the Clansman who seemed to be the ship's captain. "I am Major Michael Ryan, Draconis Elite Team Six." Ryan almost stumbled over the words. Morgan-*sama* had passed instructions that any captured Clansmen were to be taken as bondsmen, but the formal words came hard to a warrior used to killing, rather than capturing an enemy. "I formally declare you and your ship *isorla*. You are now the property of the Star League, and Task Force Serpent."

Before Ryan or the Clanner could speak again, Raiko interrupted.

"Sir? The mission."

Ryan flushed slightly. In the excitement of capturing his objective, and the sudden necessity of dealing with a captured Clan officer, he had almost forgotten where he was.

"*Hai.* Talon Sergeant, you, Carter, and Hollis will remain here to watch the prisoners. The rest of us . . ."

"Ronin One, this is Ronin Two." The sudden squawk from the commline forced Ryan to break off his instructions.

"Two, this is One, go ahead."

"Ronin, One, Ronin Two has secured secondary objective. Sir, we need med-evac. We've got a few casualties. A couple of them are pretty bad."

"Very well, Two. Stand by in the docking bay. I'll call the *Bisan* in to take off the wounded."

27

Battle Cruiser ISS Invisible Truth
Unnamed Star System
Deep Periphery
15 December 3059
1925 Hours

Morgan was beginning to feel like a spectator as he watched the battle swirling around him, played out in exquisitely detailed miniature in the *Invisible Truth*'s holotank. Though he knew that men and women were struggling for their lives aboard the ships represented by the insubstantial replicas floating around him, he felt as though he were standing in the midst of a giant hologame.

He had often heard the criticism that war was rapidly becoming a contest played out on computers, by generals who had no more regard for the lives of their men than for the multitude of electronic ones and zeros shuffled around by kids playing *Immortal Warrior*. Morgan had never really believed the accusations leveled by those he called the "peace-at-any-price-so-long-as-I-don't-have-to-pay-it" crowd. But here, standing in the middle of the holographic representation of a battle, contributing nothing more than his approval, he wondered if the anti-military critics might not have something. He was aware that the days of honorable combat were gone. They had died a violent and noisy death centuries ago.

Well, the musket and muzzle-loading cannon were

gone, too, replaced by the laser and the PPC. And with them went the last vestiges of romance, the image of the "thin red line," and fighting for a glorious Cause.

Morgan shook his head angrily. *Pay attention, blast it. You still have a job to do,* he told himself, although he had no idea what that job was right now.

Watching the cold, deadly dance of WarShips and fighters through the electronic display of the *Invisible Truth*'s holotank had produced an odd detached feeling in Morgan, a detachment he didn't like. It was far too easy to look at the insubstantial projections of the combat vessels and see them as mere objects. It was far too easy to forget that there were living men and women aboard the ships represented by the tiny flickering images, men and women for whom *he* was responsible.

Again burning frustration seared his heart. He had been a warrior all his life, used to taking the reins of battle in his own hands. Now, here, aboard one of the most powerful WarShips ever built, he was nothing more than a spectator.

Several times Morgan opened his mouth to give an order or make a suggestion, but closed it again, the words unspoken. He was completely out of his element. His vast store of tactical knowledge, built up through long years of combat experience and command, was based on ground-based 'Mech actions. In a battle between capital ships, it was useless.

Briefly, he considered departing the bridge, leaving management of the battle in Commodore Beresick's obviously capable hands.

No dammit, he told himself angrily, frustration giving even his thoughts a rough edge. *I'm still the commander of this task force, and my place is here.*

Returning his attention to the battle, he watched as the Clan *Whirlwind* rolled along her long axis, presenting her relatively undamaged starboard side to the *Invisible Truth*. The WarShips had been engaged in a close-quarters battle that alternately resembled a graceful waltz and a brutal slugging match. The Clan *Whirlwind*, with her superior speed and maneuverability, danced around the ponderous battle cruiser, pricking the *Truth*'s hide with weapons better suited to destroying fighters than attacking a capital ship. The *Truth*'s gunners did their best to answer the volleys of missile and laser fire, but the Clan ship captain always managed to evade the worst of the cruiser's attack.

Twice, the *Truth* had managed to deliver a devastating broadside to the darting, circling destroyer, but the Clan *Whirlwind*'s heavy armor had blunted most of the damage. It was like a battle between a cat and a bear. The cat was faster, more agile, but the bear was stronger, and only needed one good bite.

"He's swinging around again!" the *Truth*'s tactical officer shouted. "Cannons firing."

On a secondary monitor, Morgan saw minute flashes spring from the Clan WarShip's bow.

"For what we are about to receive, the Lord make us truly thankful," one of the bridge crewmen quipped, seconds before a volley of autocannon shells slammed into the *Truth*'s port bow.

Armor shattered. The *Invisible Truth* trembled under the impact of the explosive shells. The *Truth* replied to this attack with a PPC blast.

The stream of high-energy protons cut into the Clan destroyer's armor like a blowtorch. The ship staggered under the blow, as she failed to slough off the fire savaging her ferro-carbide skin. The thick armor held, but a steaming crater forward of her secondary sensor array told how badly she'd been hit.

"Helm, twenty degrees to starboard. All guns, fire as you bear!" Beresick shouted. Seconds later, a pair of gray-painted missiles left a thin layer of black soot on the *Truth*'s outer hull as they leapt free of their launch rails. For sixteen long seconds, Morgan watched the missiles' drive flares burn their way across the gap between the *Invisible Truth* and the Clan destroyer. Then, there was a brief explosion, as bright as the flare of a match. It faded.

"Missile number one intercepted and destroyed," the missile control officer sang out. A heartbeat later, a brighter fireball flashed into existence, expanded until it seemed to engulf the target vessel, and died out.

"Number two, direct hit."

Before the Clan *Whirlwind* could recover from the effects of the missile's warhead, a firestorm of particle, laser, and autocannon fire blasted into her hull. Armor spalled away in chunks the size of ground cars.

"Sensors indicate major damage to target vessel," the sensor tech reported.

"Put it on the screen," Beresick commanded. As the chief sensor operator complied with the order, Beresick rose from his seat to watch.

The Clan WarShip's armor had been breached. Dense clouds of ice crystals jetted away from deep holes reaching into the personnel spaces of the ship. Miniature lightning storms from the severed power feeds played across great scars in her hull. And, all along her six-hundred-meter length, fires burned through shattered viewports and rents in her hull. The total effect made it seem as though the destroyer was consuming herself in her death throes.

"Oh, my God." Morgan's whisper was a horrified prayer for a dying ship.

Out of control, the Clan *Whirlwind* canted sharply to starboard, dropping by her head as she rolled.

Beresick punched a switch on his command console.

"Clan *Whirlwind,* this is the Star League WarShip *Invisible Truth*. Abandon your vessel. We are standing by to take on survivors."

There was no reply.

"*Whirlwind,* this is no time for Clan heroics. Your ship is dead, let us take on survivors . . . *Whirlwind,* do you copy?" Cursing, Beresick slammed his fist down on the panel, shutting off the broad-band hail. "That evil, bloody-minded Clan bastard! He won't answer, even to save his crew!"

"Commodore, our comm system is out," shouted a horror-stricken crewman.

"What?"

"Sir, that last attack hit the main communications array, blew the antennas clean off. Damage control says they can fix it, but it'll have to wait until we're out of this furball first."

"Dammit." Beresick slammed his fist into his command console. "Air Boss, launch the *Integrity* and the *Honor*. *Integrity* is to lay alongside the *Truth* to act as a message-relay ship. *Honor* will assist in rescuing survivors."

It seemed like a long time before the *Truth*'s *Union* Class DropShips were detached from their docking collars, and longer still until the secure laser communications link could be established between the relay ship and her parent vessel. The relay system was slow and clumsy, but by using the *Integrity*'s long-range communications system, Beresick was able to maintain contact with the rest of the task force's WarShips.

Able to understand, but unable to contribute to, the delicate process of matching speed and direction between a 900,000-ton WarShip and a DropShip massing less than one percent of that, Morgan turned his attention, with a sort of sick fascination, back to the dying *Whirlwind*.

The *Honor* made its way, moving at "dead slow" speed, toward the burning destroyer. At several points along the Clan ship's flank and dorsal surfaces, Morgan saw tiny, brick-shaped lifeboats pulling away, backlit by the fires consuming the vessel. He counted six of the little rescue ships. He knew from his time aboard the *Invisible Truth* that lifeboats usually held only a half-dozen passengers, though ten could be crowded aboard if the survivors expected to be adrift but a short time.

Sixty men. Morgan shook his head in sorrow. *Sixty, out of what? Beresick told me there are twice that many aboard the* Ranger.

Cautiously, the *Honor* picked her way through the expanding field of twisted armor, charred structural members, and other debris. Twice, she came to a complete stop, allowing the minuscule life boats to drift into her empty fighter bay. In a display of courage as great as any Morgan had seen on the field of battle, the DropShip pulled to within five hundred meters of the wrecked Clan *Whirlwind*. The *Honor*'s captain must have known that the burning destroyer might explode at any second. Still, he held his ship close aboard the shattered WarShip as the lifeboats made two more trips each.

When, after what felt like an eternity, the *Honor* backed away from the Clan destroyer, Morgan felt an odd tightness in his chest. He realized he had been holding his breath while he willed the DropShip away from the burning Clan WarShip.

"Message from the *Honor*, Commodore," a commtech sang out. "Captain Zeco reports ninety-six survivors taken off the *Whirlwind*, including her captain. Some are badly wounded. Survivors report the ship's name was *Ursus*."

"Very well. Have them brought aboard," Beresick said. "Get the wounded to sickbay, and lock the rest in the number four cargo hold."

Morgan watched the ghostly holographic image of the *Haruna* flicker as a blast of autocannon fire smashed into her side. His limited knowledge of naval warfare told him that the Combine frigate was primarily a fighter-defense ship. The majority of her weapons had been designed to counter the threat of small attack craft, rather than trade blows with another capital ship. Only the fact that she had been joined by a pair of assault ships had saved the *Haruna* from taking severe damage.

As he watched, the massive frigate swung, crossing her opponent's stern. Despite his own frustration at not being able to join the fight directly, Morgan could not help but be impressed at the way Captain DeMoise handled his ship. A flash lit the viewscreen, as one of the *Avengers*, gaps showing in its nose and right wing, swooped in, pressing home his attack against the *Whirlwind*'s battered port side. The destroyer must have seen the disk-shaped DropShip begin its dive, because it unleashed a point-blank blast of PPC and laser fire into the attacking ship. The already-abused armor gave way, collapsing under the megajoule caress of the destroyer's laser cannons. The *Avenger* rocketed past the Clan ship, avoiding a collision by sheer good luck.

"Commodore, the *Hainan* reports severe damage to all major systems, Captain Cho is dead, and their weapons systems are out. Lieutenant Kindig is ordering 'Abandon ship.' "

Morgan felt a momentary pang as the holographic image of the *Avenger* assault DropShip flickered into a dull gray representation of its former self. As the *Truth*'s sensors tracked the crippled vessel, the holotank would continue to display its location. Soon enough rescue would stand to, hoping to recover the *Hainan*'s survivors.

The *Whirlwind*'s image flickered as the *Haruna* raked her from stem to stern with her broadside guns.

"She won't last much longer," Beresick said, gesturing at the tiny Clan WarShip as he spared Morgan a word. "Look, the *Haruna* is reversing her turn. In a few more seconds, she'll blow the Clanner out of existence."

Evidently, the Clanner knew it too.

"Unknown WarShip, this is Star Captain Manfred Snuka, commanding the destroyer *Fire Fang*," the voice-only message broke from the *Truth*'s bridge communications speakers. "My ship is no longer able to fight effectively. In accordance with your *batchall*, I concede the battle. My crew and I are your bondsmen."

"V-very well, Star Captain." To Morgan's ear, it sounded as though DeMoise was unprepared for such an occurrence. "Power down your drives and weapons. Stand by to be boarded."

"It will be as you say." Exhaustion, mixed with unbroken pride, colored Snuka's reply. "My ship and my crew are yours, as *isorla*."

As the communications link went dead, a quiet chuckle rumbled in Morgan's throat.

"What's so funny, sir?" Beresick asked, confusion evident on his face.

"Well, Alain." Morgan turned an amused grin on the naval officer. "You don't suppose the Coordinator will allow them to keep that ship, do you? To say nothing of her crew."

"Well, sir," Beresick smiled his reply. "Bushido does allow the taking of booty. It also permits keeping prisoners as personal servants. But, somehow, I think Theodore-*san* is going to ask for the *Fire Fang* as his liege-share."

"Bloody hell!" Mercia Winslow ground her teeth, as a series of explosions wracked the *Ranger*. "This Clan beggar isn't going to give up. Mr. Held, can you bring us under his stern?"

"I'm trying, Captain. He's just a little too quick for us."

In fact, the *Congress* was slightly slower than the old *Lola* Class destroyer. Her crew's greater experience gave the illusion of speed. Winslow and her crew had been trained as well as the Com Guards could manage, even to the point of drilling in full-scale replica control rooms buried deep beneath the Order's Rocky Mountain training facility. But there was no substitute for combat experience. The Clanners had been fighting each other for scores of years, and had learned the details of starship combat from actual battles. Winslow and her crew were learning as they went along.

Suddenly, the *Congress* fired all of her portside thrusters, causing the humpbacked ship to swing sharply. Autocannon fire lanced out of her gun bays, spewing a cloud of tracers across the blackness of space. Unconsciously, Winslow flinched, bracing herself for another impact. Then she realized that the Clanner hadn't fired at the *Ranger*.

There, driving in from the frigate's starboard side, was the battered shape of the *Starlight*. The *Essex* Class destroyer had finally made running repairs to the damage inflicted by the Clan ship's broadside. Gunfire sparked from the *Starlight*'s nose and forward hull, even as Clan autocannon fire laced her thin armor with smoking craters. Missiles leapt from their launchers, adding to the destruction being wrought on the *Congress*' outer hull.

Taking advantage of the Clan ship's temporary preoccupation with the *Starlight*, Winslow ordered her ship to run straight under the frigate's stern. At less than forty kilometers, every gun in the *Ranger*'s port broadside fired into the Clan ship's aft quarter.

Sensors indicated that the enemy had taken severe damage to his armor, but revealed little about which systems might have been hit inside the vessel.

"All back full."

In answer to Winslow's excited command, the *Ranger*'s helmsman slammed his hand down on his control board. With speed guaranteed to turn an old-time blue-water naval officer green with envy, the massive starship's engines went from full forward to full reverse. The *Ranger* shuddered as the quartet of Rolls LeFay interplanetary engines brought the vessel to a dead stop directly under the Clan frigate's stern.

"Mr. Fontanazza, hit him again!" Winslow yelled.

"Captain, his weapons are powering down."

"Belay that." Winslow gestured sharply at her weapons officers just in time to spare the *Congress* another shattering broadside.

"He's hailing us."

"To the commanding officer, Star League *Lola III* destroyer. I am Star Colonel Alonso Gilmour, of the Ghost Bear WarShip *Shining Claw*. My vessel has been disabled. In accordance with the *batchall* of your commander, I yield my crew and myself as bondsmen to you and your Clan."

"Star Colonel, this is Captain Mercia Winslow, of the destroyer, *Ranger*," Winslow replied, using the Clan officer's stilted speech as a model. "I accept your surrender, and assure you that you and your men will be given fair treatment. Stand by to receive a prize crew."

Winslow waved her hand, signaling the commtech to cut the connection. Taking a deep breath, she held it for a few seconds, then blew it out in a low whistle. Feeling the tension in her neck, she wearily rolled her head, massaging the aching muscles.

"Patch me through to the flagship."

"Well, Marshal, our losses were light, much lighter than I had expected," Commodore Beresick said, referring to the notes displayed on his noteputer.

Several hours had passed since the last Clan vessel was captured by Task Force Serpent. During that time, the crews of the Inner Sphere WarShips did their best to put their vessels back into some kind of fighting trim. Once repairs were sufficiently underway, Morgan called a full command staff meeting, to be held in the *Invisible Truth*'s briefing room. The first item on the agenda was the one Morgan hated the most, the reading of the casualty and damage list, the so-called "butcher's bill." Being the commander of the task force's naval assets, the responsibility for this grim task fell upon Commodore Beresick.

"Seven aerospace fighters, four of which belong to the Com Guards, have either been destroyed or damaged beyond repair. Of those, three pilots survived, although Lieutenant Bharie lost his right arm," Beresick intoned.

"One *Avenger* Class DropShip was destroyed fighting the *Fire Fang*. Half of her crew escaped, but most of them are wounded. Captain Cho is missing, reported dead. Our total casualties are twenty-six dead, thirty-two wounded, and four missing. I don't think we'll find any of the missing alive."

Beresick paused, allowing Morgan time to assimilate the surprisingly low number of casualties.

"Losses to our ships were a little heavier. As I said, we lost seven aerospace fighters and one assault ship. It's that last that concerns me the most. Fortunately, there were no special forces teams or marines aboard. Next time, we might not be so lucky. The *Haruna, Starlight,* and *Ranger* each took a couple of heavy hits, mostly to their armor. That can be repaired in the field. The *Starlight* lost her number two PPC to a missile hit. *That* can't be fixed in the field. We've got her patched up pretty well. The engineers tell me that they plan to weld a big armor patch over the wrecked mount. As you know, the *Invisible Truth* lost her main communications array. Right now, we're maintaining contact with the rest of the fleet through a picket ship. We should be back on line in a couple of hours."

"What about the Clan ships?" Ariana Winston spoke for the first time. As the task force's second-in-command, her presence at the meeting was required, though she felt awkward, having watched the battle from a safe distance away, aboard the *Gettysburg*.

"The *Invader* is a write-off. Her field initiator looks like a piece of modern art." Beresick smiled in bitter amusement. "It seems that Captain Winslow took my orders to prevent the ship from jumping a bit too literally.

"The *Fire Fang* is the least damaged of the Clan War-Ships. She's lost a couple of her weapons bays, and both of her after autocannon batteries are gone for good. Our biggest problem is her jump sail. There's a hole through it the size of Montana. We can try to repair it, but I'm not too certain of the results."

"What about using one of the sails they cut adrift before the battle?" Paul Masters suggested. "Or the one off the *Invader*?"

"Well, maybe." Beresick shrugged. "The other *Whirlwind,* the *Ursus,* cut her sail away, and it may be drifting around out there. Nobody reported running into it during the fighting. The problem is that each ship is designed to take a jump sail of a certain size. Smaller than that, and you may never get a good enough charge to make your jump. Bigger, and you won't be able to fit the array into your sail locker. Nah, it's going to have to be repair the *Fire Fang*'s sail or find the *Ursus'*."

"And the *Congress*?"

"Well, she's somewhat the worse for wear. Her starboard quarter is pretty shot up. One of her docking collars is shot to pieces. She's lost most of her after and starboard broadside weapons, and her rightside maneuvering thrusters are really chewed. To top it all off, her armor looks like a sieve."

"How long to complete the repairs?"

Beresick tapped his data unit's keyboard a few times, then said, "Fifty-two hours, assuming that all goes well and that no more Clanners show up."

"What are the prospects?"

"I'd say about fifty-fifty. The *Fire Fang* and all of our ships are definitely repairable. The *Shining Claw*? Your guess is as good as mine. And, like I said, the *Invader* is ready for a scrapyard.

"The upside is that we captured a dozen OmniFighters relatively intact. We've also got a couple of damaged *Union-C*'s and an intact *Broadsword*."

"I meant to ask you about that." Morgan leaned his elbows on the conference table. "Why didn't they ever launch that DropShip?"

"They couldn't." Beresick grinned. "It was one of those freak things. The missile that breached the *Winter Wind*'s hull warped one of her docking collars. They couldn't get the locking clamps to release, so the *Broadsword* was stuck. It'll take about twenty hours to pry her loose and strip out the *Invader*."

"There's more to it than that," Major Ryan interrupted. He explained that while securing the *Invader,* Team Five had cut into the trapped *Broadsword*. In its 'Mech bays, the special forces troopers had found a Star of brand-new OmniMechs. The DropShip's cargo bay also held several tons of consumable supplies, including ammunition for their autocannons and missile launchers.

"Hmm, that could be a bonus." Morgan turned to look at Andrew Redburn from beneath hooded eyelids. "What do you think, Andrew?"

"Yes, it could." Redburn's lips curved wickedly into a smile of delight. "I'll get the techs to working on it as soon as those 'Mechs are shipped."

"Now, wait just a minute, Morgan," Marshal Bryan snapped angrily. "Why should those OmniMechs go to your Kathil Uhlans instead of another unit? I didn't see any of them assaulting any Clan WarShips?"

"Well, for that matter, Marshal Bryan," Redburn said, "I didn't see any of your Lyran Guards out there either."

Morgan saw the scarlet flush creeping up the Lyran

officer's neck and intervened. He informed Bryan that the OmniMechs were not automatically being signed over to the Uhlans, or to anybody else. "I merely want them checked out, and I trust my own techs to do the job right. Do you have a problem with that, Sharon? Besides, if it comes down to who actually captured the 'Mechs, Major Ryan here would have the first OmniMech-equipped DEST team in history. Isn't that right, Major?"

"Well . . ." Ryan let his voice trail off, giving the command staff the benefit of an inscrutable, I-know-something-you-don't-know smile.

"Now, what does *that* mean?" Bryan demanded.

"People, let's get back to the business at hand." Morgan rapped the table lightly with the knuckles of his right fist. "We can save the cat-and-mouse games for later, all right?

"Right now, we have bigger problems than who gets a Star of Clan 'Mechs and how long it will take to make repairs. As a result of this battle, we now . . . own, I guess is the right word, roughly three hundred bondsmen. Most of those are technician, scientist, and laborer caste. Only a few dozen are warriors. The question is, what do we do with them?"

"There's more to it than that, Marshal," Beresick said quietly, fearing the reactions of those among the command staff who had been opposed to the idea of taking prisoners. "Records recovered from the *Fire Fang* indicate that this was a personnel transfer. There were almost a thousand Ghost Bear civilians packed into the *Winter Wind* and those two *Union*s."

The conference room exploded into startled gasps and exclamations.

"If I understand Clan society properly, Clan civilians are not covered by the bond-oath," Morgan explained. "But those who give their word will stick to it, just as though they were warriors. They would rather die than break their word. And I'm sure they'd rather go bondsmen to us rather than meet some worse fate out here in deep space."

"Begging your pardon, Marshal, but I don't give a rat." Captain Montjar threw out his hand in a gesture of refusal. "Oath or no, I just can't bring myself to trust a Clanner."

"Me, either." Ryan agreed.

Paul Masters, still smarting over not being consulted on the fate of the pirate leaders, was quick to voice his opinion. "Those who will give us their bond should not be disgraced any more than being forced into bond-service makes necessary. I say we accept them."

"That's all well and good, Sir Masters," Ariana Winston interrupted. "But what about the rest? What about the techs and the civilians? I want to know what's going to happen to them, before we go any farther."

Morgan shook his head wearily. "General Redburn and I have developed a contingency measure," he said. "We hoped it would never be used, or at least not before we had a chance to discuss it with the staff. We plan to hold the prisoners who do not wish to offer us their bond-oath until we jump into the next system with a habitable planet. There they'll be herded aboard a DropShip and marooned."

"All right, General," Winston sighed heavily. "I'll accept that."

"I'm sorry, Marshal," Montjar cut in. "But I can't see the wisdom of taking an enemy who was just trying to kill you and making him a trusted servant."

Before Captain Montjar could continue, Masters shot to his feet in anger. "Rabid Fox? Huh! That's a good description." Suddenly, Masters drew his sidearm. Before any of the commanders could react, the Knight threw the heavy Rugan automatic onto the table in front of Montjar. The autopistol lay there, gleaming in the diffused light radiating from the overhead panels. "If you are so anxious to see them die, why don't you do it yourself?"

For several seconds, Montjar's furious gaze flicked back and forth between Masters and the pistol.

"Dammit, that's enough," Morgan roared, shooting to his feet. Snatching up the weapon, he ejected the fifteen-round magazine, snapped back the slide to eject the round in the firing chamber, and pitched the gun back to its owner with enough force to make the Knight bobble the catch.

"I have had it with you people. What do you think this is? A bloody church social? *I* am the commander of this *military* operation. *You* are my *subordinates*. You *will* abide by my decisions, or I will bloody well court martial the lot of you.

"Those Clansmen are bound by their oath to this task force, and we will treat them properly. Some of you don't want them working on your ships or 'Mechs? Fine, you won't have them. If necessary, I'll assign all three hundred of them as my personal technical staff. Those who don't want to be part of this task force will be treated according to the Ares Conventions. We will hold them until we jump into a habitable system, where they'll be marooned.

"That . . . is . . . *final*.

"Now, get out of my sight."

Morgan sat down heavily, refusing to acknowledge the salutes or muttered farewells of the departing command staff. Soon, only Alain Beresick was left.

"Well, Marshal," Beresick said, reaching into a breast pocket of his khaki jumpsuit. "Looks like the task force won a victory for its first time in battle."

With a snort, Morgan leaned back wearily in his chair, accepting both the attempt to change the subject and the proffered victory cigar.

"Yes, Commodore, we won a pretty victory, but we were lucky. The next time we cross swords with the Clans, luck may not be on our side."

═══ 28 ═══

Battle Cruiser ISS Invisible Truth
Deep Periphery
16 December 3059
1000 Hours

Fifteen hours after Task Force Serpent's first major engagement ended, the task of repairing the ships damaged in the fight had barely begun. Sir Paul Masters and Colonel Samuel Kingston had advocated jumping outsystem immediately. The Capellan officer recommended returning to the last system visited by the task force. As much as he hated to agree with a Liaoist, Morgan had to admit that there was some wisdom to what they said. Kingston argued that they had encountered Clan WarShips in this system once already. The task force was victorious only because they had, as he put it, "gotten the drop on the Clanners."

Commodore Beresick reassured the command staff that, by assigning the undamaged *Rostock* and *Emerald* to picket duty, and deploying their fighters as a BARCAP, the fleet would have sufficient warning to either jump outsystem or prepare for a fight.

The highest repair priority had been assigned to locating the *Ursus'* jump sail. Despite its great diameter, the polymer disk proved difficult to find. Only a few millimeters thick, made of a dead black energy-absorbent material, the sail didn't show up well on scanners. It took an educated guess, a detailed visual search, and a great deal of luck to spot the drifting sail. Fortunately, the delicate fabric hadn't suffered much damage. The sail was towed back to the fleet. Extra Vehicular Activity-suited engineers mated the array to the captured *Fire Fang*.

During the search for the jump sail, the wreckage of two of the missing Com guard fighters were discovered. One was so badly mangled that the rescue teams had to cut the canopy open with a laser torch, As expected, the pilot was dead, as badly mutilated as his *Rapier*. The second fighter carried a few minor scars. When the rescuers cycled the ship's canopy open, they saw that the pilot's body was undamaged, except for a small, deep gash in her left leg. An examination of the corpse revealed that a tiny sliver of steel no bigger than a man's thumbnail had pierced her flightsuit, entered her thigh, and nicked her femoral artery. The flight data recorder indicated that she had been trying to make it back to the *Ranger* when she fainted from blood loss. The enemy had apparently decided that the drifting *Hellcat* was no longer a threat, and Flight Lieutenant Debi Petrillo had bled to death.

Of the other fighters lost in what the task force members had begun calling "the Battle of Trafalgar," no trace was found. The rescuers gave up after twenty hours, assuming that the ships had either been blasted into unidentifiable fragments or that the destroyed fighters had drifted outside their search parameters.

A single event brightened the otherwise grim and depressing search. Badly wounded, "Badger" Sarti had been rescued from the wreckage of a Clan DropShip. Unconscious, his upper body a mass of second- and third-degree burns, the young pilot was pulled from his escape capsule. It had ejected from his disintegrating *Gotha* seconds before its long-range missiles detonated, blowing the ship apart. Sarti was doubly lucky. When the rescuers finally pried open the blistered escape module, they saw that the charge on the capsule's life support system was less than five minutes.

Aboard the *Winter Wind*, some of the newly sworn bondsmen had been detailed to salvage crews struggling to free the relatively undamaged *Broadsword* from its warped docking collar. The *Invader*'s hull had been breached by the *Ranger*'s crippling attack, and several of her pressure bulkheads had been holed during the struggle to possess the JumpShip, leaving large areas of the vessel with no atmosphere. In some places, salvage crews welded pieces of sheet steel over the breaches, allowing the ship's still-functional life support system to reestablish a safe environment. The DropShip docking bay was one such area.

"It is no use," Clan tech Lennox explained, as he backed away from the open panel giving him access to the jammed locking mechanism. "The collar is so badly damaged that it will have to be cut away from the outside."

"Damnation." Lennox knew that the man who spoke was the Master Tech, one Philip Brna. As a member of a Clan lower caste, Lennox had heard plenty of profanities in his time, most of them uttered by warriors to their inferiors. Most Clan epithets tended to be based upon the rigid class divisions and the genetic engineering program, whereas those uttered by these Inner Sphere barbarians seemed to be based on everything from religion to bodily functions. Add to that the staggering array of euphemisms and half-oaths, and the direct, plain-speaking Clansman was at a loss to attach meaning to most of what one of his new masters said. Indeed, some of the coarser, truly barbaric captors seemed to utter profanities in every sentence, as though they knew no other words.

Brna pulled a black plastic box from one of the pouches hanging from his web belt. Lennox knew that the device was a long-range communicator, probably tied into some kind of communications net. The Master Tech flicked a switch and spoke in a low voice. For several minutes, he exchanged messages with the person on the other end of the link. Soon, with a look of disgust, he shoved the device back into his pouch.

"Listen up." Brna spoke loudly enough for the rest of his technical crew to hear him. "They're going to send an EVA salvage team over to work on cutting the *Broadsword* loose from this bloody collar. We're supposed to go down to engineering and help salvage spare parts."

Even before Brna finished speaking, Lennox had tugged the collar of his environment suit up around his chin. Similar to a marine combat suit, the thick cloth garment had been designed for use by technicians aboard warships. A small life support pack and a lightweight helmet allowed techs to work in hostile environments ranging from heat and high radiation to vacuum. The only drawback was that the life support units had a limited lifespan before they had to be recharged. Still, the suits were remarkably well-made for an Inner Sphere design. They were worlds better than anything the Clans had. The hostile-environment gear used by Clan techs was on the level of Inner Sphere equipment from fifty years ago, probably because it was usually the lower castes who used it.

Out the corner of his eye, Lennox noticed the bulky olive-drab figures of Inner Sphere marines. It mattered little to him that the men wore both the crest of the Lyran Commonwealth and the oddly proportioned star of House Cameron. He felt a pang of insult at the Inner Sphere commanders' inability to accept a bondsman's oath as binding. Lennox, like all who had given their oath, now considered himself to be part of the task force, in effect, part of a new Clan. Many of the bondsmen resented the implication that their oath was not to be trusted. Others, Lennox among them, simply told themselves that they would work even harder to demonstrate their trustworthiness to their new "Clan."

Once the last technician indicated that his suit was sealed, the salvage party set out, climbing through the long narrow passages between the docking bays and the engineering module. Though they were crawling feet first through the deck hatches, they weren't necessarily moving downward. Unlike a larger, more powerful WarShip, the transport vessel was unable to generate much more than the 0.2 G needed for station-keeping. In perpetual freefall, up and down were relative. By a tradition that predated the Exodus, moving forward on a space- or starship was always referred to as going up, and moving aft was going down.

In the engine room, wires of every size, description, and color hung from bulkheads, the overhead, and jutted up from the deck. Each bundle or strand showed the gleam of freshly cut metal from the places where some salvage technician had hacked a component free of its moorings.

In one corner of the dimly lit chamber, a team of bondsmen struggled, side by side with their Inner Sphere counterparts, to wrestle a massive charge converter out of its heavy steel mountings. The big chunk of polycarbon, steel, and alloys was like a huge transformer, designed to change the electrical energy created by the ship's jump sail into a form usable by the vessel's Kearny-Fuchida drives. Had the *Winter Wind* not been in freefall, the component would have weighed over three metric tons. It would have required a block and tackle to move. Lennox watched, fascinated, as five men levered the immense piece of equipment out of its brackets.

A yell of alarm, which immediately turned into a shriek of agony, pierced the hubbub of three salvage crews all working in the same space. Unfortunately, both the Inner Sphere technicians and their bondsmen had forgotten one basic principle. Although an object in zero-gravity has no weight, it has mass. As the converter unit began to come free of its mountings, a corner of the device caught against a dangling loop of power conduit. With a velocity of about three meters per second, the charge converter pivoted around the impinging cable, catching a ComStar tech between the converter and the engine room's pressure bulkhead. The massive chunk of plastic and metal struck him, crushing both legs and pinning the screaming man behind it. Metal squealed as it bent, jamming the converter against the bulkhead.

Dropping his prybar, another ComStar tech grabbed the charge converter by a torch-severed conduit. Shouting at the others to be ready to arrest the motion of the unit, he braced his feet against an empty mounting bracket and attempted to heave the massive weight off his injured comrade.

"No!" Lennox yelled, darting across the tool- and debris-littered deck. Grabbing the tech by the shoulders, he shoved the startled, would-be rescuer away from the converter.

The tech's flailing hand caught a grab-bar, arresting his tumbling flight. Fury coloring his face an ugly red, he yanked a stainless steel, small-framed revolver from a pouch attached to his tool belt.

"You malfing Clan bastard." The man's voice was a snarl, as he raised the snub-nosed weapon until it was level with Lennox's heart.

"If you move the converter, you might kill him." Lennox didn't let himself flinch, despite the unblinking stare of the weapon's black muzzle. "The converter could be all that is preventing him from bleeding to death."

For long seconds, the tech kept the evil-looking revolver leveled at the bondsman's chest. Then, shaking his head and blinking, he lowered the weapon. A marine guard lunged forward to snatch the revolver as it fell from his grasp.

Lennox released the stanchion he'd been grasping, allowing himself to float free. He was grateful for the bulky suit. It concealed the shaking in his muscles as the tension left him. Seconds later, a rescue team complete with a trauma surgeon rushed into the compartment and began working to free the trapped technician.

"Here you go, son." The Lyran soldier who stood over Lennox, offering him a zero-G canteen, was probably three or four standard years *younger* than the exhausted bondsman. The man's nasal twang did little to hide the admiration in his voice. "That were the damnedest thing I ever seen."

"I could not allow him to move that converter." The water in the plastic bottle was warm and flat, but to Lennox it tasted as sweet as wine. "The man's legs must be badly crushed, but he's probably torn arteries as well. If so, the converter was acting as a tourniquet. If that other technician had succeeded in shifting the unit, his friend would have bled to death in a matter of seconds."

Returning the canteen, Lennox turned to watch. The rescue team, after lacing a pair of inflatable constriction bands around the injured man's legs, levered the massive charge converter away from his trapped limbs. The injured tech, who had been drifting in and out of consciousness, suddenly came awake, screaming. Mercifully, the shriek was cut off when he fainted once again.

As the injured man was being carried away in a pressurized rescue stretcher, the chief emergency medtech came over to Lennox.

"You're the one who wouldn't let them take the machine off his legs."

"Aff," Lennox replied, eyes lowered to show respect.

"Good job," the woman said, admiration mixing with relief in her voice. "You probably saved his life."

Aboard the *Fire Fang,* repairs were proceeding more slowly, partly because the destroyer had suffered more severe damage than the JumpShip. The biggest reason for the slow-down came in the wake of the nearly fatal accident aboard the *Winter Wind.* Not willing to risk the lives of any more technicians, Morgan, on the advice of Commodore Beresick, ordered that any further repairs involving the handling of major shipboard components should be carried out by men wearing power suits. Neither he nor the Commodore believed that using the bulky armor would prevent *all* accidents. They merely hoped that the suits' thick skins and augmented strength would lessen the *severity* of a mishap.

That they did. Several times during the repair process, armored troopers were struck by pieces of equipment. The worst injury among the augmented soldiers-cum-repairmen was a broken nose resulting when a loose steel I-beam struck a Light Horse armored infantryman a glancing blow to his faceplate. Had the man been unarmored, he might have escaped unscathed. On the other hand, he might have been killed. Trooper Vance Davis said he'd take the broken nose rather than the fifty-fifty shot at having his head smashed in by a chunk of structural metal.

In many cases, the members of Task Force Serpent were surprised by the unexpected level of cooperation among the former Clan personnel. Some of the "barbarian techs," as they jokingly referred to themselves, were initially suspicious of their bondsmen, fearing that the ex-Clanners would sabotage any vital system they could lay their hands on. Those fears evaporated as the story of Lennox's rescue of a tech spread throughout the fleet. By the time the tale came back around to the former Clan technicians, it sounded as though he'd single-handedly lifted the charge converter off of the already-dead tech, and then, with a touch of his hand, brought the man back to life. When Lennox tried to explain the actual turn of events, he was brusquely corrected.

"No, no. The guy who told me has a buddy, whose lance mate is hot for one of the medtechs who was on the rescue team. I'm tellin' you the way it really happened."

"Get used to it, Lennox," one of the other ComStar techs said, clapping him on the shoulder, an Inner Sphere gesture of friendship which Lennox found quite annoying. "You're a hero."

"Marshal, I have a preliminary report from the repair teams."

Morgan looked up from his data display terminal. Commodore Beresick dropped into the thinly padded chair facing the task force commander's desk.

"Uh-huh." It had been nearly sixty hours since the last Clan warrior had been taken into custody. Morgan wondered if he'd managed to get more than six hours' sleep during that time.

"The work is about eighty-five percent complete. They expect to have the last bits of armor bolted down by this time tomorrow."

"Uh-huh."

"As per your order, the *Fire Fang* has been assigned to Fox Team Three. Also, as per your prediction, Marshal Bryan griped about it. They finally got the *Broadsword* pried away from her docking collar. She hooked up with the *Haruna* about two hours ago. Since then, the DEST boys and a couple of the Clan bondsmen have been working on getting the Clan 'Mechs unlocked and reprogrammed so we can use them."

"Wait a second. The DEST teams are working on 'Mechs?"

"Yessir. Seems that Ryan and company brought along some really slick code-breaking gear. He says that they'll probably have the OmniMechs ready for reprogramming by oh-nine-hundred tomorrow."

"Well, how about that?" Morgan snorted, amused. "Remind me to keep Major Ryan and his cutthroats away from my *Daishi*."

"Your *Daishi*?" Beresick laughed in return. "What about my battle cruiser? Just think what that boy could do if he set his mind to it."

They enjoyed the joke for a moment. Then Morgan turned serious.

"What about that tech, what's his name? Falconi?"

"Failoni. He'll probably survive. I talked to the doctor myself. He said the boy has an eighty percent chance, or thereabouts. Thing is, he'll probably lose his legs."

Morgan leaned back in his chair, shaking his head.

"Yessir. Doc Yohi says a Clan bondsman saved Failoni's life. Says he beat up some ComStar tech who wanted to lift the charger off Failoni's legs. Yohi says if they'd let him go, Failoni would have bled to death, and no one could have helped him."

"Okay, Alain. Thanks." Morgan learned forward and glanced at his data display, then sat back once more, rubbing his eyes. "I'll stop by and see Failoni as soon as I can. Meanwhile, I'd like to see this bondsman. What's his name?"

"Lennox," Beresick replied. "Senior Technician Lennox. You want me to send for him right away?"

"No. Tomorrow's soon enough."

"All right, Marshal." Beresick sighed as he levered himself to his feet. As the office door hissed open, he turned back toward Morgan sitting behind his desk.

"You know, Marshal, maybe you need some rest too."

"How's that?"

"Well, you're slipping. Twice now, you've called me Alain." Beresick grinned leaning against the door frame. "Gotta watch that. It's bad for morale."

Morgan smiled tiredly.

"Good night . . . Alain."

Good night, Morgan."

True to his word, twenty-four hours after he left Morgan, Commodore Beresick reported to the command staff that the last of the repairs had been completed, and the fleet was ready to start charging its jump engines.

"Good," spat Major Marcus Poling, commander of the St. Ives Lancers. "We've been sitting here for nearly three days while you navy-types played Mister Fix-it with a bunch of busted-up spaceships. We should've jumped out right away and left the wrecks for the Clans, or pushed 'em into Trafalgar."

"Settle down, Major." Morgan was growing short of patience where his painfully diverse staff was concerned. "Sitting here exposed has been a strain on all of us, so let's try not to make things worse, hmm?"

Poling bobbed his head sheepishly, wishing to avoid another explosion of Morgan's fraying temper.

"Good. New ship assignments. The *Broadsword* . . ."

"*Stiletto*."

"What?"

"*Stiletto*. That's what her crew is calling her," Beresick explained. "They thought she needed a new name."

"All right," Morgan chuckled. "*Stiletto* has been assigned to the *Haruna*. For now, we're going to leave the

OmniMechs where they are, if that's all right with you, Marshal Bryan."

Bryan took the barb, and nodded in agreement. At least the Clan war machines weren't being assigned to the Uhlans.

"We've cobbled together a volunteer prize crew for the *Fire* . . . What is her crew calling her, Commodore?"

"Fire Fang, sir." Beresick smiled broadly. "That *is* her name, after all."

Morgan laughed, for the first time in days.

"All right, the *Fire Fang,*" he said, emphasizing the vessel's name, "has been crewed by volunteers, and by those bondsmen we feel are most trustworthy. We've also assigned Fox Team Three as her security detail. Since she can't carry DropShips, and she's got a skeleton crew, we've assigned her as a fleet defense boat. If we run into a fight again, she'll stay with the JumpShips and try to knock off any enemy who leaks past the WarShips."

"Sir, that's something I wanted to talk to you about—the bondsmen," Överste Sleipness interjected. Sleipness was a native of the Free Rasalhague Republic, a state freed from the Draconis Combine in 3034 but which had been eaten down to seven worlds just eighteen years later by the Clan invasion. The sufferings of his family and nation at the hands of the invaders had left the Överste with a deep-seated hatred for Clansmen of any stripe. "Many of my men still bear the scars of our encounter with the Ghost Bears back in Rasalhague. How can you ask them to trust some of the very warriors who razed Thule, Radije, and Kempten?"

"As I said before, Överste, If you don't want bondsmen serving your unit, you don't have to take them."

"That isn't what I mean, Marshal." Sleipness locked his gaze on Morgan. "It is the very presence of the bondsmen with this Task Force that concerns me. Yes, I know that you believe their 'bond oaths,' their promise to serve the 'Serpent Clan' faithfully. I understand. That doesn't mean I agree with you."

"So what should we do, Överste? Kill them?" The edge in Morgan's voice betrayed the thinness of his temper.

"No, of course not. I think you should maroon all of them."

"No, sir. I'm not going to do that. They've given their word to this task force, to 'Clan Serpent' as they are calling us, and I've given *my* word that they'll be treated as bondsmen, and according to the Ares Conventions. The bondsmen stay."

"Very well, Marshal," the Rasalhague commander nodded. He'd made the point he'd hoped to, and it was time to accept the orders of his superior. "I respectfully request the removal of all Clan personnel from our Table of Organization and Equipment."

"All right, Överste. I can't say as how I blame you."

Bloody hell. The first time in days I get to close my eyes, and some blasted fool comes banging on my door.

Morgan rolled off his bunk. A glance in the small mirror above the stainless steel wash basin proved to be a major mistake. The man staring back looked horrible. The dark smudges under his bloodshot eyes looked stark against the drawn, pale skin of his face. A three-day stubble darkened his chin.

Morgan shook his head at the sight of himself, then laughed softly. He wondered what Kym would say if she could see him like this. The thought of her warmed him, but saddened him too. When would he see her again?

The knock, which had awakened him after thirty minutes of sleep, sounded again, jerking his attention away from the mirror. Morgan splashed cold water on his face, wiped it roughly dry with a towel, and crossed into his flag office, closing his bedroom door behind him.

"Come," he called. The croak in his voice reminded him of a crow that used to roost in a tree outside his bedroom window in his father's house on New Syrtis.

The door hissed open, revealing a slight man dressed in a stained olive-drab jumpsuit. Two thin nylon cords encircled his right wrist.

"Bondsman Lennox, reporting as ordered. Star . . . er, Marshal."

For a moment, Morgan stared uncomprehendingly at his visitor, then he remembered.

"Ah, yes, ah, Lennox, please come in, sit down." With one hand, Morgan gestured to the chair facing his desk, while with the other, he struggled to button the collar of his uniform tunic. "I *did* want to see you. Commodore Beresick told me what you did yesterday. It's quite a story."

"It was my duty, Marshal."

"Maybe," Morgan said gently. "Maybe. I think it was something more. You saved a man's life, and risked your own doing it. I don't know how it is among the Clans, but in my world, that deserves recognition."

"No recognition is necessary, Marshal," Lennox answered. "That man is an experienced technician. It would have been wasteful to allow him to die." A flicker crossed the bondsman's eyes. "I understand he will be crippled, quiaff? He will lose his legs?"

"Looks that way." Morgan saw the sympathy in Lennox's eyes. "Don't worry. The docs will stabilize him, get him fixed up as best they can, and when we get back home, we'll fix him up with the best prostheses we can find.

"In the meantime, there's something I'd like to do." A small, blue-steel knife gleamed dully in Morgan's hand. "Hold out your right hand."

Obediently, Lennox stretched out his bondcorded wrist. The short, tanto-style blade sliced cleanly through the thin nylon.

"I don't know what the words are, if there are any among your Clan," Morgan said, sliding the knife into its hidden sleeve sheath. "You are a bondsman no longer. You're a free man. And I'm transferring you to my personal technical staff."

At first, Lennox didn't respond. He stared at the severed cords lying on the deck. Rubbing his wrist, he looked across the desk at the tired, smiling man.

"Marshal, I do not know how to thank you."

"Just don't let me down, boy. Don't let me down."

It took over nine days to finish charging the last Jump-Ship's drives. Exhausted by the stressful events of the past fortnight, Commodore Beresick leaned against the waist-high brass rail surrounding the *Invisible Truth*'s holotank.

"Commodore," the Officer-of-the-Deck said gently. "The sail is sixty percent stored. The rest of the fleet will be ready to jump in an hour or so. Why don't you hit the rack for a while, sir? You look like you could use it."

Beresick turned to face the one-time Demi-Precentor, who now wore the paired green bars and silver pip of a major. The black-haired officer wore a genuine look of concern on his olive-skinned face.

"All right, Mister Karabin, the bridge is yours. Call me if anything big crops up; otherwise, I'm not to be disturbed for eight hours."

"Yes, sir." Karabin struggled to hide his relief. "Good night, sir."

"Good *afternoon,* Major." Beresick gestured at the bridge chronometer. It displayed the time in bright green numerals: fifteen thirty-eight hours—three-thirty-eight in the afternoon.

"Right. Good afternoon, sir."

The Commodore smiled and left.

Ninety minutes later, the last vessel to furl its sail, the Light Horse *Star Lord* Class *Buford,* reported ready to jump.

Major Miklos Karabin stood in the center of the holotank.

"Mister Ritt," he called to the on-duty jump engineer. "Take us out of here."

"Aye, sir. Jump drives on line. Initiating sequence."

The first of two warning tones sounded hollowly through the *Invisible Truth.* Moments later, a more urgent klaxon signaled that the ship was about to make the translation into hyperspace.

"Sir, I've got a ta . . . csaoun . . ." The sensor operator's voice, clear at first, slurred and dopplered down to nothing, as the Kearny-Fuchida drive buried deep within the huge WarShip's armored hull ripped a hole in the fabric of the universe and flung the *Invisible Truth* through it into the void of hyperspace. As the *Truth* reappeared at the nadir of the fleet's next waypoint, the shouted words seemed to run backward at high speed. ". . . shflarf . . . oming JumpShip."

"Say again." Karabin shivered as his body threw off the stomach-churning after-effects of the hyperspace jump.

"Sir, I thought I saw the EMP/tachyon flare of an incoming JumpShip as we made the jump," the technician said. "If that's what it was, there's a good chance whoever it was will know we were there."

"Play it back."

As Karabin looked over her shoulder, the sensor operator cued up the last few seconds of the WarShip's sensor log. Most sensor displays did not show a graphic representation of the area they covered. Usually, the readouts consisted of "waterfall displays," showing bright spots in places where a contact had occurred. Not as familiar with the system as Petty Officer Margaret Culp, the OOD recognized the wide white band as the electromagnetic pulse generated by a JumpShip. The trace flared to life for a few seconds before the screen, overloaded by the *Truth*'s own electromagnetic emissions, whited out. When it cleared again, the battle cruiser had already phased in at their present location.

"Any chance that it was a reflection of our jump flare?" Karabin's brow was creased with the effort to make sense of the fleeting contact.

"Possible, but I don't think so, sir." Culp replayed the short digital recording. "We've been trading log records with other ships for the past couple of months, including the sensor traces of our own vessels. I've seen the *Truth*'s EM signature from about every angle there is, and that ain't it."

The OOD knew better than to question Culp on sensor readings. The tech was said to be one of the best.

Karabin straightened, placed his hands on his sacroiliac, and arched his back, relishing the click of vertebrae falling into place. Sometimes, it seemed like he spent too much time on his feet.

"All right. I'll log it in. I don't think we've got anything to worry about. We were gone before he jumped in. Even if it was a Clanner, he's not going to be able to track us. No one can track ships through hyperspace, not even the Clans."

Returning to the watch-stander's bridge position, Karabin collapsed gratefully into the heavily padded, yet uncomfortable seat. For several minutes, he pecked away at the keyboard in the station's command console. The log entry was short and to the point. "Just before jump, an anomalous EMP was detected. Sensor scans were inconclusive." He signed the notation with a flourish, using a light-pen, and consigned the report to the battle cruiser's memory core.

Sliding away from the console, Karabin wandered around the control deck for a few minutes, looking over the shoulders of the various technicians before getting back to his position in the center of the bridge holotank. After ten minutes of watching the miniature starships floating in the air above the deck, he forgot about the incident.

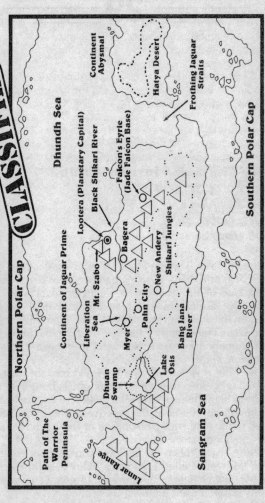

MAP OF HUNTRESS

CLASSIFIED

Northern Polar Cap

Dhundh Sea

Continent of Jaguar Prime

Lootera (Planetary Capital)

Black Shikari River

Continent Abysmal

Hatya Desert

Falcon's Eyrie
(Jade Falcon Base)

Frothing Jaguar Straits

Liberation Sea   Mt. Szabo

Bagera

Southern Polar Cap

Path of The Warrior Peninsula

Myer

Pahn City

New Andery

Shikari Jungles

Dhuan Swamp

Latze Osis

Bahg Jana River

Lunar Range

Sangram Sea

Battle Cruiser ISS Invisible Truth
Task Force Serpent
Deep Periphery
30 December 3058
1600 Hours

Morgan Hasek-Davion stood, leaning against the closed hatch of the *Invisible Truth*'s number three cargo bay. To either side of the three-meter diameter black steel hatch stood the faceless hulks of an armored infantry squad. Though the big warriors lacked the impressive bulk of their Clan counterparts, the two-meter-plus forms, with their vaguely insectoid appearance, were always a vaguely disturbing sight.

The Clan prisoners of war crowded into the cavernous cargo bay seemed to have no such unreasoning fear of the armored men. In the two weeks that these people had been the unwilling guests of the task force, there had been no break in the cold, stony resolution of those who refused to take the bond oath.

"Now, listen, this is the last time I'm going to go through this." Morgan's amplified voice echoed hollowly in the steel-welled chamber. "If you wish to give your bond-oath to this task force, do it now."

He lowered the small, hand-held microphone and waited. Other than an uncomfortable shifting among some of the MechWarriors, none of the Clansmen moved. He had expected as much, but felt obligated to give the prisoners a last chance.

"All right." Morgan nodded, feeling a certain sadness in the gesture. "You deserve an explanation of what is going to happen to you. You will be placed aboard DropShips and taken in-system. There, you will be marooned in the most survivable location we can find. We will provide you with whatever food, supplies, and tools we can spare. You will not be given communications devices or weapons, other than axes and knives.

"If this task force completes its mission, I will send someone back for you. How you survive until that time is up to you. I am truly sorry that I must take this course of action, but circumstances allow me no other option. Good luck."

Turning away from the stoic faces, Morgan thrust the microphone into the hands of a former Com Guard petty officer who began to reel off instructions.

"Listen up. As your name is called, step over to the starboard accessway. If you cooperate, things'll go smooth and quick. If not . . ." The non-comm's voice trailed off. He glanced at the waiting armored infantry squad. No one in the cargo bay missed his meaning.

"Blast, I hate this," Morgan fumed, as he approached Ariana Winston, who'd been watching the whole time. "It's nothing but a bloody waste. Surely they can see that."

"I think they can," Winston replied, as she straightened her short green jacket. "They've chosen exile rather than to help us 'Inner Sphere barbarians' in the conquest of a Clan homeworld. For all they know, we're going after Strana Mechty or Arcadia rather than Huntress. Would *you* help *them* if you thought they were going to invade New Syrtis or Kathil?"

"No, I suppose not." Morgan said, then sighed. "It's just such a waste."

"Yes, it is, but there's nothing you can do about it now. They won't hold it against you. The warriors might, but the civilians aren't going to hate you for not killing them. Let it go."

Morgan tossed a salute to the lieutenant commanding the armored infantry detachment and palmed a lockplate. The hissing whine of the iris valve cycling open sounded loud against the petty officer's drone was he reeled off the names of the Clansmen who refused bond service. As he stepped into the airlock, Morgan looked back at the captives moving to the access hatch. The scene reminded him painfully of old-time photographs he had once seen of innocent civilians being herded aboard railroad cars because some madman thought they were a threat to racial purity.

Good God, I thought we'd moved beyond all this, packing your enemies off to some out-of-the-way place where you can forget about them. Well, I won't forget.

The hatch cycled shut, cutting off his view of the cargo bay.

Aboard several of the task force's largest ships, identical scenes were being played out, with greater or lesser degrees of compassion. Aboard the Knights JumpShip *Bernlad* where, at Colonel Paul Masters' insistence, a multitude of Clan civilians were being housed, Major Sir Gainard had been put in charge of the loading process. In accordance with his commander's wishes, he made every effort to keep family units intact. The opposite was true aboard the captured *Shining Claw*. Prisoners were shoved aboard troop carriers in alphabetical order, without regard for rank, position, or family ties. The Lyran marines wanted to get the job over with fast.

Regardless of how the task was accomplished, the last Clansman, an aerospace pilot named Woart, found his place on the floor of the lower cargo hold aboard the Eridani Light Horse *Overlord* Class DropShip *Lancer* three hours after the operation had begun. Several of the largest DropShips attached to the task force were required to provide space for all of the Clansmen who would not take a bond oath. It would have been possible to complete the operation using fewer ships, but that would have required making several ferrying runs. The command staff had insisted that the task be accomplished as soon as was practicable. By using large transport ships, such as the *Lancer,* the mission could be completed in one trip. Everyone wanted to be done with the distasteful business as quickly as possible.

Unfortunately for the Clansmen penned up in the DropShip's empty cargo and 'Mech bays, "as quickly as possible" meant fourteen days round trip. The guards and support personnel assigned to escort the prisoners did what they could to make the journey more bearable. As large as the holds were, they were never intended for use as passenger compartments. The ship's crews tried to provide cots, mattresses, and blankets, but there were barely enough to go around. Food consisted primarily of combat rations, prompting kind-hearted task force personnel to share whatever they had to eat with the prisoners. Compared to their present state, most of the captives looked forward to being abandoned on an uninhabited planet, as a relief from the cold, echoing hell of the cargo bays.

Their destination was the fourth world of the eight-planet system. Commodore Beresick dubbed the world "Lee Shore," drawing the name from a term often applied to an inescapable harbor during Terra's age of sail. The name suggested an unpleasant place of hopelessness and misery.

In fact, when the *Lancer*'s crew, squinting against the evening sun, caught their first glimpse of the planet's green forests and gently rolling hills, they felt jealous of the Clansmen. The prisoners were being left to found a new colony on a beautiful, hospitable planet, while the Light Horse was going still farther from home, to launch the first attack against the enemy's homeworlds. As that sobering thought set in, the smiles and the joking banter faded away. The Inner Sphere crewmen seemed to grow angry with their captives, resenting that the Clanners were staying behind on a garden planet, while they were going on to risk their lives.

Several hours after the DropShips had grounded, the Clanners, and the few supplies the task force could spare, were offloaded. The *Lancer*'s crew made the *Overlord* ready for boost. Without a word of encouragement or a shout of good luck, the ship's captain fired her drives, lifting the mammoth steel egg skyward on a silvery pillar of flame. As the huge DropShip lifted free of the surface, the rest of the transport ships followed suit.

Watching the ground recede beneath them until it was obscured by a thin layer of cloud, Lieutenant-Commander Sally Guter, the *Lancer*'s captain, heard a stage-whispered voice cursing the Ghost Bears and the planet.

"Well, good riddance. I hope they all rot."

"Belay that," Guter snapped, not knowing who had spoken, but fighting the urge to agree with the sentiments.

The fleet was barely out of Lee Shore's gravity well, when the doors to the *Invisible Truth*'s spacious briefing room hissed open before General Winston and her regimental commanders.

"Well," she said, flopping wearily into her accustomed seat. "They're on their way back."

Morgan, already seated at the head of the conference table, nodded and sipped at his tea.

Across the room, Colonel Amis sniffed experimentally at the mug full of black coffee.

"Enjoy that while you can, Colonel." Morgan forced a smile. "That's the last of the real stuff. After this, you'll have to make do with soy."

Amis slurped a mouthful of the hot, bitter liquid.

"Marshal, I'd like to request a transfer back to the Inner Sphere. This is getting to be too hard. It's not enough that we're out of coffee. This morning, I found that I'm down to one box of cigars."

"Thank God," said Sandra Barclay.

"What's the matter, Sandy? Don't you appreciate the aroma of fine tobacco?"

"Actually, I do, Ed." Barclay smiled, adding sugar to her cup. "Do you know anybody who *has* any fine tobacco?"

"Not only does Colonel Amis not know anyone who has any fine tobacco," Antonescu interjected. "He wouldn't know fine tobacco if it grew in the cockpit of his Battle-Mech. He's been smoking those dirty rope ends for so long they've poisoned his brain and killed his taste buds."

Winston exchanged a glance with Morgan as she accepted a cup of coffee from Colonel Amis. The Light Horse commander had been worried about her staff. The farther out of the Inner Sphere the task force got, the more strained the relationships between her regimental commanders seemed to become.

The battle of Sweetwater Lake and the attack on the pirate base should have eased some of the tensions, but the disposition of the prisoners had increased the degree of stress each of her officers was feeling. She had feared that the encounter with the Ghost Bear fleet and the marooning of the prisoners would deepen the rift, but the opposite seemed to have occurred. Her only explanation for the sudden reversal lay in the fact that they had, at last, engaged the enemy, and had handed him a defeat.

The Light Horse Colonels were forced to expand the scope of their humor as the leaders of the other units making up Task Force Serpent arrived. This would be the final planning session before the Task Force jumped into Clan space.

"All right, folks, settle down," Morgan had to repeat himself several times before he could bring the meeting into some semblance of order. "We have a lot to do here, and it'll never get done if we don't get started."

Morgan laughed quietly to himself as he watched the officers find their places. No specific seats had been assigned to any of the officers save himself, Commodore Beresick, and General Winston. As the unit commanders had arrived for the first planning session back on Defiance, they'd established a pecking order. Andrew Redburn grabbed the seat next to Winston, the closest vacant space to Morgan's own. Sharon Bryan, seeming unwilling to be upstaged by a Davion commander, staked out the place next to Commodore Beresick, and so it went, until, at last, Överste Sleipness and Major Poling, of the St. Ives Lancers, took their seats at the far end of the table.

"I don't suppose you've changed your mind about a *batchall*?" Paul Masters said, kicking off the discussion.

"No, I haven't, Sir Masters." Morgan dropped his hands into his lap and leaned back in his chair, exasperation in his voice. "We've been told again and again that the Smoke Jaguars will no longer honor *batchalls* from the Inner Sphere. They got burned twice by the Combine; once on Wolcott, and again on Luthien. I guess they finally learned that old proverb."

"Proverb?"

"Fool me once, shame on you," William MacLeod of the Highlanders said. "Fool me twice, shame on me."

Paul Masters asked, "So we'll be hitting them with everything we have?"

"That's what we're here to discuss." Morgan hitched his chair forward until his elbows rested on the tabletop. "Remember, the idea is to hit the Jags hard. We want to destroy their ability to make war. That means wiping out their factories, training facilities, command and control structure, everything."

"You're talking scorched earth," Masters said, appalled.

"Well, not scorched. Not completely anyway." Morgan sensed Ariana Winston stiffening beside him as he locked eyes with Paul Masters. "We're going to confine out attacks to military and industrial targets. We'll make every effort to avoid any civilian casualties."

"I guess that means orbital bombardment is out?"

"Yes, Marshal Bryan, orbital bombardment is right out."

"Excuse me, Marshal." Alain Beresick raised his hand. "We've always known it was possible to use a WarShip's batteries for tactical support fire as well as strategic bombardment. For the past several days, I've been going over the records salvaged from the *Winter Wind* and those in the *Fire Fang*'s computer core. The Clanners managed to erase much of the information in the *Wind*'s primary core, but they never got to the off-line backups. The *Fang*'s core was intact when we captured her. I believe that there was enough information in those computers to allow us to attempt support fire. I'd suggest moving the *Fire Fang* in-system, maybe to the second or third planet, for a test fire."

"I don't know, Commodore," Morgan said reluctantly. "Firing a couple of batteries at an empty planet is one thing. Calling in tactical support fire from an orbiting WarShip is quite another. It's going to be a lot harder to direct naval support fire than it is to direct ground-based field artillery. I mean, nobody from the Inner Sphere has done it for two hundred years. We don't even have a procedure for designating targets or correcting fire."

"I know that, sir." Beresick was eager to prove his theory. "I've got my staff working on fire-direction protocols right now. We'll get it nailed down to the point that we won't even fire if we're not absolutely certain of what we're going to hit."

For several moments, Morgan rested his elbows on the table, toying with an electronic stylus while he considered his options.

"All right, Commodore," he said. "We've got a good number of jumps to go before we hit Clan space. Run your tests and get me the results. I want a full observation team both on-planet and aboard the *Fire Fang* when you try out your theory. If you can't control the shot-fall to within thirty meters, it's a no-go. Understood?"

"Understood, sir," Beresick said. "You'll see, Marshal, you won't be disappointed."

"Uh-huh." Morgan didn't sound reassured. "One more proviso, Commodore. We're talking about tactical support fire only, not bombardment. Even then, we're only going to fire if it's a choice between that and losing part of the task force. Got it?"

"Got it, sir." Beresick's joy was unabated by the severe restrictions Morgan had placed on him. Secretly, he had been mourning his role in the task force. He had thought he wouldn't be able to make a direct contribution to the mission, with the exception of chance battles such as Trafalgar. Now, with the possibility of delivering massive support fire directly into a battle area, Commodore Beresick was a happy man.

Morgan cleared his throat, preparing to move on to the next subject, when Major Ryan stood up.

"Marshal," he began. "I've been reviewing the data provided by Precentor Martial Focht's 'agent,' Trent. I believe I've located the target that should be attacked first by this task force."

Ryan paused, looking to Morgan for permission. When the Marshal nodded, the DEST commander passed a datachip to the only noncommissioned officer in the room. The yeoman accepted the chip and fed it into the front of the small, powerful data unit in a corner of the briefing room. The data unit was, among other things, a smaller version of the *Truth*'s holotank.

A map of the planet Huntress sprang into the air above the conference table. Huntress was a world of extremes, with massive polar icecaps, blistering deserts, and thick equatorial jungles. Only two continents showed green against the blue of the Sangram and Dhundh Seas. The larger, unimaginatively named Jaguar Prime, housed the planet's entire human population. Five large cities nestled among the mountains or crouched beneath the jungle canopy. One of the mountains well to the south of the planetary capital of Lootera showed the small image of a green bird, a katana clutched in its talons. The map legend revealed that this installation was the Falcon's Roost, the only enclave of Clan Jade Falcon outside of the Falcon homeworlds and the occupation zone.

A dot of white light pulsed near Lootera. Ryan spoke to the yeoman, and the map, originally only one meter in diameter, expanded until only the area surrounding Lootera was visible. The bright white area was also still visible, only a few kilometers from the city.

"As you all know," Ryan said, "there have been many

tales of hidden Star League bases capable of defending a planet against invading fleets. For years, we dismissed these stories as old wives' tales. No such base had ever been found. Ladies and gentlemen, I tell you that you are looking at one right now."

Stunned silence blanketed the room. Morgan recovered first. "Go on, Major Ryan."

Ryan continued, "As most of you are aware, these space-defense systems were originally developed to protect Terra. The theory is, a computer system tracks and interrogates all incoming ships. If they're not transmitting the proper Identify-Friend-or-Foe code, the system launches remotely controlled drones that are programmed to destroy the intruder. Originally, these drones were powerful robot warships. Unfortunately, or fortunately for us, depending upon how you look at it, these drone cruiser-based systems were too complicated and too expensive to build in large quantities. Subsequent systems were designed with smaller and smaller drones, until the final version boasted an automated ship no more powerful than an *Overlord* Class DropShip. Some of these systems even launched 'suicide' ships—fast, fightersize robot bombs designed to pull alongside their target vessel and detonate a nuclear warhead. Some of these robot attack ships were programmed to crash into the intruder before detonating their warhead. Most of these space-defense systems, or Reagan Systems, as they were called, were deactivated around 2750. The information provided by ComStar and the Explorer Corps leads me to believe that we are facing an *operational* system of this last type."

"What?" Commodore Beresick jumped to his feet. "Are you telling me that I'll be taking my fleet into a system protected by a Reagan defense grid?"

"No, Commodore." Morgan laid a hand on Beresick's arm, noticing the twitching muscles in it as he guided the man back to his seat. "I think what Ryan's telling us is that he has a plan for preventing us from jumping into the teeth of a space defense system. Isn't that right, Major Ryan?"

"Yes, sir." Ryan asked the petty officer to bring up another display. "As you can see from this map, the projected location of the SDS control center is directly beneath this large peak, Mount Szabo. According to information ComStar obtained from the defector Trent, the facility is lightly guarded. Trent's briefing tells us that the

Jags consider the possibility of a strike against their homeworld to be nonexistent.

"What I propose is this: detach the *Haruna* for this mission. We'll go in via a pirate point while the rest of the fleet emerges at the jump points. We'll make a fast in-run, hit the control center, disable it, and withdraw into the mountains above Lootera.

"Come to think of it, you may want to send in the Fox Teams at the same time to hit the C-3 installations, sensor sites, and aerospace fighter bases around your LZ. Who knows? We might get lucky and whack a couple of high-ranking Clan officers."

Morgan steepled his fingers, pressing them against his lips as he considered the DEST commander's plan.

"Okay," he said at last. "I think Major Ryan's plan has merit. Now, I hesitate to do this, but, comments?"

"Marshal, the plan to take out the SDS system is a good one," Paul Masters said. "So is the idea of destroying Command, Control, and Communication installations. What concerns me is the cold-blooded assassination of unsuspecting people, Clan leaders or no."

The Knight Commander's objection earned him a muttered *"Baka"* from Major Ryan.

Morgan shot him an angry glance. Calling Masters a fool was a breach of military courtesy, even if Ryan *had* spoken Japanese. Ryan lowered his eyes.

Commodore Beresick said, "I recommend launching the strike as Ryan outlined it, with just a few alterations."

For half an hour, the staff discussed the merits and faults of the DEST leader's plan, until Morgan passed his final judgment.

"Major Ryan, I want you and Captain Montjar to go ahead and plan your operations. Give me a list of potential targets and their importance; timetables, force and equipment requirements, the lot. Top priority should be locating and destroying the Reagan System. After that, you can hit whatever targets of opportunity may present themselves.

"If a Clan officer happens to be present at one of your targets, I'm not going to forbid you to shoot him, but your teams may *not* go hunting. Is that clear? Captain Montjar, that goes for the Fox Teams too."

The special forces officers looked across the table at

each other, then at Morgan. Their faces wore identical expressions of wounded innocence.

Morgan shook his head slightly and smiled, but the look he gave them left no doubt that he meant what he said.

Ariana Winston asked the petty officer to pull back the scale of the holographic map until it showed the entire Huntress system.

"The only thing that concerns me, Marshal, is Major Ryan's three or four days. I understand that it may take that long to locate and penetrate the Space Defense System control center, but, if it doesn't, two things are going to happen. First, the special teams are going to be cooling their heels on-planet until the rest of us get there. Second, the Jags are going to have advance warning that something is about to happen. It may not be enough time to whistle up reinforcements from Strana Mechty, or wherever else, but they could certainly get off a shout for help or slap together a defensive plan.

"My suggestion is to go ahead and launch the commando strikes. Aim them at the SDS system, C-3 sites, and the like. Ideally, the 'Mech forces should be halfway planetward before our sneaks set off their bombs, or whatever they plan to do. The strikes, timed to coincide with our assault, would certainly throw the Jags off balance and prevent them from mounting an organized defense."

She studied the glowing map for a moment. "I do agree with Major Ryan on one point, though. The first major landings should come just outside Lootera, on this surrounding plain. Look at it, it's a natural landing field. Wc could drop 'Mcchs, ground DropShips. For pity's sake, we could even land fighters if we had to. To top it all off, they've got that 'eternal laser' thingy." Winston laughed at the idea of a laser burning eternally into the sky above a planetary capital. While it was intended to honor heroes to whom the Jaguars had apparently built massive monuments in the capital, the laser would also make a nice landing beacon in a stormy, cloudy atmosphere like Huntress'.

Colonel William MacLeod stood and walked around the narrow conference room, keeping pace with the slowly revolving holographic globe. "You know, Marshal, I'm thinkin' that each outfit in this task force should be assigned its own area of operation. That way, we can hit the maximum number of objectives, while spreadin' th' Jags out thin."

He halted his pacing and gave the map a few more moments of thoughtful examination. Giving a satisfied nod, MacLeod straightened.

"Our man Trent says there's some kind of 'Mech production facility here at Pahn City. I'd kinda like t' take my Highlanders and shoot th' place up a bit. I think we may be able t' draw some o' th' Jags off there. Maybe even some o' th' *sassanach* who'd be opposin' th' main landings.

"I'm sure my Highlanders can hold out against the Jags fer a couple o' weeks at least. Especially if we fight them a run-an'-gun battle." MacLeod grinned slyly at Morgan. "Just like we did with your boys on Northwind a few years back, eh, Marshal?"

Morgan smiled thinly at the jibe, then shook his head. "Now, Colonel, you know I had nothing to do with that operation. If I had, Northwind would belong to the Federated Commonwealth."

MacLeod nodded but did not return the smile. The attempted takeover of his home planet of Northwind still had the potential to become a sore spot.

After several hours of planning, discussion, revision, and argument, the staff had come up with a rough operational plan. Afterward, Morgan reviewed the dozens of electronic pages of notes he'd taken during the long, arduous session.

"All right, that's enough for today," he said, gesturing at the chronometer above the petty officer's computer terminal. The bright green numbers showed that they'd been in the conference room for over ten hours. A clutter of dirty coffee cups, crumb-covered plastic plates, and half-eaten sandwiches competed for table space with hard-copy maps, noteputers, and data chips.

"I want you to review your individual phases of the operation and try to polish up any rough edges. We'll reconvene tomorrow morning at oh-eight-hundred, and try to refine this monster into something workable.

"Thank you, people. Dismissed."

With a chorus of "goodnights," the various commanders filed out of the briefing room, stretching and yawning as they headed for the shuttles and DropShips that would carry them back to their respective JumpShips.

=====30=====

Morgan sat back in his seat, watching his officers file out of the meeting room until only Andrew Redburn and Commodore Beresick remained.

"We got a lot accomplished today," Redburn said as he closed the cover of his noteputer. The command staff had spent the last two days ironing out the last details of the invasion plan. Finally, they had settled on a basic framework for the battle plan.

"More than I'd expected," Morgan agreed. "If we can get the same amount of work done tomorrow, we might even have a workable plan hammered out before I retire."

"Retire? You can't retire yet, sir," Redburn said with a laugh. "You're far too young. Don't you know that a Davion can't retire before he's a hundred and two?"

"It's not the years, Andrew," Morgan groaned as he levered himself out of his chair. It felt as though his backside had gone to sleep. "It's the mileage."

As the three officers strolled down the passageway connecting the *Truth*'s main briefing room with the bridge, they were startled by the hiss of opening lift doors. A pair of young able-bodies stepped out, still wearing the circle-

star and white Greek letter Q that had once marked them
as Com Guard ship's crewmen. The youngsters snapped
to rigid attention. The younger of the pair, a tow-headed
youth with slightly protruding teeth, whipped his hand up
in what he obviously hoped would be a smart salute. So
vigorous was his motion that the snappy gesture of respect turned into a blow to the forehead.

Before the scarlet creeping up the youth's neck had time
to reach his ears, Morgan came to a complete halt, executed
a crisp right face, and solemnly returned the lad's salute.

"At ease," he said, extending his right hand. "What's
your name, son?"

"Acolyte . . . er, Private Frank Seremet, Marshal, sir."
He took the proffered hand as though Morgan were offering him the throne of the Federated Commonwealth.

"And you?"

"Private Steven Kalp."

"Nice to meet you, gentlemen." Morgan shook Kalp's
hand as well. "Carry on."

For a moment, the young men didn't move. Then, in a
rush, they saluted again, this time accomplishing the maneuver without injuring themselves, and strode down the
corridor, smugly pleased with themselves.

"Y'know, Morgan," Redburn grinned. "That's what
makes you a good commander. You care about your men."

Now it was Morgan's turn to color slightly. "Don't start
with me, Andrew." The smile on his lips gave the lie to the
growl in his voice. Turning to Beresick, he rolled his eyes.
"Tell me, Commodore, what would *you* do with a subordinate who insisted upon embarrassing you in public?"

"Well, sir," the Commodore grinned wickedly at Redburn. "There's an airlock just across the bridge . . ."

"Nah, I couldn't do that. There'd be an inquiry."

"Yeah, but I'd vouch for you. You weren't even on the
Truth when General Redburn wandered into the lifeboat station without a vacsuit on." Beresick laughed. "Tricky
things, those airlocks. Push one wrong button, and whoosh!
Out you go."

"Marshal," Redburn said in a mock tone of fright. "You
wouldn't really blow me out into space. Would you?"

"Only if you start trying to run me for the High Council
again."

Beresick laughed along with the FedCom officers. Obviously, the issue was a long-running joke between the two of them. What Redburn had said was true, though. Morgan *was* a good commander, because he *did* care about his men; his, and every other unit in the task force. Beresick had seen it time and again: a commander who loves his men, but understands that, in order to be a good soldier, he will eventually have to order some of those men to die. The commander knew that the first rule of warfare is that young men die, yet when a man died in a battle planned by that commander, the commander took it personally. What made a good officer was the ability to strike a balance between the love and compassion for one's men, needed to assure that they weren't thrown away needlessly, and the strength and detachment needed to preserve one's sanity in the midst of death and destruction.

As the doors to the *Invisible Truth*'s bridge whispered open, Morgan's laughter stopped. As long as they were in the corridor, with its featureless, pale blue-gray bulkheads, he could forget where he was and what he was about to do. As soon as he stepped onto the control deck, with its holotank, sensor, and weapons stations, reality came flooding back. The grim mask of a seasoned commanding officer snapped back into place.

With it came a tightness around the eyes that Andrew Redburn had never noticed before.

Morgan crossed the bridge, going, not to the holotank as was his wont, but to the main viewscreen. There, all the glory of the universe was displayed in its diamond brilliance against the black velvet of the void.

Here and there, Redburn saw the faint gleam-and-fade of the fleet's starships, as the light of the nameless, numberless star far below was caught and reflected by them. The three officers stared silently at the scene before them, each lost in his private meditations.

How far we've come. Redburn's thoughts echoed in his mind. *From the Garden to the stars, twenty thousand years of human history have all led up to this point.*

Suddenly, a deep sigh escaped Morgan's lips. Startled out of his reverie, Redburn whirled around to see his friend and commander leaning heavily on the narrow lip surrounding the viewscreen, his eyes closed, head down.

"Morgan?"

"Oh, I'm sorry, Andrew. I didn't mean to startle you," Morgan said softly as he lifted his face toward the viewer once again. "I'm just a little worn out.

"Whuhh," he sighed again. "We could all use some rest, but I don't think there'll be much to go around until this business is over with."

A distant look came into Morgan's eyes as he straightened, running his hand through his hair. Then he seemed to come back to the moment, a tired smile tugging at the corners of his mouth.

"I'm all right, Andrew." Widening his gaze to include Commodore Beresick, Morgan gestured at the viewscreen. "Why don't you two turn in? You've both worked hard these last couple of days, I think I'd like to stand here and watch the stars for awhile."

Beresick bade Morgan good night with a short, formal bow, but Redburn lingered for a moment. "You sure you're all right?"

"I'll be fine, Andrew. I'll be fine." Morgan laid a hand on his friend's shoulder and guided him gently toward the bridge pressure lock. "Don't worry about me, old friend. We've seen it all, and we'll make it through this one too."

As the lock cycled open, Morgan turned back toward the viewscreen. Redburn paused and watched him for a moment. For the first time in his life, he noticed the toll that had been taken on his friend in the service of his nation. Lines of care had etched themselves deeply into his face. Like most soldiers of his generation, Morgan had a perceptible darkening of the skin on his face, hands, and arms, even after months of isolation aboard a starship. The permanent sunburn was a legacy of too many hours spent in the sun, either on parade or in battle. Still, his back was as straight, his step as sure and strong, and his green eyes as clear and bright as the day they'd met thirty years before.

Briefly, Redburn considered returning to his friend's side, but the love and respect he felt kept him from doing it. Bidding Morgan a silent good night, Andrew Redburn stepped into the lock and headed for bed.

Morgan stood in front of the viewscreen, staring at the glittering stars. His thoughts ran in many channels. He thought of his father, gone these thirty years. He thought of Kym, again wondering how long before he'd see her again. He thought of the mission before him, and wondered when he would see his home once more.

The Com Guard Officer-of-the-Deck stole several surreptitious glances at Morgan as he leaned on the viewscreen's edge.

Abruptly, Morgan straightened, and saw how the OOD flinched. He could see that the man had been about to reach for the button labeled "General Quarters."

Realizing that he'd startled the OOD, Morgan smiled sheepishly. Reading the nametape stitched over the man's right breast, he called him by name.

"Good night, Mister Frei."

"Good night, sir."

Without another word, Morgan adjusted his tan uniform jacket and walked off the bridge, feeling the accustomed spring in his step.

During the short trip back to his cabin, Morgan encountered no one. It was the middle of the watch, and most of the *Invisible Truth*'s off-duty personnel were either asleep or relaxing in one of the battle cruiser's eight rec rooms. In a way, he was grateful for the solitude. His time of meditation at the viewscreen had left him feeling more relaxed and refreshed than he had been in a long time. Running into someone he'd have to talk to would have ruined the quiet, almost dream-like peace in his heart.

Upon reaching his quarters, he keyed in a request with the ship's central computer for an 0600 wake-up call.

It'll be good to get up early, he told himself. *Maybe I'll even get in a couple of kilometers before staff meeting.* He laughed briefly at the thought. Morgan hated the stationary treadmills located in the officer's rec room, preferring instead to run laps around the *Truth*'s number one cargo bay.

Tossing his jacket over a hook bolted to the back of his bedroom door, he rummaged around in a drawer of the wood-veneered night stand next to his bunk, eventually coming up with an odd-looking contraption of tubes and valves. Opening the lower, locked compartment of the night stand, he shoved the big, blue steel Colt auto pistol out of the way, extracting a three-sided bottle half-full of a rich, amber-colored liquid. The gold foil label proclaimed the contents to be Glengarry Black Label, Special Reserve. Though some, Colonel MacLeod among them, might argue the point, Morgan believed that the natives of

Glengarry produced the finest single malt whiskey outside of the Scottish Highlands.

Taking a small nightcap was one of his few vices. He'd taken to it recently to help ease the aches and pains of age. It was something he wouldn't allow the less than one quarter gravity of a recharging JumpShip to interfere with. Pulling the real cork stopper from its mouth, Morgan attached the device to the bottle. The turn of a valve allowed compressed gas to hiss from a small cartridge through the tubing and into the bottle, where it forced the golden liquid through a second set of conduits, which carried the whiskey into a plastic squeeze bulb. As the bulb filled, Morgan closed the valve and removed the transfer system from the bottle.

Taking a deep breath of satisfaction, he sat back on his bunk, not even removing his boots first. His Com Guard steward had often groused about his habit of lying down not only fully clothed, but still wearing his boots. The highly polished synthleather, according to steward, left black scuffs on the sheets, though Morgan had never been able to see them.

Taking the plastic bulb's nozzle between his teeth, Morgan gently squeezed out a mouthful of the liquor. Closing his eyes, he rolled the whiskey around his tongue, savoring the smoky, faintly iodine taste imparted to the malt by the slow peat fires over which it was roasted. A second, long, slow sip emptied the bulb, which Morgan carefully replaced in the drawer, along with the high-low pressure transfer system.

As he relaxed against the thin foam pillow, he felt a slight numbness in the roof of his mouth and tongue. *Brother, they brew it strong on Glengarry.*

As he was closing his eyes, a light, polite rap sounded at his door.

I knew it was too good to last, Morgan thought as he sat up.

Or tried to. Something was wrong. His arms refused to obey. Summoning all his will, Morgan tried to swing his legs off the bunk, but failed. There was a tightness in his chest, as though a thick leather band was being slowly tightened about his torso.

Fighting the raw edges of panic, he tried to call out for help. A faint, rattling gasp escaped his lungs.

As his sight began to dim, his thoughts flashed between

the wife and family he was leaving behind and the mission he was leaving unfinished.

Blackness collapsed in on him, leaving only one bright spark at the center of his vision. Then, it too went out.

══════ 31 ══════

Battle Cruiser ISS **Invisible Truth**
Task Force Serpent
Deep Periphery
03 January 3060
0845 Hours

"Let him sleep." Andrew Redburn told an orderly as Ariana Winston entered the conference room. "Yesterday was a long day. We can get by without him for awhile."

"Morgan?"

"Yeah." Redburn turned to her. "He was really beat. I don't ever remember seeing him look so worn out. You're the second-in-command, General. How about if you take over this meeting?"

"All right," Winston agreed. "But it seems a little strange, like I just launched a coup or something."

In ones and twos, the rest of the staff wandered in, some of them clutching noteputers, others nursing steaming cups of soycaff, a bitter coffee substitute common to military rations. Most looked like they hadn't gotten much sleep. Winston felt almost as tired as they looked. She and her regimental colonels had spent several hours after leaving the *Invisible Truth* going over the Light Horse's phase of the assault against the Jaguar homeworld. Edwin Amis and Sandra Barclay both had dark smudges under their eyes, and the Twenty-first's veteran commander wore a heavy stubble of beard. Only Charles

Antonescu showed no outward signs of fatigue, appearing to be as fresh as though he'd enjoyed ten hours sleep, instead of the four they'd all had. Winston had purposely avoided looking in a mirror before she'd left the *Gettysburg*. She knew that she was looking just as bad as the rest of her staff.

At least I can't get dark circles under my eyes, she told herself, grateful that her dark skin hid some signs of fatigue.

In spite of the fact that the weariness gripping the commanders limited the amount of joking and chatter that usually marked the slack time before staff meetings, it took Winston a long time to bring the session to order.

"Where's Morgan?" Marshal Sharon Bryan asked.

"Marshal Hasek-Davion is indisposed," Winston answered quickly, forestalling any response by Andrew Redburn. "As the executive officer of this task force, I'll be taking over today's sessions until he can join us." The sharpness in Winston's voice offered a challenge to anyone who might dare to oppose her.

Bryan decided not to push it.

"When we broke up last night, I believe Marshal Hasek-Davion asked us to refine the plans for our individual phases of the operation. Major Ryan, your people will be going in first, so we might as well start with you. Let's have it."

Ryan rose to his feet.

"As we discussed yesterday, my teams will be going in a few days ahead of the main assault force." Ryan ran down the operational outline the staff had established for his commandos the previous day. He explained the changes he and his staff had made in order to make the plan more workable, and more survivable.

"We'll start by making a HALO insertion pass, as discussed. The *Haruna* will jump in and out at the zenith point. I'd rather use a pirate point, but our system maps just aren't accurate enough. We'll be using recognition codes supplied by Agent Trent and masquerading as Clan ships. Our original plan called for us to use the *Bisan*. But since we captured a Clan DropShip, we may as well use it. The *Stiletto* will detach and make a normal burn for the planet. After deploying the teams, the DropShip will ground in a concealed location in the Lunar Range on

Abysmal. The *Haruna* will go through a standard recharge and jump outsystem again."

Ryan answered questions concerning the special teams' targets, schedules, and operating procedures, until the staff was satisfied with the plan. By the time he took his seat again, the first phase of the Huntress assault, code-named "Stalking Tiger" bore only a passing resemblance to the one he'd initially presented. Ariana could tell that Ryan was unaccustomed to having "amateurs" planning special forces operations, but admired the way he gave no sign. She wondered if he was just putting on a good face now, but would simply conduct the operation his own way later.

And so it went, for several hours. Each commander presented his refined operational plan, and suffered while the command staff mutated it into something else. Several times during the course of the session, Winston caught Redburn glancing anxiously at the door.

She knew he was watching for Morgan. She couldn't stop glancing at the door now and then herself. Where could he be?

Halfway through the meeting, the conference room door slid open to reveal a man wearing a khaki jumpsuit of a junior petty officer. The single blue stripe on his shirt cuff marked him as a cabin steward. Quietly, he circled the table, cutting behind Colonel Samuel Kingston as the Capellan officer was delivering a self-aggrandizing lecture on his unit's role in the overall operation. Approaching Winston, the steward leaned over and spoke into her ear in a hurried whisper.

Twisting in her seat, Winston stared at the young man, forgetting the documents she'd been examining. They slipped from her fingers and bobbled around her in the zero-G.

"General, are you all right?" asked Beresick.

"Yes, Commodore," Winston replied, gathering up the sheets of hard copy that had escaped from her fingers. "Will you please take over the meeting until I return?"

Without waiting for a reply, she rose quickly and elbowed her way out of the crowded briefing room, the cabin steward close on her heels.

As she was leaving, Winston heard Commodore Beresick

try to cover the awkwardness of the moment with a joke. "So, who's going to take over when I have to leave?"

In the lift car, Winston turned to the steward.

"Are you sure?" she whispered, as though she didn't want someone to hear the answer.

"Yes, ma'am," The steward's voice was also hushed. "It looks like it happened sometime last night."

Winston squeezed out through the widening gap as soon as the lift doors began to open and darted down the passageway. Rounding the corner, she saw a pair of Com Guard marines standing outside Morgan's stateroom door.

Rorynex needle rifles cradled in their arms, they stared up and down the corridor, looking as though they would fire at any suspicious sound.

Striding through the open stateroom door, Winston ignored the marines' stares. The flag office looked the same as it always did; clean, but untidy. Stacks of hardcopy files and datachips littered the desktop. Morgan's personal data-reader sat untouched on the sideboard. Incongruously, a fresh pot of coffee sat steaming next to the reader, brewed automatically by the timer-controlled machine.

In Morgan's stateroom, the scene reminded Winston of a sequence from some bad detective holoshow. The *Invisible Truth*'s chief medical office, Captain Joel Donati, was standing beside the Marshal's bunk, gazing sadly at a sheet-covered form. Glancing up at Winston's breathless arrival, he blinked a few times and shook his head.

"How did he die, Doctor?"

"I'm not sure, General." Donati shook his head. "It looks like his heart just gave out."

"I didn't know Morgan *had* a heart problem," Winston said.

"I didn't, either." Donati shrugged, but he was obviously having difficulty maintaining his air of professional detachment. "It happens that way sometimes. . . ." His voice broke. He cleared his throat, and said, "Some hidden flaw suddenly manifests itself, and bang, you're gone." He shook his head again, refusing to meet Winston's eye. "It just happens."

"All right. Blast." Ariana felt as though she should say something else, but her mind was reeling. She tried to think about what to do next. "I suppose you'd better take him to sick bay. I've got to tell the staff."

She surveyed the stateroom. The room was as neat as the flag office had been cluttered. Not a single object was out of place. Already, the presence of the man who had occupied this space was beginning to fade. It looked as though it could be anyone's room. Sorrow began to well up within her. The pain and sense of loss was almost as great as she'd felt when her father died.

Steeling herself, Winston squared her shoulders and marched out of the stateroom, passing a pair of white-clad hospital stewards. Something familiar about the man carrying one end of the stretcher caught her eye. The man must have felt her curious stare. He turned to face her. Tears fell from the steward's almond-shaped eyes, but there was no flicker of recognition. Perhaps she'd encountered him during one of her visits to the flagship. With a bow of apology, she turned the corner and made her way to the lift.

Unexpectedly, General Ariana Winston bobbed her head at him in a token of respect and apology. For the first time in his career, Kasugai Hatsumi was thrown off balance.

In the shuffling of personnel that had followed the battle at Trafalgar, the nekekami leader had received orders transferring him to the medical staff aboard the *Invisible Truth*. The message said that his mission was at hand, and he'd be given his target once the fleet was safely away from the battle area. They'd been in-system for less than three hours when a long coded message was sent to his data unit. Translating the message, he saw that the mission assigned was indeed of great importance. It took all of his skill at *hengen-kashi no jitsu* to maintain the false persona of a ComStar hospital steward that had been created for him. Fortunately, his study of personality traits, which was so much a part of that discipline, was sufficient to see him through. When Captain Donati called for a stretcher to be brought to Marshal Hasek-Davion's stateroom, Hatsumi was one of the stewards assigned to the task.

Briefly, he'd been afraid that Winston had recognized him as the technician who'd serviced her *Cyclops* on Defiance, but then she hadn't seemed to remember him.

"C'mon, Yee," Corpsman Leland Newell said, calling Hatsumi by his cover name, and nudging him with the stretcher. "Let's get this over with."

*   *   *

Ariana Winston felt as though she couldn't think. As she returned to the briefing room, she only wanted to get what she had to do next over with quickly. She leaned for a moment against the bulkhead alongside the door, taking a moment to collect herself and put her thoughts in order. Drawing in a few deep gulps of air, she straightened, and strode purposefully through the door.

The shock etched into her face betrayed her.

Commodore Beresick, the first to see her enter, jumped to his feet.

"General, what's wrong?" he asked.

Stepping mechanically into the room, Winston grabbed an empty chair and leaned against its metal frame.

"Give me your attention." Her voice started out strong, but caught in her throat. Twice, she coughed, trying to open up her swelling throat. Finally, a third cough freed her voice. "Sometime last night, Marshal Morgan Hasek-Davion died of an apparent heart attack."

Someone gasped in disbelief.

Paul Masters bowed his head, his lips moving in a whispered prayer.

"Chief Medical Officer Donati says that Morgan may have had a hidden defect that suddenly manifested itself, causing a fatal episode. That is all the information I have at this time."

All the commanders sat in stunned silence, until Paul Masters broke in, saying what everyone was thinking.

"What now, General?"

Her head came up. She fixed the Knight with a burning stare. Her voice uncharacteristically sharp, she said, "What now, sir? We carry out our mission. That's what. This is a military operation, and we do not turn back because our leader has a heart attack."

Winston glared at the unit commanders as though defying them to challenge her decision. Then, as quickly as it had come, the anger left her. She felt a sick weariness. She wanted nothing more than to return to the *Gettysburg* and lock herself in her quarters, but she knew she had to go on.

"As second-in-command, I will assume the post of task force commander. Commodore Beresick, I will be moving over to the flagship as soon as quarters can be prepared for me. General Redburn, you will be my executive officer. You can either maintain command of the Kathil Uhlans or pass that post on to one of your subordinates, as you see fit. Just tell me which it is to be. I, likewise, will decide whether or not to relinquish command of the Eridani Light Horse. Everyone else will remain at their original posts.

"I am going to postpone this session until thirteen hundred tomorrow. I'd like each of you to return to your respective commands, and inform your people of the Marshal's death. That is all. Dismissed."

The commanders filed out of the briefing room, each of them expressing sorrow and condolences to Andrew Redburn, who had known Morgan longer than any of them. Ariana Winston tried not to stare at Redburn as he wrestled with his shock and grief. Grief was natural, Morgan had been one of his closest friends, but there was something else in Redburn's eyes, something fierce, almost predatory.

As Samuel Kingston, the last to leave the room, closed the door behind him, Redburn glanced at Winston. His face still showed pain, but had taken on the hard, unyielding quality of flint.

"General Winston, I've known Morgan for most of my life. I knew him better than anyone in this task force, maybe even better than Kym."

"I know that, Andrew. I understa . . ."

"No, ma'am, you don't." He cut her off. "Right after the Whitting Conference, Victor Davion made him get a complete physical: blood work, stress test, the works. Victor said he wanted to be sure Morgan was in shape for this mission. I don't think Victor was actually worried about Morgan's health. He just wanted to be sure."

"And?" Winston suddenly felt as though a frozen metal hand was squeezing her stomach.

"The doctors passed him with flying colors—a clean bill of health."

"Andrew, what are you driving at?"

Redburn paused for a moment, his green eyes locking with hers. "I believe Morgan was murdered."

Winston's felt all the blood drain from her face. For long moments, she stared at Redburn.

"General, did you hear me? I said . . ."

She cut him off with an angry gesture. "Come with me," she said curtly.

Redburn got quickly to his feet and followed her out of the briefing room. In a cold fury, Winston walked to the lift and punched the call button. She crossed her arms, tapping her foot angrily as they waited. When at last the doors slid open, she pointed for him to enter the car.

Redburn nodded and complied. A few minutes later, she ushered him into the small office that had been reserved for her aboard the flagship. Ironically, the room was right across the passageway from Morgan's flag suite.

As Redburn entered Winston's office, she barked out for him to have a seat. As he began to lower himself into the chair she'd indicated, she secured the old-fashioned mechanical lock on her door.

"Now, General Redburn . . ." Winston's obsidian gaze never wavered. "Would you care to repeat what you just told me?"

"Yes, ma'am. I said that I'm afraid Morgan's been murdered. General, Morgan had a complete physical right after the Conference. The doctors said he passed it more easily than some men twenty years his junior. I checked. It's my job to check. The report gave absolutely no indication of heart trouble. So, if Donati thinks it was his heart, but he didn't have heart trouble, what does that make it?"

Winston stared past him at nothing. She felt cold and dead. Then, she reached across her desk and keyed in the ship's intercom system. She had the tech route her call to docking bay three, where Captain Roger Montjar was preparing to board a shuttle back to the *Fire Fang*. Without preamble, she asked Montjar if the Rabid Foxes had brought any counter-surveillance equipment with them. After being assured that they had, she ordered Montjar to get that equipment and bring it straight to her office.

"General, what is this all about?" Montjar's confusion was evident despite the metallic distortion of the intercom.

"Not now, Captain. You'll find out when you get here."

Severing the connection, Winston tapped in another command.

"Sickbay."

"Doctor Donati? This is General Winston. Report to my day cabin immediately."

Without waiting for a reply, Winston switched off the communicator and sat back.

Sitting there, waiting for the officers to arrive was one of the longest, loneliest times of Ariana Winston's life. Hard as it was to believe, to accept, Morgan was dead. Silent tears welled up inside her, but she could not give in to any of that right now. First, she had to find out what had really happened.

Looking across the desk at Redburn, she saw that he, too, was fighting for composure.

The office door chime sounded. Winston and Redburn both jumped, startled. She got up and unbolted the door.

She had been expecting Doctor Donati to arrive first, assuming that Montjar would have had to send to either the *Fire Fang* or the *Antrim* for his electronic surveillance equipment. But she was wrong. Seeing her surprise, Montjar explained that he had developed the habit of carrying a portable scanner/jammer to every staff meeting.

"It may be a bit paranoid, but you never know who might be out to get you."

"Captain, I want you to sweep this office for bugs," Winston said.

"Sweep for bugs? Why?" Stopped short by a look from Winston, Montjar shrugged, and dug a thick, six-by-ten-centimeter black plastic box out of his nylon briefcase. After fiddling with a few tiny controls, he paced around the office, waving the device at the bulkheads, ventilation ducts, furniture, even the coffee pot.

In the middle of his performance, the door chime bleeped again. As the door opened, Doctor Donati entered. Winston saw him suddenly clamp his lips shut as though seeing Montjar in the cabin made him decide not to say whatever he'd been about to. Instead, he took a seat on the edge of Winston's sideboard until Montjar finished his scan.

Giving the instrument a last critical gaze, he switched the device off. Pulling a small, gray plastic mushroom out of his kit, he set it in the center of Winston's desk. At the touch of a stud, a low, whistling hum filled the air.

"There. That'll cover our voices, as long as we're quiet," he said. "If we talk louder, the jammer will distort anything we say. It'll also scramble any bugs I may have missed." Montjar picked up his case and turned to go.

"Wait a minute, Captain," Winston said. "This concerns you, too."

Montjar shrugged and set the case down again.

Donati pushed himself upright, placed his hands behind his back and said, "So, General, what's this all about?"

Winston looked pointedly at Redburn. "Andrew?"

Getting to his feet so he could face the newcomers, Redburn carefully repeated everything he'd said earlier to Winston. When he finished, Montjar nodded thoughtfully. Donati, though clearly shocked by the allegations, recovered quickly and promised to begin an autopsy immediately.

"That's good, Doctor," Winston said. "Can you cover it under some kind of bureaucratic red-tape, like 'standard practice in case of an unusual death'?"

"Of course. I'm the chief medical officer of this task force. If I say a post-mortem has to be done, who's going to question me?"

"It's not questioning you she's worried about," Montjar put in. "It's security, right, General? If it *was* murder, there's a more-than-even chance the assassin will pick up on what we're doing. He can't run far. Where's he going to run to? The problem is, we want good, clean evidence for when we hang the son-of-a-buck."

"That's right, Captain," Winston said grimly. "The killer may not be able to escape, but we still have to catch him and prove he did it. So I don't want this to leave this room."

"What about the other commanders?" Redburn asked. "Shouldn't they be told?"

Again, Montjar answered for Winston. "What if one of the other commanders was behind the murder?"

"That's right." Winston looked sharply at Donati. "Doctor, do you have enough people you trust to help with the autopsy?"

"Yes, ma'am," he said with a nod. "My people are almost all old-time ComStar. They've been trained to keep their mouths shut."

"All right," Winston said. "You'd better go ahead and get started. Captain Montjar, I don't suppose you've been carrying around any forensics gear?"

"Some. Not much."

"Well, go fetch what you have, and send for what you need." Winston rose from her chair as she spoke. "General Redburn and I are going to have a look at Marshal Hasek-Davion's quarters. We'll meet you there."

"Okay." Montjar was already on his way out the door. "Just be careful. Don't touch anything. I don't want you to destroy evidence."

In the short time that had passed, Morgan's stateroom had somehow become like a room in a museum, which, although it recreated his home, captured none of his personality. An unpleasant burnt odor stung their nostrils, evading identification until Winston remembered the pot of soycaff she'd noticed earlier. The warming plate hadn't been switched off, and the brown liquid had begun boiling down to sludge. With a grunt of disgust, Winston slid the switch into the Off position.

Redburn and Winston crept around the flag office, using writing styluses to open drawers and cabinets to keep from damaging any possible fingerprints. Not knowing what else to do, they left the data-reader for Montjar.

Moving into Morgan's bedroom, Redburn used his pen to tug open the nightstand.

"General, you'd better come in here."

Winston closed the cabinet she'd been inspecting, and walked through the adjoining door.

"Did you find something?" she asked.

"It's what I didn't find," Redburn said bitterly. "Morgan had a newly acquired vice he refused to give up, even though Kym hated it. Every night, he has a small glass of scotch just before going to sleep." Redburn didn't notice that he'd spoken as though his friend was still alive.

"He keeps a bottle of Glengarry Black Label in the nightstand next to his bunk. The other night, he offered me a drink. He had to open a new bottle. But when I looked in the stand, there was only one unopened bottle— no sign of the open one. Morgan didn't drink enough to empty a whole bottle of whiskey in two days.

"There's something else. He had this contraption rigged up so he could have his nightcap even in zero-G. It uses a high-low pressure system to fill a plastic squeeze bulb. Well, the system's still there, but the bulb's gone."

"What bulb?"

So unexpected was this third voice that Redburn started violently, and Winston dropped to one knee, spinning to face the door over the sights of the laser pistol she snatched from a concealed holster. She snapped the weapon up as soon as she saw it was Roger Montjar.

"Captain, if I didn't need you . . ."

"Sorry, General." Montjar said. "Now, what bulb?"

Redburn repeated his tale of Morgan's single foible.

Montjar thought for a moment. "Did either of you touch the bottle or the transfer system?"

"Uh-uh," Redburn answered.

"Good," Montjar barked, his voice becoming professionally detached. "If you didn't touch them, I may be able to lift some prints."

The special forces officer went to work, dusting, probing, sampling, and examining everything in sight. For over an hour, he searched the stateroom and the office. The data unit he set aside, explaining that he wasn't very good with computers. Montjar promised to allow a Com-Star technician to access its memory at a later date, with Winston, Redburn, and himself in attendance.

Other than discovering that the bottle and squeeze bulb were missing, the search of Morgan's quarters proved fruitless.

As they turned to leave, Winston noticed Redburn lagging behind. She stopped too and watched him. For a long moment, he stood in the doorway, staring at the empty, unmade bunk. Turning away, he shook his head, blinking to clear his eyes. Unashamed of the tears that threatened to stream down his face, he turned to his new commander.

Winston nodded sadly.

"He was the last of the old order of things," she said. "We'll never see his like again."

About the Author

Thomas S. Gressman lives with his wife, Brenda, and four-and-a-half cats in the foothills of western Pennsylvania.

When not chained to his computer, he divides his time between leather crafting, living history reenactment, and a worship music ministry.

The Hunters is his first novel, and he is currently writing the sequel, *Sword and Fire*.

'Mech Repair Field
Coventry
Jade Falcon Occupation Zone
18 June 3058

"**W**hat the hell. The *hell*. This is one hell of a hellish hellhole, quiaff?"

Horse grunted. When Joanna was in an irritable mood, it was not easy to respond in any way to her unexpected outbursts. This time, though, through the use of the ritual interrogatory, *quiaff,* she was demanding a response.

"I said, quiaff!"

"Aff, Joanna. Whatever you say."

"And what did I say?"

"Whatever you said."

"You do not know what I said. You were not listening. That shows no respect."

"Whatever you say."

"That is on the verge of insubordination, Horse."

"I am always on the verge of insubordination. Do not take it to heart."

Joanna sighed. An unusual trait among warriors, sighing.

"We have the same conversations, Horse. Over and over."

"What it is, is that we have known each other so long we are beginning to sound like coffin-mates."

Joanna shuddered. Coffin-mates was a term common to most of the seventeen Clans, though rarely used. By Clan standards it was one of the most obscene insults one could say to another and still survive—which was why Horse had used it. It referred to two people who formed a lasting relationship. While such relationships, whether or not formalized into some legal arrangement like (ugly word) marriage, were more common in the castes beneath the warriors and even popular in some rural areas, Jade Falcon warriors found the idea of a lasting relationship of any kind disgusting.

Coffin-mates was an archaic term which suggested a relationship so permanent it would last to the grave and beyond. Jade Falcon warriors could not accept such a notion, since their desired fate was to be recycled after death for various uses. The highest honor for a warrior was to be accepted into the Clan's gene pool and used for new sibkos. Thus, burial was no longer seen as desirable in the higher Clan castes.

Burial was even repellent to think about, the subject of deep insult. The sight of a village graveyard nauseated warriors. The custom harked back to a pre-Clan era when burial was the accepted way on Terra, humanity's planet of origin. Most warriors believed that the humans of the past had been extremely wasteful in burying their dead. It was sickening to think of how much of the planet had been taken up with wasteful graveyards. But Terra, they knew, had been a wasteful planet, populated by wasteful civilizations whose careless practices had nearly destroyed the planet in the times before its people branched out into space. Sometimes Joanna wondered why there was such an urge among the Clans to reclaim Terra. Even if the first Clan to set foot victoriously on Terra would have the honor of becoming the most important Clan, the ilClan, the Clan leading all the other seventeen Clans, what would they be reclaiming? No, Terra held little allure for her.

Horse and Joanna had served together for many years, and had often argued with each other. Somehow the arguing brought them closer, but not too close. There had never been a sexual moment between them. Even though Joanna, impatient when the need was upon her, generally chose the closest available male warrior, she had never chosen Horse. He had never selected her either, though she had never noticed him going off with anyone. His apparent celibacy may have been governed by his caste. As a freeborn he could not easily approach a trueborn for the purpose of coupling, so his choices would usually have to be among the few freeborns in the unit or among the lower castes. Joanna, on her part, could not even bear touching a member of any caste below warriors.

After Horse had called them coffin-mates, she had an unwelcome image of the two of them being put to their final rest in side-by-side coffins, lids slipping open, skeletal hands reaching for each other and missing, winding up drooping from skeletal wrists. A bad way for a warrior to end. Her ideal image of death was burning up in a flaming 'Mech, leaving in her wake about a hundred other smashed 'Mechs.

"You know, Horse, when I think about it, although I always thought of you as a low freeborn bastard, you are worse than that—you are beneath the lowliest of the low, scummier than dirty oil trapped in a 'Mech joint, lousier than—"

"Joanna, I get the point. This does not work anymore, this more trueborn than thou attitude."

"Well, of course I am more trueborn than you, lousy freebirth."

Horse stayed silent, gnawing on his lip, a gnawing that was not obvious beneath the abundant growth of hair on his face. Although he would never tell her, Joanna was one of the few trueborns he actually *liked*. Even then, there were times when he would just as soon kill her as look at her. And these days looking at her *was* becoming more of a task. It seemed that freeborn warriors were like trueborn warriors in one way: both types hated signs of age, in themselves and in others. The signs of age were increasing for Joanna.

In general, Clan warriors did not expect to grow old. The few who did battled the shame attached to advanced years. Every so often Joanna endured slurs about her survival as a Clan warrior, all caused by her obvious age. There were snide implications that her warrior skills were over-rated, that perhaps she took sneaky ways out of battle, protected herself in situations where most warriors would be daring.

They knew her reputation for bravery but wondered: if so brave, how could she *survive* for so many years?

The question, while expressed occasionally, was never allowed to linger. Even her enemies had to admit that there were few Clan warriors who rushed into battle so recklessly, who slew her quarry with so much ferocity. Her defeat of Natasha Kerensky, achieved by incinerating that fabled Clan Wolf hero in the cockpit of her 'Mech, was already legendary. Even worse, she was so hated within Clan Wolf that there were rumors of parties of assassins out to infiltrate Falcon ranks and kill her.

Horse did not often look directly at Joanna. When he did, as now, he had trouble focusing on the rows of wrinkles beside her eyes and on her forehead. He could not shut out the tight thin line her mouth had become, the sallow valleys in her cheeks, the mottled leatheriness of her skin, the half-hidden age lines of her neck. A few warriors dyed their hair, as if to put off oncoming age, but Joanna could not abide such fraud. Her hair had wide gray streaks in it.

Joanna stared at the valley where techs worked on damaged 'Mechs from Coventry's battles. This expanse of repair, fallen 'Mechs looking like corpses, techs scrambling around them like insects, had probably induced her to call Coventry a hellhole. It was the right word, all right. The scene below even had specific hellish elements in it. Fires burned and sparks flew from 'Mech surfaces. Some fallen 'Mechs were arranged in distorted positions. They looked very much like suffering sinners, with the workers in the role of minor spirits whose job was to torment them. Some techs roamed the battlefield, searching and supervising, discovering new ways to punish the sinners. Those who were not repairing damaged BattleMechs were on salvage duty, making sure that usable parts of unusable 'Mechs were not being wasted.

Studying the scene, Joanna's rage flooded through her. Two days ago she, along with the rest of the Jade Falcon warriors on this planet, had been primed for battle with some Inner Sphere forces. After Tukayyid, the warriors longed for the chance to win against an Inner Sphere unit, even if the conflict was minor.

The first blow to Jade Falcon expectations occurred when the Inner Sphere invaders were allowed to assemble on Coventry's surface and join the depleted nearly-defeated armies already on the planet without any sort of Clan retaliation. They had achieved this privilege because their leaders had invoked _safcon,_ a revered Clan custom. Safcon meant that the Clan had to allow the Inner Sphere safe passage to the surface of Coventry.

Then, seeing that the two sides were matched evenly and that any battle victory would be narrow with extensive loss on both sides, Victor Steiner-Davion, the Inner Sphere commander, had offered _hegira_ to the Jade Falcon Clan. Hegira was another Clan custom, this one allowing an army to withdraw from the battlefield with honor. Honor was everything to the Clans, and hegira was a means by which one Clan contingent, which respected the abilities of its enemy Clan, could allow it honor without further bloodshed.

Hegira was rarely used among the Clans, for whom a fight to the last 'Mech left standing was more venerable, and it had never been used before by any force that was not Clan. Horse told Joanna that the word came from ancient Terra, where it stood for some kind of flight. Flight was certainly what this particular hegira had felt like, even though no Clan warriors had actually traveled anywhere.

The hegira tactic had caught the Falcons off-guard. Nobody could have expected the Inner Sphere leader to invoke it. Who would have expected someone from the enemy to even know these Clan customs? There had to be a spy somewhere, Joanna thought. It was unthinkable that anyone from the Clans would even give information to the enemy. Certainly no Jade Falcon warrior would perform such a traitorous act. The treason must have come from some other Clan. Wolf Clan, maybe. Joanna, like most Jade Falcons, hated the Wolves. Even among them, though, it would be hard to find someone as treacherous as this spy. Maybe it was that former Wolf Khan, Phelan Kell. He was Inner Sphere in the first place, a lousy freebirth who unfortunately had been allowed status within Clan Wolf as a bloodnamed warrior.

Her anger at the Wolf Clan was minor compared to the rage she felt at her own Khan, Marthe Pryde, for _accepting_ the offer of hegira. The official Khan version of the incident was that Khan Marthe saw no gain in two large armies exhausting their ranks against each other. The casualty rate would be too high, especially for the mere gain of a minor planet just within the truce zone. Coventry, while strategically located, did not have sufficient military value to lose so many good warriors fighting for it. So many warriors had already been lost during the invasion. *Stravag,* Joanna thought, no Jade Falcon worth his salt should ever consider previous losses as a reason for retreat.

Joanna and others of the dissenting minority saw no honor in this hegira. Not now, not after all they had been through during the invasion. She recalled vividly the desperate battle for Tukayyid, where Aidan Pryde had entered Clan legend, and a place in the Clan saga, *The Remembrance,* through his heroic efforts. His genes had been accepted into the breeding pool early because his valiant acts had returned honor to his unit, the Falcon Guards, who had been so disgraced in the Battle of Twycross. She remembered her own victory on Twycross over the Clan Wolf legend known as the Black Widow, Natasha Kerensky. The triumph had made Joanna suddenly famous throughout the Clans. That did not matter to her. What mattered was that it avenged her own earlier shame as a warrior in the disgraced Falcon Guards on Twycross.

To Joanna, hegira was wrong. The courageous acts of Falcon Guard warriors during the long invasion deserved more than a diplomatic maneuver that marked an exit from a major battle. Further, she thought it dishonored the memory of the Khan's sibkin, Aidan Pryde, whose heroism had salvaged Jade Falcon dignity on Tukayyid. Perhaps she should not have been surprised. After all, this Khan, the revered Marthe Pryde, had capitalized on the cadet Aidan's miscue during their mutual Trial of Position. Her win there, a double victory, had allowed her to enter Clan ranks as a Star Captain, a significant first step that precipitated her quick rise through the hierarchy to Khan level. Deviousness then, deviousness now—it was not so startling.

What frustrated Joanna more was the realization that most Jade Falcon warriors, experienced warriors perhaps exhausted from their ferocious battles, endorsed the hegira. Joanna feared that the action was merely a symbol of the overall weakening of the Clan caused by certain measures encouraged in the upper echelons. There were, for example, the warriors she thought of as "the new breed," arrogant youngsters fresh from sibko training who never let up on their unearned assertions of superiority over veteran warriors. Joanna did not really mind their arrogance—Jade Falcon warriors were *supposed* to be arrogant—but she despised the way they set themselves apart from other warriors. Even more, she hated the hero worship they gave to the Falcon Guard commanding officer, Ravill Pryde. Joanna thought the new breed much too cultish, especially with their attitude that the old warriors were outdated. She was especially angry at Ravill Pryde for encouraging the division in the ranks with his obvious approval of the new breed. Joanna would not accept new breeders into her Star, feeling she would rather have solahma warriors at her back. Solahmas were over-the-hill warriors usually used as cannon fodder in battles.

Still, she would accept a new breeder before she would accept one of the sibbies, the name given to warriors who had been rushed from their sibkos directly into battle without having qualified through the Trial of Position. These half-formed creatures were not *real* warriors. To Joanna, the sibbies' arrogance was even less earned than that of the new breed. In battle they were dangerous.

She knew she should be more sympathetic to sibbies, since she had been a training officer for so long, working with many sibkos; however, she simply did not like to have unqualified warriors in a battle zone. Horse insisted that the sibbies had acquitted themselves adequately, sometimes bravely, in the Coventry warfare, even with poor skills and a lack of combat instincts. She told Horse that she felt it was insulting even to use the term *warriors* for sibbies. It was wrong, she said, to rush unfinished trainees into battle, even if Jade Falcon forces were depleted from the invasion.

Some sibbies had gathered at the foot of the hill, talking eagerly among themselves. That was one of their nauseating characteristics, eagerness. They remained eager in spite of their heavy losses in battle. The group below, merely because they had survived probably saw themselves as seasoned warriors, even if hegira had diminished their chances to prove it. She could see in their easy manner and their comfortable faces that they considered themselves sufficiently initiated, just from getting through the

Coventry skirmishes. Who knew what future blunders they were capable of?

Joanna was contemplating writing a report (and she never wrote reports except under duress) that would recommend the return of the sibko warriors to their homelands in order to resume warrior training.

The more she thought about the current state of the Jade Falcon forces, ravaged and diluted by events since Tukayyid, the more her anger grew. As she watched the happy sibbies below, she felt it rising to an unendurable point. It had to be released in some way. Sometimes she attacked rooms of furniture or ripped branches off trees and punished them. This time, though, chairs and branches would not be enough. She needed to punch out a few people. She needed to see bloodstains on her freshly-bruised knuckles.

Abruptly, she started down the hill.

"Where are you going?" shouted Horse, caught off-guard.

"I want to kick some sibbie butt."

"Joanna, do not be an—"

His insult was drowned out by the sound of the rocks she purposefully kicked so that she would not hear.

The sibbies were moving away from her, walking in the direction of a severely damaged *Night Gyr* that was being busily worked on by a pair of techs. One of them pointed toward the 'Mech, while another made a clearly disparaging gesture. What was being disparaged was not clear.

On the *Night Gyr,* the techs were apparently scavenging for usable parts. Joanna, her attention concentrated on the sibbies, paid little attention to what the techs were doing with welding tools and the odd clamplike tool known as the Peeler because it could be used to peel off large sections of metal from a 'Mech surface. It was a monstrous tool, something like a pliers with exceptionally sharp teeth. It pulled off thick layers with minimal guidance from the tech operating it. It could be readjusted to peel off thin strips as well.

Joanna did not like this new type of 'Mech, the *Night Gyr.* It was too fancy for its own good. Equipped with the new laser-based heat sink technology, which did add to its lasting power during a battle, it had a distracting aura of light around it during night combat as laserlight bounced off mirrors and out cockpit windows and other openings.

In action it looked more like a walking monument than a BattleMech. This particular _Night Gyr_ had apparently been in some heavy battle. It was scarred, dented, twisted, and generally unfunctional. Good salvage, good riddance, she thought.

Joanna picked up her pace, as she closed in on the sibbies. She tried to form a plan of attack that would not look like picking a fight. Cantankerous as Jade Falcons were, the idea of officers picking fights with subordinates was officially frowned upon. Some commanders might discreetly approve, but among them would never be the stiff-backed, by-the-book leader, Star Colonel Ravill Pryde.

She hated having to think so sneakily. It was too much like Pryde and his new breed. She _wanted_ to smash a few sibbie heads, and that was that.

Near the bottom of the hill she spotted one of the small but heavy black rocks so common on Coventry. It was said that black rocks rained onto Coventry during thick swirling storms. As far as Joanna knew, this was just country superstition and not an observed phenomenon.

I do not know any of this bunch, she thought as she drew near the sibbies. _None of them are from my Star, anyway. Good. Now I can get in trouble with their star commanders. Nothing like a little boil in the pot. Anyway, trouble clears my head, always has._

"Hey, you," she shouted.

Well, that is an original opening. Does verbal facility decline with age, too?

The half-dozen sibbies all seemed to whirl around at once. Their faces copied each other's surprise. A couple of them stepped forward and eyed her up and down.

I must be a sight. Still in battle-torn uniform. Dirty. Hair like twisted wire.

She tossed the rock from hand to hand.

"What is it, Star Commander?" said the warrior on the right, a muscular young man with a childlike face that reminded her that these sibbies were just like the ones she used to train. The only catch was, these stravags had left training without going through the qualifying trial, the one that turned ordinary cadets into warriors. This sibbie even looked bizarre, since he had clearly ripped off his shirt arms to show off his thick arms.

Really, he looks like a baby in an overgrown body.

"No freebirths allowed in a repair zone. Too dangerous, quiaff?"

The other warrior in front, a woman with a long plait of blonde hair hanging down almost to her waist (a sibbie fad), stepped forward and shouted in a voice so low it was almost bass: "How dare you call us freebirths? Do you see the insignia? We are trueborn!"

This one really looks ridiculous. She has on just enough uniform to satisfy dress code requirements in a battle zone. She looks disgusting, with that low neckline. How dare she even show the beginning of her breasts? Does she not know that warriors believe exhibitionism is foul?

Since trueborns were genetically engineered and birthed from vats, then nurtured by various devices that carefully measured their nutrition intake, some felt that breasts were unnecessary and should be eliminated in genetically engineered female warriors. They were neither nursed by females nor did a warrior ever nurse a child. The argument given to this view was that not all trueborn warriors succeeded. Many failed training and chose to become mothers in their new lives. Even though it was difficult to overcome their natural revulsion for it, some of them did nurse their children. It struck Joanna that Peri, natural mother of Diana, must have suckled her, and the thought brought on a faint nauseous pain at the pit of her stomach.

As if she read Joanna's thoughts on the matter, the woman rubbed the exposed part of her neckline. Joanna tossed the rock from her right hand to her left so hard that the palm of her hand was badly stung.

"You are not warriors," Joanna shouted, "only half-warrior—and therefore the same as freebirth by my accounting. Later you will have the honor of accepting your trueborn heritage, when you succeed in proper trials. You wish to argue with that?"

The woman took another step forward. "I do. I do wish to argue, Star Commander. I know who you are, and I know you to be an old woman. I can see the age in your face and it sickens me!"

Joanna wanted to lunge at the woman immediately, but she saw that she would be at fault. By Jade Falcon interpretation the sibbie woman was stating an obvious fact and had every right to say what she had. If roles had been reversed, Joanna might have said something similar to an ancient version of this upstart. This thought lessened her rage, and she had to struggle to maintain it. Fortunately, she was an expert at rage and, though it seemed illogical, she could even control its surges and falls. Horse had once accused Joanna of being the ilKhan of rage.

"Freebirth scum like you have no right to judge me!" Joanna shouted.

The woman started toward her, but the muscular warrior rushed to her and held her back. She struggled fiercely within his grasp. The man whispered something in her ear and she stopped. He let her go and she retreated to the others at a gesture from him, not once taking her eyes off Joanna.

The man addressed Joanna. "We do not wish to do battle with you, Star Commander Joanna. As Carola stated, we know who you are, and we value your defeat of the despised Wolf Khan, Natasha Kerensky. You are a hero to us, and we do not wish to battle our heroes, quiaff?"

In spite of his words, Joanna wanted to ram a knife into the man's throat.

How dare he be polite? How dare he show respect? Using the quiaff is despicable. It forces me to reply. If I do not reply, I will be at a disadvantage. I do not like that.

"Aff," she muttered reluctantly.

The man nodded. "We are here because we know we are still, as you say, unformed. We believe we can learn from observing these techs work on 'Mechs. We will become better warriors for it. We would like to remain in the work arca, with your permission of course."

This one turns my stomach. He is too polite for his own good.

"What is your name, sibbie?"

She saw a flicker of anger in his eyes, but his voice remained calm. "I am Shield."

As she stared into his cold eyes—cold eyes in a child's face—she realized that Shield was a good name for this one. Underneath the shield of his politeness was a dangerous sibbie.

"You were not spilled from the vat with the name Shield assigned to you, I suspect, quiaff?"

He nodded. "Aff. My given name was Shaw, but I received the name Shield when I began cadet training, and I have taken it as my own. Shaw did not seem a warrior name to me."

"I am sure other warriors have borne it with honor, sibbie."

There was a ripple of annoyance among the group, but it was clear they deferred to Shield in most matters.

This child with the cold eyes might be a fine leader someday. Still all this talk is not doing anything to give me a good fight.

She rubbed the rock harshly against the skin of her hand. If she examined her skin, she knew she would find it raw and peeling.

"If it pleases the Star Commander, you may call me Shaw."

"I do not have to call you anything but sibbie scum, freebirth!"

"Scum, if that is the way a superior officer wishes to view us, but never freebirth!"

Joanna nearly smiled. *I have done it, riled this calm bastard. I can do more.*

"Scum *and* freebirth, if I wish it."

"I challenge your right to malign us."

Joanna felt almost joyful, a rare feeling for her.

"You would like a circle of equals, quiaff?"

"Aff!"

"I like to make children happy. What area shall we designate for the—"

"Right here, old woman."

Shield sprang at Joanna, who was quite ready for the move, who had longed for it. She did not even try to dodge him in order to make a calculated blow. Instead, she accepted him almost like a lover and allowed him to put his surprisingly powerful arms around her and push her backward onto the ground. He landed on her chest. It felt as if the pressure might have cracked a rib. The pain was sharp—and welcome.

She did not move within his grasp and looked up at him stoically. He was clearly puzzled and, with puzzlement came a letting up of pressure that Joanna took advantage of. She tightly gripped the rock, now in her right hand, and brought it up forcefully against the side of Shield's head. At the same time she kneed Shield in the crotch, for a moment glad of at least one physical difference between female and male warriors. Both actions loosened Shield's grip further, and she was able to squirm sideways. She cast him off her body. Instead of jumping to her feet, she rolled toward Shield, her right arm high, and slammed the rock even more firmly against his cheek. She heard something crack beneath her blow and smiled. Shield had initiated the kind of fight she wanted—one where, according to all warrior tradition, she could punish her adversary as severely as she knew how. And, more than most, Joanna knew how.

Viewing the damage she had already caused, her rage abruptly subsided. From now on, she could function on warrior instinct. The fight no longer came from her desperate need; it was merely exercise.

Shield scrambled to his feet. His eyes were dazed. Apparently, though, his will was not affected. He managed a fairly weak kick against Joanna's side, and she laughed at him in response. Getting to her own feet, she stood calmly, not even egging Shield on. She did not have to. He vaulted toward her. She went into a sudden crouch, catching his stomach with her shoulder, rising, and flipping him past her. He landed on his back. In recoil, his head went upward, then down so quickly that it hit the ground hard.

Joanna decided to show him the kind of fierce warrior assault that an *old woman* could muster. She leaned down, picked Shield up by the collar and yanked him to his feet. He had some trouble planting his feet and she had to keep holding him up. She ran forward with him, dragging him by the collar toward the *Night Gyr*. His feet finally managed a kind of drunken stumbling run.

When she reached the 'Mech, she gave Shield one powerful wrench and slammed him against it, so hard that the *Night Gyr* rocked a bit from the blow. Up above them, the tech holding the Peeler, who had been distracted by the fight below and come to the edge of the work area, lurched sideways, almost off the 'Mech. He regained his footing with obvious difficulty.

Joanna released the sibko warrior, expecting to see him slide down the side of the 'Mech, unconscious. Instead, his eyes displayed a rage that duplicated what she had felt. For a moment Joanna felt an absurd bond with this Shield.

Shield pushed himself away from the *Night Gyr* and at Joanna. She was not prepared for the sudden counter-attack, and he caught her with a strong roundhouse right to her jaw. The force of the blow was increased by the momentum of his rush at her. For a moment it dazed her but, before he could land another blow, she yelled with a voice that could rattle the armor off most of the 'Mechs in the valley and pushed Shield back against the _Night Gyr_'s side. The tech with the Peeler, who had barely regained his footing a moment ago, slipped sideways, off the Mech. As he fell, he lost control of the powerful tool and it fell straight down, right at Shield, who was shaking his head, trying to clear it. Joanna saw the falling Peeler and tried to leap forward to push Shield out of the way, but she was too late. It landed, heavy end first, on top of his head. Next to her, the tech landed a split-second later, just missing hitting Joanna by millimeters.

Joanna grabbed for the tool as Shield fell. Her hands wrapped around the handle, she tried to knock it aside. The end which resembled a large pliers locked onto the skin of Shield's forehead and began to peel it, raggedly, away.

Cameron Class
Battle Cruiser

Kyushu Class Frigate

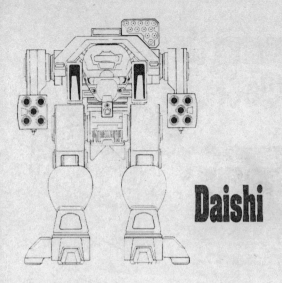

Daishi

Hercules

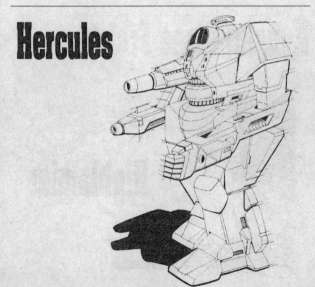

Cyclops

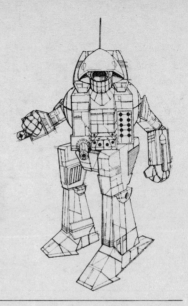

Highlander

Firestarter

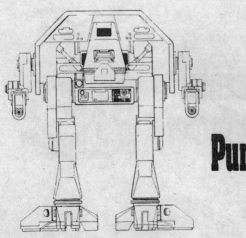

Puma

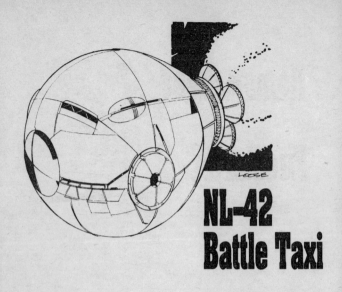

NL-42
Battle Taxi

Elemental
Battle Armor

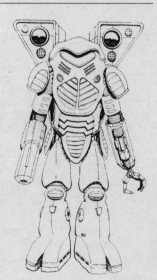

Hammerhead

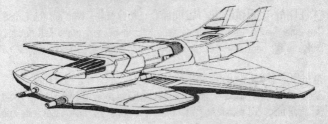

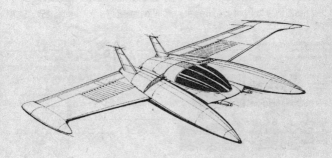

GOTHA